Torsten

The Naming

The 13th Paladin

Volume II

Dear Reader,

if you like my books, spread the word and share my links.

There's nothing more enjoyable than experiencing a tale for the first time.

www.tweitze.de

www.facebook.com/t.weitze

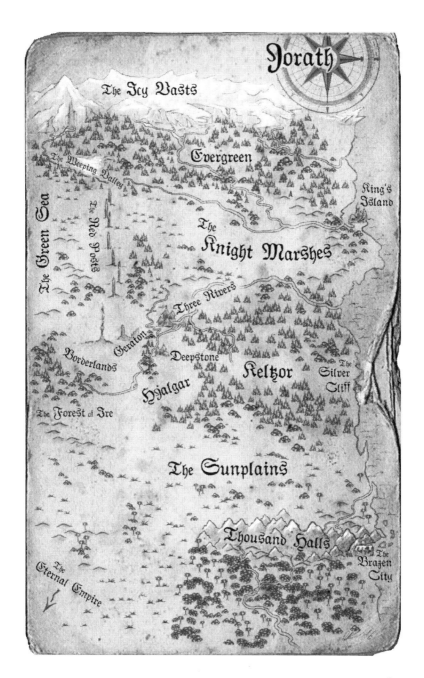

Chapter 1

The rays of morning sunshine shone brightly on the vast leafy roof of Eathinian. The treetops of the elf forest, which people called Evergreen, stretched in all their majestic glory in front of Ahren's eyes. He had woken up early and his need to be alone had been overpowering. He was familiar with this feeling from an earlier and darker chapter in his life, when he had regularly sought refuge from his drunken father in the forest. Of course, he was now much happier as Falk's apprentice, and his master treated him fairly. But so much had happened over the previous days and weeks that he really needed time to take in all the events that had so suddenly befallen him.

And yet everything had started so quietly and unobtrusively two years previously. Falk, by profession an experienced Guardian of the Forest with more than fifty years' experience fighting, had taken Ahren on as his apprentice completely out of the blue and had begun to teach him everything a would-be Forest Guardian needed to know: endless hours of running and climbing, not to mention lessons on plants and animals and all the minor details pertaining to survival, which meant the difference between aimlessly wandering around in the undergrowth and being a proper Forest Guardian. Those two years had been the happiest in his young life, even taking into account the ribbon-tree, the enormous king oak-tree on which he had had to practise for hundreds of hours until every bone in his body had ached.

Everything had changed when he had touched the stupid rock at the Spring Ceremony. The silly thing had to pick him out as the Chosen One, and so he had become the candidate for the position of the Thirteenth Paladin. He was now one of the warriors handpicked by the gods, who, along with twelve other similarly blessed men and women, was to destroy HIM, WHO FORCES.

It was true that his task sounded like one of those heroic ballads, but the reality was considerably more laborious and complicated. When the Thirteenth had died on account of being betrayed, the Twelve had, only with great effort and with the help of the immortal wizards, chained the dark god to a sleeping bane. Since then, they had been waiting for a new Paladin to be chosen so that HE could finally be conquered. Unfortunately, it had taken the sleeping gods of Jorath over seven hundred years to gather enough strength to choose Ahren as the new Paladin. During this time the free peoples had become used to the deceptive peace, and it was only stories and legends of the Dark Days that remained with them. The huge armies of yore had long been disbanded or were now fighting in mortal wars. The names of the Paladins were either only found in legends or were long forgotten, and those warriors of the gods continued living over the centuries, free to pursue their own ambitions.

Which meant nothing but trouble for Ahren. As a Chosen One he had to undergo his Naming, a magical ritual that would prove to the gods and the people of Jorath that he was a worthy successor. In the past it had been merely a matter of form but now he was on a treacherous treasure hunt. Ahren needed the approval of a human, an elf and a dwarf, each of whom carried a holy artefact of their deity with them.

The human had been an easy one. Uldini, the immortal wizard who looked like a child, had sought out Falk in Ahren's home village of Deepstone, and had brought along an artefact of HIM, WHO MOULDS.

Unfortunately, the grumpy wizard had also brought along some bad news with him. A swarm of Fog Cats, sent by HIM, WHO FORCES was coming their way to kill them and finish Ahren off too. Once Ahren had been chosen, the self-proclaimed god had gradually awakened, sending his henchmen to track down the apprentice Forest Guardian, while he gradually sucked the magic of the gods out of the young boy. And so, the three had headed straightaway for the elves of Evergreen so they could win the high priestess Jelninolan and the elf artefact Tanentan for their cause. That too had proved far from easy, but they were successful in spite of the attacks and the intrigues of the adversary's servants.

An indignant barking interrupted Ahren's train of thought and he looked down the enormous trunk he had climbed in the early morning so he could think in peace. Culhen, his young Blood Wolf, whom he had freed from the spell of HIM, WHO FORCES, was jumping up at the tree and barking in a half-ordering and half-sulking tone. Culhen hated it when prey flew into the branches of a tree, and this feeling obviously also applied to horrible Forest Guardian apprentices who left their four-legged friends too long on their own on the ground. Ahren looked with affection down at the bundle of energy making giant leaps up at the tree trunk with his shiny white coat. Ahren couldn't see everything on account of the branches, but from time to time the young man caught a glimpse of the wolf's clever yellow eyes filled with silent reproach at having been left alone for so long.

Ahren smiled and called out, 'Don't worry, my friend, I'm coming down!' As he began his descent, the barking became friendlier and the apprentice couldn't stop smiling. Culhen was true, courageous and loyal, not to mention vain, greedy and easily offended. The elves had organised a feast in his honour two days previously and Culhen had enjoyed every bit of the attention – as well as half a dozen rabbits. The wolf had slept the whole of the previous day, except for occasional binge eating sessions when he devoured the previous day's leftovers, which the elf children had brought by. Ahren really hoped that the little ones would stop spoiling his wolf, or the next part of their journey would be punctuated by whining and begging for rabbit.

They had to journey on, and more quickly than they had wanted to. Ahren was still in need of the dwarf and the artefact of HIM, WHO IS, the patron god of the little people. So they would travel on to the Silver Cliff, a sort of trading enclave on the coast of Kelkor. Uldini had made it perfectly clear that time was of the essence, and Ahren was sure they would be heading off soon. Their enemy was growing stronger by the day and the blessing on Ahren was growing weaker. The Naming would have to be carried out to stop this process and cut the connection between the young man and the dark god,. And it would have to be before HE, WHO FORCES had sucked too much strength out of him, giving the free peoples no time to prepare for the dark god's awakening. It was already the beginning of autumn, even if this was impossible to tell in Eathinian (which had no seasons), and Uldini wanted to carry out the Naming before the winter solstice if at all possible because Ahren would surrender a huge amount of strength to HIM on such a magically significant day.

The apprentice reached the forest floor with a sigh. Before the dark thoughts of such a monumental undertaking could overpower him, a friendly, barking and slobbering wolf, stinking of rotting rabbit, planted his paws on Ahren's chest, knocking him to the ground before licking the face of his human companion.

Ahren couldn't stop giggling as he turned his face one way and then the other so Culhen could lick him all over. Experience had taught him that it was better to succumb to a quick wash than to defend himself.

Otherwise he would spend the next hour being stared at by an offended animal that looked for all the world like an unloved and rejected whelp.

Culhen growled contentedly and climbed off Ahren's chest once he was satisfied that every inch of his master's face was sopping wet. The young man wiped himself with the sleeve of his linen shirt and vowed to take a bath in the nearest river. He loved Culhen above everything else but the thought of smelling of rotting rabbit for the rest of the day was too much to bear.

He fell into a steady trot, something he had learned to do by watching Falk and had become used to. It was useful when he was in a hurry but still had to conserve his strength. Ahren's strength and endurance had developed significantly through his training, and although he could still only run half as fast and as far as his master, he was delighted with his progress. He soon reached the river which gurgled quietly as it flowed between the trees of the elf forest. There was no-one to be seen, so Ahren peeled off his clothes and slipped contentedly into the cool water. Culhen joined him with an almighty splash and soon they were playing happily in the water.

'If you've no objections, we do have to save the world from a destructive god. Unless of course, you and your wolf are too busy playing.' The voice was that of a child but with the biting tone of someone much older and Ahren didn't need to turn around to know who was hovering there.

'We'll be straight out, Uldini. But it's the perfect opportunity. Who knows when we'll have fresh water available to us again on our journey', answered the apprentice.

'Alright, alright. But hurry up. We're going to head off after breakfast and Jelninolan has a surprise for you before that.' The wizard's tone had softened a little.

Ahren turned around and looked at him with interest. A surprise? What could it be? He knew the wizard well enough not to persist with questions. He'd get nothing but a sarcastic comment in return. Instead he simply nodded at the bald dark-skinned boy, who really did not look at all like having centuries of knowledge and wisdom. Then he pushed Culhen away from him so he could quickly scrub himself. He had climbed into the water to get rid of the smell of rotting rabbits, but not to come out smelling of wet dog. Culhen snorted in disgust before scrambling onto the riverbank. Uldini was on the point of turning back to head for the guest accommodation, which the elves had put at their disposal, when the young animal leaped nimbly to his side before energetically shaking off the excess water. Ahren dived with a snort under the water just as the wizard, now soaking wet, let out a scornful yell. Culhen would have no problem avoiding Uldini's rage by disappearing among the trees, but Ahren would be the perfect target if the wizard spotted him laughing at his misadventure. He came back to the surface once he could control his facial gestures and looked at the darkened face of a master wizard, whose childish build was covered by a sopping wet robe. Ahren's face betrayed no emotion and he was very proud of himself. Uldini's dark eyes bored sternly and questioningly into his for a moment, then the magician threw his arms into the air and he stamped away, muttering to himself. Of course, Culhen was nowhere to be seen. Ahren had always been of the opinion that the wolf was unusually intelligent.

Laughing quietly to himself, Ahren climbed out of the water and dried himself off with his shirt. Then he slipped on his trousers before bending over the river to have a quick look at himself in the reflection. He could see his dark hair was falling over his eyes, which were a soft brown, and his face was alert in a way that it hadn't been before. His features were no longer childish and the fifteen-year-old was pleased to spot a little stubble on his chin. His shoulders were broader now and although his frame wasn't particularly muscular, it was sinewy. Satisfied, he stood upright and looked cheerfully into the trees.

'You can come out, he's gone,' he called quietly, and in an instant saw Culhen fifty metres away, trotting out from behind one of the massive trees which were scattered all over the forest and lent Eathinian a noble atmosphere.

The wolf tilted his head and his tongue lolled. Ahren could almost swear that Culhen was laughing.

'A few days ago, you took on a giant snake and now you're goading an immortal wizard. You're either very brave or very stupid,' said Ahren mock seriously. Then he slapped his thigh and Culhen ran over to his right side and trotted beside him.

They returned together through the forest to the knotted tree houses of the elves, and with every step Ahren enjoyed the peace and harmony that filled this place, and dissolved his troubles just as the early morning mist dissolved in the sunshine. He had no idea of what lay ahead of him, but Ahren was convinced that he should absorb every pleasant memory he could lay hold of.

The others were already waiting for him when Ahren arrived back at their accommodation. Uldini, as was to be expected, looked irritated – his black robe was already dry again – and stared at Culhen with a severe look. The wolf whimpered and pressed himself into Ahren's leg while the apprentice looked in concentration at his master.

Falk was leaning, arms folded, against the outside of the hut and looking at the wizard with an amused expression on his wrinkled face with its grey beard. The short grey hair of the muscular man was wet. He too must have taken the opportunity to refresh himself, and he was already dressed in his leather gear with his bow slung over his shoulder.

Ahren was suddenly uncomfortably aware of his naked torso and the crumpled shirt in his hand. He was about to hurry inside to prepare himself like his master had. He didn't want to give Falk the chance to list out Ahren's flaws in his gravelly voice, but the old man calmly raised his hand and smiled at him.

'Don't worry, Ahren. Wait here with us for a second. Jelninolan is just preparing your surprise,' he said in a friendly voice.

Ahren was taken aback. Of course his master was still intolerant, strict and intimidating, but since Ahren's successes in Evergreen, there were moments of leniency among the persistent criticisms from the old man.

The apprentice had been able to save the Voice of the Forest, the sacred animal of the elves, from a Swarm Claw. It was true that he had defeated the monstrous bird for other reasons and had known nothing of its prey's significance, but afterwards he had, with Culhen's help, nursed the newest incarnation of the Voice of the Forest - a little chipmunk – back to health. Everyone had been amazed and overjoyed when he produced the animal, now fully recovered, from his rucksack. Ahren was stunned that all of a sudden he had been promoted to the status of a hero.

The fabric that served as the entrance door to the tree house was moved aside and Jelninolan stepped out. The plump little elf with her dark red hair and green eyes smiled merrily as ever. Ahren thought yet again that this was how he would have loved his late mother, whom he had never known, to have been. The high priestess of the elf-goddesses,

SHE, WHO FEELS, was carrying a bundle in front of her. She addressed Ahren with a solemn look.

'The Evergreen folk want to express their gratitude once again, and so I present you with this gift: a suit of elf ribbon-armour put together by our best magic-craftspeople.' She pressed the bundle into his hands, and he looked down at it in amazement.

The reward he had asked for had been the suspension of his master's enforced exile from the elf forest, an exile that had been imposed because after his training, Falk, being a human, had spent far too much time with the elves. He couldn't believe he was getting a second reward.

He moved the finely woven cloth (gift enough in itself) aside and stared down in confusion at a complex assembly of leather bands and over two dozen variously formed leather panels. None of the panels was larger than a wooden plate, and Ahren was unsure if this was one of the impressive elf suits of armour he had seen worn by the tree top guards of this forest folk.

'Is it magical?' he asked hesitantly, only to be met with a disappointed shake of the head from his master and a derisive comment from Uldini.

'Not even two days a hero and he's already getting greedy,' interjected the boyish figure in a dry voice. Jelninolan however, smiled and dismissed the wizard's words with a wave of her hand.

'This armour has been designed to fit you perfectly and will adapt as you develop but it isn't magical. It takes more than one day to create a magical object – many weeks, in fact.'

'I didn't know that,' mumbled Ahren and gave the two men an accusing look. He had already complained to them before that he had been left in the dark about too many things, and after having innocently carried around the Voice of the Forest in his rucksack for many days, the others had promised him that they would keep him in the loop and give him more information.

He laid the bundle on the ground in embarrassment and gingerly pulled at one of the leather bands. Jelninolan gave a warning sound but it was too late. The individual bands seemed to be interconnected in a confusing way and as he pulled randomly at one, the others gathered together, and he was left with a complex knot of leather bands surrounded by an irregular, tightly knit combination of leather panels.

Uldini laughed like a billy goat, Falk covered his eyes with his hand and Jelninolan looked on with sadness. Ahren stared in shock at the chaos he had created.

'Have I broken it?' he whispered in the stillness, whereupon Falk let out another sigh.

'No, you haven't. But it will take quite a while to untangle. The ribbon armour is an elf masterpiece, made of interconnected leather panels, a network held together by these leather bands in a perfect balance of weight and counterweight. It takes a lot of practice to put on this armour without help. One of the reasons I never wore it', his master explained in a tired voice.

Uldini gave a derogatory snort and suspended himself with his customary magic a half pace in the air, where he stayed hovering.

'I'll tell the elves we'll be leaving as soon as you've cleared up the lad's mess. Falk, tell Selsena she should meet us, and organise the necessaries for the journey. And this time a little more than the bare minimum, please! There's nobody on our heels, unlike the last places we travelled through. We'd better disappear from here before your apprentice riles everyone up against us.'

The disapproving tone disappeared from the wizard's voice as he spoke and was replaced by a mild mocking tone. It seemed that Ahren's new position within the group meant that the honeymoon period was over, and he was now fair game for the moody wizard's biting humour.

Ahren sat quietly in the corner, watched Jelninolan as she slowly and patiently began to unpick the leather bands. He thought over Uldini's words. It was true, they really had been chased from one place to the next. They had defeated the Fog Cats in Deepstone and had fled so the villagers would be free of further danger. Then they had been hunted by Swarm Claws. Cut-throats had been after them in the large trading city of Three Rivers on account of falsified wanted posters that had been hung up around the place. And to top it all, they had fallen victim to an ambush half-way to the elf forest, organised by a High Fang, an intelligent servant of the Adversary. It was only here in Evergreen that they had found a little peace, and this was the first time they would be continuing their journey in a leisurely way.

He was jolted out of his thoughts by a hand clipping the back of his head. Jelninolan looked at him sharply, then pointed tellingly at the tangled armour.

'If I'm going to the trouble of sorting this for you, then the least you could do is look and learn,' she said testily.

The High Priestess had never been stern towards Ahren and it took him a second to recover from the shock. The look on his face, it seemed, caused the elf to laugh out loud. She tickled his cheek and her look softened before she turned her attention once again to the armour.

'You wanted us to treat you like an adult. Uldini is over a thousand years old and still gets a rap on the head from me. So, don't be surprised if I put you in your place when I think it's deserved,' she said absently, as she pulled at the bands in concentration. Ahren nodded in agreement and wished for the first time he hadn't insisted on being treated differently within the group.

'But I didn't know something like that would happen,' he said, trying to defend himself.

The stern look reappeared in the elf's face as she looked at him again.

'You demanded the right to ask questions and to receive answers. The only question I heard was if this present were magical. Then you started to play around with it.' She stopped speaking, but her summary of the situation made Ahren feel as if he had behaved like a three-year-old.

He harrumphed and addressed the elf as Uldini always did when wanted to get on her right side.

'Sorry, Aunt Jelninolan.'

The red-haired woman had freed Uldini from slavery and had begun teaching him at the time the Arch Wizard's talent had been awakening when he had, at the tender age of nine, accidently unlocked the secret of immortality. He had been imprisoned in the body of a child ever since, and Ahren was convinced that the wizard's deeply sarcastic behaviour was as attempt to counter his outer appearance.

Ahren was heartened by the effect of his familiar address because Jelninolan gave him a warm smile.

'Don't think I don't know what you're up to. Better not let Uldini hear you say that. He's the only one who addresses me like that. He hides it well, but there's a jealous streak in him. I'm sure you don't want to spend the rest of the time until your Naming being a potted plant,' she whispered conspiratorially.

Ahren swallowed hard. He decided to change the subject and not to address her like that in future.

'What's this band for?' he asked and pointed at one of the leather bands, which had a stylised wavy line engraved on it.

'That's the water band, sometimes also called the hip band,' Jelninolan answered. 'That's the first one we have to untangle, then the fire band and the cloud band will loosen themselves.'

The priestess and Ahren spent the best part of the morning going through the various panels and bands, and it struck the apprentice that every piece and connection had been well named. With every new piece, he asked about the deeper meaning behind the name and discovered that the elves had woven a story into the armour. Once you knew the story and used the order of the individual motifs, it was much easier to figure out how to assemble the armour.

Ahren was deeply impressed by the stunning nature of the pictures and the intricacy of the story. The water band, for example, represented the river and its various levels, not to mention its relationship to the sun and the rain. This was reflected in its dependency on the sun and cloud bands. All of the bands were dependent on several connections and when you understood the story, then you began to make sense of the armour.

Ahren asked question after question until finally all the knots had been undone and the leather panels lay cleanly on top of each other.

'Right, let's get on with it. Best if you put your shirt on or the armour could really chafe your skin when you're wearing it,' Jelninolan said mischievously and indicated his naked torso.

Ahren's face went a deep red and he ran into the hut so he could throw on a fresh linen shirt. Evergreen spoiled its inhabitants with its mild temperatures and pleasantly warm sunshine, and so Ahren had completely forgotten that he had been sitting there half-dressed. He came out of the tree house again and found the elf still sitting cross-legged with a smile on her face and the present, which they had untangled together, in front of her.

Ahren still hadn't got used to the natural way the elves followed their own inclinations wherever they found themselves. They had been sitting there for quite a while on the path in front of the house and any elves that had passed them had acknowledged them with nothing more than a polite nod. Ahren had seen elf craftswomen and men asleep in the communal square so it was little wonder that no-one had taken a blind bit of notice of their little disentanglement game on the path.

Jelninolan giggled when she saw that Ahren was still blushing.

'I've seen many more exciting things over the centuries than the chest of a mere boy, you know,' she commented, laughing at his timidity.

Ahren scratched his head in embarrassment and he wisely decided not to pursue the matter.

'We should finish this before the others come back. Uldini wants us to set off immediately and my mishap has cost us a lot of time,' he simply responded.

Ahren was well aware that he was using one of his failings to distract from another, but his time as Falk's apprentice had shorn of him of any false pride he may have possessed in the past.

Ahren's master had allowed him to make as many mistakes as he wanted, so long as he made the effort to learn from them in the future. 'Don't pick to pieces what you don't understand,' was one of the many pieces of advice he had taken to heart and tried to follow.

Jelninolan nodded and gingerly lifted the first layer from the pile.

'Step into it with your left leg and be careful not to touch the other bands,' she said in a concentrated voice.

Ahren nodded enthusiastically and a feeling of joyful anticipation came over him. Keenly and carefully he followed the elf's instructions and after a remarkably short time all the leather panels were in position. He realised that the main part of the work lay in the preparation. Once he stepped in and followed the order of the segments, the bands then did the rest of the work, pulling and lifting the individual panels into place.

Ahren turned around in a circle, moved his shoulders, tried a leap into the air and dropped into a crouching position.

The leather panels worked in perfect harmony with his movements, sliding elaborately over and under each other so that his body was always protected by at least one layer of leather. Of course, you couldn't compare it to Falk's solid knight armour but on the other hand you could hardly feel any weight and he was certain that it would prove less of a hindrance travelling through the forest than the simple leather gear he had worn up to now.

The leather panels were dyed a greenish brown, which would be useful as camouflage in the forest if he didn't want to be seen. His face was a picture of happiness as he gave the elf priestess a little bow.

'Thank you for this wonderful present. It almost feels like a second skin.'

Jelninolan bowed briefly in return and her voice took on a formal, almost ritualistic tone.

'Presented with joy, received with thanks and to be used with harmony,' she intoned.

Then she straightened up with a smile and patted his cheek again.

'Now you really look like a Forest Guardian. We would have made you a new bow, but an adult elf bow takes several moons,' she said regretfully.

Ahren stroked the leather in wonder. 'It doesn't matter,' he answered absently.

'When you're finished stroking your armour, there are more things to be packed.' It was Falk's stern voice, and the grey-haired man appeared from around the bend in the path.

Ahren disappeared guiltily inside and began to pack up the group's possessions.

'Surely you could have left him another few minutes with his new toy,' said Jelninolan to the old Forest Guardian in a reproachful voice.

He shrugged his shoulders and looked contentedly after his hardworking apprentice while he leaned in towards Jelninolan conspiratorially. 'At that age you have to keep bringing them back down to reality. That dreamy look in his face reminds me of the dangers of all those silly stories of valour and hunting griffins,' he said airily. Then he became serious.

'Our undertaking is dangerous enough as it is for his young shoulders. He has come some way already, but he still has much to master. I want to hammer as much as possible into that skull of his before things get really uncomfortable, or he stops listening,' he added quietly.

Jelninolan placed her hand on his strong arm and pressed it gently. 'You're concerned for the boy and only want what's best for him. I'm very proud of you. You've found your centre again since that time, and looking after him has done you good,' she said in a warm voice. 'Do you know what he wanted as reward for saving the Voice of the Forest?' she continued and looked at him expectantly.

Falk shook his head and the high priestess looked deeply into his eyes. 'Only one thing – that we would lift your banishment from Eathinian. That shows you're doing a good job.' She emphasised this with a smile.

Falk had listened intently to her words and now stood stock-still. 'He did that?' he asked incredulously. 'And what have you decided?' he added fearfully after a few heartbeats.

Jelninolan shrugged her shoulders and looked at him innocently. 'You know what the elders are like in these matters. I spoke on your behalf, but in the end it's a group decision.' She gave him a quick hug and then continued. 'First, be thankful for your apprentice's loyalty. Everything else will take care of itself.'

Falk nodded. He was moved as he looked over at the young man who was hard at work. 'We would like to head off today if it were convenient for the young gentleman.'

'Yes, master,' called Ahren respectfully and redoubled his efforts. Falk gave a satisfied grunt and Jelninolan looked at the old man sternly. He stared back at her defiantly for a few heartbeats, then mumbled, 'I'd better give him a hand, or this will take all day.'

Chapter 2

It wasn't long before they had packed up all their belongings and made their way down the tree, Falk unceremoniously misusing the free hanging ribbons of fabric as a slide. In the beginning Ahren had found it bizarre that everything in the elf settlement was folded, knotted or woven together out of fabric, even the walls of the houses. But in the meantime, he had become used to it, and he was surprised to find that he missed the feathery bounciness under his feet as soon as they were back on the forest floor.

A large group of elves had turned up to send them off and Ahren saw laughing and merry faces all around him. Culhen was smothered by a gang of elf children and it pained Ahren that he was taking the young wolf away from his new playing partners. The animal had everything he needed here, and for a second, he was tempted to leave Culhen behind, but the thought of heading off into the wilderness without the wolf at his side was too much to contemplate, and he rejected the idea in an instant.

They now had considerably more things to bring with them than before, partly because Jelninolan was travelling with them, and partly because Uldini and Falk had gathered together additional equipment. Ahren was amazed by the little mountain of gear and was relieved when Falk produced two pack horses and gestured to his apprentice that he should load them up. For a moment Ahren had seen himself weighed down with an enormous rucksack, puffing and wheezing as he trudged behind the others while his master explained that this was a part of this training. So he quickly got down to work and loaded the two good-natured animals.

Jelninolan had joined them but Ahren couldn't see any travelling clothes on her. She was still wearing the same pale green linen clothing as in the morning. Somehow, Ahren found this disappointing.

He knew that the elf priestess had fought alongside Uldini and the Paladins in the Dark Days, and had assumed that Jelninolan would appear as a resplendent heroic figure, sparkling with magical items and heading off into the world on an armoured Titejunanwa.

Instead, there she was, sitting on a piebald mare and looking, but for her pointed ears, for all the world like the farmer's wife from next door. Even her magic staff looked like any normal stick.

'You're not riding an elf-charger?' he asked as politely as he could.

Jelninolan laughed and shook her head so wildly that her red hair flew in all directions.

'Estelian never leaves Evergreen. In fact, neither does any Titejunanwa. After all, they are the custodians of the forest,' she said airily. 'Only when the elves go to war, then the Titejunanwas stand by their side.'

'And what about Selsena?' he responded. He'd seen the unicorn for the first time in the Eastern Forest of Deepstone when she had saved him from a Blood Wolf's attack – Culhen's mother, in fact – and he also had Selsena to thank that he had succeeded in freeing the whelp from the curse of the dark god. She had been Falk's companion for decades, even though a bitter dispute between them had kept them apart for years.

'She is a special case,' said the elf, and was about to continue but Falk intervened.

'The old girl has always had a stubborn streak and doesn't take a blind bit of notice of what others say or think.' Then he tilted his head as he always did when he and the unicorn communicated silently and said in a resigned voice, 'I should have known.'

With her mane billowing in the wind, Selsena galloped out from the trees, her silver eyes fixed on Falk and a wave of disapproval streaming out of her.

The Titejunanwa could only speak telepathically with Falk, but she could sense others' feelings and transmit her own to them. And at the moment she was expressing her feelings towards Falk's sarcastic commentary in no uncertain terms.

The Forest Guardian turned and stood awkwardly for a couple of heartbeats before tickling the animals head, above the protective bone plate, from which protruded one long spiral horn and two small curved dagger-like ones. They were arranged one beneath the other, and Ahren had seen what havoc the mighty elf charger could wreak in the heat of battle.

Nothing of her fighting strength was evident now as Falk's devotion towards her transformed her displeasure into a wave of blissful contentment. Ahren stepped up to the animal, two paces in height, and put an arm around her neck.

'I haven't seen you since you helped us combat the Warden of the Weeping Valley. I haven't had a chance to thank you for your help yet.' Then he pressed himself against her and she reciprocated his affection.

'Any chance of you finishing your group hug and sweet-talking? There's a dwarf waiting for us out there and we still have to find the place of ritual for the Naming. Unless of course you want to carry on canoodling until a certain bad-tempered godhead has awakened.'

Uldini's little tirade ruthlessly ended their joyful reunion with the unicorn. Self-satisfied, the little figure looked spitefully at the group and was greeted with scornful looks in return.

'What?' he asked innocently. 'Someone has to keep a clear head here or you'll spend the whole day patting each other on the back.'

He turned dramatically to face the assembled elves and called out in a magically strengthened voice: 'Dear friends, sadly the time has come for us to leave you. We shall take good care of Jelninolan. For your part, please spread the tidings throughout Evergreen that the time of the Thirteenth has come, and we shall soon need the strength of the elves to succeed against HIM,' he intoned formally.

'Complaining about us and then immediately going all sentimental during a little farewell speech,' murmured Falk, loudly enough for everyone in the group to hear.

The others sniggered and Uldini spun angrily around to face the old Forest Guardian.

'I was speaking not only to the elves but also to the pages of history. My words will find their way into every relevant historical document. Not everyone is content with a 'let's get this job done,'' said the Arch Wizard sulkily.

Falk gave a disinterested shrug of his shoulder. 'I thought it was the right thing to say at the time and it hit the nail on the head,' he responded drily.

One of the older elves stepped forward before Ahren could ask what the pair were arguing about now.

'We have discussed young Ahren's wish and reached a decision. We, the Eathinian folk welcome into our fold the Guardian of the Forest known to us as Falk, once he has fulfilled the task that has been bestowed upon him.' Then he placed his hand on his heart and made a gesture towards Falk. A wave of similar gestures rippled through the crowd of elves and Falk responded with same gesture. There were tears in his eyes. A gentle wind wafted through the solemn silence that held everyone in its charm, and it almost seemed as if the forest itself was giving the Guardian her blessing.

Finally, Jelninolan embraced the old man and Ahren too couldn't resist the impulse. The silence was broken by the joyful laughter of the forest folk. All the elves congratulated Falk, Selsena whinnied and sent her triumphant feelings out into the world while Culhen jumped around the group, barking happily.

'Oh good, more canoodling. We're never going to get away from here,' Uldini sighed, resignation in his voice. Then he floated up and over to congratulate his old friend too.

A short time later and they were on their way.

They all sat on their horses and Jelninolan led them on the broad paths through the trees of Evergreen, and so they trotted along at a comfortable pace. The sun was high in the sky and they had only another half a day's journey.

Falk had pulled himself together again and every now and then threw a look of gratitude towards Ahren, something that slowly made the apprentice uneasy. He wasn't used to this prolonged friendliness from his master and didn't know how to deal with it, so he sought refuge by asking Uldini questions.

'How does our plan look exactly?' he asked.

Uldini shrugged his shoulder and raised an eyebrow. 'We conquer HIM, WHO FORCES?' the wizard said nonchalantly.

Ahren suppressed a sigh. When the wizard was in a mood like this, he had to be more precise with his questions. He tried again. 'Where exactly are we going and what do we have to do there for my Naming to be fulfilled?'

Uldini became serious and started counting off the stages of the journey on his fingers.

'Well, first we have to make our way through Knight Marshes to King's Island. That's the only harbour in this region from which ships take a direct course to the Silver Cliff. The alternative would have meant a several weeks detour, and we want to avoid wasting time. So, we're going to sail southwards from the main town along the coast and disembark when we reach the dwarves. Then we come to the vague part of our plans. We don't know what task our currently nameless dwarf has to perform on his Lonely Guard or Watch as it's called. According to dwarf laws only other dwarves are prohibited from helping him in his task. We'll take advantage of this loophole and give the poor chap a helping hand. Our group has enough exceptional talents that the dwarves are lacking in, so I'm pretty sure we can quickly help him,' explained Uldini. 'Then it will get easier. We'll travel by land through Kelkor, grab ourselves a member of the Wild Folk, preferably a fay, and ask him or her to lead us to the Place of Ritual.'

Uldini was silent and looked at Ahren expectantly. The apprentice mulled over what he had just heard, then stopped short.

'Won't the dwarves be furious if we as outsiders interfere with the Lonely Watch? It sounds a bit like cheating.'

Uldini hesitated briefly and then shook his head.

'Not really. The Lonely Watch is there to prove to the community the worth of the individual dwarf. If the candidate succeeds in organising help from outside, then the commonality has been helped, without other dwarves having to assist him. The little people would see that as being pragmatic. As long as things can be completed and it doesn't cost anything, then they're happy,' said Uldini with an admiring undertone in his voice.

Jelninolan snorted and slapped her thigh in protest as she looked over at the magus. 'Just don't admire them for their cold-heartedness and callousness as well. They're little barbarians who send their own children to certain death while these children are trying to earn their right to a name,' she said angrily.

Uldini merely smiled in return and shrugged his shoulders.

'You know me, auntie. I always had a leaning towards the practical. I find a certain amount of efficiency very refreshing. Not everyone lives in a magical forest and has a natural sensitivity towards harmony and balance. We others can only come to insight through hard work. And simply put, our ways are not your ways. The free peoples are fundamentally varied, and that's good. The Adversary would have won that time if everyone had followed the elf method, and you know that yourself,' he responded.

Ahren was amazed to see the Arch Wizard arguing so vehemently with his erstwhile mentor. The elf had always seemed to appeal to his softer nature until now, but Uldini seemed to be iron-willed regarding this topic.

Jelninolan was silent and Ahren was convinced this was not the first time they had had this discussion. He didn't want to make the argument between them any worse, so he asked another question that had been gnawing at him.

'How much time are we going to need? It seems like a very long way, and if I've understood you correctly, the Naming should have been completed by the winter solstice.'

The thought that the sleeping god was nourishing himself with every breath that Ahren had taken since the blessing of the gods – and that the sleeping charm on the Adversary was thereby being shortened – made the hairs on the back of Ahren's neck stand up. He himself didn't sense anything, but the wizard's assurances that this invisible connection was present and active, worried Ahren no end.

Uldini rubbed his bald head absently with his hand.

'This is the very reason I'm pushing things along. I looked at the stars last night – it's ninety-eight days until the winter solstice. The journey alone to King's Island, then on to the Silver Cliff and after that through Kelkor will take a good two moons. That leaves us a little over thirty days to release the Lonely Watch and to find the Place of Ritual, and of course there are the inevitable delays. We could be dealing with Dark Ones as soon as we're out of Evergreen. As you can see, it might be tight,' he explained.

'How is it that you don't actually know where you are to perform the Naming Ritual,' asked Ahren, a little anxiously.

Up until now he had seen the Arch Wizard as someone infallible, but the more Ahren asked, the more he realised that even the eternally youthful magician didn't have the perfect answer to all the questions. This realisation made him deeply uneasy.

'At any normal Naming, the old Paladin passed the power on to their son or daughter. The parent then became mortal again and the next generation carried on the fight. The place was more or less irrelevant. But in this case, there is nobody who can transfer the power to you. Instead of that, the blessing of the gods has been bubbling out of you since the Spring Ceremony. We have to find the suitable place where we can anchor the power within you. There we will use the Naming as a channeling ritual and then you will be a Paladin. No more ebbing away of power and no more strengthening of the enemy. But finding a suitable place is far from easy. Something like this has never been done before. We have no point of reference to show us the right direction. That's why we need the help of the Wild Folk. The Wild Folk are practically made of magic. They can point us to a Place of Ritual without any bother, one that will fulfil our objectives.'

The voice of the childlike Arch Wizard was sounding much more confident again and Ahren breathed a sigh of relief. He had enough to be thinking about, and the last thing he needed was a clueless Uldini.

There was one more point however, that he wanted clarified.

'We don't have to be finished with everything by the winter solstice, do we? It isn't that HE, WHO FORCES wakes up immediately at that point, is it?' Ahren's questioning sounded more fearful than he liked.

Having, it seemed, got over her previous argument with Uldini, Jelninolan now joined in the conversation.

'No, HE wouldn't wake up at that instant. But during the winter solstice, the longest night of the year, HE will be able to misuse a large part of your blessing for his purposes. HE would awaken completely, considerably more quickly after that, and up until that point, his attacks on you and the other Paladins would be far clearer and more focussed than at present. HE has not yet even left the deep sleep, but you have already seen what barriers HE has put in your way. Uldini's approach is totally correct. If we want to have a decent chance of uniting the free peoples against HIM and gathering the Paladins at the Pall Pillar, we are going to need as much time as possible.'

The elf's tone of voice brooked no opposition and once the wizard had nodded in agreement, Ahren vowed to himself to do everything to carry out the Naming as soon as possible. The young man had no idea what would follow that, but at least he had a tangible goal he could now aim for.

Chapter 3

Ahren awoke the next morning from an uneasy sleep. He had been plagued by a recurrent nightmare in which a skeletal hand reached into his chest and squeezed his heart slowly and endlessly, while he wandered through the starless night, calling in vain for help.

Ahren rubbed his face and shook off the effects of the nightmare. The fact that he was so used to these dreams now should have given him food for thought, and if he were honest with himself, he was thankful that he had learned how to live with them.

He stood up and stretched as quietly as possible. It wasn't sunrise yet and everyone was still asleep.

Well, almost everyone, he corrected himself. The blanket on which Jelninolan had been lying was empty.

Ahren assumed that the elf was saying goodbye to Evergreen. According to Uldini they would return to the Knight Marshes during the course of the day. They would make better progress on the trade paths and save themselves long distances than if they were to continue travelling through Evergreen.

They had travelled a considerable time the previous day until it had become too dark. The atmosphere had been pensive and subdued.

Ever since hearing that he would be allowed to return to Eathinian, Falk had been smiling happily, and as they had ridden onwards, he had seemed to be conversing with Selsena. The rest of the group had been lost in their own thoughts, and Ahren had been digesting the news he had learned that day and forging plans whereby he could help them make good progress.

One of which he would now put into effect. Of course, he couldn't speed up their journey significantly, but he could ensure that the others wouldn't be waiting for him, and he could prepare himself in so far as it was possible for any potential dangers.

He grasped hold of Windblade and sought out a small secluded clearing where he could practise what he had learned from the armourer Falagarda a few weeks previously in Three Rivers when she had drilled into him in the basics of attacking and parrying.

Culhen woke up as he was leaving their camp and Ahren gestured to him to be quiet. The wolf immediately crouched down and crept over towards the apprentice. Ahren tickled him between the ears as a reward and then they slipped away.

Ahren spent a moment finding his bearings before deciding on a clearing they had ridden by the previous day, shortly before they had set up camp. He was stretching and loosening his muscles as they approached when suddenly he stopped stock still.

He could hear sounds that he couldn't identify coming from the training spot he'd picked. A sort of rhythmical beating was reverberating through the forest and it certainly wasn't a natural sound.

He moved towards the sound carefully, and Culhen did the same. Crouching in the undergrowth, Ahren slowly crept forward and spied out the clearing, ten paces in diameter and barely visible in the early dawn. Surprised, he gave a sigh of relief and stepped out of the branches once he saw the source of the sounds.

Jelninolan was standing at a fallen tree and was making a dazzling array of movements with her magic staff, hitting the branch in ever-changing angles and thrusts, the staff circling her body in breath-taking patterns. Even as a neutral spectator, Ahren couldn't predict where the next hit would come from.

Ahren could see that the elf's linen clothing was already soaked with perspiration and he reckoned she must have been laying into the tree trunk for some time already. He stepped out of the undergrowth and his relaxed posture was a signal to Culhen that he too could let down his guard. The wolf leaped into the clearing with his tail wagging and raced towards the elf, yelping joyfully. She reacted with an immediate spin around, and her staff came down at lightning speed towards Culhen's nose.

Before Ahren had a chance to shout out a warning, the staff stopped a hand's width over the head of the stunned-looking young wolf who sat on his hind legs in shock and whimpered quietly at Jelninolan.

The elf priestess dropped the staff with a laugh and grasped Culhen's white fur in her comforting hands. He allowed himself to be cuddled, and she looked over his shoulders at Ahren.

'I really must be rusty if I didn't hear you from such a close distance,' she said breathlessly. ' It still isn't very clever to sneak up on a trained warrior in the half light. If my reflexes had become even more dulled over the years, the wolf would have a nice big lump on his head now.'

Ahren lifted Windblade to show her.

'We'd planned on practising here too while the others were sleeping. I have to admit, I never expected to see you training with weapons. Aren't you a priestess and magician?' he finished somewhat lamely.

'And are they not supposed to protect themselves? What strange ideas you people sometimes have. My magic covers many things: illusion, healing, mind-reading. But I've never been able to create fireballs like Uldini. I've never had the will to inflict deadly damage, and so my battle magic is rather weak and passive. I prefer the staff when it comes to the crunch. It can be very effective when used properly, and with the necessary precision you can put your opponent out of commission without having to kill him, she said emphatically.

Filled with curiosity, Ahren stepped closer, all the while fiddling around with the scabbard of Windblade.

'Dark Ones have to be killed though, don't they? Aren't you just postponing the inevitable?' he asked carefully. He found it difficult to contradict the priestess.

She always seemed so noble and in harmony with everything so it was hard to believe she could be wrong about anything. But her confrontation with Uldini yesterday had shown that even the knowledge of an ageless elf priestess wasn't limitless.

She looked thoughtfully down at Culhen and only said, 'so every Dark One must be killed? What do you think Culhen would have to say to that?'

A feeling of shame overcame Ahren for what he had said. He himself had gone against his master when he had found the Blood Wolf's whelp and had refused to kill the pup. His four-legged friend wouldn't be here now if he hadn't believed in finding a solution that didn't involve the spilling of blood.

Before he could answer, the elf continued speaking.

'Of course, I know what you mean, but I'm trying to limit the damage I will cause. Who knows what will happen to all the creatures HE has in HIS power when you and the other Paladins impede HIM. Do they turn back into what they were previously, do they die, or do they have their own free will at last? Imagine you exterminate all the Blood Wolves only to discover you could have saved them all – free of blood lust, taking their place in the great scheme of things.'

She stroked Culhen's fur as she spoke and meanwhile the young wolf had rolled over on his back so the elf could tickle his tummy too.

Ahren bit his lip thoughtfully and decided to mull over the priestess's words. He had realised from the day before that whenever she spoke, it was as an elf, and elves always felt a natural affinity with all things. Ahren shared her conviction that one's first duty was to preserve life.

He gave her a nod in agreement, cleared his throat and pointed apologetically at his weapon.

'I need to do my morning practice before the others wake up. I don't want to be the cause of another delay'.

The elf looked at his sword with curiosity.

'That's a Windblade, isn't it? I haven't seen one in such a long time. Did you know that it was originally an elf weapon?' she said.

Surprised, Ahren shook his head. 'I thought Windblades came from the Eternal Empire,' he answered.

'Well, yes, since then. But they were developed by us at the start of the Dark Days. The people of the Eternal Empire had a talent for handling them and developed them further, both in their form, and technically. We elves decided to pull away from the horrors of close combat and so we lost the art of manufacturing them. Instead we concentrated on the art of making bows and arrows.'

She seemed to be lost in thought for a moment, then she looked at him alertly.

'Show me what you can do,' she said. 'The foot technique is practically the same as with stick fighting and maybe I can give you a few useful tips.'

Ahren nodded, somewhat embarrassed, and pulled the weapon out of its scabbard. The first rays of sunlight raced silently through the leafy roof of the elf Forest, and one of them sparkled on the curved blade of the weapon.

Ahren floated into the state which Falk called the Void. It was a form of meditation which enabled him to blank out all forms of distraction. Even though the apprentice was now able to achieve the Void regularly when he was practising, this ability often failed him when it came to the crunch. Mostly it lasted for only a few heartbeats but, as during his confrontation with the Warden of the Weeping Valley, an enormous snake, even that short time was enough to do the necessary damage. Instead of tackling the monster head on, he had tricked it. He had shot the magic lute from the tree on which it was hanging, so that Culhen could bring it to Jelninolan while Selsena had distracted the enormous monster.

Jelninolan was impatiently shifting her weight from one foot to the other while looking quizzically at him, so Ahren shook himself awake from his daydreaming and began to glide through the various movements.

The elf watched him silently, without saying anything at all. When Ahren was finished, he stood breathing heavily in front of her and she merely nodded.

'Very good. Now do the whole routine again. Only this time backwards.'

The young man gasped.

'Backwards?' he asked in disbelief.

'Yes. Reverse the order. The last parry first, then the penultimate attack and so on.' She gave a smile and waited expectantly, leaning on her stick.

Much to his horror, Ahren stumbled painfully slowly, back through the movements. The transitions were clumsy, his footwork was all over the place and his thrusts were jittery. When he was finally finished, his confidence had evaporated.

'You've never changed the order, am I right? Which means that the technique looks beautiful, but it doesn't fulfil its task. You must learn to vary things. Then you must learn how to react. The parrying and attacking must happen when you need them, not when it's their turn.' Her voice was soft and free of criticism, but Ahren still felt the need to defend himself.

'Falk never told me to change the order.'

Even as the words were coming out of his mouth, he realised how childish it sounded, blaming his master, but he felt that he had been betrayed. The young man had really begun to see himself as a passable swordsman, but the priestess had shattered his illusions in the blink of an eye and with a simple variation of his exercises.

The red-haired elf smiled good-naturedly and gave him an encouraging pat on the back.

'Falk isn't to blame. His own training was more in the classic military style. Practising the basics until they became second nature, and then the rest followed. That's what he's done with you and he can't be blamed for that. But now we have to break the pattern before you get stuck in a rut. Don't look so sad. Look on it as progress. You're now ready to climb the next rung of a very tall ladder,' she said, encouragingly.

Ahren was feeling a little better now and gave her a smile in gratitude. He was determined to master this new challenging phase of his swordsmanship.

Jelninolan stood upright in front of him, took her stick in both hands and swung both ends back and forth.

'Right, then. Now try to hit me,' she commanded.

Ahren looked doubtfully at the naked blade in his hand and said hesitantly, 'but…but I don't want to hurt you'.

An energetic smile creased Jelninolan's face.

'Then I had better be careful.'

Daylight had re-established itself in Evergreen, and Falk and Uldini had decamped when a merry, whistling elf and a badly beaten, hobbling apprentice returned to the horses.

Falk couldn't believe his eyes and asked in disbelief, 'what happened to you? Did a tree fall on you?'

'Something like that,' muttered Ahren and felt one of his molars with his tongue. It was feeling a bit loose since it was hit with a particularly mean blow.

'We were just doing a bit of training', said Jelninolan airily.

'Auntie, if you're determined on dismantling our would-be Paladin here and now, then do let us know so we can spare ourselves the long journey,' said Uldini sarcastically.

She glanced over at Ahren and pensively placed a finger to her lips.

'I'm a little out of practice and I hit him more often than I had intended,' she said regretfully.

Then she went over to Ahren and carefully put his head in her hands. She whispered something in Elfish and the pain disappeared, while a gentle coolness spread throughout his body. Jelninolan gave him a critical look, then nodded in satisfaction.

'As good as new. Everything should be healed by midday. Thank you dear, I think we'll do the whole thing again tomorrow morning,' she said sweetly.

Ahren looked at his master in horror and pleaded silently for help.

'If you're planning on beating my apprentice to a pulp, then please ask me for permission beforehand. In fact, I'd planned on taking a hard line with him today, but if I overdo it, he'll break down altogether. You can thrash him…sorry, I mean train him, every second day.'

Ahren was flabbergasted and looked at his master, who was holding out the prospect of the priestess torturing him regularly without batting an eyelid. Falk looked back at him and his voice took on a serious tone.

'I'm doing you a favour. Jelninolan has more experience than all of us in fighting and that means something. She can teach you a lot, especially the fundamentals, and if you're in this state after such a short training session, then you could certainly do with the practice. Now, get ready and have a bite to eat. We're setting off shortly,' he said firmly.

That was the end of the matter and Ahren realised soberly that his cranky old master was back again after only one day of high spirits caused by the lifting of his banishment. Maybe Ahren should have wished for something different as a reward.

He went over to his armour and bent down to put it on when Culhen suddenly stopped and fixed his eyes on the bundle of leather panels and bands. Ahren looked suspiciously at the bundle and spotted a barely perceptible movement among the narrow leather ribbons. He strained his neck forward very slowly to see what was hiding in there when a small wraithlike shadow jumped towards him. All Ahren could see was a collection of furry legs and a red barb that was bounding towards his face. His reflexes, ingrained through exercise, kicked in immediately and without thinking he dropped straight to the floor.

The thing, whatever it was, whooshed over him and landed with a slight rustling sound on the forest floor.

Ahren spun around and saw how the thing was crawling to him at lightning speed on its eight legs, when an arrow whizzed past the apprentice's head and landed with a satisfied crunching sound in its little black body, pinning the thing to the ground. Ahren thought he heard a furious hissing, and then the creature moved no more. Just to be safe, he crawled back half a pace before picking himself up.

'What sort of a thing was that?' he gasped. His arms and legs were shaking, and he suppressed a shudder with difficulty.

'That was a Needle Spider,' said Falk with disgust. 'I haven't seen one in a long time. I didn't know they lived in Evergreen as well.'

'They don't' responded Jelninolan, who was clearly in shock. 'At least, they haven't until now'.

Uldini made a gesture with his hand and the arrow released itself from the spider's body. Another wave of his hand and the insect was lifted into the air where it turned slowly on its own axis.

'The common Needle Spider is actually to be found only in the southern jungles. HE, WHO FORCES made a tiny alteration to their needs, and as a result they have spread out into every region. The beasts are naturally aggressive and extremely territorial. They were a real plague because, being normal animals, they are immune to Magic Charms against Dark Ones.'

Uldini had fallen into his lecturing voice, all the while turning the suspended animal so that Ahren could examine it properly. He could see eight long hairy legs protruding from a dull-black, knotty body. A fiery red barb stuck out of the spider's back, which looked quite flexible. Ahren could make out neither eyes nor head, just an enormous mouth on the underside of the spider, in which were several rows of teeth, all of them barbed. Feeling nauseous, he took a step backward.

Uldini made another hand movement and the body was consumed by magic flames until nothing was left but a heap of ashes.

'The things are extremely poisonous, both the barb and spittle. One sting or bite and within ten heartbeats your lungs have stopped working and you suffocate. I think Culhen has just saved your life, young man,' said Falk seriously.

The wolf sat down on his hind legs and tilted his head when he heard his name. And when Ahren embraced his furry friend, he gave Ahren's face a good lick with his tongue.

Uldini addressed them again with a look of alarm on his face.

'I don't think this was a coincidence. I wouldn't be surprised if HE harried the animal into your armour with an insinuation,' said the wizard, tensely.

'An insinuation? What do you mean?' asked Ahren nervously.

'A little suggestion, rather than force. You can ensure that a creature performs an action that it would willingly do anyway, given the right circumstances. A hungry person eating a loaf of bread, or an exhausted animal resting under a palm. But with an insinuation you can decide which loaf of bread or palm the object of the magic will seek out. This is a very subtle kind of magic which, if I'm not mistaken, isn't really part of our enemy's armoury,' Uldini responded.

Jelninolan interrupted with an edge in her voice. 'Then it can't have been HIM. Someone whispered to the spider how warm and snug the bundle of armour was. I'm thinking it was more likely a Doppelganger.'

Ahren froze. Doppelgangers were the most dangerous of the Dark God's weaponry. They were a spurned experiment of the gods, and the only living beings in creation who served the Adversary of their own free will. They were highly intelligent, dangerous and completely unscrupulous. And their master could transform into any form that suited his plans. They were his most important agents, generals and assassins.

'You think one of the elves here is an assassin?' Ahren asked Jelninolan, his voice trembling.

Falk responded by shaking his head. 'That's impossible. The emotional connections among the elves would immediately alert them to the alien spirit of a Doppler. I'm thinking more in terms of an animal.

Something small and unobtrusive that one mightn't even notice,' he mused.

Jelninolan made some hand movements and spoke a long and complicated Elfish sentence. A ball of blue light appeared above her hand and she addressed it.

Ahren recognised the object as a Rillan, a magic ball that could deliver messages. Jelninolan finished her torrent of words, the ball rose up from the palm of her hands and flew off into the forest at speed.

'The others have been informed and are going to comb the forest with a magic net. The Voice of the Forest will stay where he's safe for now, in case another attempt is made to kill him.'

Uldini nodded in agreement. 'Well done. This Doppelganger is in for a hard time. I'm pretty sure the Titejunanwas will be furious about his meddling and will be searching for him too,' he said gleefully.

Selsena reacted with a snort and everyone felt her indignation clearly.

Jelninolan watched the Rillan disappear and her concern for her home place was written in her face.

'Don't be afraid,' said Falk calmly. 'Evergreen can look after itself well. It always has done so. By this time tomorrow every elf, every plant and every animal in the forest will be hunting down the intruder. In two days at the latest the Doppler will be dead or will have fled.'

She smiled at Falk in gratitude and turned away from the disappearing Rillan. Then they silently packed up their things and strode off, leaving only a little pile of ashes behind them, which was finally caught up in the gentle spring breeze of Evergreen. It wasn't long before the ashes had been scattered and lost to memory.

The rest of their journey through Evergreen that day went without incident. Jelninolan was true to her word: the strange coolness had disappeared from Ahrens body by midday and he realised that all his wounds had disappeared. He briefly wondered what it would be like if she had been his teacher. Then she would have been able to heal him any time he was injured. It wasn't long however, before the unfortunate realisation dawned on him that Falk's method was more effective. Whenever he had made a mistake or injured himself, he had been urged by his master to be more careful and skilful. Ahren's instinct constantly drove him to internalise the Forest Guardian's instructions quickly so he would avoid further injury. Even when the young man couldn't move anymore because of cramps, Falk found a way of turning this into a lesson, describing to Ahren how he could run more economically, climb with more ease, and shoot with more precision. The fact that Jelninolan could make all traces and consequences of Ahren's missteps disappear with a few gestures of her hands also lessened their significance. It was true that at this moment he was only too happy to be uninjured again, but in the long run he would become careless and neglectful if he had a teacher who cured him in the blink of an eye every time.

He smiled in gratitude over at Falk, who responded with an irritated frown. The old man signalled to Selsena to drop back until he was riding beside his apprentice.

'Are you alright again?' he asked shortly.

'Yes, master. The next time I practise with her, I'll be more careful', responded Ahren, eager to please. He wanted to show Falk that he had learned his lesson.

'What exactly happened?' the Guardian wanted to know.

'I was supposed to attack Jelninolan with Windblade because she wanted to practise. But I was very careful because I was afraid of hurting her. She swung her stick in complicated patterns and parried every one of my blows. Then it became painful.' Ahren winced at the memory of it.

'She said now it was her turn and I should parry. I didn't see half of her attacking blows coming. And she hardly said a word. You're always shouting at me and telling me what I'm doing wrong. But I only heard her say individual words and they weren't connected, so I didn't understand a thing. "Left", "lower", "more from the middle", those sorts of things.' Ahren shook his head in frustration.

Falk laughed out loud and looked at him in amusement. Selsena too seemed to be greatly amused.

'It seems as though your master isn't that bad after all, what?' And without waiting for an answer he continued, 'Elves teach in a completely different way to humans. Because of their emotional connections they need considerably fewer words in many situations. Jelninolan was probably just as annoyed as you were because you weren't listening to her, but were just allowing yourself to be beaten to a pulp. When I learned from the elves in those days, they had to invent specific exercises for me because I didn't understand things that every school elf would have picked up on the first day. So, remember that, the next time you're cursing your master.'

Ahren nodded eagerly and then looked a little guilty.

Falk started to ride to the front of the group but then dropped back again. 'Thank you for ending my banishment. That means a lot to me and Selsena,' he murmured in an almost inaudible voice. The Titejunanwa sent a wave of deep gratitude to him, then galloped forward so that the two them were positioned one again at the head of the group.

Ahren looked thoughtfully after his master. The old man might not have realised it, but he had certainly adopted a few of the elves' traits. When it came to expressing emotions, he didn't say much either.

By afternoon they had reached the edge of the forest. Even from a distance they had already seen the two defence towers rising into the sky near the trees and trying in vain to defy the majestic treetops of the elf forest. Ahren was surprised that the defence fortifications were so near the trees. When they had travelled along the trade path alongside the Red Posts, there had been a respectful distance between the last manifestations of human military power and the elf forest.

He was about to make a point of this to Falk when his master sat bolt upright in his saddle and signalled to the others to halt.

'What's up, old man?' asked Uldini impatiently, drawing up beside him.

'I'm not sure, but it looks like trouble', said Falk, hesitantly.

Ahren pushed his way forward as far as possible to just behind the pair and peered beyond the wizard. He could see a mounted posse of armed soldiers wearing tabards, who were keeping their eyes peeled on the forest border. Their weapons were not drawn but the expressions on the men and women were grim and almost hostile.

Uldini turned to Jelninolan with a quizzical look.

'Is the local baron in conflict with Evergreen? That doesn't look like a normal border patrol. The next convenient crossover to the Knight Marshes, which becomes a plastered road, is two days' journey away. It isn't really much of a detour but after having found Ahren's visitor in his armour, I would suggest getting away from these trees while the Doppelganger hasn't been found.'

'Actually, Baron Gralon always had a good relationship with us. We haven't heard anything from him over the last five summers, but we never thought it odd. You know how slow elf diplomacy is. If we don't like a ruler, we just wait a generation and talk to his successor. Five summers is a blink of an eye.' She looked suspiciously at the towers.

'The fact that he's manned the towers again however, is new and disturbing. They've been unoccupied for over two hundred years,' she added.

'We should turn around. It can't be a coincidence', implored Falk.

Uldini didn't seemed convinced and rubbed his bald head thoughtfully.

'Let's give it a shot anyway. The baron won't risk starting a war by attacking guests of the elves. If the worst comes to the worst, we'll have to turn around, but at least we'll know what the border watch means. The best-case scenario – they're just trying to catch a thieving tramp who's slipped into Evergreen, thinking he might try his luck among the elves,' said the Arch Wizard.

They strode slowly nearer and Ahren's hands began to sweat. He fidgeted with his body armour and straightened his sword and bow, all the while indicating to Culhen that he should disappear into the undergrowth. There were too many guards and he didn't want one of them to get nervous because he saw a wolf, and fire off a bolt at him.

He relaxed a little once he couldn't see the animal anymore and concentrated on the guards in front of him. They had taken up position and presented a row of bodies, blocking the route.

A woman with a plume of feathers in her helmet stretched out her arm towards them and thundered in a commanding voice, 'halt! In the name of Baron Gralon, ruler of the Northern High Marshes, I command you to stay still or we will use force!'

'Would it have been better if I'd put on my knight armour again?' whispered Falk to Uldini.

'We never thought anyone would be here, not to mention a small army. No, I don't think we'll reveal your title, this is all a bit too bizarre. We'll find out what the problem is and disappear back into the forest.

46

They look really angry. Even if they let us through, I wouldn't like to have any of these armed guards behind me,' answered Uldini quickly.

Falk nodded and sat up straight in his saddle as he trotted a few paces forward to show that he was their speaker. The reaction of the guards was immediate and surprisingly aggressive. Swords were drawn, crossbows raised, and shields positioned at the ready.

Ahren gasped while Falk slowly and deliberately raised his hands and his eyebrows.

'The hospitality in the Knight Marshes seems to have deteriorated rapidly since the last time I was here,' he said furiously. 'What has happened exactly to make you so hostile towards innocent travellers?'

The chief guard gestured with her hand and the rest of her troop relaxed a little.

'We are under orders not to let anyone enter or leave the elf forest. Farmers along the forest border have been found murdered. Whole families have been cut down, bored through with arrows. The baron is of the opinion that the elves are about to start a war and so he is preparing accordingly,' she said in a strained voice.

Ahren noticed that most of the hostile looks were trained on Jelninolan and so he pushed his horse forward, shielding the elf's body.

'Let's get out of here,' hissed Uldini.

Falk nodded imperceptibly and addressed the chief guard again. 'We spent quite a few days in the company of the elves and didn't notice any tension in the air, and the trade route along the Red Posts is still open and secure. Perhaps there are bandits wreaking destruction around here. I wouldn't judge the Evergreen elves quite so quickly.'

The Forest Guardian was about to continue when the woman cut him off with a commanding gesture.

'Enough! I will brook no more discussion concerning my master's commands. Turn around or bear the consequences. Brother Ansilmus has warned us that friends of the elves would try to lull us into a false sense of security. The Illuminated Path is only for the righteous – the elves are no longer considered such.'

Murmurs of agreement could be heard coming from the armed ranks.

Ahren had tensed up when he heard the woman's words, and the others had too.

The Illuminated Path was a religious cult used as a smokescreen by the Adversary's servants to lure the desperate and the foolish into his control.

It was only recently that one of their recruiters had spoken to Ahren at a trading post. Later, the man had been discovered to be a High Fang, a man under the dark god's control, who had then set a gang of highway robbers on the apprentice and his companions. The fact that the cult had extended its influence as far as the border patrols was certainly an ill omen.

Falk acknowledged the guard with a silent bow and Selsena turned and trotted back into the forest. The others followed, turning their heads every so often to make sure a bolt hadn't been fired off by an excitable guard who had lost his or her self-control.

As soon as they were out of sight of the forest border, Uldini stopped and let forth a terrifying torrent of maledictions and obscenities.

Ahren couldn't suppress a grin at the wizard's unflattering commentary concerning the family trees of the guards in general and the baron in particular. The apprentice was about to join in, but as he was about to issue his own invective, he was stopped by a steely look from Jelninolan.

Falk listened carefully and when the childlike figure paused for breath, he asked softly, 'are you feeling better now?'

'Not really, but it was necessary. Otherwise I would have ridden back to them and transformed them all into turnips,' grumbled Uldini and carried on with his cursing.

This went on for another while until Culhen started running around them whining, and Jelninolan's face took on a pained expression as the expletives became ever more creative. Finally, even Ahren didn't find the wave of obscenities entertaining anymore and so he tried somehow to stop the Arch Wizard's tirade.

'Why turnips?', he asked, unable to think of anything better.

'I hate turnips!' Uldini spat out, stopping his own torrent of words.

Jelninolan used the pause by raising her voice while giving Ahren a look of gratitude. 'This development is really disturbing. The peace between the Knight Marshes and Evergreen was always fragile. I bet you anything the Illuminated Path are responsible for the murders and have set us elves up. This has to be stopped immediately.'

Falk scratched his beard ruminatively and looked off into the forest.

'You have to admire their tactics. They incite a baron to turn against the elves. Either the other barons will support him and we have a war between the Knight Marshes and Evergreen, or they go against him and it comes to a skirmish amongst the barons. If the rest of the nobility are squabbling, it could end up in a civil war. Either way, the Knight Marshes will be weakened, and many people will have lost their lives for nothing, for absolutely nothing,'grumbled the Forest Guardian.

Uldini had calmed down and now he conjured his crystal ball to rise up until it was floating in front of his eyes.

'I'd told Elgin weeks ago to take care of the Illuminated Path, right after the High Fang's ambush attempt. How, by all the hells, can they operate so openly?' he spat.

Then he mumbled an incantation and the inside of the ball glimmered red. Uldini shook his head, rubbed his eyes and repeated the incantation. Again, there was a red glimmer. Exasperated, he pushed the crystal ball aside, until it was floating unnoticed over his right shoulder.

'I can't make contact with him. What's going on?' he complained.

Jelninolan's face betrayed complete disapproval as she began to scold the wizard, gesticulating wildly.

'You know exactly what's happened. Elgin is working at some magic again so that he can outstrip you. I'm sure your little job for him was embarrassing and so he ignored it. Or his self-delusion regarding his own importance led him to believe that you only set him on the Illuminated Path to sabotage his own plans because you were afraid you might be knocked off your pedestal,' she responded forcefully.

Ahren had never seen the elf so angry before and he was glad that he wasn't the object of her rage.

'Who is Elgin?' he asked quietly, looking over at Falk.

'One of the Ancients. There are seventeen of them at the moment if memory serves me correctly. There's a definite pecking order among them. Whoever has the most magical power is the leader and can dictate to all the others what to do. Added to that, a more senior Ancient can give commands to one lower down the pecking order as long as these don't run counter to a more senior Ancient's commands. And so, the pair have been tussling over the higher positions for centuries like two dogs fighting over a bone. Uldini has been at the top for so long that most of them have given up trying to replace him as leader. But every few decades, Elgin tries to push his way past with an exotic ritual of a particularly powerful magic spell,' explained Falk.

The other pair had stopped talking and the Arch Wizard turned towards Ahren.

'The perfect example of an obsession that is out of control. Elgin is so obsessed with his goal that he hasn't the least idea, I'm absolutely convinced, of what he's meant to do if he gets to assume command over the Ancients. Remember this, Ahren: first, be sure you know why you want something, then how you can achieve it.'

The childlike figure rubbed his face with both hands.

'This is a great start,' he said in a resigned voice. 'We'd better travel a bit further eastward. 'There's a fortified road in Baron Restelan's territory which reaches as far as Evergreen. As long as the Illuminated Path's influence hasn't reached anyone there yet, we can go from there back to our planned route. If that doesn't work, then we'll stay in Evergreen until we've reached the coast and then we'll battle our way through to King's Island.'

He waited for a few heartbeats, then looked expectantly around him.

'Any better suggestions?', he asked curtly.

Nobody answered and then they all nodded. Satisfied, Uldini set off on his horse.

Ahren was surprised that his master hadn't said anything. It was normal for the old man to take every opportunity to contradict the wizard, almost as if it were an ingrained reflex.

Ahren thought the matter over for a time, and then the penny dropped. Uldini's authority, it seemed, was being challenged by one of the Ancients. The last thing he needed was further criticism. To his surprise, Ahren was beginning to understand that Uldini was still only a man, in spite of all his power and his long life. Falk was sparing him. When the apprentice gave his master a look of understanding, the Forest Guardian winked back at him.

A moment later and Falk's expression had changed completely. He pointed sternly at Ahren's saddlebags.

'Now that we'll be riding for another while, you might as well be using your practice arrows. We're not here on a pleasure trip and your training is far from over. So, get up, you lazybones and hit that branch over there, or I'll be looking for a good high tree this evening that you'll have to climb up ten times,' he said severely.

Ahren quickly pulled out the blunted arrows and raised his bow. He sighed quietly. This was going to be a long ride today.

Chapter 4

The next three days passed by with a calm regularity.

They kept an eye out for the Doppelganger and any surprises he might have in store, but the harmonious, peaceful air of Evergreen still had a relaxing effect on them.

Ahren's days were filled with training exercises given to him by Jelninolan and Falk, which he was allowed to carry out while riding along. Sometimes it was target practice, sometimes it was balancing a pinecone on the fingertips of his outstretched arm. Sometimes it was something as banal as untying his saddlebags without looking. Before decamping, he practised his swordsmanship, and in the evenings, Falk made him climb until he was exhausted. Ahren was sure that he was only allowed to remain on horseback because it would have cost too much time otherwise. At least his master exempted him from gathering wood, cooking, setting up camp and dismantling it.

Ahren was impressed by the equanimity with which Uldini and Jelninolan, who were hundreds of years old, performed these simple, everyday tasks and he vowed that he would perform the tasks given to him with the same stoical calmness.

Uldini continued trying to make contact with Elgin, but to no avail. The Arch Wizard's demeanour remained sour and Ahren avoided burdening him with questions. Jelninolan too was tight-lipped, and Rillans whizzed back and forth several times a day, exchanging news with the elves in Evergreen on the fraught situation and ideas on how to deal with it. Falk viewed each of these magical spheres with concern and when the Forest Guardian was riding a little away from the others, Ahren seized the opportunity and rode up to him to quiz him on the situation.

'Why doesn't Uldini simply ask one of the other Ancients to investigate the Illuminated Path? He has the power to do that.' It seemed illogical to him that the Arch Wizard was spending so much time and energy trying to contact this Elgin, instead of giving one of the others the order.

Falk looked over at him and smiled wearily.

'It's not that simple. Elgin has been advisor to the royal house of the Knight Marshes for over two hundred years. He is highly rated and respected everywhere. He has the necessary influence and knows exactly whom he must talk to and how, in order that the barons will enforce a prohibition of the cult. As far as Uldini is concerned, if he sent any of the other Ancients to King's Island to involve themselves in the destiny of the country, they would meet with considerable resistance. The Illuminated Path has already used very devious tactics, and any failed attempt at prohibition would only draw more followers into its grasp.'

Falk took a deep breath and gathered his thoughts.

'I can only hope that Elgin will keep his ambitions in check this time and act promptly. Uldini holds him in high regard in spite of the way he's been cursing him. I, on the other hand, think Elgin is indeed scheming, just enough to allow the Illuminated Path to operate, so that Uldini will appear weak, thereby damaging him.'

Ahren's heart raced, and the thought that one of the Ancients would consciously play into the enemy's hands made him incandescent with rage.

'How could he do something so horrible?' he whispered, grinding his teeth.

54

Falk shrugged his shoulder and gave a tormented scowl.

'Elgin is still young for an Ancient. He has been ageless for slightly more than two hundred and fifty years and never experienced the Dark Days. I think he's underestimating the damage he's causing. Or he's over-estimating his ability to control the cult once it's gained a foothold. Or both. Whatever his motives are, we're carrying the can for the cock-up.

The old Forest Guardian glanced over at Jelninolan.

'At least the Elf Priestess has been responding in the right way. She has informed the other Ancients, so that the cult won't spread out beyond the frontiers, and the elves are going to offer their wares at much lower prices for the foreseeable future. Good trading relations always mean your neighbours are more likely to support you than attack you. Apart from that, a delegation of elves is going to travel to the Green Sea to strengthen their alliance with the Clan Folk. We need to be able to strike quickly and hard in the event of the Knight Marshes falling under the control of the cult,' said Falk darkly.

Ahren was appalled. His master was talking of war with a whole kingdom. And not just that, but one that was supposed to be their ally in their conflict with the Adversary.

'We have to find a way of stopping that!' he called out in a louder voice than he had intended.

The others turned their heads and Uldini spoke in a grave voice. 'We'll do that, Ahren. You will become the Thirteenth Paladin as soon as it's feasible. When news of your Naming spreads, courage and hope among the people will be reignited. The Illuminated Path feeds on those who are desperate or who can't find their place in the world. Your Naming will reduce the basis on which the cult can act.'

Jelninolan and Falk nodded in encouragement, and this calmed Ahren somewhat. The apprentice was beginning to understand that the world was considerably more complicated than he had previously experienced, and that even ageless Arch Wizards couldn't command kingdoms willy-nilly. His face took on a determined look and he saw a look of pride in his master's face. Falk understood that his apprentice was taking on this additional burden without complaint. Up until now the boy had seen the battle against HIM, WHO FORCES as something isolated, detached from the affairs of the world. The realisation that everything that they achieved or failed to achieve had an effect on countless lives was a heavy burden, and Falk would gladly have spared his protégé from this. Since this was not possible however, there remained only one thing to do.

'That's enough questions for today. This branch up here can't just strike itself. I want to see three arrows hit it before we're beyond reach and I want your lazy wolf to get his act together by bringing them back to you again.'

Then Falk picked up speed and smiled as he saw through the corner of his eye Ahren frantically drawing his bow.

The old Forest Guardian might not be able to spare Ahren his fate, but he'd be damned if he was not going to prepare the boy as well as he possibly could.

The edge of the Evergreen forest lay before them again when they reached the trade road that would lead them into the heart of the Knight Marshes. There wasn't a soul to be seen far and wide and the moss path of the elves was seamlessly replaced by the rough cobbled road which wound its way through fields of golden wheat.

Ahren saw that it wouldn't be long until harvest and he realised sadly that there wouldn't be any Autumn Festival for him this year. He felt a stab of pain in his chest as homesickness suddenly hit him. He had a lump in his throat as he thought of Likis and the others he had left behind in Deepstone. He yearned for the days when the Eastern Forest had seemed to him to be high and vast, and his friend had lived a stone's throw away. Now, with his brief impression of the sheer size of Eathinian, the wood in which he had begun his training seemed no more than a motley collection of trees, and Likis many leagues away.

They pulled up and Falk began his transformation into Knight Falkenstein, a sight that had dumbfounded his apprentice only a few weeks before. His master put on his shimmering whitish armour, covered Selsena's head with the decorated battle armour, which gave her the appearance of a horse armoured up as a unicorn, and pulled a tabard over himself.

Jelninolan, in the meantime, had some good news to report: a herd of Titejunanwas had spotted the trail of the Doppler in Evergreen and had ascertained that the creature had left the elf forest two days previously and had gone in a south-western direction, away from their planned travel route. It seemed as though they could continue their journey reasonably safely.

'Now that Jelninolan is with us, our group is just that little bit too colourful for any meaningful disguise, so we'll try to make our appearance as worthy of respect as possible. When a knight travels through a village in full regalia, then his followers are usually spared inquisitive questions,' Falk explained.

Uldini didn't seem particularly persuaded but didn't have any better tactics at the ready.

Jelninolan, on the other hand, leaned down towards Culhen, whispered something Elfish into his ears and performed some magic on him. The effect was as surprising as it was subtle. The colour of his fur changed ever so slightly, took on a darker and slightly dappled tone here and there, just enough so that within a few moments Ahren's companion looked like one of those wolfhounds that are used for shepherding. The young wolf sat on his hind legs and looked at his dappled grey forelegs. He snorted scornfully and gave Ahren a begging look, all the while whining pathetically.

'Our vain little friend doesn't seem to think much of his clothing. It seems he wants his glorious old self back,' laughed Falk, and Selsena showered them all with a wave of merriment.

'Good job, auntie,' said Uldini in wonder. 'The shadings hide his origins, without the necessity of changing his form. A true masterpiece of illusion.'

Jelninolan smiled, gave a little curtsey and ruffled Culhen on his head as he continued to whine.

'Stop behaving like that. I'll undo the spell once we've reached the Silver Cliff. The dwarves love wolves, and there are so many more dangerous creatures in Kelkor that a wolf doesn't bother anyone,' she said airily.

Ahren felt queasy when he heard her last sentence, but he had decided to tackle only one thing at a time on their journey and so he refrained from asking questions.

'It's for your own good, and you're still my magnificent favourite wolf,' he said, trying to cheer up the deeply unhappy Culhen. He threw him a bit of dried rabbit from the provisions he had stored in his saddlebags, and the wolf snatched it out of the air before it could reach the ground. The whining stopped, and now the wolf scampered around Ahren's horse, barking and begging for more. His master noted to his delight that Culhen's vanity was outstripped by his gluttony.

The attack came suddenly in the middle of the night. Figures with smouldering red eyes raced with surprising agility towards them from all sides. When Ahren awoke, they were already visible in the light of the campfire, and on top of the travellers. Ahren could see deformed bodies with grimaces distorted in pain, long arms and long legs, all ending in claws. All of the creatures were unique looking, each was terrifying in its own way and yet they all had one thing in common - they had tusks. Nauseated, Ahren noticed that they had eyes where no eye should be, whether on the forehead, behind the ears or even on their shoulders. The same was true for mouths, noses and ears. Even the number of arms, legs and hands seemed to vary from creature to creature.

Even as the attackers were raising their weapons, Ahren realised what he was looking at. These were Low Fangs, the shock troops of the dark god, people who had fallen under the control of HIM, WHO FORCES, and who had been formed into these monstrosities by the power of HIM.

Ahren shook off the drowsiness of sleep and let out a cry of warning. But he was already too late. A Low Fang, with tusks like those of a wild boar under three red eyes, sank its crude blade into Jelninolan's throat with an appalling crunch.

Ahren's eyes welled with tears and he sprang forward screaming in rage as he attempted to corner the killer, but two others had already stepped forward from right and left and were raising their ugly swords. He had to leap back quickly to avoid being hit, then at last he drew forth his weapon. He gasped as he saw Uldini and Falk surrounded by ten attackers. His master and the Arch Wizard had just pulled themselves up and a fierce fire was burning between Uldini's fingers. Hope burgeoned within Ahren, and with difficulty he parried the threatening blades of the Low Fangs.

Then the circle of bodies closed in around the old Forest Guardian and the childlike figure, and furiously and insanely, the Low Fangs struck their blades again and again into the centre of the circle.

Ahren dropped his weapon as if paralysed and stared at the horrific performance in front of him. His assailants smirked at him from their dreadfully distorted faces, and just as he heard in the darkness Culhen cry out in pain and Selsena's wheezing whinnying, he felt a strange, cold resistance in his chest and his legs gave way beneath him. He looked incredulously at the bloodied blade sticking out through his chest.

The Low Fang that had crept up behind him, yanked the blade back out and a fountain of blood sprang forth from Ahren's chest. His world darkened, he tumbled to the ground and he could hear the unfamiliar, fragile whispering of an old woman saying to him, 'wake up.'

Gasping for breath, Ahren's eyes shot open and he looked in panic around him.

This nightmare had been more realistic than any he had experienced before. He felt his chest, which was uninjured and revealed no gaping wound. Culhen grunted in annoyance. The wolf had settled in beside him as he did every night, and the young animal's digestive sleep was being disturbed. The wolf had been feeling sorry for himself the previous evening and had been comfort eating as a result.

Relieved to be alive, Ahren couldn't resist the temptation to look at the others in the weak light of the dying embers. All were sleeping, untouched on their blankets, and slowly the apprentice calmed down.

'Only a bad dream,' he whispered into Culhen's ear and looked into the darkness with relief. He stroked the wolf's fur to calm himself down and Culhen grunted again, but this time in contentment, and snuggled in closer to Ahren.

The previous evening, they had set up camp on a little hill surrounded by a few fallow fields. The local farmers were giving the land time to recover, and so there was only grass and weeds. Ahren had almost dropped off again when he saw a red glimmer flaring up in the darkness.

The light disappeared as quickly as it had flashed but Ahren's pulse was now racing. He forced himself to be as cool, calm and collected as his master had taught him, and peered carefully around him, making sure not to look at the campfire but to accustom his eyes to the surrounding darkness. A few heartbeats passed by and then another glimmer flared up briefly, but this time in a different spot.

Now that he knew what he was looking for, he spotted more of these strange flashes and understood immediately what he was looking at. The eyes of the Low Fangs, who were creeping towards them under cover of darkness.

His first impulse was to jump up but then he thought better of it. Another of his master's lessons flashed through his terrified brain. 'Don't be a terrified prey who takes flight without thinking when it comes to the crunch. Fight or flight, every situation should be considered rationally before taking the required action. If you don't know what you're doing, then your enemy will decide: then the hawk will catch the timorous rabbit, but the *clever* rabbit will escape the voracious bird of prey. The fate of most battles is decided in the head.' Falk had explained all this to him one sunny morning while they were crouched down in a field watching a hawk as it hunted.

If he stood up now, his silhouette would be clearly visible in the weak light of the campfire and their attackers would know they had been discovered. For the moment they were creeping slowly forwards and Ahren hoped to prolong the situation as long as possible. He calculated that the Low Fangs were still at least a hundred paces away and so he had sufficient time to act in a clever and judicious manner. Jelninolan was lying closest to him, hardly two paces away.

'Jelninolan,' he whispered several times as quietly as he could, until the elf opened her eyes. The priestess looked at him sleepily and Ahren put a finger to his lips.

'Low Fangs,' he whispered and made a faint hand movement, indicating that they were surrounded. Jelninolan nodded silently and pointed at Uldini, who was lying beside her, and then back to herself. Ahren gave her a thankful look and began very slowly, and in his lying position, to draw his bow and Windblade into position.

Culhen was awake at this point and began to growl. Now that the young wolf was no longer asleep, he could sense the Low Fangs. Ahren tapped him gently on the bridge of his nose and the wolf became silent. He looked at his master questioningly and Ahren indicated that he should lie perfectly still. The hunting fever could be seen in the animal's eyes, but he behaved and waited, crouched on the ground, every muscle tensed, ready to spring into action.

Jelninolan had in the meantime woken Uldini up, who, with a few little movements, rang an almost inaudible bell sound in the ears of the others. It seemed the others recognised this signal, for Falk's and Selsena's eyes opened wide but they didn't move any other muscles.

'Low Fangs, eighty paces, in ring formation.' Ahren heard Uldini's voice right beside his ear, although the Magus hadn't opened his mouth.

Falk nodded and everyone began preparing their weapons while Selsena stood stock still. Uldini moved his fingers in incredibly complicated and serpentine movements over his crystal ball, which began to emit an irregular flickering violet light. He nodded in satisfaction and looked at the others, one by one. Jelninolan and Falk nodded back at him, but when the Arch Wizard looked at Ahren, he was only met with a questioning look. The rest of the group might well have had practice in this before, but the apprentice had no idea what to do next. He had reached the Void with difficulty and his fears and worries were like a sea of chaotic emotions crashing against the cliff of calmness to which Ahren's spirit had retreated.

Uldini's murmuring magical voice whispered commands into Ahren's ear. 'On my signal you grasp your bow and kill as many as you can until they're at the foot of the hill. Then change to the sword and we'll position ourselves back to back. There are too many, so Culhen will stay with you and keep himself ready.'

Ahren nodded and within a heartbeat Uldini tossed the ball into the air, where it hung ten paces above them. The Wizard closed his eyes and his companions leaped to their feet.

Falk and Jelninolan were holding their bows in their hands and Ahren did likewise. For a moment he wondered where the elf had got her bow from but then he remembered the heavy bundles she had been carrying with her. Of course, the priestess would have a bow in one of them. Perhaps she preferred the staff, but it was a relief to Ahren that Jelninolan didn't hesitate using other weapons if it were necessary.

The others had already shot three rounds of arrows, and the night air was filled with the screams of pain coming from the Low Fangs surrounding them. The pack started moving forward, and the apprentice could see a line of glowing red eyes staring at him scornfully. The attackers had to have been looking down at the ground up to that point so as not to reveal their presence, but now they looked at their prey and charged forward.

Ahren could see at least two dozen eyes fixed on him, but to his horror he was unable to calculate the number of attackers. Here were three eyes in triangular formation, over there eight eyes in spider formation, and yet another creature with only one large eye.

'Less staring and more shooting, boy!' snarled Uldini as the wizard continued to concentrate on his magic with his eyes closed.

Ahren raised his bow and began shooting arrow after arrow into the darkness, targeting the glimmering eyes of the enemy. Much to his satisfaction, almost every arrow hit its target and at least eight Low Fangs fell to the ground. But the fact that the eyes were not necessarily in the heads, but in various parts of the bodies, meant that over half of the wounded kept moving forwards to him, if considerably more slowly.

Ahren kept firing until his quiver was emptied. He had shot twenty arrows, and yet five wounded and two uninjured Low Fangs were coming up his side of the hill.

'No arrows left!' he shouted over his shoulder and he could see that both Falk and Jelninolan had none left either.

Uldini's eyes were still closed and he was smiling.

'Good. Then it's my turn now', he said with thrilled anticipation.

'Take the healthy ones first if you don't have enough for all of them', said Falk firmly.

'I have done this before you know, old man', snarled Uldini venomously.

Ahren knew that magic influenced the emotions of the performer in different ways, depending on what purpose it was being used for. When Uldini had weaved a Fireball that time in Deepstone, he had gone into such a rage that Ahren had been afraid the Arch Wizard would turn them into a pile of ashes if they put a foot wrong.

Whatever the wizard was planning now, it was probably going to be just as destructive.

Ahren laid down his bow and drew out Windblade as the beasts were storming up the hill. It was a very shallow hill so their attackers were already only a few paces distant and Ahren, with an uneasy feeling in the pit of his stomach, could see that from where he was standing that there were over ten attackers moving with disturbing speed towards them. He seized his sword with more strength and banished the nightmarish pictures of his dying friends from his mind, pictures, which were constantly trying to break through into the Void so that he would succumb to his own fears.

Uldini called out a single unrecognisable word and for a brief moment a lilac light broke through the darkness, as if, for a brief heartbeat, a strange light from another world was casting its colours over the heavens. Then narrow arrows of dark violet light landed on the distorted creatures below. Eight attackers were hit by the arrows, which travelled in gentle arcs before landing perfectly and burying themselves into the creatures' heads. In an instant, the Low Fangs had fallen to the ground and were completely still.

Surprised and overjoyed, Ahren gave a gasp of relief, and confidence overcame his fear. There were only three of the dark god's downtrodden servants storming at him now. Each of the grotesque creatures had tasted at least one of his arrows and was injured accordingly. One of them had two arrows in its eyes that were positioned in its shoulders. Its face, however, made up entirely of a circular mouth full of needle-sharp teeth, was untouched. Curved horns were sticking out of the creature's chest and it was slowly coming towards Ahren. The other two Low Fangs would reach him first and so Ahren reached a decision.

'Attack, Culhen!', he shouted and pointed at the four-eyed creature. It seemed to be considerably more injured than the other two and Ahren hoped that Culhen would be able to finish the weakened Low Fang off.

Culhen shot off and there was no more time for thinking. The other two Low Fangs had arrived and Ahren was horrified to see that he recognised one of them. The wild-boar tusks were unmistakable, as was the derisive, toothy grin playing around the monster's mouth. This was the Low Fang that had killed Jelninolan in Ahren's nightmare.

The Void was beginning to crumble, but then a wave of anger carried Ahren forward and into the midst of his enemies. He struck with his sword, quickly and with economy, all the while skipping towards the right and around the Low Fang. His blows were only there to keep his enemy on the defensive, and smiling scornfully, Ahren could see how awkwardly the monster was parrying them. Blood was streaming from a wound where Ahren's arrow had dug itself into the Low Fang's upper body. The apprentice's sidestepping had brought him to the creature's right side, so that the route for the third Low Fang was blocked, as it first had to manoeuvre its way around its companion. This gave Ahren precious breathing space. From the corner of his eye he could see how Culhen was snapping at the back of the third Low Fang's knees, all the while prancing nimbly around the awkward creature.

Then Ahren's opponent raised its sword, bloody foam dribbling out of the mouth of the monster with the wild-boar tusks. Ahren's arrow must have penetrated its lung. Ahren stepped in front of the Low Fang, his blade positioned laterally in front, one hand grasping the hilt, the other pressed against the back of the blade. He aimed towards the thing's raised attacking arm, and when the blade made contact with the armpit, he simply pulled the blade sideways and turned behind the Low Fang. The creature collapsed with a grotesque squeal as the length of the sword moved along the armpit, causing devastating damage. Ahren knew that he had mortally wounded his enemy and that his fighting arm was completely useless, and so, after he had risked a sideways glance at

Culhen, Ahren turned his attention to the remaining Low Fang. The wolf had already overcome his adversary and was snarling and biting into the martyred creature's neck. Ahren could see that Culhen's fur exhibited some cuts from the being's claws and this sight enraged the apprentice.

The Void gave way to a red mist of fury and a thirst for action. Snarling, he raced up the slope towards his remaining opponent, an appalling face made up of two eyes, one above the other, accompanied by a far too wide mouth and two flat noses. A third arm came out of its chest and was hanging lifelessly. It was carrying a heavy club full of spikes, which it now raised in challenging anticipation.

None of this made any impression on Ahren at all. He was intent on attacking this grotesque travesty of a human, and ran forward. His sword stroke was quick and strong, the blade bore into the Low Fang cleanly and with precision. Ahren's movement brought him within range of the club, however, and as he was about to dance away, the creature's third arm lifted itself suddenly and grasped his underarm with strong, knotty fingers.

Ahren screamed out in surprise and tried to tear himself away as the club was swung in a high arc over and down towards him. His sword was still stuck in the creature's body, and he couldn't dodge out of the way, the third hand's vice-like grip was simply too strong. And so, he fell to the ground, at the same time pulling with all his might at the hilt of his sword, his body weight pulling the blade downwards in the creature's body. The creature shuddered and buckled as the strength of its knees gave way, but the club continued to race downwards and smashed into Ahren's back with a shuddering power.

The apprentice felt how two of the spikes had penetrated his body, and an appalling pain spread through his torso. The third hand's grip loosened eventually, and Ahren rolled to the side, so he wouldn't be pinned under the collapsing body. He was alert enough to pull his blade out of the gaping wound that his manoeuvre had inflicted. His back was burning like fire and he could feel blood seeping through his linen shirt. In his rage it had never occurred to him that he was carrying no armour and was therefore virtually unprotected.

Annoyed with himself and grimacing with pain, he looked around him and struggled slowly onto his feet. Culhen was standing at the ready a few paces to his side, guarding Ahren with watchful eyes and looking at the carnage around them. The wolf had defeated the third Low Fang and was watching his surroundings furtively, ready to spring into action should any of the attackers venture near his wounded friend. Ahren slapped his thigh and Culhen jumped over towards him and positioned himself beside his master. Not a single Low Fang was moving anymore. Relieved, Ahren turned towards the others.

Jelninolan and Falk were combating four Low Fangs in total, and Ahren wanted to rush towards their aid, but before he'd reached the crest of the hill, two of the attackers were already dead, sent to the ground with the well-practised blows of broad sword and fighting staff. Then Selsena ran forward out of the darkness and ran down the two remaining attackers. Her mighty hooves smashed their bodies into the ground with a crunching sound. Then the hill was silent.

Ahren could only hear the sound of his own painful breathing and the others panting for breath. Uldini was sitting, his face distorted with anger, in the middle of the encampment, looking at the others with hostility. Ahren remembered the reason for the emotional chaos which was engulfing the Magus and went over to him carefully, making sure to leave his sword gently on the ground.

Uldini pulled a face and snorted.

'Well you're some Forest Guardian, allowing yourself to be wounded by a simple Wild Fang. We might as well all lie down and give up if you're supposed to be the saviour of the Free Peoples,' he scolded, his face distorted with scorn.

Ahren turned away without saying a word. What the wizard had said was hurtful, but he knew that it was Uldini's emotional recoil to the battle magic that made him like that. He pulled his blood-spattered shirt over his head with a sigh, and a few heartbeats later he saw it lighting up behind him.

Uldini was screaming out the magic formula, a mixture of defiance and rage in his voice. Constructive healing magic was the best antidote to the negative emotions that destructive magic brought with it. The Arch Wizard always tried to keep his distance on account of his unstable emotional condition when he used too much battle magic.

Ahren could feel his wound healing as Uldini continued to scold.

'Why didn't Selsena or the wolf know the horde was nearby? The mangy cur could at least make himself useful after eating all that food.' The wizard continued to complain but his words were gradually softening.

Culhen whined at Uldini's comments and Ahren tickled him gently between the ears. Then he pushed the wolf under Uldini's healing hands.

'Are you serious? Those few scratches require the healing service of an Ancient?' grumbled the youthful figure, and Ahren had to suppress a laugh. Uldini was always sulky and behaved like a spoiled nine-year-old in the moments before he regained his spiritual balance.

Ahren looked at the others, who all appeared to have escaped unharmed.

Uldini finished his incantation and Culhen thanked him by licking his hands and looking up at the Arch Wizard with his loyal golden eyes.

'Alright, alright,' he grumbled. 'Happy to have obliged,' and he stroked the wolf, who threw himself on his back enthusiastically.

While Uldini was rubbing Culhen's stomach and trying to hide a smile, Jelninolan chuckled and leaned over conspiratorially to the others.

'If he has to work his battle magic again, we'll just give him Culhen to tickle. That seems to help,' she said quietly.

Everyone laughed, but then Ahren became serious.

'What will we do in an emergency if he gets into an uncontrollable rage? We can't just allow ourselves to be injured so that he can heal us.' He frowned and his back tensed up at the memory of the recent wound.

Falk looked up at him sternly and was about to launch into a tirade concerning Ahren's negligence during the battle, but Jelninolan intervened.

'Uldini's self-control is considerably better than it appears. He releases his anger and scorn immediately and in a controlled fashion. He can spend weeks in this state if he needs to. But it's true that if it comes to a battle at that point, it is possible that he will lose himself in his emotions,' she explained.

Ahren's anxiety was plain to see and she made a reassuring gesture with her hand.

'There are many things we haven't tried yet. Selsena can calm him down and, if necessary, I can soothe him with Tanentan,' she continued.

Ahren had completely forgotten about the artefact that had caused them so much trouble when they had been retrieving it from the Weeping Valley. The lute influenced the emotions of those who heard it and was extremely powerful.

'Why didn't you use Tanentan earlier? You could have prevented unnecessary bloodshed,, said Ahren deferentially. He didn't want to sound as though he were accusing the elf, but he wanted to understand better the tactics of his new travelling companion. Every time he thought he understood the elf, something new turned up.

Jelninolan looked down sadly at the grotesque bodies lying around them. Luckily, most of them were only recognisable as outlines in the darkness.

'Low Fangs are immune to suggestive magic. Their natures have become so corrupted that nothing human is left. Which is why Uldini's magic was so effective.' She broke off and put her hand to her heart, and then quietly murmured something in Elfish.

Falk pointed to the enemies that Uldini had slain and were lying at the foot of the hill.

'He calls them Night Arrows. But don't be fooled, the magic works during the day too, but it becomes damned dark when he unleashes it. I've never really understood it, but Uldini manages to cut the connection for a heartbeat between HIM, WHO FORCES and his servants. Whoever has been hit by one of these missiles is free from his influence.'

He scratched his beard and continued. 'The Low Fangs die immediately. Their bodies have been so deformed that it is only through the Will of the Adversary, who has forced the deformations on them, that they can exist. One heartbeat without HIS control and their insides are torn asunder,' said his master.

Ahren shivered. Only now did he fully understand how absolute the dark god's power was. He felt a wave of pity for the creatures. Who could say which of the poor souls lying around them had just strayed too near the Pall Pillar, the prison of smoke and shade, where HE, WHO FORCES lay imprisoned? The nearer you got to the pillar, the greater the risk was that you would fall under HIS control. Which was why only fanatical individualists lived in the Borderlands, the area surrounding the Pall Pillar.

Falk cleared his throat and Ahren listened again to his master.

'On the other hand, the magic only confuses High Fangs for a moment. They are briefly in control of their own free wills and most of them have no idea how to react. The changes that have been made in them are not so drastic and so they don't die when the connection with HIM, WHO FORCES has been temporarily cut. But they are so used to his commands that they simply wait until the magic wears off,' explained the old Forest Guardian. 'And Dark Ones are hardly affected by the magic at all. The alterations that the Adversary has made to them are subtle and usually only intensifications of tendencies they already possess. His orders to them are usually only short impulses. Things like "hunt in this valley!", or "there's the prey!", and he leaves the rest to the Dark Ones' instincts,' said Falk, finishing his explanation.

Ahren nodded and looked down again at the Low Fangs that were barely visible in the flickering firelight.

'So that's why you resorted to the bow and arrow without hesitation. Even if we are victorious against HIM, WHO FORCES, all of the Low Fangs are destined to die?' he asked, turning to Jelninolan.

She nodded and placed her hand on his shoulder while she looked deeply into his eyes.

'That was one reason. But if it is necessary, I will shoot at anything and anybody if it means protecting this group. I would prefer not to do it, though', she said quietly.

Ahren nodded thankfully. He found her assurance that she would defend the group as well as she could, very reassuring at that moment. He gave Falk and Jelninolan a grateful smile and then turned to Uldini.

'Thank you for your help, both in the battle and in healing my wound,' he said sincerely and even a little solemnly. If positive words helped Uldini come back to his old self, then a few words of gratitude could hardly do any harm.

Uldini rolled his eyes and threw his hands up to heaven.

'I swear by all the gods, if this touchy-feely business starts again, I'm going to throw up!' he called out, grumpily.

'Look, he's back to his old self,' said Falk drily.

<u>Chapter 5</u>

93 days before the winter solstice

Ahren spent the rest of the night in an uncomfortable half-sleep.

Uldini had cast a small magic net to ensure that there were no further servants of the Adversary in the area, and after they had rolled the lifeless bodies down the hill, they had all lain down again,. But now the elevation was surrounded by corpses and the wind kept blowing the stench back up to them. When dawn began to break, Ahren had had enough. Anything was better than this half-sleep from which he was constantly waking in fright every time he had visions of glowing red eyes in the distance.

He stood on the slope of the hill and began his sword training. It had struck him that he had had problems fighting on a slope the previous night, and his steps had been awkward and uncertain. If he were honest with himself, one small stone in the darkness would have been enough to have caused him to stumble just at the wrong moment.

The thought that he had only survived the night by chance shook him to the core, and so he trained as hard as he could while the sun slowly rose, all the while ignoring the corpses of the Low Fangs as much as possible.

In the middle of his second routine, he heard steps behind him. He was about to break off but then recognised Falk's quiet voice from the brow of the hill.

'Keep going, boy. Good idea to practise on an uneven surface. Could have been an instruction from me.'

Ahren turned his back to his master while continuing his manoeuvre and allowed himself a broad grin of satisfaction.

'Stop smirking!' snapped his master, and Ahren forced his face to become impassive, all the while asking himself how Falk could possibly know that he'd been grinning.

'I wanted to talk about your escapade last night. You do know what I'm talking about?' asked the old Forest Guardian.

Ahren nodded and then waited for his master to give him a dressing down. But nothing happened. Then Ahren realised that Falk was waiting for him to explain his own mistakes.

'I fought in a rage and ran into my enemy with too much gusto. I forgot to keep up my guard in the process and ignored the fact that I wasn't wearing any armour. I underestimated the capabilities of the Low Fang in my anger and so he was able to take me by surprise. Because I administered an unnecessary blow, I found myself unable to parry.'

There was a harshness in Ahren's voice, and his dissatisfaction with himself was clearly to be heard. He couldn't see Falk smirking but he could hear it in his master's voice.

'I see you are developing something like ambition. And your description of your deeds was open and honest and without any attempt to cover up. It had been my plan to punish you for yesterday's mistake by forcing you to run around the hill six dozen times, but a reasonable young man like yourself would be willing to do it voluntarily, isn't that right?'

Ahren nodded respectfully and dropped his sword. Then he heard the voice behind him again. 'First you will finish your practice session. We wouldn't like you to neglect your swordsmanship', Falk ordered merrily.

'Yes, master' said Ahren and suppressed a sigh.

When Ahren returned to the camp, everyone was ready to leave.

He prepared himself for the accusations that he had held everyone up, but the other three were standing around an object which seemed to be taking up all of their attention.

Ahren moseyed over to them, all the while trying to bring his quick breathing under control by drawing in his breath and expelling it in a slow and concentrated manner. Hectic breathing wasn't just an impediment when it came to the hunt, as it could easily reveal your whereabouts, but it also slowed down your recovery time. If Falk caught him panting like a dog, he'd make him do another ten laps of the hill. As Falk liked to say, 'there's nothing worse than a breathless Forest Guardian.'

Ahren joined the others, trying to be as relaxed as possible and glanced down at the object at their feet, only to look away immediately in horror. Lying there was a Low Fang, one considerably smaller than its companions. When standing it would scarcely reach up to Ahren's hips. It was completely covered in obscure symbols that had been scored into its skin and Ahren could have sworn that they were moving!

The hairs stood up on the back of his neck, and he noticed that his hands were shaking. This thing seemed to be emitting a real danger, and Ahren would have taken a few steps backwards were it not for the fact that the others were looking down at the body so calmly.

'A Bane Bearer,' said Falk into the silence.

Uldini nodded and tipped the body gently with his foot. The symbols puckered and contracted where Uldini's shoe made contact with the skin.

'The sigils are still fresh, no more than two days old,' he said. Then he laughed like a billy goat. 'I think I know where our not very successful Doppler from Evergreen has got to,' he added. Then he looked demonstratively up at the cloudy skies.

'What a wonderful day,' he said merrily.

Jelninolan threw him a reproachful look, then took pity on Ahren's uncomprehending face and decided to explain the situation.

'Doppelgangers who fall out of favour are transformed by HIM, WHO FORCES into Bane Bearers. These poor creatures are nothing more than empty shells, who have more than a half dozen spells burned into their essence. Wherever they go, these spells are put into effect. In the Dark Days, one Bane Bearer alone could strengthen a whole army. Luckily for us, HE is still in a deep slumber, so HE only managed that.'

She pointed pitifully at the corpse and continued.

'That explains why Selsena didn't sense the Low Fangs. Or why Uldini's magic net didn't find them.'

She pointed at different parts of the complex drawings. 'This drawing here indicates camouflage from wizards and this one is for a tireless forced march. The rest are conjurations summoning all Low Fangs, Swarm Claws, Fog Cats and Blood Wolves to come under the control of the Bane Bearer.'

'We were very lucky', interjected Falk. 'Had there been more Dark Ones in the area, it could have ended very nastily for us.'

Ahren nodded thoughtfully and suppressed a shudder. The thought of being attacked here in the open field by hundreds of Swarm Claws was horrifying. The birds could slice a person's throat open with ease using their razor-sharp claws and beaks in a nose dive. Without magic it was practically impossible to fend off a swarm.

He swallowed hard and pointed over at Uldini, who was cheerfully mounting his horse. 'And why is he so happy', he asked in wonderment.

'Doppelgangers are rare. They cannot reproduce themselves and HE, WHO FORMS had only made a few hundred before HE realised his error. Any time a Doppler dies, it's a great victory. By our calculations there are less than sixty of them left,' she said sadly.

Ahren remembered her talk about the extermination of a species and he understood her feelings.

Falk too seemed to understand what the elf was feeling and so he came over to them and spoke softly to her.

'Remember that the Doppelgangers serve the Adversary willingly. It is their own decision that has put them on their course, not coercion. It is their hunger for a concrete form and purpose that drives them into the abyss.'

Ahren thought over his master's words and they seemed to ring true. He himself found it very hard to know who he was and what he wanted to be. How would a being then feel, who couldn't take on a permanent form without external help? The offer from the dark god must simply be too tempting for the Doppelgangers.

Falk clapped his hands together and jolted Ahren out of his musings.

'We've no time for dawdling. Uldini, will we throw the bodies into a heap so you can burn them?', he asked.

The Arch Wizard shook his head. 'Not necessary. Our little friend is still emitting a little camouflage magic. I should be able to practise a few little finger exercises without us having to get our fingers dirty and letting anyone locate my magic.'

Then he made some sweeping gesticulating motions with his hands, and within a couple of heartbeats, the fallen Low Fangs raised themselves into the air before slowly stacking themselves into a large heap on top of the hill. Uldini made a swift hand movement and uttered a quick magic charm. The bodies immediately ignited and burned brightly, causing Ahren to step back in surprise. The others mounted their horses showing no concern, so Ahren did the same. Only Jelninolan stayed for a moment beside the magical burial place and spoke a few words in Elfish.

Ahren leaned over towards Falk. 'What's she saying?' he whispered.

'She's asking for forgiveness for the souls of the poor devils who were trapped in those bodies. Whether they were willing or not, I'm pretty sure that after one day as Low Fangs, each one of them hoped for redemption. I imagine that the gods will give it to them now', answered the old man.

Ahren looked sadly at the blazing pyre and silently added a prayer of his own.

The next few days flew by. In the mornings, Ahren was taught by either Falk or Jelninolan, and during the course of the day, he would practise his archery skills. If other people were in the vicinity, he would have to balance objects or a full rucksack on his outstretched arms until they felt like frayed elastic bands. Ahren began to search out the healing herbs on the sides of the path - the ones that alleviated the worst of the pain and that he had already begun to learn about in the Eastern Forest. His master looked on approvingly as he used all his knowledge of the healing arts as remedies and to strengthen his tired body. Jelninolan also gave him a few tips along the way and it wasn't long before the apprentice always had a flask of herbal tea hanging on his belt, which helped his body recover from the daily lessons. But the exercises were becoming more challenging, and Ahren began asking himself if improving his bodily regeneration was really such a good idea. After all, his master and the priestess would invariably come up with even more difficult things to practise.

They usually slept in the open, or whenever possible, in one of the many farmhouses they passed by. Now and again Ahren would see a castle in the distance, but it seemed to him that the Knight Marshes consisted for the most part of farmyards, charcoal burners and the odd artisan dwelling. The little villages they travelled through reminded him of Deepstone, and he regularly found himself thinking of his old friends. Once he even thought of his drunken father. He wondered how he was getting on. Doubtless, the money he had wangled from Ahren's master for his son's apprenticeship was petering out, and Ahren doubted that his father could have found his way back onto the straight and narrow without the crutch of alcohol. Falk seemed to be able to read his apprentices gloomy thoughts because he was constantly showering Ahren with new exercises which challenged his mind and distracted him from his musings.

The inhabitants of the Knight Marshes hardly batted an eyelid as they passed by. Falk's noble appearance as a knight of the kingdom ensured a respectful distance, and even if from time to time Jelninolan was looked at suspiciously, the elf was free to continue on her way.

They did, however, come across many priests of the Illuminated Path, who could be found holding forth in the village squares, speaking to the simple folk. Falk would make a big detour around them so they could never overhear what was being said, but the mistrustful looks that Jelninolan received spoke volumes.

In such villages Falk and Uldini too seemed to arouse suspicion and one evening as they were sitting around the campfire, the Arch Wizard spoke. 'I used a little magic to listen in. It seems the cultists are trying to stir up the simple folk. "The taxes are too high," "the elves are to blame," or "it's all the knights' fault," things like that. Nice and simple, easy to learn and perfect for anyone who wants to blame everyone else for their own inadequacies. Unfortunately, those are just the sorts of people who will willingly accept the next step in the enticement: "submit yourself to the Illuminated Path and we will free you from all your cares."'

The Wizard's concern was written in his face and Jelninolan whispered almost inaudibly, 'that's how it always starts. They lay the foundation for a senseless war between their own people and their allies. A war which nobody can win.'

The rest of the group pondered this before all retiring anxiously to their beds.

As if to confirm the Wizard's words, they were met the following day by a procession of people.

Two dozen haggard, filthy figures in plain linen garb were being led westwards by a cultist in a white robe who was carrying a golden book under his arm. The faces of the believers were glowing with fanaticism and more than one of them made a point of spitting in Jelninolan's direction.

There was such a sad look on the elf's face that Ahren automatically gripped his sword without knowing what he was doing. Falk pointedly cleared his throat and the apprentice loosened his grip before deliberately looking off into the wheat fields, which were being harvested.

Once the group of pilgrims were gone, Ahren turned towards the others.

'Did you see their grim faces? I really thought they were going to attack us. And where on earth are they going?' he spluttered hurriedly.

The others looked at him with serious looks and then strode on without answering his questions. His nose out of joint, he spurred his horse on, and the rest of the day passed by in a dark mood.

He received his answer that evening, when they had retired to the barn of an old, half-deaf farmer, where they were to spend the night. A light drizzle was coming down and the smell of damp straw surrounded them.

'What you saw there was a purification procession,' said Uldini with barely contained rage. 'Which means that the people are on their way to the Pall Pillar where they intend to purify the Adversary with their solemn prayers. The power of their prayers is supposed to direct the power of the THREE directly towards the Pillar and destroy the sleeping god within.'

Ahren stare in open-mouthed irritation at the Arch Wizard. When he didn't continue, Ahren pursued the topic.

'But surely that doesn't work. If they go too near to the Pall Pillar...'

'...he will force them into his charm.' Falk had interrupted the young man and his voice was rough. 'Every one of them out there will become a Low Fang, or even a High Fang if his will is strong enough to be able to survive the touch of the enemy's spirit.'

Ahren stared, shaken, into the fire. The fact that more than twenty living beings, each with their own hopes, memories and dreams, were going on their way to be tricked in the most devious manner imaginable, stunned him into silence. When he had finally collected himself, he looked pleadingly at the others.

'But why didn't we intervene?' he asked frantically. 'We could have saved them!'

Jelninolan shook her head wearily.

'That was tried before. They are convinced they are doing the right thing. Of course, we could have attacked the cultist and even slain him and scattered the group, but what then? An elf and a knight kill a man of the cloth and prevent believers from purifying the Pall Pillar. That would be exactly the story they would relate to the others. And then there would be more recruits, ten times more than before. This conflict cannot be won by impetuous action,' she said. Then she pulled her knees into her chest and looked ruefully into the flames.

'There are only two ways of getting at the Illuminated Path. Either by sending out hundreds of volunteers to go through the villages and confront the cultists as they are preaching, or by revealing a high ranking priest of the Illuminated Path to be a High Fang – as publicly as possible, so that the story will spread of its own accord,' explained Uldini.

Ahren plucked up his courage. 'But can't we do that to the priest who's leading the procession?' he asked excitedly. He was on the point of jumping up and running to his horse so that he could help the poor souls before they marched to their destruction.

Falk nodded. 'We could do that indeed. If he was one,' the old Forest Ranger answered drily.

Ahren looked helplessly at his master. 'So, he isn't a High Fang?', he asked in a low voice.

Uldini shook his head and gestured helplessly with his hands.

'I'd tested him with some magic. He was just as human as the rest of them. Only considerably more fanatical. Can you see our problem now? The Enemy is making us do his work for him. Either we let them go on, and he gets more followers, or we hold them up using force, and he still gets more followers.'

The voice of the Arch Wizard was filled with scorn and he took his crystal ball and called for Elgin again. Again, the ball glowed red until with a yell of fury, Uldini hurled the sphere against the wall, from where it ricocheted with a crash before floating slowly back to his hand.

'Behave yourself, Uldini,' said Jelninolan but with such a maternal voice that Ahren couldn't help smiling in spite of the dreadful dilemma they were in.

The Arch Wizard gave her a furious look, but it was only a few heartbeats before he gave in.

'Yes, auntie,' he mumbled, and Ahren looked away so nobody could see him laughing.

Then he thought of the hopeless group on their way to the Borderlands, and the smile was wiped off his face.

They continued their journey eastward, into ever more densely populated stretches of land. The buildings were becoming older and bigger, the roads wider and the villages more full of life.

'The Knight Marshes have their origins on the east coast of the country,' Falk explained to his apprentice. 'From there they pushed their way ever deeper in to the west, as far as the Red Posts. If they hadn't been held up by the clans from Kelkor and the Green Sea, the Knight Marshes would probably have become the next human empire. Every stage we're taking eastwards is bringing us closer to the heartland, the Old Marshes.'

It was becoming more and more difficult for the group to avoid the larger villages, until finally they couldn't bypass them. They strode through side streets or through outlying farms, always trying to avoid unwanted attention. At least they didn't have to worry about Dark Ones, as Falk had assured him. Because of the high number of knights and patrols, the Old Marshes was one of the most secure areas in north-eastern Jorath.

Unless you were an elf, that is.

As they were riding through a little town, hardly more than a collection of forty huts, they were suddenly confronted by an angry mob of people, blocking the way. They were speaking so loudly it was like bedlam and everyone was gesticulating. Ahren could see behind them a thick pall of smoke rising from a granary, and the attitudes of the farmers ranged from stunned shock to incandescent rage.

'Back, back now!' hissed Uldini, but it was already too late. One of the farmers saw their group and pointed with a shaking finger at Jelninolan.

'The elf! Of course, it was the elf who set fire to our provisions. They want to starve us before they attack us!'

The words were tumbling out of the accuser in a mixture of fear and wild blood lust. To a man and woman, the villagers turned to face them and began to approach. Ahren was horrified to see pitchforks and threshing flails being raised in the midst of the outraged mob, before the improvised weapons were distributed among the growing gang.

Falk looked around him wildly, but the farmhouses right and left offered no way through with the horses, and the way back only let them to a larger town. If anyone received news of the accusations there, they'd be dealing with more than a few angry farmers.

He drew his sword.

'There's nothing for it, we'll have to push through them! Uldini and I will try to create a passage; you two ride through as fast as you can!'

Magical energy was already beginning to glow between the Arch Wizard's fingers.

'Are you sure you want to do that? I mean they are totally innocent people, even if they're not behaving that way,' he asked Falk uncertainly.

'Do you have a better idea? If I use the broad side of the sword, and you try something with a strong gust of wind, then we'll only injure a few of them at most,' argued the Forest Guardian.

Jelninolan was sitting, white as a sheet, on her saddle, staring at the raging mob, which was moving closer and closer and demanding the head of the priestess.

Culhen was leaping back and forth in front of the horses and barking furiously at the villagers.

Ahren thought feverishly of what they could do. He really didn't want to injure anyone, but he knew in his heart of hearts that he would do anything to protect his travelling companion if anyone were to attack her. His eyes flashed in every direction and suddenly he had a brainwave.

'What about Tanentan?', he called out quickly and fumbled at the elf's saddlebag. She had taken it out twice during their journey to check for any damage, so he knew where he had to look.

Jelninolan nodded vehemently and helped him to take out the oil-soaked cloth as quickly as possible. Ahren unwrapped it and held the musical instrument out to the priestess, so she could take it in her hands and begin playing it immediately.

Just as during the Elvin Feast, no sound was emitted once the strings of the lute were plucked. Instead, Ahren could hear the individual notes in his head, so clear and so pure that they drowned out the screaming and shouting of the farmers.

'I need time for it to be effective!', called out the priestess, and Ahren reacted immediately. He leaped off his horse, planted himself in the middle of the path and began to carry out the most impressive looking sequence of parries and thrusts with Windblade. It would have been totally ineffective in a real fight, but it looked remarkably threatening.

The mob hesitated as they came closer, and Ahren glanced back.

'A little help would be appreciated,' he called over his shoulder. The others didn't hesitate for a heartbeat. Falk planted his armoured body beside his apprentice and swung his broadsword in terrifying-looking circles through the air, while Selsena reared up on her hind legs and whinnied threateningly.

Meanwhile Uldini was causing little flashes to light up between the two Guardians and the mob, an illusion that had served him well when he was trying to make an impression on the elves in Evergreen.

The rows in front were intimidated and stopped, but they were being pushed forward by the farmers behind who were secure in the knowledge that they weren't in the front line.

Ahren performed more dangerous looking manoeuvres with his blade, hoping all the while that Tanentan's magic would soon take effect. The otherworldly musical notes were sounding more and more clearly in his soul, and he could feel an uncontrollable happiness overcoming him. He had to suppress an impulse to throw the sword aside and dance, and he did this by pulling his spirit back into the Void, in an attempt to insulate himself from the effect of the music.

His master was obviously feeling the same effects, as was Uldini, because the sparks were now flashing in time to the ethereal song, and the Arch Wizard was humming, unknown to himself.

Ahren clenched his teeth and concentrated on further intimidating the mob.

There were no more than two paces now separating master and apprentice from the nearest pitchforks and clubs when Ahren noticed the behaviour of the gang of farmers changing ever so slightly – like a gentle breeze that disperses a fog.

First the weapons began to move in time to the music, then the feet, which rhythmically began to stamp the ground. Then the rows of villagers broke up, the weapons were thrown aside, and the villagers were linking arms, laughing and dancing around in a circle.

The Void burst and Ahren was laughing too, he laughed until the tears were running down his cheeks. All of his cares were gone, far away and forgotten, as if after a summer thunderstorm, when the skies are clear and blue again.

The young man threw himself into the arms of the dancers and was passed along from one to the next while the whole village rejoiced in celebration. He kept spotting the pall of smoke coming from the burning granary twelve dozen paces away, but this didn't bother the apprentice in the least.

The music in his head had drowned out everything else, leaving only a joie-de-vivre and exuberance. In the corner of his consciousness he saw some knights riding past, and he asked himself briefly if he shouldn't invite them to dance too, but then the fleeting thought was gone, like all other thoughts, for the music made him happy and his cares had evaporated.

Suddenly, two strong arms hoisted him up and placed him athwart his saddle. He didn't find this as much fun as dancing, but he hummed on and bobbed his legs in time to the music.

In the distance he heard a sarcastic voice saying 'Oh, I'll rub his nose in this for a long time to come yet.'

Chapter 6

75 days to the winter solstice

Once they had ridden on a mile, Jelninolan stopped playing and the music in Ahren's head died away. The levity with which he had just looked on life was gone as he regained control of his emotions.

Strangely, it seemed to Ahren as though some of his troubles had disappeared. It was true that he was conscious of all the difficulties and problems he had to overcome, but his worries weren't pressing so hard on his young spirit anymore. He could still hear the echoing of his carefree laughter in his head and he felt a remarkable lightness within himself.

Ahren pulled himself awkwardly up in his saddle and sat upright. The others were grinning at him and the apprentice prepared for an onslaught of ridicule. He jutted out his chin aggressively and stared thunderously at them.

'So what if I was dancing and laughing? It felt good and now I feel fantastic.'

At the last second, he remembered not to cross his arms like a spoiled little brat. Instead he rested them in a deliberately relaxed manner on the pommel of his saddle and quietly hummed the melody of the song that had sparked the storm of joyfulness within him.

Uldini opened his mouth in a nasty grin and drew in his breath to speak, but Jelninolan gave a warning hand gesture and smiled caringly at Ahren.

'Leave him alone, the two of you. Tanentan seems to have really moved him and that is a priceless experience.'

She looked deeply into Ahren's eyes with a look of satisfaction.

'Sometimes, when the soundless lute is played, you pick exactly the right song at the right time, which gives the listener a genuine feeling of peace. A feeling that lasts beyond the length of the song. And so, the melody helps to repair what is broken and to bring order to chaos.'

She lovingly stroked the instrument in her arms

'It seems you needed a good portion of joy with all the hardships you've had to endure in this world. We older ones forget so quickly what it's like to be young. Perhaps we're not aging physically, but nonetheless we're getting older. I'm delighted that Tanentan was of help to you,' she concluded.

Falk considered briefly what she'd said, and Ahren could see that the old man stopped himself from making a biting commentary, and instead, he could feel a wave of benevolence from Selsena, which presumably was directed at his master.

'Selsena would like to tell you that it was a good idea to use the lute as a means of solving our problem with the farmers.' He cleared his throat and hesitated before continuing. 'I can only say "amen" to that. That was very good work, boy.'

Ahren beamed with happiness.

'With a bit of luck, you might eventually become a half-way decent Forest Guardian in the far distant future,' his master concluded.

That wiped the grin off the young man's face, only to appear instead on the faces of Falk and Uldini, who nodded to each other in satisfaction.

Jelninolan rolled her eyes and ruffled Ahren's hair.

'Don't listen to those two old grumpy bears, they're only jealous because they didn't have the idea and were on the point of harming innocent people,' she said pointedly.

Her words were like a bucket of icy water being thrown over the two men, and both fiddled around in embarrassment with their saddles.

'Better a grumpy bear than a dancing bear,' said Uldini finally. He and Falk strode ahead laughing coarsely, leaving Ahren and the priestess in their wake.

The apprentice and the elf moved off too, and Ahren asked a question that had been bothering him.

'Why did the lute have such little effect on all of you? The farmers and I were completely out of control,' he asked.

'We have been under the spell of Tanentan quite a few times already and so we have much more practice in handling it. In Evergreen, a few weeks ago I only evoked a memory but no emotions. Today was a foretaste of Tanentan's real power. That's why I so rarely put it into effect,' the priestess answered.

'But why not? It was so beautiful!', answered Ahren so vehemently that he was almost shouting. He clapped his hand on to his mouth and was amazed at the strength of his own outburst.

Jelninolan smiled indulgently and packed the artefact back into her saddlebag.

'There are several reasons. For one thing, I can also release negative emotions with the lute. You've seen the unbridled joy it can cause. Now just imagine in the heat of battle if I were to release rage or grief. The consequences would be devastating. The more I use it, the more I fall into the temptation of using it again. And so I use its power only sparingly. Also, there are two things one needs to be aware of. You can become addicted to the emotions it releases, and it can unwittingly damage you.'

'Because it can drive you into a rage,' stated Ahren, who now understood how dangerous the lute could be.

The elf shook her head. 'That's not what I mean. Tanentan did you good. But imagine someone has just lost a loved one. And now, all of a sudden, they are full of the joys of life, dancing and laughing until their grief disappears. The natural emotions are overcome by what they're experiencing now. There have been listeners whose lives have been broken by the effects of the lute. It's possible that I have spiritually wounded two or three farmers. I hope not, but it's a heavy responsibility.' Jelninolan's voice died away and she seemed to be lost in thought or in her memories.

Ahren thought over what he had just heard. He was glad he didn't have to bear the responsibility for such a mighty artefact, and his respect for the priestess grew even greater.

They caught up with the others in silence and rode on, deeper and deeper into the Old Marshes and towards King's Island.

They were coming across more half-timbered houses and merchant's dwellings every day, while the number of farmhouses was decreasing.

Ahren saw an increasing number of town walls on the horizon, and although they avoided the larger settlements, it was clear to him that the towns he could see in the distance were as big or bigger than Three Rivers, the trading town they had gone through on their way to the elves. The thought of how many people lived in these towns made Ahren dizzy. And he'd spotted at least nine such towns as they travelled through the Old Marshes!

As they continued eastwards, there was more and more evidence of the unrest that was shaking the Knight Marshes.

One midday they happened upon makeshift gallows from which five farmers were hanging. Their cadaverous bodies were swinging in the wind and their threadbare linen clothing hardly disguised the torture they must have experienced before their deaths. Horrified, Ahren looked away.

He came from a village where the ultimate punishment anyone could suffer had been abolished. Although the death penalty was sometimes carried out in his homeland of Hjalgar, it was only on an individual basis, never a gruesome mass punishment like this, which had been carried out in a seemingly causal manner at a country crossroads.

The others looked as darkly as he did. Falk pointed at a sign that had been put up beside the gallows.

Ahren squinted his eyes and read the proclamation. *Condemned for High Treason* had been burned into the wood. Someone had also smeared *Elf Friends* in pig's blood on it as well.

'It's getting serious. Now they seem to be inciting neighbour against neighbour,' murmured Uldini.

They had encountered several processions of believers over the previous few days, and each time Ahren's heart bled as he saw the pious faces of the pilgrims and thought of the gruesome fate that awaited them.

Jelninolan kept her hood pulled over all the while and let her red hair hang loose. She didn't have the tell-tale white hair and grey eyes of the other elves, and her simple disguise as a farmer's wife proved effective as long as nobody looked directly into her face. Nevertheless, the tension was rising within the group. It was true that they probably didn't need to fear any Dark Ones, but every passing farmer, every little town, every armed group – of which there were more and more – was potentially a deadly danger.

The conflicts between neighbours, villages and whole baronies were certainly on the increase, the closer they came to the capital. The latest news was exchanged with angry faces and it seemed as there was an increase in the number of larger granaries being burned to the ground, and the Knights Marshes had to prepare for a hungry winter. Fear and rage were written on the faces of many, and rumours that elves had been responsible for carrying out the arson attacks were doing the rounds. Voices of reason could scarcely be heard, and when Ahren thought back to the hanged farmers, he could see why.

The mood among the travelling party was growing darker and Jelninolan would often ride the whole day without speaking a word. From time to time Ahren would squeeze her hand with encouragement and would receive a weak smile in return. He remembered how harmonious and communally woven the Elvin way of life was. The lies and suspicion that the priestess was being confronted with here had to be devastating. Ahren recognised on more than one occasion that he was ashamed of his fellow human beings. The worst traits of human culture were coming to the fore here, and the helplessness in which he found himself once again nagged at him.

Then one rainy autumn afternoon, they strode onto the brow of a hill and Falk gestured for them to stop. Loud cries rang out towards them, and the wind carried with it a curious smell. Ahren joined his master and at first, he couldn't make out what was happening before them in the field below. Initially, he thought it was a funfair, for dozens of people were pushing against each other down there, all in colourful clothing. A moment later he realised his error and despaired.

Two small armies were laying into each other with pitchforks, threshing flails and scythes. Even from this distance Ahren could make out dreadful red stains, which looked like blossoming flowers, appearing on the unfortunate bodies of those who were unlucky enough to be hit by the weapons. The bodies on both sides were tightly packed, the rows behind pushing those in front forward. Ahren realised to his horror that all his sword skills would be of no use in such a squeeze. What good was the best technique if you couldn't move your arm properly because you were pinned in by two of your fellow warriors, who were pushing you into the enemy? Left and right of the throng could be seen men and women in full armour striking their foes with broadsword and spiked mace and contributing their share to the bloodbath. Now Ahren recognised the faint scent in his nostrils. It was the blood of the dead and the wounded.

Falk wearily shook his head and scratched his beard with one hand.

'Now even the barons are beginning to fight each other. If this madness isn't stopped, it will end up in a full-scale war. Then all the desperate, the homeless and the hungry it creates will turn in their need to the false promises of the Illuminated Path.'

'I hate when that happens,' added Uldini sadly.

Ahren spun his head around. 'You mean it's happened before? I thought it had been stopped that time,' he blurted out.

Uldini shrugged his shoulders helplessly. 'When the Illuminated Path appeared the first time during the Dark Days, we were completely blindsided. Nobody knew what was happening until the first empire, destroyed from within, fell apart. Where do you think the Borderlands come from? HE, WHO FORCES all of a sudden had a whole kingdom in the middle of the Northern Lands under his control, and just at that very moment when we thought we had come to grips with him. Suddenly, the armies of the Free Folk had a hostile area right in their battle lines, full of Low and High Fangs who would ambush their ranks. It took us a full two summers to adapt our tactics – and the logistics were an absolute nightmare. The Dark Days had already lasted many centuries. And HE lengthened it by another two hundred years with this gambit,' he said darkly.

' They can also return at any time. Even if it all seems to have been forgotten,' added Jelninolan in a melancholy voice.

Everyone looked over at the elf priestess sadly. Selsena sent out a wave of pity and the elf's drawn features relaxed momentarily.

'Can you take us down there with Tanentan?' asked Falk in a mild voice.

'No. There's a full-scale battle raging and the knights will have hacked us all to pieces by the time the lute's song has taken effect,' she answered despondently.

'But we have nothing to do with them. Why would they attack us?' asked Ahren fearfully.

His master pointed down to the battle below. 'You see how it's going down there. Do you seriously think they would give it a second thought? We're not wearing the right tabards, so we are the enemy, for both sides. No, so long as the fight goes on, we won't be able to make our way through.'

He thought for a moment, and then pointed with his thumb back in the direction from which they had come.

'Half a mile behind was a guesthouse. We'll stay there for the night and hope they'll have finished knocking themselves about by tomorrow. Then we'll be able to ride on.' He gave a loud curse, then added: 'I love my homeland, I really do, but sometimes we can be incredibly stupid.'

The rain fell continuously that evening and through the night, only to transform into a full-blown autumnal storm the following morning.

Ahren looked out through the bedroom window and saw how the trees fought futilely to hold on to their few remaining leaves. The wind whipped over the countryside in powerful gusts, and window frames and doors of the lodging house clattered violently. The uneasy muttering of the guests could be heard through the cracks in the wall and was intermingled with the ire of the storm.

Travelling on that day was out of the question and the apprentice sensed clearly that an uneasy tension was building up among the guests who had sought shelter. It was still only early morning but already he could clearly hear the first loud quarrels. The apprentice had spent the night battling the horrific images he had been subjected to the previous day and the atmosphere in the lodging house didn't improve his mood.

Pale and concerned, Ahren looked over at his master, who had a similar demeanour.

'We should go and check on the others,' the old man said cautiously.

Ahren nodded and went over to the door. Sitting around wore him down. He always had the feeling he was just hanging around waiting for something bad to happen.

'I'll go over to Jelninolan and then I'll look into the stable,' he said firmly. Uldini was bound to be in a bad mood and anyway, he could try to cheer the elf up a little. He also missed Culhen, who wasn't allowed into the house and had spent the night with Selsena. Once he'd visited the elf princess, he'd check up on the young wolf, storm or no storm.

Before Falk had a chance to object, he slipped out and after a few steps he knocked on Jelninolan's door.

'Come in!' sounded the voice of the elf. Her voice sounded strangely other-worldly and when Ahren entered he almost started back in surprise. He quickly closed the door and observed the drama in front of him.

Jelninolan was sitting on her knees in the middle of the little room and she was playing with barely moving fingers on Tanentan. Much to Ahren's surprise he couldn't hear the sound of the lute in his head. Rays of golden morning sun were shining through the window although Ahren could still see the storm raging outside. The contrast was disconcerting, and it wasn't the only peculiarity within the room. An intense aroma of springtime filled the air, and the wooden furniture looked strangely young and fresh, as if the trees from which the pieces were made had only recently been felled.

He shook his head in wonderment and it took him a few heartbeats to digest what he was looking at. The elf finished her lute-playing and opened her eyes.

Ahren had recovered his senses again and now examined his travelling companion's face. He was pleasantly surprised to see that life had returned to the elf's features again. Her eyes were sparkling with vigour and she had some strong lines in her face which he hadn't seen before, which gave her face more of a striking look and took away some of her motherly features. She stood up gracefully and Ahren gasped. The elf seemed to have grown by half a head during the night, and her figure had become more muscular and was less plump than it had been.

He blinked twice in disbelief and Jelninolan laughed, her voice clear as a bell.

'I think I owe you an apology.' The vitality in her voice was unmistakable, and although he was taken aback, Ahren was delighted that the priestess had found her centre again. He nodded slowly and she pointed to her bed where he gratefully sat down and from where he continued to stare at her in astonishment.

'We elves are strongly influenced by emotions, as you already know. SHE, WHO FEELS gave us an overabundance of them, whereas we were left a little short of form and essence.'

She bit on her lower lip and seemed to be searching for words as she looked at Ahren.

'Members of the Elvin Folk are shaped by the role they have to play in our society. The expectations and demands that work on us, through the emotional connections our people put on us, permeate right through us, and that gives us the necessary shape with which we can fulfil our role in the community.' She looked at Ahren expectantly, but he only gave her a baffled look in return.

'You people also have the expression 'to grow into a role,' don't you?' she asked, trying a different approach.

Ahren nodded hesitantly, and she continued cheerfully.

'That expression comes from us elves. Yet we don't just grow metaphorically into our roles, but we also grow physically. All the tree guardians grow tall, with long arms and legs and our magic craftsmen and women have slim, agile figures. In the last few centuries, I've been the motherly, caring centre of our village, and my appearance has reflected the emotional image of my role.'

She paused and looked out the window where now only the storm could be seen raging. The morning sunlight had disappeared along with all the other contradictory impressions that had been in the room.

'I spent the whole night with the aid of Tanentan living through my memories of the Dark Days. Painful but necessary, so that I could remember what I once was and must be again.' She looked at herself thoughtfully in the reflection of the window. 'Most of it has returned. If you wait for another three or four decades, I'll probably have all my white hair back as well as my silver eyes,' she joked.

At least, Ahren hoped she was joking. The change in her appearance was shocking, and the idea that nothing in an elf, whether male or female, was unchangeable made him deeply uneasy. Ahren remembered the time in his home village when everybody had seen him only as the son of a confirmed drunkard, and he also remembered the feeling of being defined by others' perceptions, but at least nobody had been able to physically change his body. He could hardly believe that this was possible in the case of the elves, and the very thought of it sent shivers down his spine.

His thoughts were clearly written all over his face because the priestess laid a comforting arm on his shoulder in the same caring manner as she had done over the last few weeks.

'I know how difficult that must be for a human being to hear. But your changeability frightens us too. Each human being is constantly developing, either through their own impetus or because they are being forced to by society. But it comes across to us as chaotic and uncontrolled, because not all of you have a harmonious purpose to go along with your development. When we come across a human being, we never know if we're dealing with a brilliant inventor, a merchant or a cut-throat – not until we've dealt with them, that is. It took us centuries before we understood how to read the signs. For example, your fashions change so quickly. Hardly have we begun to recognise a merchant by his outfit, when the next generation comes along and he talks and dresses in a completely different way.'

Ahren could hear genuine frustration in Jelninolan's voice and he began to understand what she was saying. There was no exclusion amongst the elves because they sensed one another's emotions. If an elf was by nature solitary, then he would probably become a spy. However, this being tied together in a mesh of emotions and community, robbed the individual elves of certain elements of their personality, elements which Ahren would never like to surrender.

Now he understood how the elf folk had had to overcome difficulties over hundreds of years in order to live together in harmony. He also understood how easily this mutual tolerance that they possessed could be destroyed.

He looked deeply into Jelninolan's eyes and took her hands in his own.

'I will stop HIM, I swear that to you! Somehow, we're going to stop a war between the humans and the elves,' he said passionately. His task had never seemed as important and significant as it did now. He thought of the maltreated faces of the Low Fangs, the farmers who had been hanged, and all the other living beings he could save if they were to be successful. Suddenly all the dangers and obstacles that lay in their way seemed to be a small price that he would be willing to pay.

Even if it cost him his life.

After Ahren had spent some time in the stable cuddling Culhen and digesting his conversation with Jelninolan, he went back into the guesthouse. He knocked on Uldini's door and went in without waiting. His new strength of will made him courageous, but within a heartbeat he wished his courage had also been accompanied by wisdom. For in front of him was a tornado of magical energy, scattering lightning flashes of blue, which scorched everything they touched, whether walls, the floor, the furniture or even foolhardy apprentices. He was hit in over half a dozen places and slammed against the very door he had closed so firmly in his over-enthusiastic entrance.

Uldini finished the magic exercise with a curse, and both the Arch Wizard and Falk stared at Ahren darkly. Both were standing in the back part of the room, which had obviously been safe from the flashes the Arch Wizard had been discharging.

'Tell me, are you weary of life?' hissed Uldini enraged. 'Do you know where the magic could have taken you?'

Falk's look clearly promised Ahren a lesson on the wisdom or otherwise of entering a wizard's room unannounced, and this lesson would doubtless involve a lot of sweat. Ahren bowed his head in embarrassment.

'What sort of magic was that?' he asked, partly trying to change the subject and partly because he was in enough trouble anyway so he might as well be hanged for a sheep as for a lamb.

'I finally know what's up with Elgin,' said Uldini, still indignant but sounding a little self-satisfied too. 'The oaf is in some sort of trance, some ritual that has been taking all his attention for weeks on end. No magic can reach him there. At least he's not ignoring me deliberately.' He rubbed his head and looked crankily up at the ceiling. 'I'm asking myself what he's up to there. Maybe it's something useful for a change.'

Falk snorted in disbelief and said: 'you really dote on this wizard, don't you? Anyone else would have been on the receiving end of a furious messenger spirit by now; instead he's still playing you like a fool.'

Uldini looked deliberately over at Ahren.

'Don't talk to me about apprentices. All the things your pupil has got up to already, it could fill volumes, and yet you still drag him around after you.'

Ahren recognised that it was just the usual squabbling between the Arch Wizard and the Forest Guardian that was kicking off and he decided to ignore the barb.

While they were involved in verbal jousting, he curiously stuck his head out into the hallway. Jelninolan had said she would join soon but there was no sign of her. The pair were still at each other's throats and he could hear more arguments coming from downstairs. What if one of the other guests had discovered the elf? Then a real fight would ensue in no time. He stepped out into the hall and walked anxiously to Jelninolan's room.

She didn't react to his knocking, so he opened the door gingerly, just a tiny bit. After all, he'd just learned a painful lesson on the dangers of entering a magical figure's room without being invited.

Jelninolan was lying on the floor, her arms and legs were bound, and she was writhing helplessly. Ahren's worst fears seemed to have come true and he burst into the room, his hand on his knife, which he always carried with him after some particularly bitter experiences.

He looked around wildly, ready to attack whoever had done this to the elf in the blink of an eye. But the room was completely empty apart from the elf and himself. He turned to her and saw her pleading look.

When he realised her dilemma, he burst out laughing. No matter how hard he tried, he couldn't resist giving in to the hilarity.

Jelninolan was lying before him, tied up in a tangle of leather bands, clearly, Elvin ribbon armour that she had tried to put on by herself. Ahren was looking at a half dozen bands that had become twisted, thereby upsetting the balance of the armour to such an extent that with every movement the elf was simply tying herself up in more knots.

He panted and tried desperately to draw breath and wiped the tears of laughter from his eyes, but the deadly look from Jelninolan confirmed what he'd already suspected – how their next practice battles would turn out. A small part of him saw the painful days ahead, but most of him continued to laugh hysterically.

Finally, he managed to pull himself together. He hastily closed the door so that nobody could see the priestess in her unfortunate state, then, still laughing, hunkered down beside her.

'You have to stop thrashing about, you know that yourself. Otherwise, I can't help you,' he said, catching his breath and trying to calm her.

Jelninolan's eyes were green slits that were almost paralysing him. His merriment drained away completely, and he asked as respectfully as possible: 'shall I loosen the bands, or can you help yourself by using magic?'

The priestess maintained her furious look for a moment before giving up and rolling her eyes.

'Not without using my hands, which unfortunately isn't possible at the moment,' she finally admitted.

Ahren simply nodded and began silently recounting the Elvin tale of the Merry River, whose leitmotifs helped him to gradually work his way through the leather bands of the elf armour.

It wasn't long before he had freed Jelninolan's hands and she immediately performed a few hand gestures and murmured a complicated Elfish sentence. The armour slid into position, although Ahren noticed that the elf cheated a little by moving the leather panels to adjust the bands. He said nothing however, but stood up and took a few steps back.

The armour was sitting perfectly on her now, and the priestess gracefully got to her feet.

Ahren could now study the quality of the leather panels in some detail and what he saw amazed him. The leather was dyed green throughout and covered in complicated patterns, just like the Tree Guards who protected Evergreen. But he also noticed there were gaps here and there in the armour. It seemed that Jelninolan hadn't quite succeeded in transforming herself back to her earlier form, because it appeared as though the armour was designed for a slimmer body.

She saw the look on his face and her scowl suggested an immediate and painful death if gave so much as a hint of a giggle. Ahren's forehead broke out in a sweat and he froze like a rabbit caught in the torch light. Finally, Jelninolan threw a loose robe over herself, which hid the armour. He recognised the shimmering of Elvin material, but then the priestess cast a spell and the robe was transformed into the everyday linen garment worn by a farmer's wife.

With head held high she imperiously swept past him, meanwhile hissing into his ear in a whisper: 'Not a word now!'

Ahren could only nod weakly and didn't move a muscle until he heard her voice from the corridor calling back into the room, 'stop dilly-dallying, Ahren! The others are sure to be waiting for us!'

He sensibly didn't ask the question that was nagging him: why hadn't the elf simply used the magic from the outset to clothe herself in the armour? Instead, he followed her in silence. Jelninolan gave him another warning look before they reached Uldini's room. He shrugged his shoulders and decided to forget the whole incident as best he could.

Ahren followed the elf into Uldini's room and noticed sulkily how she swept in unannounced and didn't receive a hint of a rebuke. Ahren wasn't particularly looking forward to the following few days as he now feared that both Falk and Jelninolan had a bone to pick with him. He carefully slipped into the room behind the priestess and retired as invisibly as possible into a corner.

The two men stared at Jelninolan in shock until finally Uldini walked towards her and gave her an awkward but genuine hug.

'I'm so sorry, auntie. I know how much you had got used to your new form and role in the community. This must be a bitter blow,' he said kindly.

To Ahren's surprise, there were tears in the eyes of the cynical wizard. He thought over what he had heard earlier. Elves changed their form because of the demands placed on them by their society, but this process was normally a gradual one. Now the elf had used powerful magic to force herself into her previous form because she felt it suited best in their present situation.

Ahren imagined if he had to go back to his previous form, as the timid boy without any prospects - the one he had been in Deepstone before being trained by Falk. The thought was unbearable and now he really understood the sacrifice the elf had made.

Falk too had laid an arm over the priestess's shoulder, and was now comforting her as she looked at the two men with her eyes full of determination. Her features were harder and more resilient, and Ahren caught himself thinking that he missed the old Jelninolan already.

Uldini cleared his throat and turned back to the window to point demonstratively outside.

'We can't leave in this weather, but by staying in here, we're tempting fate. The voices below are getting louder all the time and I don't think this day will pass without fisticuffs or a real fight. And if one of the patrols comes in and finds us here then we're in real trouble,' he said darkly.

Falk nodded in agreement. 'Better to be wet in safety than dry in peril.'

Ahren had got very familiar with wet weather in the course of his training and nodded in agreement too.

'I spent the whole night reliving a memory with the help of Tanentan. So the lute can't be used as an aid to calming the hot-heads below. Its effect was very powerful as you can all see, so I should really avoid using it for at least one lunar month – or it could damage me badly. I think we should leave immediately too,' she explained in a steely voice which sounded more like an order than a suggestion.

And so, a short time later they were all in the saddle and riding off into the autumn storm while suspicious eyes stared at them through the windows of the hostelry.

No sooner had they left when they were drenched by a squall of rain. It hit Ahren like a massive wall of water and within a few heartbeats he had fallen behind and was soaked to the skin. The cold wind pulled and tore at his clothing and after two hundred paces his whole body was shivering with cold. He carefully pulled out his flask, took a swig from it and grimaced. He had created his herbal drink from a medicinal perspective, and was still trying to find a way of bettering the taste without lessening the effect.

The apprentice caught up with Falk and offered him the flask.

'There's Gorge Weed in it, which should protect us from a cold or worse,' he said, his teeth chattering.

Falk gave him a searching look, then shrugged his shoulder and took a large draught of the herbal brew. He returned the flask to Ahren with a look of self-satisfaction.

'I taught you something useful anyway. It's good that not all of my lessons have gone in one ear and out the other,' he grunted.

Ahren looked suitably contrite but he was jumping for joy inside. The apprentice had begun to understand that Falk liked to be sparing with his praise because he didn't want Ahren to become cocky. He was slowly learning to look behind the mountain of criticism which the old Forest Guardian was constantly heaping onto him.

The young man strode over to Uldini, granting himself a little smile that none of his companions could see. Then he gave the flask to the wizard, who drank from it too. Finally, he dropped back to Jelninolan, but she declined with a little hand gesture.

'Elves never get colds. The weather can never get the better of us, whether rain, snow or sun. SHE, WHO FEELS is also the goddess of nature,' she said modestly.

Ahren, shivering from head to toe, put away the flask and wondered morosely if, when he was a Forest Guardian, he might not be able to change deity if he prayed hard enough for it.

Chapter 7

64 days to the winter solstice

They passed through the previous day's battlefield without any problems. To his left and right Ahren saw tell-tell signs of the bloodbath, but the bodies had been taken away. A few torn and discarded tabards, some broken shields and the churned-up earth were the only clues to the battle that had raged on so recently.

Only one day earlier people had died on that spot, but the piece of land lay there innocently, as though nothing unusual had ever occurred, and the storm was scattering any remaining evidence of the slaughter. This impression of transience both frightened and angered Ahren. They rode on silently, leaving the field behind them.

The weather hardly improved over the following days, and neither did Ahren's mood. He was constantly on the lookout for medicinal plants so that his supply of herbal tea wouldn't run out. The others left its preparation to Ahren although Falk and Uldini helped themselves to generous amounts. His task was made more difficult by the fact that the surroundings were becoming more urban.

They spent most of their days moving from one village to the next, or if it couldn't be avoided, along the outside of town walls. All this meant it was more difficult to find the necessary plants. Then, to top it all off, there were the nasty exercises Falk had thought up for him, which all had to be carried out in rainy conditions. Ahren practised pulling the arrows out of his soaking quiver, then he had to fletch his arrows anew or untie wet leather knots. Their nights were spent in draughty barns or by the side of the road in the small tents the elves had given them. Uldini and the others were afraid of another hostelry full of combative guests, and Ahren acknowledged the wisdom of their decision with sadness.

At least Uldini ensured they were warm every evening. He would always intone a magic spell over their campfire, which ensured a constant natural warmth so they could dry their clothes and warm their bones. Herbal brew or no herbal brew, Ahren was convinced that without this magical intervention, they would be sneezing their heads off the following day.

Finally, after a stormy but dry autumn afternoon, they arrived on top of a hill from where Ahren caught his first glimpse of King's Island. Large clouds were scudding across the sky, and every so often, through the gaps in the rays of sunlight, it would brighten the capital in a golden hue, just for an instant, before the city would cloud over again.

Ahren was amazed by the sight of this impressive, silhouetted city rising up out of a craggy island. There must have been a promontory once, connecting King's Island with the mainland, but now it had been replaced by a gaping chasm filled by the swirling ocean brine. An enormous drawbridge, rising upward at a slight incline, connected the mainland with the egg-shaped island, which had been the seat of the Knight Marshes royal house since time immemorial.

The city walls seemed small and delicate when compared to the cliff-faces, but when he spotted the sentries positioned on the battlement's walkways, Ahren calculated that the fortifications had to be at least fifteen paces high. Splendid buildings with shimmering roofs soared upwards here and there from behind the walls, but what impressed Ahren the most was the palace, which he could see in the distance. The broad main street beyond the drawbridge stretched straight as an arrow directly up to the palace, so that any visitor entering the royal city had an unhindered view of the building. It seemed enormous, almost threateningly so, and was at least fifty paces high and almost five furlongs in length. A square-shaped tower stretched high into the air, seeming almost to touch the heavens.

Ahren gaped and Uldini seemed unusually contented.

'It's best if we keep going. It would be a pity if we were to get drawn into any trouble just as we're about to arrive,' said the Arch Wizard.

The mood among the populace had changed over the previous few days. It was no longer that of open squabbling, but now there was an intangible brooding feeling of resentment against the authorities. It seemed as though the ever-present King's Guards still had the surrounding baronies under control, but the general atmosphere reminded Ahren of the humming of an angry beehive just before the swarm bursts forth.

They travelled quickly on towards the drawbridge, which marked the end of the first stage of their journey. Ahren was excited and curious, and kept craning his neck as they approached the enormous wooden structure. Dozens of merchants, farmers, knights and guards crowded the wide bridge, at least twenty paces wide, whose beams were formed from mighty old oaks which had been cut into rectangular shapes. Ahren looked in amazement at ropes, as thick as your forearm, and iron heads as large as your fist, which bound each enormous plank of wood to the next. The chains, with links bigger than Ahren's torso, stretched tautly into the heights above them, disappeared into holes in the wall, as large as a fully grown human. As they approached the opening in the wall, he heard the mighty surge of the waves, fifty paces below them, and racing through the narrow strait before they would crash into the coastal cliffs.

Ahren felt queasy when he looked down at the ocean beneath him and he could hardly wait to set foot on King's Island. Falk's training had not, up to this point, included any swimming lessons. The apprentice, it was true, could keep afloat in a still pool, but Ahren was under no illusions concerning what would happen if he fell into the maelstrom of water below and crashed into the jagged cliff-face.

The passersby pushed and jostled each other in a hectic hurly-burly motion from one side of the bridge to the other and Ahren was surprised that not one out of this seething mass had fallen off. Personally, he would have been delighted if there were some form of barrier left and right, but its absence didn't seem to bother anyone. It was like a complicated dance where everybody seemed to know the rules, and the edges of the bridge was always clear of people.

A massive ox cart pushed by them while the cloth merchant on the coach box urged on the animal, causing the crowd to separate, only to join together in a wave of bodies, moving forward again as soon as it had passed.

'Why is there such a coming and going? I know this is the capital, but I can see so many merchants. They can't possibly all sell their wares on this small island?' he asked Uldini quietly.

The Arch Wizard eyed him merrily.

'Well spotted, boy. To make sure that the trade isn't completely taken away from the capital city, every merchant who doesn't sell his wares on King's Island has to pay a higher tribute. In this way the political and economic power of the kingdom has been centralised in one place for centuries,' answered Uldini. 'Also, the largest harbour on the north east coast is here. The currents are normally favourable and at night a mighty beacon in the palace tower guides the sailors on their way. Ships are becoming more daring and are even docking and unloading at night, so that there's a constant hubbub at the harbour. A third of all goods from Evergreen, Kelkor, the Knight Marshes and the Green Sea are channelled through King's Island before being shipped off to the Sunplains or into the Southern Jungles. Or indeed to the Silver Cliff, which is exactly why we're here. It should be easy enough for us to find a ship that will take us to the dwarf enclave,' said Uldini hopefully. 'But first I'll pay a visit to Elgin. He has to put a stop to the activities of the Illuminated Path before the cult plunges the Knight Marshes into chaos. Senius Blueground is a good ruler, but I really don't understand how he could have let things come to this pass', said the Arch Wizard grimly.

'That's the disadvantage of King's Island,' answered Falk. 'It's set apart. Trade and politics dominate day-to-day life and the voices of the common folk are scarcely heard here. The next baronial convention won't be until winter and by that time the situation will have worsened considerably. The King may be hearing about isolated unrest here and there, but it will probably be too late by the time the barons present him with the full picture.' Ahren noticed an urgent, almost pleading tone in his master's voice and it reminded him clearly that his master's original home was the Knight Marshes.

Ahren glanced over at Jelninolan to see if she had anything to say on the matter, but the elf kept her head hidden under her hood, trying not to attract attention.

Culhen was whining, and Ahren looked down at his friend with concern. The wolf was continually looking quickly from left to right and back again. The hordes of people, their smells and the noises they made unsettled the young animal. Ahren quickly dismounted and led his horse by the reins, while at the same time commanding Culhen to walk by his side, and so the wolf's attention was concentrated on his master and his commands, and this put him at his ease. Thanks to Jelninolan's illusion,

113

Culhen wasn't attracting any attention and the apprentice was eternally grateful to the priestess.

They pushed their way closer to the end of the drawbridge and now Ahren calculated that the enormous wooden construction had to be over forty paces long. He realised that he had miscalculated with the rest of his measurements concerning the dimensions of the city walls and the buildings. It would never have occurred to him that houses could be so tall. The two towers left and right, which soared in front of him and contained the chain winches, seemed to stretch unbelievably far up into the heavens, and Ahren could only compare them to the mammoth trees of Eathinian.

The elves would allow a tree to grow and then build a shelter among its branches, which would be harmoniously intertwined with the qualities of the tree, whereas the humans would simply build their dwelling place wherever and however they wanted, without compromising on anything. Humans had to seem very strange to the inhabitants of nature, and Ahren could see how easy it was for the Illuminated Path to drive a wedge between them.

'Why does the capital city not have a proper city gate, but only a hole in the wall?' he asked Falk curiously.

His master grinned and pointed at the two towers, which were rising up before them. Ahren saw three openings in the sides of the fortifications.

'In the case of an attack the drawbridge is simply pulled up, and three enormous bolts are pushed out of the wall. The bridge itself is the gate. In times of peace the island is open to all day and night,' replied the old man.

'One of our better ideas,' said Uldini contentedly. Ahren looked questioningly at the Arch Wizard, and Uldini gestured to the whole city.

'The Ancients used to intervene considerably more openly in the lives of humans than nowadays. During the Dark Days the king of Knight Marshes asked us for a defence of the capital. We destroyed the promontory that time and built this bridge instead. Ye gods, how I miss Belsarius,' said Uldini wistfully.

Ahren looked over the edge of the bridge and was dumbfounded by the thought that this strait was once a land-bridge. Then he remembered the remains of the exploded mountain they had ridden past when they were travelling along the Red Posts on their way to Eathinian, and the thought of what the wizards had done here seemed more plausible. The thought that the miracles and also the destructive powers of those days could be repeated once HE had awakened made Ahren dizzy, and so he tried to turn his thoughts in another direction as quickly as possible.

'Who's Belsarius?', he asked.

'He was one of the Ancients. An exceptionally gifted visionary and at that time the first among us. My predecessor, so to speak. Although I couldn't hold a candle to him in so many areas. He fell in the war.' There was sadness in Uldini's face, and he became lost in thought.

Before Ahren could ask any more questions, they reached the castle walls and pushed themselves along with the other travellers onto the dry land of King's Island. Ahren was looking in amazement around him at the soaring buildings with their neatly tiled roofs, when ten armed city sentries broke away from their companions and marched quickly towards them.

'Master!' whispered Ahren fearfully and looked pleadingly over at Falk.

His demeanour was grim, but he made a placating hand gesture.

'Everyone, stay calm. They seem relaxed and they're not holding their weapons. Let's follow their example,' he muttered firmly.

The sentries arranged themselves in a semi-circle in front of them, their looks were alert but respectful. Their hands were clasped behind their backs and they stood erect, while the leader of their troop stepped forward and with his closed fist, punched his armoured chest with a clatter, presumably a military greeting.

'Uldini Getobo, first among the Ancients, and Baron Falkenstein, I greet you. The King of Knight Marshes, blessed be his rule, requests hereby most graciously your attendance. It is therefore my honour to escort you forthwith to the palace,' he said with a loud voice which was familiar with giving orders.

Even Ahren recognised, in spite of his limited experience of military or political protocol, that this was no request. The soldiers arranged themselves into a guard of honour and they marched together at a trot along the main street and up to the monumental building, which was the physical manifestation of the regal seat of the King of Knight Marshes.

While Ahren, who was surveying the imposing building which rose up before them ten furlongs ahead, had a queasy feeling in his stomach, he heard Uldini's furious voice mumbling darkly, 'well, this was all we needed!'

Ahren was sitting in the saddle again and looking around nervously. Culhen, on the other hand, had fully calmed down and was trotting beside the horse and was sniffing the scents around him. Every time the young wolf caught an interesting smell, he would try to move away from the soldiers that surrounded and were escorting them to the palace, and Ahren kept having to whistle orders to make him come to heel. Luckily, their guards of honour were more amused than annoyed at the animal's escapades and they maintained their relaxed air.

In contrast, pedestrians' eyes from all directions kept looking at them as they proceeded along. Ahren saw haggling traders, eager craftsmen and aristocratic nobility, who were for the most part sitting in splendid, open coaches. Ahren tried not to stare open-mouthed at the luxury, but Falk's grumpy stare suggested the apprentice was unsuccessful in this regard. Many of the coaches were richly decorated in silver or gold, and every so often a gemstone, artfully set, would sparkle. The aristocrats themselves were dressed in the finest clothing, whether extravagant or noble. Any aristocrat who wasn't in a coach was surrounded by an army of attendants and guards, and all the wealth that Ahren observed made him quite dizzy. In Deepstone there were precisely three gemstones and every villager knew to whom they belonged, how long they had been in the family, and how they had been come by. In the last five furlongs, Ahren had seen certainly over fifty diamonds, emeralds or rubies.

It wasn't long before he began to concentrate, not so much on the wealth he was seeing, but rather on the people who possessed that wealth, and his amazement was now accompanied by disquiet. The expressions on their faces ranged from curious to hostile. It wasn't Jelninolan who was the target of their mistrustful looks, but rather Falk and Uldini. The wealthier the onlooker of their little procession, the more disgusted the look appeared to be.

'Why are the really wealthy people looking at you so angrily?' whispered Ahren, who had ridden up as closely as possible beside Falk.

His master shrugged his shoulders.

'Uldini and I are well-known here on King's Island. Everybody here knows Selsena, and because they know her, they also know me, which has led all these gentlemen and wealthy merchants to ask themselves why we are being given a parade of honour to the palace. Everyone that you see here has three or four devious plans or intrigues in their minds that

117

they are just trying to implement. We two, turning up out of the blue, presents a potential problem for their machinations. The resentment is less aimed at us than at the political turbulence we might cause,' explained the old man calmly.

Ahren was confused. Politics was foreign to him and he couldn't really follow what he'd just heard. While he ruminated over what his master had said, he tried to ignore the people around him but instead he looked curiously at the city itself.

The main street leading straight up to the palace was at least fifteen paces wide and covered with cobblestones, which had been so artfully set into place that there were none of the weeds that would customarily be growing in the gaps. Trimmed trees, set at intervals of ten paces, lined the street on both sides, and were carefully pruned, and curbed by cobblestones. The contrast to the wild and powerful vegetation of Eathinian couldn't have been greater, and Ahren sensed what Jelninolan would feel about these constricted plants. Everything smelled somehow sticky and claustrophobic, while the overpowering perfumes of the wealthy, mingled with the sweat of the oxen, horses and craftsmen, combined into a horrible mixture of hypocrisy and egoism.

The buildings left and right were, in contrast, breathtakingly ornate. Ahren saw frescoes, reliefs, mosaics and many gargoyles or crenellations on the outer walls, and even turrets stretching up from the enormous stone houses. Each house seemed to want to outdo its neighbour and Ahren could sense the intense competition between their residents. The side streets they passed by were wider than any of the trade routes they had travelled on. Ahren saw no narrow lanes nor communal yards, all houses had their own private gardens, protected through high hedges from curious passersby. There were watchmen everywhere and every building seemed to be guarded.

118

Ahren felt a cold shiver run down his spine and suddenly he yearned to be back in Deepstone, where there were precisely two bailiffs and where a house door was only bolted in the darkest of dark nights. The jealousy and mistrust that was so clear already as they strode along made Ahren feel uneasy and he turned once again towards his master.

'It almost seems as if everybody hates everybody else here,' he said a little indignantly.

Falk grinned and looked at Ahren kindly.

'Hold onto that insight, my boy. I learned to understand a long time ago that power is always accompanied by a dark side. And concentrated here, over an area of just a few streets, is the political and economic power of the Knight Marshes. The noble district is laid out like an upside-down horseshoe with the palace at the end of the bow. The harbour area, loud and filthy, is situated behind the royal residence, and it's a lot more honest and open than this nest of vipers here!'

The old Forest Guardian nodded his head towards Uldini.

'Look at Uldini. He's loving it here. You can be sure he's gathered together over two dozen useful bits of information just by studying the family coats-of-arms on the houses, which belong to the aristocracy we've been observing. Our magical friend lives and breathes politics. Wait and see how he lives it up once we're in the palace.'

Now Falk was grinning broadly and Uldini threw him a withering look before saying snidely, 'Not everyone is content to spend his life in a filthy mud cabin and watch from afar how the world continues to turn.'

Ahren was surprised at Uldini's sudden arrogance, but then he saw a twinkle in Falk's eye. The apprentice noticed that the guards were listening in on their every word, and within a few heartbeats the penny dropped. Falk and Uldini were playing roles in front of the guard of honour. Obviously, they were supposed to think that Uldini was an overbearing, powerful man of the world. The young man had no idea what good that was supposed to do, but as he also didn't what role they'd thought out for him, he decided to keep his mouth shut and to have a good look at the palace instead.

The closer they got to it, the clearer it became to Ahren that there were five buildings rising up in front of him, all behind a gold and silver bordered ceremonial wall. The main building was without doubt the actual palace, but the surrounding buildings were no less impressive, bar the fact that they were considerably smaller, which is why he had only now really noticed them.

The royal residence was a rectangular building, which, in spite of its ornate surface, looked well-fortified.

The four short towers, one at each corner, radiated a threatening presence, an impression which was further strengthened by the four enormous crossbows they contained, which were recessed into wrought-iron mountings. Ahren could also see the guards, who looked frighteningly small when compared to the defensive installations.

Falk noticed where Ahren was looking and indicated to one of the guards.

'A gift from the dwarves of Thousand Halls. These things are called Dragon Bows, because supposedly they can bring down a dragon from the skies. That's nonsense of course, but these weapons are very effective against conventional armies,' he said.

Ahren swallowed hard as he imagined that one of these constructions with its iron staff, three paces in length, sharpened and ready for action in the guide-shaft, could shoot straight at him. He looked away from the deadly weapon and turned his attention instead to the tall central tower, which dominated everything else, looking for all the world like a tall finger pointing up from the centre of the palace. An enormous open archway crowned the top, above which was a small, golden roof. Even from this distance Ahren could see an enormous cauldron standing within the archway. He remembered what Uldini had said and concluded that it had to be the beacon for the seafarers. Most likely it held oil, which burned at night. Ahren pitied the poor souls who had to carry the fuel up to it day after day.

The other four buildings that made up the palace complex were completely different to each other. One of the buildings exuded pomp, and its bell tower had the sign of THE THREE embedded in it. That building had to be the cathedral. Ahren had never seen such a place of worship before and he calculated that hundreds of people could gather together there and worship HIM, WHO MOULDS. He couldn't figure out what the other buildings were for. It was true that they were decorated, but all in all, they looked rather simple.

'What's the point of those three buildings?' he asked his companions.

'The one at the back is the barracks, with its monument to the knight in front of its portal,' Falk answered.

'In front of it are the servants' quarters. All the servants who work in the palace complex live there with their families. That's why an appointment there is a dream job. Not only because the pay is very good, but also the sleeping quarters are roomy and secure. Anyone who works in the palace doesn't have to worry about his family.'

Falk scratched his beard. 'One of the better ideas of past kings. The servants are extremely loyal and if there's an emergency, they are all together in one place, so palace life continues smoothly in spite of any crises.

He pointed at the last building, which was closer to the palace, and was connected to the royal residence through an archway.

'The administration building. Whatever the king decrees is published in a proclamation and then divided among the heralds. They also process the tithes that every baron has to submit to King's Island, and they deal with all the minor activities that the royal house either can't or doesn't want to tackle,' said Falk, finishing his presentation.

'If you disregard all the pomp and circumstance, then this is the most important building in all the Knight Marshes,' murmured Uldini.

They arrived at the ornate palace wall, which wasn't quite three yards high, but had pointed, copper-coloured spikes at the top. They were granted entry through a large open doorway which was lined with twenty alert-looking palace guards, all of whom were equipped with halberds, small under-arm shields and light crossbows, which were hanging across their backs. Both the men and women were all wearing shimmering scale armour.

They all radiated discipline and purpose, and Falk said under his breath, 'Another good idea from the old days: veterans who have earned their spurs on the field of battle make up the squadron of palace guards. No spoilt sons and daughters of the nobility who want to live the easy life of an officer, but battle-hardened soldiers.'

He gave a deep sigh.

'Somehow it's nice being here again,' Ahren's master mused nostalgically.

The guard of honour stopped at the door and gave a brisk salute, hitting their closed fists against their chests. The gatekeepers replicated the gesture and allowed the soldiers and their guests through.

Ahren could hear snatches of conversation. Things like: 'Is it really him?', 'I thought he'd fallen,' and again and again he heard his master's official title – which he'd only heard the first time himself a few weeks previously – Dorian Falkenstein, Knight of the Marshes.

The others still called him Falk, and that's what he'd continue to be to Ahren unless his master told him otherwise. It still didn't fit in with the apprentice's idea of the world, that his master actually had a different name and that he had lived a completely different life before his time in Deepstone, and so the apprentice ignored this fact as much as possible.

They strode in under the shadow of the palace, and the high building seemed to be looking down on Ahren and impressing on him the insignificance of his existence. They dismounted their horses on a step so wide, the whole population of Deepstone could have stood on it, and their horses were led away by some liveried stable boys. One of the young lads tried to grab Culhen by the neck, but Ahren immediately ran over and slapped his hand away.

'What do you think you're doing?' he growled angrily.

While Falk threw Ahren a warning look, the trembling stable boy pulled himself together.

'Animals are not permitted in the palace. Your wolfhound must stay in the stables with the horses,' he explained timidly.

Their guard of honour were suddenly a little more alert and watched Ahren with interest. Up until that point Ahren had been almost invisible, but now the situation had changed.

'Nobody touches this wolf...hound,' Ahren corrected himself quickly.

He knelt down in front of Culhen and looked into his loyal, intelligent eyes.

'Go with Selsena. If anyone touches you or tries to lock you in, defend yourself,' he said loudly.

Culhen gave a yelp, then licked Ahren's face. The apprentice looked over at the Titejunanwa,

'Promise me that you'll take care of him.'

A calming wave of serenity came over Ahren as Selsena conveyed her reassurance telepathically.

He stared into the eyes of the war horse, gave a nod, then patted Culhen on the back, and the wolf trotted off obediently beside Selsena.

Ahren looked after them briefly, then caught up with the others, who were waiting for him at the entrance.

'What was that supposed to mean?' snapped Uldini.

'There are too many people here with cross bows. As far as I'm concerned, Culhen shouldn't be left to fall into a trap', said Ahren gloomily. He felt vulnerable and unsure without the wolf at his side.

'Leave my apprentice alone. If I didn't know that Selsena could sense if anybody was approaching with evil intent, then I wouldn't have left them on their own,' said Falk, defending the young man's actions.

Uldini glanced over at their escorts, and then came to the conclusion that a prolonged discussion might only damage his esteem. Instead he remained silent, flew up a little into the air so that he was hovering half a pace over the ground, and floated towards the throne room, whose enormous double doors, decorated in blue, stood open in front of them at the end of the long hallway.

As they moved forward, the honour guard captain turned to Jelninolan.

'M'lady, you can take off your head covering if you so wish. Elves are safe within these four walls as long as my people and I are keeping watch,' he said respectfully.

Jelninolan immediately pulled back her hood and gave a thankful nod to the captain.

Falk slapped him on the back. 'Good man!' he growled appreciatively.

The effect of this simple gesture was amazing. The captain blushed like a Godsday schoolchild and proceeded to fidget, embarrassed at his uniform. Finally, he pulled himself together and clasped his hands behind his back.

'The least I could do, m'lord,' he said modestly.

While Ahren was digesting the respectful treatment which his master had received, they stepped into the throne room and he immediately became distracted by his surroundings. The room was spacious. Four mighty load bearing pillars divided up the room symmetrically. The first two pillars seemed to mark the boundary beyond which the common courtiers and petitioners couldn't pass. Here, right and left of the blue carpet which led up to the throne, there was a colourful crowd of men and women of all ages and from every level of society, ranging from the simply dressed to the richly ornamented. Ahren only spotted three farmers, who were ill at ease in these surroundings although they were clearly wealthy. The less important petitioners were presumably fobbed off to the administration building and could never hope for an audience with the king.

The space between the first and second pair of pillars was presumably for the king's guards. Twelve heavily armed figures stood there, covered in armour plating, with their faces hidden behind visors. Each of the guards was large and broad shouldered and radiated a steady readiness, which nipped any thought of rebellion in the bud.

As the group moved forward, Ahren noticed crossbowmen standing behind arrow-slits that were discretely positioned at the upper end of the high walls. The far end of the throne room was dominated by the throne itself and the person sitting on top of it.

Senius Blueground was a man of middle years with sandy hair and a well-manicured beard. He wore a deep blue robe with a heavy cape which

125

draped over the arms of his throne, which was also blue in colour. His head was adorned with a golden crown with a simple blue diamond at its centre.

The hubbub died down and was replaced by total silence as Uldini floated into the room, and everyone stared at the little figure, who stopped three paces in front of the king and gave a single loud clap with his hands. Left and right of the regent stood the nobility and advisers to the king, charmed into stillness by the bombastic arrival of the Arch Wizard.

'So, Senius, you wanted us to come, and here we are. Even though I'm delighted to see you, we are rather in a hurry. I suggest we skip the protocol and get straight to the point,' said Uldini in such a matter-of-fact manner that none of those present believed that the wizard had actually made a petition.

In his mind's eye, Ahren could already see swords flashing and bolts flying, but to his amazement the king simply laughed and stood up immediately.

'I've missed you, old Magus. I see your tongue still cuts through all the ceremonials,' said the monarch with amusement.

Uldini shrugged his shoulders. 'When necessary,' he said drily. The silence that surrounded them had now taken on a new quality. It had been curiosity and wonder that had stopped those present in their tracks, but now there was an air of indignation and forced respect. The majority of the courtiers were baffled by the fact that the king allowed himself to be spoken to like that, and that he was apparently even amused by the carrying on.

The monarch performed a strange formal gesture with his hands and suddenly the throne room was filled with movement. All the visitors and even the nobility left the room without saying a word, every one of them hastily bowing before disappearing back through the doors. Ahren noticed that behind the throne there were doors left and right and it was through these that the higher nobility and advisers made their exits.

As the crowds were leaving the throne room, Falk grasped Ahren by the forearm and steered him to one of the pillars.

'You stand there and don't say a word unless you're asked something. I want to see the perfect imitation of a Forest Guardian statue, is that clear?' his master ordered in a hard but low voice.

Ahren swallowed hard and nodded in awe. The doors closed behind the last few stragglers, and now only the travelling party and the king were left in the room. The throne room seemed enormous and Ahren dared to turn his head ever so slightly right and then left. From the corner of his eye he could see that the king's guards were all strategically placed. A minimal glance upwards confirmed what Ahren suspected, that the crossbow men and women were still at their places and even had their weapons at the ready. One of them was pointing directly at Ahren, which promised a quick end if a decision was made to shoot. Ahren broke into a sweat and he stood stock still, eyes looking forward as he concentrated on the discussion now beginning.

Uldini, Falk and Jelninolan bowed briefly before the ruler, who acknowledged this gesture of respect with a gracious nod. Then he leaned forward and fixed his eyes on them.

'You've surely got wind of the unrest that's been besetting the kingdom for the last few weeks. Rumours about marauding elves are doing the rounds, and there's discord between the barons, the towns and the villages. Long forgotten feuds are igniting again, and all my efforts are in vain.' And with that, King Senius fell back into his throne and rubbed his face. Suddenly, he didn't seem the awe-inspiring authority but rather a man plagued by difficulties looking at Uldini with tired eyes. His shoulders were slouched, and his face was drawn. Ahren realised that he was now looking at the real Senius Blueground, the man behind the royal mask. He could sense the daily effort of will it took for the ruler to present an impression to the world that here was a man of strength and steely determination, and Ahren felt a wave of pity for him.

Every young boy had dreams of killing the dragon, rescuing the damsel in distress and becoming the king – just like in the old tales. But just at this moment, Ahren could think of nothing better than to be running freely through the forests with Culhen at his side and the fresh wind in his face.

'We did stumble across a few complications, yes,' said Uldini drily in response to the king's summary. 'And what measures have you taken to deal with the problems?' the wizard continued tensely.

'I had proclamations delivered which exonerated the elves from all the incidents that have been taking place. I sent special messages to the northern barons ordering them not to break their ceasefire with the elves, and I also sent out religious leaders, who are travelling through the towns and villages, bringing spiritual peace to the inhabitants and calming their outraged passions.' The king listed off his actions in a weary voice. 'Brother Wultom has been an invaluable help in view of the fact that Elgin is incommunicado, now of all times,' he added with gratitude in his voice.

Uldini was standing with his back to Ahren, but from where the apprentice was standing, he could still see how the wizard had tensed up.

'And who is Brother Wultom? Is old Conrad no longer in charge of the cathedral of THE THREE?' asked Uldini, all innocence.

The king's answer shook Ahren to the core and was worse than the worst of his forebodings.

'Yes, yes, Conrad is still the abbot of the church. Brother Wultom belongs to a small religious community whose aim is to assist the poor and the desperate. They call themselves "the Illuminated Path". They established a soup kitchen in the harbour last year and they give out clothing to anybody who is in urgent need. When tidings of the unrest reached us, Brother Wultom presented himself to me. He said he was prepared to send his brothers and sisters out to reconcile any of the warring parties, and as I had heard nothing but good things about their work in the harbour, I happily assented.'

The king turned towards Falk.

'You know what the barons are like – good with their swords and at the ready when ordered, but when it comes to the worries and needs of the common folk, we've always depended on the church. It was a real godsend having over sixty men and women of the cloth ready to travel the length and breadth of the kingdom to help in these difficult times.'

Falk frowned but said nothing. Uldini, on the other hand, seemed to be on the point of venting his spleen in an explosion of magical discharges.

Jelninolan noticed the wizard's demeanour and quickly intervened.

'I am grateful that you haven't given credence to the rumours concerning my folk. I can assure you that Eathinian is still bound to the Knight Marshes in a spirit of friendship,' she said formally but sincerely.

King Senius looked at her half-relieved but also half-ashamed.

'I am happy to hear it and apologise for any injustices you may have experienced at the hands of my subjects on your journey here,' he said contritely.

Uldini had his emotions under control again and turned to the monarch again to ask further questions.

'Would it be possible for us to get to know this Brother Wultom? His help in this crisis seems to be all-embracing, and it would be sensible to consult with him concerning any further measures,' said the wizard, his voice as soft as velvet.

Ahren only recognised the threatening undertone because he had been travelling with the cantankerous immortal through the country over several lunar months.

The king, innocent of all, smiled broadly.

'But of course. I shall send for him immediately,' he said loudly.

Ahren heard the door of the throne room quietly open and close. It seemed the monarch did not even need to give the order, for someone to rush off in search of the priest.

'Brother Wultom's religious duties take him all over the harbour so it may take some time. I have put a room at his disposal here in the palace, but due to his modest nature he rarely makes us of it. So, I propose that you freshen yourselves up and allow my steward to go through the protocol. Then you can disarm yourselves so that my guard of honour won't have to be pointing their weapons at you all the time, and there won't be any talk of the king being led a merry dance by one of the Ancients.' The ruler gave Uldini a piercing look. 'You understand the necessity of keeping up appearances to hold the rabble in check.'

Uldini nodded in agreement and stepped back from the king.

'Just one request before we retire. Don't mention us to Brother Wultom. My reputation can be quite intimidating, and I'd like him to be as relaxed as possible when he approaches us,' said the wizard in a neutral tone. Ahren admired the wizard's ingenuity, and not for the first time, swore silently never to underestimate him.

The king nodded, a look of understanding on his face, and made another gesture with his hands. Immediately the doors were flung open and the mass of people that had been waiting outside streamed in. Senius Blueground went through his wondrous transformation again and was now sitting upright and serious on his throne, every inch the king and commander.

Ahren's companions bowed again and the apprentice followed suit. Then they all stepped out of the throne room.

Ahren's thoughts were in turmoil. Not only was the Illuminated Path rapidly plunging the country into chaos, but it had the backing of the well-meaning king, who was completely in the dark concerning its true motives.

A large, portly man of thirty summers or so was waiting outside the throne room. He had a carefully cultivated moustache and his clothes were resplendent. This had to be the steward, for he began to shower the surrounding servants with a litany of commands, all of which were connected with the travel party's clothing, hairstyle, length of beard, accommodation and cleaning. He had an open, kindly way about him which made him difficult to refuse. Ahren was sure that much of the advice he was now giving them as they walked through the palace halls was rather more binding than the steward made it sound.

Ahren was dazzled by the speed at which he was being smothered by instructions regarding etiquette, use of language and palace regulations. In all his young life he was never so happy to see a door which promised safety and quiet, when they finally stopped in front of the guest rooms. Almost fleeing, Ahren rushed into the room only to stop suddenly, frozen in shock. There had to be some mistake, for Ahren was undoubtedly in the wrong room. Although, the word room was surely a misnomer.

Ahren was standing in a space, ten by ten paces, whose walls were made from dark wood and bright stone. Beautifully decorated pieces of furniture were tastefully positioned, and the high ceiling added to the sense of spaciousness. Bright sunlight shone through the crystal windows, and the bed was enormous beyond belief.

He took another uncertain step into the room - and then his master whooshed past him, and with a deliberately relaxed face turned towards the steward and said, 'this suits us perfectly, thank you.'

The steward stepped back with a bow, then closed the door behind him, leaving the master and apprentice alone together for the first time in ages. If you ignored the pomp surrounding them, it was almost as if they were back in the cabin in the forest, thought Ahren. He smiled at his master.

'It suits us perfectly? Are we going to be staying here?' he asked in disbelief.

'Us? No, of course not. This is my room. My servant sleeps over there,' said the old man matter-of-factly and pointed to his left.

Ahren saw a little door and went up to it curiously. He opened it and looked into a tiny cell. A chair, a table, a narrow bed with a thin mattress and a tiny window filled the musty room.

'I should have known,' he murmured and fell back into the straw mattress. From the next room he heard Falk laughing merrily.

132

Chapter 8

60 days to the winter solstice

Ahren spent most of the rest of the day surrounded by liveried servants who made him feel as if he had just come out of a dark cave after decades of neglect. They looked after every aspect of his appearance with an unsettling attention to detail.

He and his master both received a haircut and a shave, they were bathed thoroughly, their nails were cut and finally they were clothed. While Falk was given a dignified outfit in blue and silver, decorated with the Falkenstein crest, Ahren was given an earth-coloured linen garment which also had his master's crest, but the form and style was more reminiscent of a brand mark. Annoyed, he fidgeted with the rough material, and his annoyance increased when the old Forest Guardian laughed heartily at his discomfort.

When they were finally alone again, Ahren felt like a completely alienated version of his former self.

'Is all this really necessary?' he grumbled crossly.

'Are you seriously asking if you needed a bath?' answered his master mischievously, and smiled at him.

'Of course not. I mean, it's nice being clean again but this clothing is so…impractical, and how I'm ever going to be able to untie a leather knot, I'll never know,' complained Ahren.

'Is this the same boy who was overjoyed to get clean leather clothing?', asked Falk, this time with an edge to his voice.

Ahren wanted to respond but then thought better of it. His master was right. Without having noticed it himself, his sense of entitlement had grown, and now he felt ashamed. Then his linen garment chafed his skin, and he scowled again.

'The leather clothing was at least a decent fit. I'm going to be scraped raw in this,' he predicted gloomily.

Falk slapped him on the back. 'It won't be for very long. We're only staying here for a few days until we've got the king out of his difficulties, and then we set sail for the Silver Cliff. You'll just have to stick to the protocol until then,' said Falk sympathetically.

They waited until early afternoon, during which time Falk examined and repaired his equipment. Ahren had half-expected that Dorian Falkenstein, the noble knight, would have ordered the army of servants to perform this work, but then he realised his assumption had been unfair. His master had drummed into him never to depend on anyone else when it came to your own equipment, and he followed this rule with iron discipline. Ahren had quickly understood the wisdom of this approach. If you examined everything yourself and made sure it was in good order, then you would know every quality, every knot, and every weak point in the objects your life depends on when you are in the wilderness or out hunting. So he followed his master's example, and when Uldini arrived in the early evening sunshine, he found the two of them sitting cross-legged on the floor surrounded by sewing kits, leather patches, weapon oil, and all the necessities essential for keeping their gear in tip-top shape.

'You can take the Forest Guardian out of the wild, but you can't take the wild out of the Forest Guardian,' said the wizard smirking. 'Come with me before you stain that expensive carpet with weapon oil, and the steward has a heart attack.'

Ahren and his master grinned at each other, then stood up and left the room with Uldini. The quiet feeling of togetherness with his master which he had experienced as they had worked in concentration at their familiar tasks had done Ahren good, and he found it sad that the wizard had put an end to it.

Uldini was the same as ever, just his black robe was clearly new and made of high-quality material. The arms and seams were sewn with a gossamer golden thread that subtly sparkled here and there whenever the wizard moved. Otherwise, the appearance of the Arch Wizard was as timeless as ever.

They knocked on Jelninolan's door, and as soon as the elf opened it, Ahren was speechless. She was wearing a green robe cut in the Elvin style, and it seemed to be of the same material as that used to make the Eathinian houses and paths. Her red hair was plaited up into an artistic beehive shape and only two strands fell left and right of her face, framing and highlighting her pronounced Elvin cheekbones.

Falk and Uldini paused for a moment. After a heartbeat, the Guardian gave an elegant bow while Uldini raised his eyebrows in admiration.

'I'd forgotten how beautiful you're capable of looking when you put your mind to it, Auntie,' he said mischievously.

She grinned at their reactions, but then she furrowed her brows.

'The Knight Marshes are certainly civilized but not particularly progressive. I'd rather be coming in my ribbon armour but when the ladies-in-waiting continued to giggle after my third time mentioning it, I gave up. If a woman is not a soldier in this kingdom, it seems she will only find a sympathetic ear as long as she's wearing a dress,' she said irritably.

'I'd prefer to be able to go around in my own clothes, but that doesn't seem to be an option here,' grumbled Ahren crossly, and pulled at the scratchy collar of his linen jacket.

Falk ignored his apprentice's interjection and gave Jelninolan his arm.

'At least you seem to have prepared yourself very well for this situation. Or did the royal court really have an elf dress lying around the place that they could lend you?' he asked cheekily.

'I thought something like this might happen and planned ahead. Unfortunately, I didn't know before we started this journey that I'd be going back into my old form again. I spent half the afternoon charming this dress until it fitted me properly,' she said, linking arms with the old Forest Guardian.

Uldini floated on ahead and Ahren trotted unnoticed behind them. He missed Culhen and promised himself he'd pay the wolf a visit at the earliest opportunity.

They headed for the throne room, and in the meantime, Uldini brought them up to date on the latest news.

'Elgin isn't in his rooms. His ritual chamber is sealed up and I have a feeling he's been sitting around in there for weeks. However, without blowing up half the palace, I can't get in there. It will take me a full day to release the protective spell so that I can see how he is. So, we're going to have to deal with Brother Wultom on our own this evening,' said the Arch Wizard quietly.

'Is he in the palace already?' asked Falk.

The magus nodded and a devilish grin lit up his face.

'He's reporting back to the king at the moment. It's going to be such fun later,' said the wizard, with a disturbingly euphoric tone in his voice.

'Don't overdo it, Uldini. We don't want a battle and a smashed-up throne room. It's true that the king knows you, but for many, you're a stranger in the court. First there will be speaking, and everything will be explained, and then you can have his guts for garters. If you attack him without explaining yourself first, then all people are going to see is an enraged wizard attacking a man of the cloth. There are too many swords and crossbows in there to be the target of a misunderstanding,' he said calmly to the little figure.

'Spoilsport!' said the wizard with a twinkle in his eye.

'Sometimes I really wonder how you've survived for hundreds of years,' interjected Jelninolan, rolling her eyes in mock dismay.

'Well, it was obviously my devastating charm and noble demeanour,' replied Uldini cheekily.

Ahren was sure the verbal sparring would have continued, but for the fact that they had reached the throne room and everyone became serious.

The first thing Ahren noticed when they entered was that there were far fewer people present than in the morning. All the petitioners had left, and half of the courtiers. There were no more than two dozen people in the room, including the king and his guards. A few heavily decorated members of the nobility and advisors were gathered together in twos and threes, and a gaunt man in a white robe was standing before the king and speaking to him in a deep, soothing voice.

'...and unfortunately, our efforts have borne no fruit as yet, your majesty. We simply need more time to close the deep chasm that is dividing your people at this time. And it pains me to say that there seems to be some truth to the accusations that have been levelled against the Elf folk. There is some evidence that Evergreen is not quite the true friend you have been led to believe it is.'

'I'd like to hear this evidence,' said a strong voice.

Amazingly, it hadn't been Uldini who had spoken, but Jelninolan. She stood there, bolt upright, and stared demandingly at the haggard man with her hard, green eyes.

The priest spun around and looked in shock at Jelninolan and Uldini while the king stood up, took a step forward and opened out his arms.

'Welcome, indeed! Brother Wultom, let me introduce my guests to you. This is Uldini Getobo, the first among the Ancients and favourite of the gods. This elf of breath-taking beauty is none other than Jelninolan, priestess of the elves and also an Ancient. And I don't think you need any introduction to Dorian Falkenstein.'

Ahren felt completely invisible as the king ignored him and so he positioned himself at one of the pillars, where he remained motionless and watched what was unfolding.

The king's words and the sight of the three companions had a devastating effect on the cultist's mood. His eyes flashed quickly from left to right as he tried to digest the situation and work out a strategy.

'I'm listening, Brother Wultom. What harm exactly have the elves of Evergreen done to the brave citizens of the Knight Marshes,' Jelninolan persisted, and Ahren saw Uldini smirk as the haggard man shifted uncomfortably at the elf's words.

'Harm is such a harsh word, m'lady,' he answered quickly. 'I'd prefer to say that there has been a whole succession of misunderstandings which could have been prevented if your folk had been more diplomatic.'

Jelninolan gave him a merciless look, but the cultist turned to the king and stepped towards him while making an imploring gesture with his hand.

'Your majesty of course can see the wisdom in the counsel that suggests we should carry on with our efforts. We have served you loyally up until now, and with the help of these distinguished visitors here we are sure to find the necessary answers which will again bring peace to your kingdom at last,' he said, indicating to Ahren's companions with a wave of his hand.

While he was speaking, Ahren saw a slight movement of the brother's hanging arm. The others' attention seemed to be focussed entirely on the gaunt man's words and not on his gesticulating hand. The young apprentice was also certain he was the only person standing at just the correct spot, for visible to him alone was a little black thorn sticking out of Wultom's palm. The palm that was hanging unnoticed and seemingly innocently, within striking distance of the king's throat.

Ahren reacted instinctively. His hand immediately gripped the small dagger he always had on him and which was hidden under a fold of his jerkin. Without pausing, he drew the weapon and flung it with a sudden movement at the man in the white robe.

Then everything happened at once. There were screams as people pointed at Ahren. The priest raised his barbed hand in an effort to slice at the distracted king, the guards aimed their weapons at Ahren, who raised his hands and stood stock-still at the pillar while his knife bored with a crunch into the cultist's leg. He buckled with a scream of agony, and this involuntary movement caused his hand to fly in a harmless arc right in front of the stunned monarch. The moist, jet-black thorn glistened in the sunlight streaming through the windows. Uldini made a gesture with his hands and the priest was thrown against the wall while Falk positioned himself imposingly and protectively in front of Ahren and roared to all in the room, 'don't shoot!'

Ahren's hands were shaking uncontrollably as he realised the mortal danger he was in. To his left and right were two heavily armed guards, whose swords were drawn and aimed at him, ready to thrust at any moment. He quickly glanced around the room and saw at least six crossbows aimed at his head. Half of the guards present seemed to believe he had mistakenly hit the priest, and that his intended target had been the king.

The apprentice was glad that his back was against the pillar. He was weak at the knees and at least he could get support by leaning against the cool stone. If he collapsed to the ground now, one of the fraught guards would surely shoot him. He closed his eyes and concentrated on the Void. There had been no time for it earlier, but now he really needed the peace and calmness that the trance-like state promised. But it was impossible, he was too distracted, and his body was so tensed-up that he gave up after a few heartbeats. Well, at least he was still alive.

He opened his eyes and saw that Falk was continuing to fix his eyes on the guards while he moved around in a circle so he could look at each of them individually, all the while placating them with hand gestures.

Ahren was relieved to see that the tips of the swords were now pointing downwards and that the crossbows were no longer aimed directly at him, but the strained concentration could still be seen in the king's bodyguards. The two sword-carriers positioned themselves close to him and each grasped one of his arms in an iron grip and pushed him hard against the pillar.

Ahren looked at them in relief and he gave a smile which they returned with impassive looks. Nonetheless, they loosened their grip somewhat, so blood flowed into Ahren's hands again.

Once Falk was certain his apprentice's life was not in imminent danger anymore, he turned towards the king and the wounded cultist.

Now that Ahren was breathing easily again and could see around him, he realised that the throne room was in a mixture of turmoil and shock. Half of the courtiers were attempting to flee the hall in a panic but were being stopped by armed guards who were running in. The other half were either cowering on the floor or had retreated to the walls.

A circle of shields and swords had formed around the king as the rest of the king's guards had moved in to protect him. Uldini and Jelninolan were standing near the priest and were using their magic to press him against the wall. The elf had clasped her hands in a complicated pattern and the air around the two Ancients was flickering. Two crossbow arrows were lying on the polished throne room floor and Ahren was horrified when he realised that they had been aimed at the elf. Thanks to her protective magic they had bounced off the sparkling wall of magic and the priestess had been uninjured. The prejudices whipped up by the Illuminated Path must have infected some of the Palace Guards, who in the confusion of the moment had seen the elf as a danger.

'How does it look, Uldini?' called Falk, still keeping his eyes fixed on the guards.

'Our Brother Wultom is a surprisingly strong magician. I can keep a tight rein on him here, but no more than that. You'd better concentrate on explaining the situation here,' said Uldini in a strained voice. The little figure's arm was still raised in a crooked shape that was pointing at the wounded cultist, who was being pressed against the wall by Uldini's powers but was thrashing around in an attempt to escape the wizard's control.

Falk tried to catch the king's eye, which was next to impossible on account of the wall of guards. He crossed his arms and spoke in a powerful, commanding voice. 'I am Baron Dorian Falkenstein. You know what that means. Allow me to pass.'

Much to Ahren's amazement, the wall of blades and steel parted, revealing Senius Blueground, who looked at Falk with joy on his face.

'You have taken on your title again, Baron? This is indeed a joyful day for the whole kingdom!' And he stepped forward towards Falk and grasped both forearms in a ceremonial greeting. Whatever fear for his life the monarch may have been feeling, this news seemed to cheer him so much that everything else was apparently forgotten. Ahren was confused and at the same time curious.

'Welcome back to the court, Baron Falkenstein!' said King Blueground cheerfully.

Then he turned, looked at the chaos around him, frowned, and his good spirits vanished.

'I think an explanation would be appropriate,' he said shortly and looked at Falk with a questioning look.

The old man scratched his beard, uncertain of what to say, before looking over at Ahren.

'I think perhaps we should ask my apprentice. I didn't see everything, but he can probably relate exactly what happened.'

Suddenly Ahren was once again the centre of attention in the throne room. King Senius came over to him with a mixture of curiosity and no small element of annoyance written on his face.

'Now, young man. Why did you draw a weapon in front of the king, something which is totally forbidden, and why did you attack and injure a man of the cloth, and why have you caused such uproar in my throne room? Speak quickly or it will be my head jailer putting the questions to you.'

The guards had tightened their grip on the young man again when the king had approached him. Ahren's hands were going numb again and the words 'head jailer' had him worried. He looked helplessly at the monarch, his knees gave way, and he only managed to stay upright with the help of the guards. Falk looked at him firmly, and his master's warning stare helped Ahren clear his mind sufficiently to be able to answer.

'I suddenly saw a small, sharp thorn jutting out of Wultom's right hand. He was about to stab Your Majesty, and from my position at the pillar, I was the only person who could see this. I am sorry for throwing the knife but I had no time to warn anyone of what was about to happen,' the young man summarised as quickly as he could.

The king studied Ahren's face and for a few heartbeats Ahren was terrified that the ruler didn't believe a word of what he'd said. Then the king became thoughtful.

'I did spot something black earlier, but my attention was distracted by our knife-thrower here,' he said and frowned. 'I find it difficult to believe that a friend of the crown, who has served me loyally over the past few months and who is furthermore a holy person, would try to harm me,' he said sceptically.

'But he belongs to the Illuminated Path, they are followers of HIM, WHO FORCES. They stir up the people against the elves and bring pilgrims to the Pall Pillar where HE transforms them into Low Fangs.' The words tumbled out of Ahren's mouth.

A wave of murmuring spread through the assembled crowd as Ahren's accusations rang out in the hall, and soon the place was in tumult again. The king looked over at Falk with a serious look. It was clear he did not believe Ahren.

'The boy is speaking the truth. This is why we wished to speak to Your Majesty and to Brother Wultom. This man is neither your friend nor a friend of the kingdom, nor a friend of the people. I think he is a High Fang, if my apprentice's observations were accurate,' said Falk, speaking in measured tones.

King Senius stumbled backwards as if he had been hit.

'A High Fang? Here…are you certain…?' he stuttered before pulling himself together and ordering in a commanding voice: 'bring Brother Wultom here!'

The guards who had circled the king now gathered around Wultom and Uldini. Jelninolan stepped to the side, still keeping her shield upright as the crossbow men and women eyed her.

The king made a threatening hand gesture.

'Put down your crossbows! If anyone aims it at Lady Jelninolan, they will no longer see the light of day!'

All of the king's fury and uncertainty seemed to be expressed in this command and the guards reacted immediately. Jelninolan looked at him in gratitude and then dissolved her magic shield.

'And let go of the young man! He can hardly stand up as it is. In the worst case scenario, he made a mistake and did the wrong thing for the right reason, and he can work off his punishment in the quarry,' he added lightly.

The quarry? Ahren swallowed hard, broke into a sweat again and looked pleadingly over at his master, while the guards loosened their grip on his arms and he clung clumsily onto the pillar behind him so he wouldn't slip down to the floor.

Falk turned again to the ruler.

'I'm sure everything will be clarified,' he said in a placatory tone.

In the meantime, the priest had been dragged into the middle of the throne room. There, where the apprentice's knife was still lodged in his leg, an accusatory red stain was spreading outward on the priest's white robe.

'Nothing but lies and false accusations', he whined, as soon as the king turned his attention to him. 'These people want to lead you away from the Illuminated Path and drive a wedge between you and your most loyal follower,' and he raised his pleading hands in so far as it was possible considering the guards' firm hold of him.

'I never had a dagger or thorn or anything in my hand. This is a conspiracy, aimed at discrediting me.'

'I've had enough of this masquerade,' growled Uldini and uttered a charm which covered the cultist in a violet hue, only to vanish again within a heartbeat.

The gaunt man stiffened up immediately and a moist, shining, black tooth shot out of the middle of his right palm, where it had been hidden under a fold of skin.

The king gave a start and the guards grasped the holy man in a tighter grip and forced him down onto his knees. The courtiers screamed in fear and made a dash for the doors in an attempt to escape the throne room, and this time the guards let them pass.

While the king was gathering himself together again, Falk turned furiously to Uldini.

'Why hadn't you noticed beforehand? Thanks to you I could have lost a halfway decent apprentice,' he said grumpily.

Ahren was pleased to receive this hidden compliment from his master while Uldini rubbed his bald head in bewilderment.

'He is undoubtedly a magus, and incredibly strong. A High Fang successfully camouflaging itself in front of me should actually be impossible.' Searching for help, he looked over at Jelninolan.

The elf closed her eyes and for an instant the room was filled with a silver glow. 'His camouflage is perfect and now I know why. He is receiving his strength from another magus. And you can guess who it is,' she said and opened her eyes.

'Elgin,' said Uldini darkly.

'Exactly right. Elgin hasn't woken up from his charm ritual for weeks because this monster has been drawing his power and using it for his own purposes,' said Jelninolan furiously.

The king had recovered from his shock and began to speak.

'So, he is responsible for our Court Wizard not being available for so long?' he asked with outrage in his voice.

'And for the fact that your kingdom is on the brink of war. The Illuminated Path preaches hatred against the elves and sows discord between the common folk and the barons. We also suspect that they are behind the arson attacks on the granaries throughout the kingdom. Starving people are easier to influence. The letters that you gave to the missionaries have in all probability never reached the barons.'

Senius Blueground stared wide-eyed at Falk. Then he looked at the black tooth that was still jutting out of the white robed cultist's hand. Without saying a word, he drew his ceremonial sword and rammed it into the chest of the High Fang. The creature's expression was one of surprise, before it went limp a moment later.

Ahren had never been present at an execution before and the cold-heartedness of the monarch overwhelmed him. He felt nauseous and turned away. Falk too had made short shrift of the High Fang who had ambushed them that time, but at least the apprentice hadn't had to look on. Ahren knew that the servants of the Adversary were beyond redemption, but they were so human in appearance. He forced himself to look at the black barb, and almost threw up.

Uldini looked down at the lifeless figure with satisfaction.

'And about time,' he said contentedly.

The sudden, violent death of the High Fang didn't seem to bother Falk or Jelninolan either, and Ahren asked himself if he too might end up

146

being so callous sometime in the future. He found the idea disturbing and pushed it to the back of his mind.

Senius wiped his sword clean on the deceased's robe and then put it back in its scabbard.

'Is our esteemed Court Wizard going to wake up now?' he asked impatiently in a raw voice.

Uldini, a picture of worry, shook his head and indicated to Jelninolan. 'The two of us will unseal his Ritual Chamber, and then we'll have to awaken him slowly from his trance. If his strength has been continuously sucked out of him for months, then he is quite probably at death's door.'

'Then hurry,' ordered the king. 'Baron Falkenstein can give me all the answers I require.'

The two Ancients hurried out of the throne room, and Jelninolan gave Ahren an encouraging wink as she left.

'And now it's your turn,' said King Senius and turned to face Ahren, at the same time drawing his sword. Ahren looked around in panic. His majesty must have come to the conclusion that throwing the knife had been an unforgivable act.

But before the apprentice could do anything silly, his master's large hand had landed unceremoniously on his shoulder, and he was gently pushed down onto his knees.

'Keep your hair on, Ahren. Nothing's going to happen to you,' he said quietly.

With flowing movements borne from years of practice, the king landed the flat of his sword, first down on Ahren's left shoulder, then down on his right.

'I hereby anoint Ahren, Squire of the Falkenstein Barony. May he continue to serve his master with such distinction as he has served me this day.'

Ahren, completely taken aback, looked up at the good-natured smiling face of the ruler until Falk pulled him gently back up onto his feet.

'Many thanks, your majesty,' he stuttered in a daze.

The king gave him a brief nod, then turned to concentrate fully on Falk again.

'Tell me everything, Baron. I want every piece of information you have, concerning this matter, no matter how insignificant,' he commanded.

'Certainly, your majesty,' said Falk obediently, and bowed slightly. 'But first, have my squire brought back to my rooms so that he may rest. I think what he's experienced has overcome him,' said the old man, ordering the guards. Then he turned back to the king to continue their conversation.

'The boy has put on a good show,' said Senius, and the young apprentice almost burst with pride as he walked out the door of the throne room.

'You're right. Normally he just passes out or throws up,' said Falk, and both men laughed.

The palace corridors seemed endless now to the exhausted apprentice. He had the feeling he'd been walking an eternity to Falk's rooms, accompanied by a friendly guardsman who was making sure that the exhausted young man would find his way.

He went through all the events in his head again and wished, not for the first time, that his body would become accustomed to the excitement of his new position in life. He pulled himself together as much as possible and decided to quiz the guardsman a little.

'What exactly does being a squire mean?' he asked uneasily. He couldn't make head nor tail of the title and really hoped his new position wouldn't make life more complicated.

The guardsman raised an eyebrow.

'Where do you come from that you don't know that?' he asked, baffled.

'Hjalgar. A small village called Deepstone', answered Ahren.

'Ah...', said the guardsman and there was a look of comprehension on his face, almost as though Ahren had just told him he had been raised by swine. 'A squire is the lowest title in the nobility you can achieve, and it's the prerequisite to becoming dubbed a knight. Now that you have become noble, you have the right to carry a weapon in court.'

At this point he paused and gave Ahren a meaningful look.

Ahren stared back at him, holding his ground, and almost a little defiantly. Had he not been carrying his knife, then the king would probably be dead by now. There was no way he was going to apologise.

When Ahren didn't respond, the guardsman continued.

'Also, you're only allowed to be tried in the palace if you have been accused of committing a crime, and you receive a monthly wage from the baron to whom you swear fealty,'

'You mean I still have to obey Falk?' asked Ahren, 'I mean, Baron Falkenstein', he added quickly, correcting himself.

The other man nodded and Ahren gave a sigh of relief. So really, nothing was going to change, except that he might get a better monthly stipend. Which wouldn't be difficult considering Falk hadn't given him a penny since they'd left Deepstone. However, if Ahren were to be honest with himself, he didn't really know when he could have bought anything, let alone what. All in all, his master and the others had provided for him.

'Is it no problem then that I come from Hjalgar? Because, actually I am not a subject of the king,' he said after some moments silence.

The guardsman shrugged his shoulders. 'You didn't object earlier, which means you are his subject now. The king will have the traditional gold coin sent over to Hjalgar. The laws of your country are…well…pragmatic.' Ahren again had the feeling that the guardsman considered the neighbouring country to be a better class of pigsty.

Now that Ahren knew how easily Hjalgar let its subjects go, he could understand the guardsman. Even his father had demanded Falk give him three gold coins for Ahren's apprenticeship years. It was ironic, thought Ahren, that his worth had apparently dropped so dramatically since then.

They reached Falk's rooms and Ahren stepped inside. The guardsman stood at the door respectfully and paused.

'May I ask you a question?' asked the man shyly.

Ahren nodded absently and turned towards him.

'What's it like to travel with a living legend?' There was a note of deep respect in his voice.

'Uldini? Well, mostly he's a cantankerous, fractious old so-and-so, who has an answer to everything, whether you want to hear it or not,' said Ahren, shrugging his shoulders.

'I actually meant the baron. The rest of the world might have forgotten his name, but here everyone still remembers the deeds of the Paladin Dorian Falkenstein. So, what is he like?' the guard asked curiously. Ahren stood there, struck dumb, and stared in shock at nothing in particular. In his mind's eye the apprentice tried to recall all the clues from the past and to digest this new information. His body was frozen but his mind was racing.

When it was clear that he wasn't going to receive an answer, the guard bowed once and closed the door, leaving a young man behind, whose world had once again been turned on its head.

Chapter 9

'How could he do that?!' shouted Ahren for the umpteenth time as he stormed back and forth.

Culhen answered with a dutiful bark while Selsena didn't seem able to stop swamping the young man with waves of cheerfulness.

'More than two years as his apprentice! I am the chosen THREE'S Thirteenth Paladin!' he almost screamed.

Culhen responded with a yelp, which echoed through the royal stable, where the apprentice had sought refuge. His own room had been too quiet and empty for his whirlwind of emotions and so he had fled to his wolf friend where he could give out to his heart's content about his dishonest, stubborn, and - to top it all - immortal Paladin master.

'Oh, by the way Ahren, I'm a Paladin too and I know exactly what you're going through,' he muttered deeply, imitating Falk's bass voice, then threw his hands in the air. 'It really isn't that difficult!'

The stable boys and girls had long fled the scene. Ahren had put on his ribbon armour and armed himself in his room because he felt the desperate need to just be Ahren the apprentice Forest Guardian. But his deed in the palace and his dubbing as squire must have done the rounds in no time at all, and as soon as he had begun giving vent to his feelings in the stable, all the servants had discretely withdrawn. He was sure they were still listening in on him, and that the rumour mill would exaggerate everything. But just at this moment, he didn't care a whit.

He was about to launch into another tirade, spurred on by Selsena's seemingly endless cheerfulness, which she underlined every now and then with a whinny, when Culhen sat down on his back paws, whimpered quietly and stretched out a foreleg to tap Ahren's shin.

The apprentice lowered himself and buried his face in the wolf's fur, stroking his loyal friend and breathing deeply. Then he sprang up and indicated to the wolf to follow him.

'Come on, Culhen, let's explore the city. I need to blow off steam and clear my head. The palace just feels like an up-market prison,' he said loudly. Anyway, it would be better for him to avoid his master until he had calmed down and knew exactly what he should say to him.

Selsena emitted a warning to Ahren, who turned back towards her.

'Tell the Lord Paladin that Culhen and I are taking a look at the city,' he said determinedly. 'We shall be back later in the evening and, yes, I'll be careful, I promise,' he added when Selsena radiated serious concerns.

The Elvin war horse seemed far from convinced. However, she had no choice but to let the apprentice go. And so off he went, with his boisterously romping wolf across the green palace lawns, hotfooting it to the golden gates of the palace, behind which lay the city, ready to be explored in all its glory.

Ahren hadn't felt so free in a long time. He wandered through the streets of the capital until dusk, rounding the palace, exploring the living quarters of the merchants and workers, not to mention the many marketplaces full of hidden nooks and crannies, where goods from all over the world were offered for sale. The sounds and smells surrounding him were many and varied and strange, and thankfully they distracted him from the afternoon's events.

Ahren had already spotted quite a few dwarves and elves, some Clansmen from the Green Sea, and ferocious-looking warriors from the Kelkor Mountains, wearing thick pelts, and with their hair held in thick plaits. Because he had promised Selsena that he would be careful, he made sure that he kept his distance when admiring the large and small sights. Three Rivers had seemed enormous to him that time, but the Hjalgar trading town was smaller than even the old town of King's Island, which he had walked through earlier. The wide trading road, which had led them up to the palace, divided in two before the royal residence and flowed like a river east and west around the palace complex. Ahren had followed the broad roads that had branched off the trading road, always keeping his bearings by the commanding palace signal tower. When the night finally drew in, Ahren had sat down on a low wall and watched the enormous flame, which was burning in the enormous cauldron and had been lit at the onset of darkness. The flames were reflected in the golden roof of the signal tower, which increased the power of the light. It was an awe-inspiring sight and Ahren could well imagine that the sailors at night were grateful for this beacon which promised them safe harbour.

Now, with night replacing day, some of the merchants had packed up their wares and left their stalls, but to Ahren's surprise most remained and continued to offer their wares by the light of the torches that were hanging on walls everywhere throughout the city, and were now being lit by the night-watchmen. The streets were just as busy now as they had been during the day and wherever Ahren went, the hostels and taverns seemed full to overflowing. Patrols and town watches were a common sight, and the young man was impressed by the fact that so many people seemed to be living together in peace. Large towns had always had a bad reputation among the people of Deepstone, and Ahren now asked himself if this had been just the villagers' prejudices.

He wandered another while through the streets of King's Island, absorbing the impressions of the city until he noticed that he was coming closer to the city harbour. He considered going on, but then thought better of it. It would take him a considerable time to get back to the palace, and it was better for him to head back or he'd have to bear the wrath of his master.

Thinking of Falk led him back to his dilemma. How was he to confront the old man? What was he going to ask him? Over the past two years he had felt an increasing attachment to the Forest Guardian, but his certainty concerning their relationship had been severely shaken by this latest revelation concerning his true identity. This breach of faith on his master's part hurt him deeply.

As he made his way back, he mulled over what he knew about the old man, who had taken him under his wing. Falk had been born in the Knight Marshes, that was certain. He had told Ahren that he was the son of a noble lady, the Baroness Falkenstein.

He stopped for a moment. Falk had never explained to him when he had been born. The baroness must have been a Paladin and Falk was her successor. The time he had spent with Uldini had been in the Dark Days. And when Falk had had enough of fighting, he had gone off and had a row with Selsena. He had then travelled throughout the world and ended up with the elves, who had made him into a Forest Guardian. It all made sense if you substituted centuries for the years and decades that Falk had talked about.

Ahren was turning these facts over in his mind when Culhen suddenly stopped. Ahren had taken the shortest route back to the palace and was just passing through the workers' area, which was squeezed between the harbour and some of the smaller marketplaces, where it seemed the poorer inhabitants of the city bought their goods. There were smaller side streets here and narrower laneways and Culhen had stopped before one of them and was growling at the shadows that were lurking within. An uneasy feeling crept over the apprentice and he walked carefully up to the wolf, adopting the silent, stalking steps he had practised endlessly during dozens of hunts.

The laneway lay in darkness and only shadows could be seen, but just twenty paces away Ahren could see three figures who had circled a fourth, and he could hear scornful voices.

'Come on, Culhen, this is none of our business. We'll find a town watch and tell him what the story is.' He had had enough excitement for one day and wasn't going to get mixed up in a row between a few drunken workers.

Just as he was turning, he heard a low shout of anger echo down the laneway. It was the voice of a young woman. Ahren stopped frozen and looked back with narrowed eyes, trying to make out as many details as possible.

The three silhouettes looked considerably larger than the fourth, which they were surrounding. He saw the smaller figure trying to duck out underneath the arms of one of them, only to be pushed back roughly. He heard raw laughter and Culhen growled and took a step into the laneway, at the same time looking back impatiently at Ahren.

Ahren stepped stealthily into the narrow street and gave Culhen a gesture to remain quiet. The wolf wagged his tail once in delight and began stalking forward, hunched low. The house walls on either side of the street were scarcely two paces apart and Ahren could smell rotting refuse, and saw that the ground was full of rubbish. Their silhouettes stood out in the light of the street they had just entered from, and Ahren was under no illusion that they could pounce without being spotted. A fleeting glance in their direction would give the game away, but the nearer they approached, the clearer the picture he would have of how they would deal with this situation.

They were now less than ten paces from their target and Ahren could clearly hear the fight that was unfolding before them.

'Now don't be like that, dearie,' he heard a deep voice say, husky through alcohol and the desires that Ahren knew spelled trouble. 'Everyone knows that a girl from the Eternal Empire only comes to King's Island with one thing in mind.'

'She just wants to drive up the prices,' said a second, nasally voice.

'Me, no scars. Me, no touchable!' the girl cried out in anger, and tried to escape once more. She almost managed to squeeze out between two of the men but then the man with the deep voice boxed her hard in the stomach and she tumbled backwards.

Ahren was stunned. And impressed by the fact that she hadn't screamed in pain.

'If it's scars that are stopping you, then of course we can help,' said the third voice in the gang, his voice almost as deep as his companion's. A knife blade flashed in his hand and the circle moved in closer.

Ahren was filled with blind fury and he drew out Windblade.

'Let go of her immediately!' he roared and stepped forward. A little voice in his head told him he'd thrown away the element of surprise, but now it was too late.

The three figures spun around, the third pressing the blade against the girl's throat.

'Who are you?' said the first, his voice slurred. 'Her boyfriend? Put that blade away before you hurt yourself.'

The girl saw the sword in Ahren's hand. Her eyes widened in surprise and she called out to him in a strange, melodic language that he didn't understand.

'Shut your gob!' roared the man with the knife and strengthened his grip on her neck.

'How about you pay us, and we let the girl go?' grunted the second man maliciously.

Ahren was suddenly reminded of Sven, the miller's son in Deepstone. He understood that situations like this came to pass when people like Sven met up together and were left to roam unopposed.

Well, he would just have to oppose them.

He raised his blade and pointed to the man with the knife.

'Let her go and be on your way or I will have to harm you.' That sounded pretty impressive to Ahren, and those kinds of warnings always worked in the legends of brave heroes. But the three just laughed at him and looked decidedly unimpressed.

Ahren shifted from one foot to another, unsure of what to do next. He couldn't attack without the girl getting injured. And so he decided to do something completely unheroic.

'Help! Town Watches!' he roared with all his might.

'Gag him!' hissed the third. 'I don't want to end up in the dungeons again.'

The first two drew their jagged short swords from their jerkins and Ahren realised that he had a problem. The short weapons were more suited to these narrow confines than Windblade. For sideways strokes he would have to push himself against one of the walls and then wouldn't be able to protect himself from a counter strike. That only left blows and thrusts from above. Furthermore, the two had separated and were now approaching him from right and left, protecting their bodies with their

158

weapons and using the wall as cover. They obviously had experience in this type of combat. There was nothing to be done, he just had to finish one of them off before both of them reached him.

'Attack, Culhen!' he shouted as he quickly tried to strike his opponent on the left. His blade was parried effortlessly aside, but the attacker on the right was caught unawares by the wolf, who had been lurking quietly in the shadows.

The animal's powerful jaws bit into the forearm which was holding the weapon and Ahren shuddered inwardly when he heard the crunching, grinding sound that the bone made as Culhen began to shake his head, tossing the screaming man here and there.

The girl took advantage of the confusion and banged the back of her head into the face of the man who had the knife at her neck. At the same time, she wrapped her fingers in a most unusual way around the wrist of the knife-bearing hand. Then she twisted her hand and Ahren heard the wrist splintering loudly and clearly.

The knife-carrier let out a scream of pain and tumbled backwards, but the girl followed him and pressed her fingertips into his throat and in the bat of an eyelid, he was making rattling noises on the ground. Then she kicked him in the nether regions and the rattling noise was now intermixed with choking sounds as her attacker vomited through his agonised throat.

The whole manoeuvre had lasted no more than three heartbeats and Ahren could only look on, open-mouthed. His opponent took advantage of Ahren's inattention, lunged forward and thrust his knife in. The blade scraped over the leather panel of his armour and slipped in between Ahren's ribs.

An icy coldness radiated from the spot, and through his whole body. Instinctively, Ahren raised Windblade in a flat upward sweep and it hit his tormenter in the face before Ahren fell backwards, his legs having lost all their strength.

Culhen howled in rage and fell upon the attacker while the apprentice could only stare up at the sky, a narrow strip between the tall houses. A few stars seemed to be twinkling in the night - they seemed to be winking at him and somehow everything seemed peaceful. He coughed and suddenly his mouth was filled with blood, while the feeling in his chest changed from cold to hot. Now every breath burned like fire and suddenly the pain was unbearable. Ahren couldn't breathe and thinking clearly was impossible.

The sounds of fighting had ceased and now the girl's face came into focus. Ahren saw smooth black hair which brushed against his face and tickled his nose. He saw two dark, almost black eyes which were strangely slanted. A small nose puckered disapprovingly as she said 'Susekan.' Her tone of voice reminded him of his master and, whatever the word meant, it was certainly not complimentary.

'Help,' Ahren managed to say, accompanied by another gush of blood. 'Palace,' he rattled weakly.

Then his world went black and Ahren hoped fervently that the last thing he would ever see wasn't a contemptuous look from a strange girl that he had just barely saved.

He felt a cool face cloth on his forehead. The birds were twittering. Uldini and Falk were quarrelling loudly. If this was what the paradise of the gods was like, Ahren would have to have some serious words with the next available priest.

Glad to be still alive, he opened his eyes and looked woozily around. He was in his master's chambers and lying in his enormous bed. He felt as though he were floating, so soft was the mattress under him.

160

Ahren carefully tested his lungs by breathing in slowly, but the pain was gone. He gingerly raised his arms and that too was possible without hurting. He felt after his wound, and found only smooth skin. Jelninolan or Uldini must have worked their charms on him.

'Oh look, he's awake,' said Uldini in an irritated voice. 'I'd love to stay here and listen to you congratulate your apprentice for his deed, but I've heard more than enough of your bluster for one day. I'll go and look after our other patient and you can take care of this hero.' The way he emphasised his last word suggested that it hadn't been meant as a compliment. The little figure waved at Ahren, said 'good luck, Ahren,' cheerfully, then went out the door, leaving the young man alone in the room with a furious Forest Guardian.

Falk stepped towards the bed.

'What have I told you about your choice of battleground?' he grunted.

'Determine the battlefield or the battlefield will determine you,' said Ahren nervously.

Falk nodded and came a step closer.

'You decided on a narrow alleyway, and you had a long sword in your hand. And what is the lesson concerning the beginning of a fight?'

'Only fight when you can do nothing else or when you are sure that you will win,' came the timid answer from the bed. Ahren resisted the temptation to hide his head under the covers. The image in his head of a four-poster bed containing a cowardly apprentice being flung out through the palace window forced him to keep his eyes on the old man as long as he could manage to do so.

'And you had to go and take on three cut-throats, and utter pithy slogans while wiggling your sword instead of decommissioning one or two of them with a couple of arrows before they even knew you existed,' said Falk, continuing his analysis.

'What have I told you about the goal of battle?' he asked and took another step closer.

Ahren swallowed hard. His master had almost reached the bed and the fact that the old man was composing himself with difficulty brought the apprentice almost into a panic.

'Always be aware of your goals. Why you are fighting and how can you end the battle as soon as you have reached your goal,' he said, repeated his master's explanations.

'You wanted to save the girl, which is why you made sure that she had a knife at her throat and all were able to draw their weapons at leisure.'

Falk took the last step towards the bed, then gave Ahren a fatherly look.

'And what lesson did I teach you regarding life itself?' he asked as if butter wouldn't melt in his mouth.

Ahren cast his eyes around the room, furiously trying to remember what piece of advice his master was referring to. The old man's eyes narrowed and Ahren decided on one that he thought might pass the test.

'Always act with courage or don't act at all?' he suggested timidly.

A fraction of a heartbeat and Falk's head was right in front of Ahren's nose, the veins in his head were about to burst and his face went a deep red before he roared with all his might, 'DON'T...BE...AN IDIOT!!'

His hands gesticulated wildly, and his fingers were claw-like as he roared.

'Everything I've taught you has that as its foundation. And you're running around the place like a character created by a third-rate bard, brandishing fine speeches, allowing yourself to be stabbed to death because you want to save a girl without the planning that you damn well need to do!'

162

Falk snatched the tobacco container from the table beside the bed and smashed it with such force against the wall that it shattered into tiny pieces.

'You put yourself and the little one into danger because you didn't think things through' he shouted. 'How in the name of all the gods did you manage to take every wrong decision you possibly could within the space of ten heartbeats? Why not just give them your sword the next time and ask if you can't just dance your way out of it?'

Falk drew breath and Ahren took the opportunity to try and defend himself.

'I wanted to frighten them so that I wouldn't have to hurt them. And I was distracted. I'd just found out that you're a Paladin', he blurted out.

Ahren was furious now and he jutted out his chin. Perhaps he had acted irresponsibly, but his master wasn't perfect either and the apprentice really felt like cursing and shouting himself now.

Falk stared at him for three heartbeats and Ahren tried to gather his thoughts together so he could confront the Paladin, but then his master started shouting again.

'SO?! You're supposed to become a Paladin too, damnation! The whole point is not to be killed! I've spent centuries trying not to, just like the others too. And because we were waiting for you! I saw my daughter die during the Night of Blood. I saw my wife grow old and die because we swore that we would wait until the Thirteenth appeared! AND YOU SERIOUSLY TRY AND GET YOURSELF GORED IN A FILTHY ALLEYWAY?!'

Falk lifted up the table and smashed it against the wall too, so that the wood splintered into a thousand pieces.

'I swear by the THREE, I will not see you die. You'll wish you were dead when I send you blindfolded and with a fully packed field kit on your back up and down every single tree in the palace park, but I will not see you die!'

The old man slumped down at these last words and fell on his knees, weeping bitterly.

'I'm not going to see you die too,' he whispered, sobbing.

Ashamed and bewildered, Ahren clambered out of the bed and embraced his master. All thoughts of a scornful confrontation had melted away at the sight of the age-old sorrow that held his master in its grip.

'I'm so sorry,' he whispered again and again, rocking the old man, who was crying over his centuries old troubles and grieving once again over his family that had died in a different age.

They were undisturbed for the rest of the day. Falk told Ahren of his earlier life, of the time he had spent with his wife, of their wonderful daughter who should have been next in line. He described the dreadful events of the Night of Blood and of how the traumatised Paladins had imprisoned HIM, WHO FORCES and how they, disillusioned, had disappeared in every direction under the sun.

Ahren believed that only very few people had ever heard this story from the mouth of the old Forest Guardian and he listened quietly, without asking a single question.

When Falk had finished, he gently placed a hand on Ahren's cheek and said, 'You must not die, do you hear me? All those centuries and all those victims cannot have been in vain.'

Ahren could only nod, his eyes full of tears.

Falk nodded in return.

'Good. Come!' he simply said.

The young man followed the Paladin and wondered what revelation was awaiting him now. They went out into the park. And Ahren spent the rest of the day blindfolded and with a fully packed field kit on his back, climbing up and down one tree after another.

With a smile on his face.

Chapter 10

58 days to the winter solstice

That evening, they were sitting at the supper table, Ahren was brought up to speed on what had happened. Khara, for so the girl in the alleyway was called, had apparently dragged him all the way to the palace, while he was bleeding like a stuck pig. He would never have survived were it not for the combined healing arts of Uldini and Jelninolan. And even so, it had taken two days of a healing sleep before he had fully recovered.

The room in which they were sitting was in Jelninolan's living quarters. The fittings were all in bright wood or white marble, and everything was decorated with nature motifs and carvings. They were at a long table. The windows were thrown open and a gentle autumn breeze wafted the last remaining warmth of the year into the room.

Ahren could only lift his fork to his mouth painfully slowly because every bone and muscle in his body still ached, and so he concentrated fully on eating, and let the others talk. Khara was sitting slightly apart and was similarly quiet and unobtrusive, apparently concentrating completely on her food. Ahren tried to give her a quick smile, but the girl seemed to be ignoring him and the others.

'How is Elgin?' Falk had just asked.

Uldini gave a sour look before biting hard into a drumstick.

'It will take a while before he's his Ancient self again.' Then the wizard laughed at his own word play, and everyone else in the group groaned.

'The Illuminated Path had sucked most of the strength out of him, and the enforced trance of many months has done terrible damage to his body,' continued Jelninolan. We were able to heal his heart and vital organs, and his muscles are on the road to recovery. But for the next year, he'll have to do a lot of exercises to aid his recuperation, both physical and spiritual.'

'Have you any idea how he was trapped?' inquired Falk curiously.

'Somebody had sold him an antique book which supposedly describes a powerful ritual whereby you can increase your powers,' explained Uldini. 'The blunderhead had never met the seller before but he still jumped on it. The snares in the magic were very well hidden and he was so enthusiastic, he didn't even notice until it was too late. Once he was trapped in the trance, his aura was as open as a barn door and Wultom could help himself to Elgin's powers. The more power he stole from Elgin, the deeper Elgin fell into the trance. Without us, he wouldn't have had a hope in hell of ever waking up again. When we jump helter-skelter into something without thinking, then things like that are bound to happen,' he continued with emphasis.

Ahren knew that he was the target of that last remark, but he decided to ignore the barb, and with his head lowered he concentrated on his meal.

'By the way, there is a celebratory banquet in your honour in three days,' said Uldini to Falk casually. 'Apparently all of the Knight Marshes citizens are delighted that their national hero has returned to them.'

He looked up at the ceiling in mock concentration.

'Perhaps I too should have disappeared for a couple of centuries so that the people would be overjoyed when I finally decided to be interested in the fate of the world again.'

Suddenly there was a tension in the air, and Falk and Uldini stared daggers at each other.

Ahren knew that the two of them had argued repeatedly over Falk's decision to turn his back on the world. He cleared his throat and decided to risk becoming the target of their contrariness.

'I've been thinking about that, you know. If Falk hadn't lived in Deepstone, then I would never have become an apprentice, but would have ended up as a farm hand. Then my father would never have let me go to the Spring Ceremony because he hates the church. Then I would never have been chosen. And that would have been bad, wouldn't it?'

Uldini looked at him thoughtfully before answering.

'Sometimes you really do surprise me. First you save a king's life - by the way that's why you're the second guest-of-honour at the feast – then you make an absolute idiot out of yourself when you meet a couple of scoundrels on the street, and finally you come up with an insight that really hits the mark. You're like one of Trefan's lucky bags. One never knows if utter nonsense or a flash of genius is going to come out of your mouth.'

Ahren suppressed the sarcastic answer that was on the tip of his tongue and chewed on his potato.

'But he's right all the same. The Gods' Stone only revealed to us where he was. Even without the ceremony, the blessing of the gods would have awakened in him, undiscovered and unchanneled. HE, WHO FORCES would have appropriated his power and that would have been the end,' said Jelninolan.

She beamed at Falk.

'So, your rebellious phase did have its advantages,' she said in a motherly voice.

168

Ahren nearly choked on his potato with laughter, and got a warning look from Falk which suggested yet more climbing lay in store.

'The good news is that we've solved the problem of finding a ship to take us to the Silver Cliff,' said Uldini cheerfully. 'The king has put a swift frigate at our disposal for the journey. We can set sail the morning after the feast. And with this ship we'll get to the dwarves faster than we'd expected. And so we can make up time for some of the delays we've experienced here.'

Ahren stared over at Khara with curiosity. The girl was sitting quietly at one corner of the table, hardly moving at all. From time to time she would put a grape in her mouth, but she spent most of the time looking down at her plate. He studied her carefully. Her skin had a bronze undertone that he had never seen before, nor had he seen such almond-shaped eyes, which were so dark they were almost black. Her shoulder-length jet-black hair seemed to almost swallow the light as it fell straight like a curtain. She was smaller than he was, probably by as much as a head, but seemed to be the same age. She was a little thin, and Ahren couldn't help thinking she must have had a difficult life.

She sensed his eyes and looked at him with hostility. Then she said something in that strange language she had already used in the alleyway.

Ahren looked at her uncomprehendingly and turned to Jelninolan.

'What language is she speaking?' he asked.

'It's the language of the Eternal Empire. Quite complex but not dissimilar to Elfish. I can speak it very well, as can Uldini and Falk,' the priestess answered.

Both men gave a dismissive wave as they continued to eat.

'My trips to the Eternal Empire were over two hundred years ago and the same goes for Uldini, so we're a little rusty in the language. The

Eternal Empress banished all Ancients and all Paladins from her empire. You know, she was always a difficult customer.'

Ahren started.

'Wait a minute, you know the Eternal Empress?'

'She's one of us. A Paladin, I mean,' said Falk.

'At the same time, she is also an Ancient. This combination is peculiar and makes dealing with her difficult,' Uldini threw in.

Ahren nodded absently and his gaze went back to Khara.

Her cheekbones were unusually pronounced, her nose on the other hand was small, and it all gave her an exotic look, which Ahren had to get used to. She looked up again and said something in a sharp tone.

'What is she saying?' asked Ahren, frowning.

'She's asking if it isn't rude to stare at people in your country,' translated Jelninolan, without batting an eyelid.

Annoyed, Ahren lowered his eyes and concentrated on his food again.

'Why is that girl still here? Not that I'm not grateful she rescued our little hero here, but still, a street urchin has no place in the palace,' said Uldini in his inimically sensitive style.

Jelninolan slapped her palm on the table, and everyone looked up in shock.

'She's staying with us,' she said firmly. 'Khara came to King's Island as a stowaway, which means that if she gets work at all here, it can only be as a Touchable. And I'm certainly not going to let that happen. We'll take her with us to the Silver Cliff and then take things from there.'

'She used that expression in the alleyway already. What are Touchables?', asked Ahren.

'Touchables are ladies in the Eternal Empire who provide certain services. You recognise them by the scar on their right cheek,' explained Falk curtly.

170

'What kind of services?' Ahren persisted.

'Services in which they are touched. Hence the name,' interjected Uldini drily.

'Oh', said Ahren. Then the penny dropped.

'Oh'.

'Precisely', said Uldini.

'If she stays here, she has no choice. But I want to offer her one,' said Jelninolan forcefully.

'Your decision, your problem,' answered the Arch Wizard and raised his hands defensively.

Falk merely nodded in agreement, and Ahren breathed a sigh of relief. He wouldn't like to see Khara suffer such a fate if it were in the power of his companions to prevent it. He gave her an encouraging smile and she looked at him disdainfully. The apprentice sighed. It was going to be a long crossing.

Ahren was sweating like a pig. Falk had been shooing him around the training ground all morning and was badgering him constantly with his broadsword, which put a whole new intensity into the day. Up until this point, Falk had been implementing swordsmanship as one element of many and had been happy that Ahren had mastered the basics. But this morning the lesson and manoeuvres were considerably more complex.

The apprentice was aware that something had changed between them since the previous day's talk. It was true that Falk was not his father and Ahren was not his son but there seemed to be an unspoken agreement on both their parts to ignore these facts.

And Ahren's opinion of his own swordsmanship had changed. All heroic dreams of combat had been driven out of him by his near-death experience. He thought of Falagarda, the armourer, and how she had presented him with Windblade that time. She had shown Ahren his first thrusts and parries and had taught him well. One of her phrases, that he had forgotten in all his excitement at the time, came back to the apprentice now with a new clarity. 'The graves are full of warriors who recognised what heroes really are.'

At the time, he had had no idea of what those words really meant, but now they had a totally new significance for him. If he really wanted to avoid killing anybody when at all possible, if he really wanted to protect those who were close to him and yet still deal with the horrors of the battlefield, then he still had a very long way to travel. Most fighters paid for this realisation with their lives. He was lucky that he was surrounded by such powerful friends. He had been given a second chance and he was determined to take advantage of it.

The flat side of Falk's broadsword crashed into his ribs and he was flung upwards before crashing into the dusty ground. He coughed and pulled himself onto his knees. Falk looked down at him sternly.

'Philosophising is an admirable quality, but when you're training, stay in the here and now. How else are you going to learn?' he instructed.

Falk was still completely inflexible, but his tone had taken on a hint of warmth which Ahren appreciated, and so he was listening more carefully now, than before.

He nodded and was about to get up when he heard a laugh of derision behind him. He recognised Khara's voice, who said something in her own language to which Jelninolan laughed. Ahren turned around as he was getting up to his feet and saw the two women approaching. Khara was wearing one of Jelninolan's garments that had been shortened in a make-shift manner but still looked baggy and fluttered in the breeze, but this didn't seem to bother the girl. She had tied up her hair in a tight, intricate plait, and she walked lightly beside Jelninolan, who was carrying her armour and held her staff in her hand.

'I thought I'd find you two here alright. How are you getting on?' she asked.

Falk grimaced.

'When he's not dreaming, he's complaining, and when he's not complaining, he's making mistakes. And when he's not making mistakes, he's sprawled on the ground,' said Falk, grinning all the while.

Ahren stuck his chin out sullenly and silently went back to the starting position, where he held Windblade in front of him, his knees slightly bent, just as Falk had taught him. Behind him he heard Khara snorting, but he ignored it.

Falk's broadsword was heading for him at lightning speed, but Ahren feinted a thrust and the flat sword headed in an arc towards the ground.

Ahren had avoided the thrust but he realised too late that it had only been a trick. The flat side of the mighty blade smashed into his ankle and the swing swept him off his feet. Again, Ahren was spitting out dirt from the ground, and again Khara was laughing scornfully. He jumped to his feet and threw her an enraged looked, but she looked back at him impassively.

'Susekan', she said mockingly.

Ahren looked at Jelninolan questioningly and she chuckled.

'That means something like 'milksop.' It's what they call someone in the Eternal Empire who had no military training but still holds a weapon in their hand.'

'She can count herself lucky that I don't hit girls. If she was a boy, she'd really get what's coming to her,' he grumbled.

'Very adult,' was his master's dry commentary.

Khara gave Jelninolan a questioning look, and the elf translated what Ahren had said. She had hardly finished speaking when the girl charged towards the apprentice. He just managed to throw Windblade aside and raise his arms to parry her first blow. More followed and the young man avoided the blows only with great difficulty. She still managed to hit him three times in the stomach and ribs, and he felt her elbow in his jaw. He backed away two paces and she stared at him expectantly.

'You defied her, and that's something that's taken very seriously in the Eternal Empire,' explained Jelninolan. 'If you want to give up, just put your flat hand on the ground.'

Ahren was torn between pride and common sense. It was clear as daylight to him that Khara was far superior to him in unarmed combat and so there were only two possibilities: either to allow himself to be beaten to a pulp in the presence of his master or to surrender. Slowly, he went down on his haunches and placed his hand on the ground.

'Good choice,' said Falk and there wasn't a hint of sarcasm.

Even Khara seemed surprised and she bowed while hitting her open palm with a fist. She went over to Ahren's Windblade and picked it up.

'Hey, that's mine!' shouted Ahren weakly. Somehow this girl brought out his worst qualities.

'Not anymore, to be precise. She defeated you in a duel and so has the right to your weapon. At least, according to her traditions,' said the priestess, clarifying the situation.

Ahren was about to protest, but then Khara began performing a complex sequence of manoeuvres while she danced from one fighting position to the next. Her movements were as flowing as water, and after ten heartbeats her performance was over and Ahren was standing there, open-mouthed.

'By the THREE, that wasn't bad!' Falk called out.

174

'But she has a bit of work to do on her foot positions and her back is strangely inflexible,' said Jelninolan thoughtfully. The elf clapped her hands once and Khara reacted instantly, falling to the floor and sitting on her knees.

Jelninolan imitated the same flowing fighting movements with her staff, and, while Ahren couldn't see any noticeable difference, Khara blushed a deep red and bowed forward in her sitting position until her head was touching the ground.

Ahren looked in amazement at his master, who grinned back at him.

'I think we should introduce that gesture when I'm showing you what to do,' he said jokingly.

Jelninolan began speaking to the girl in her own language and the men listened in. Falk followed the conversation with some difficulty and frowned at the effort while Ahren could do nothing but stand there and wait. He looked around him, bored, and spotted Culhen, who was frolicking around the palace park which adjoined their training area. Ahren called his friend over, and the wolf hurtled into his arms, and Ahren gave him a tickling all over. The wolf greedily searched Ahren's pockets – the servants were still not used to the animal's enormous appetite, and so Culhen was always looking out for extra portions. Ahren made a mental note that he should have a word with the stable boys later.

Jelninolan's tone was growing harsher now and Khara's answers meeker, which made Ahren turn his attention back to their conversation.

'Can you follow what they're saying?' he asked Falk.

The old Paladin shook his head.

'I'm too out of practice. Jelninolan is asking her about her past and where she comes from, but Khara's answers are very vague.'

Jelninolan was become angrier, and when Khara gave a bow of apology, the elf grasped the girl's clothing and revealed her neck and shoulder-blades.

Ahren couldn't believe what he was seeing and turned away in horror. Khara's skin was covered in scars, elevated and grown together.

'She was a slave,' whispered Falk, stunned.

Khara hid her face in her hands and her head was bowed. Jelninolan continued speaking to her, and drew further hesitant answers from her. Finally, the conversation was over, and the elf priestess looked at the two Forest Guardians angrily.

'I'd forgotten how much I abhorred some elements of human culture,' she said passionately.

Falk slowly raised his eyebrows.

'Now take it easy. What did she say?'

'She was a slave in one of the rural areas. She was born and grew up there, and when her mother died in the wars, she inherited the debts. Last year she succeeded in fleeing and she survived on the streets of Thulasthan by begging and stealing. When she got the chance, she smuggled herself onto a ship which was leaving the Eternal Empire, and spent several months as a stowaway on the seas before she jumped overboard in King's Island harbour and swam ashore,' explained Jelninolan.

Ahren was dizzy at the thought of the hard existence the girl had already endured in her young life. Suddenly, life at home with his father seemed like a walk in the park, and Falk's training methods were heaven on earth! He looked thankfully at his master.

'But why does her back look like that?' asked Ahren.

'An elementary part of slave training is the imposition of pain. If you make a mistake, you're whipped, burned or you have acid poured on you.

176

That's how they break the wills of the poor souls and at the same time ensure they will never be as flexible or as well able to fight as their guards,' said Jelninolan darkly. 'Any movement they make causes terrible pain in their backs. And I'm certain their legs and arms look no better. If I ever see Qin-Wa again, I'm going to demand an explanation as to why she allows such horrors in her empire,' she blurted.

Falk looked awkwardly at the girl who was still huddled together in shame.

'And now?' he asked helplessly.

Jelninolan looked back at him with blazing eyes.

'Now it's time for magic. Tell the soldiers the training ground has been closed. I need the area for myself.' Her tone brooked no dissension, and Falk's centuries of life experience taught him to follow her orders to the letter. He left in silence to carry them out. Ahren was about to follow him but the elf stopped him.

'You stay here and make sure that nobody disturbs my circle.'

He nodded obediently and went to the edge of the circular area, roughly sixty paces in diameter.

Jelninolan led Khara into the centre and began speaking to her. The girl knelt in obedience and then went back onto her heels where she remained immobile. Jelninolan took her staff and began tracing drawings and patterns in the sand at the girl's feet. The girl looked down uneasily, and Ahren positioned himself on the edge of the area so that he was standing directly in her field of vision. He made comforting gestures towards her and pointed at where the short sword had penetrated his breast. Then he pulled up his jerkin and stroked the smooth skin, which now revealed nothing of the terrible injury he had suffered. He was quite a distance away and he wasn't absolutely certain that the ex-slave understood what he was communicating, but she seemed to be less anxious.

The following hours felt endless. Jelninolan drew, fully concentrated, step by step, lines and waves in the sand, at the same time creating a deliberate, ever widening spiral. There was a gentle breeze, but the symbols remained clear and sharply delineated. Ahren walked the perimeter, shooing away inquisitive servants and curious soldiers. His title as squire made the task easier because everybody obeyed without complaint, if a little hesitantly. Only once did an officer, who was doing an exercise with a troop of the palace watch, try to override Ahren. But the apprentice gave the man an apologetic smile and said in a disarming voice, 'I'm only following the orders of Baron Falkenstein. You'd need to discuss the matter with him.' At which point the grumbling officer withdrew.

Jelninolan was finally finished in the early afternoon. The practice area was strewn all over with the elf's magical symbols and now she stood beside Ahren with a tired face, smiling wanly, but with a look of satisfaction on her face.

'Does the magic begin now?' he asked excitedly.

She gave a weak laugh.

'Oh, my dear boy, that was the magic,' she said, correcting him.

Then she stamped her staff once into the tiny circle that marked the end of the enormous pattern, and a blue flame blazed inside it. The tiny flame sped along the line, tracing it as it ran along, with the symbols vanishing behind it as though they had never existed. The blue light worked its way backwards, through each of Jelninolan's designs, erasing more and more of the ritual circle while the flame grew steadily with every symbol it passed through. Khara stared petrified at the approaching fire, and Ahren tried to make calming gestures towards her, but now she wasn't reacting. The girl became increasingly anxious and Jelninolan called out, 'she must not leave the circle while the charm is working or it will all have been in vain!' The priestess had slumped over after the outbreak of the charm and she was leaning heavily on her staff. Ahren could see that the elf could help nobody in her present condition.

The apprentice tried to establish eye-contact with Khara, and when he succeeded, he saw a wild, almost primitive terror in her eyes. With a moment of inspiration Ahren passed his hand through the blue flame. It felt surprisingly cool and his skin was completely undamaged, just as he had hoped. This calmed Khara down a little and he gave her an encouraging smile.

Behind him he heard Jelninolan groan.

'Don't do that again. That type of interruption drains my strength.'

Khara looked spellbound at the flame, which was now racing through the remaining symbols and was bearing down on the girl in shortening circles. The fear was back in her face, and as the two paces high flame extinguished the last symbols, he saw her body tense up. She would jump up at any moment! With an elegant leap he jumped past the flame and landed just behind the girl as she was beginning to stand. He threw his arms around her upper-body, the flames engulfed the girl and she screamed out in fear and tried to break free. Ahren knew what damage she could do in hand to hand combat so he lifted her into the air for a heartbeat and then let go.

Khara was now completely surrounded by flames and as she threw herself to the left, still screaming, the magic fire stuck to her and flared into a ball. It seemed to creep under her skin where it blazed from within for a moment. And then in a flash, it was gone.

The light had vanished in an instant, leaving behind a sobbing girl lying on a humdrum training ground. Ahren bent over her to calm her but she grasped his wrist, twisted it forcefully, threw him into the air, and he landed with his nose in the dirt.

Jelninolan gave a tired laugh and called out hoarsely, 'well done, Ahren. It may take her a while to understand that you helped her, but I, at least, thank you.'

The young Forest Guardian spat the dirt out of his mouth and gave Khara an accusatory look, but she ignored him and looked, spellbound, at her exposed forearms. Ahren could see that the blue flame hadn't quite gone out, but was running along the web of scar lines, extinguishing all visible and invisible injuries in the same way that the fire had obliterated the lines in the sand. Left behind was bright, perfect skin, that looked as smooth and untouched as the ground on which she was lying.

Ahren stood up, and a weary Jelninolan walked towards him. When she saw his baffled face, she pointed to the training ground and then at Khara's arm.

'This is how Elfish magic works best. We create a mirror of what we are trying to achieve. A rugged, scarred field that smoothes itself. First on the ground. Then on her skin.'

The girl was weeping with joy, and she tried to have a look at her back by taking off her clothing. Ahren blushed a deep red and turned away while Jelninolan knelt beside Khara and held her up. She was talking insistently to the girl, and Khara threw herself down at the feet of the elf and stuttered a ritualised phrase through her tears.

'Oh dear' said Jelninolan and frowned. She shook her head sadly. 'I never thought of that.'

'What happened?' asked Ahren curiously and turned back to them.

'Khara has just sworn me service until her guilt has been atoned for. In my hurry, I'd forgotten to offer her healing as a present,' she said,

180

looking down at the figure, who was still kneeling with her head on the ground.

'What's the problem? Give it to her as a present now,' said Ahren with a shrug of his shoulders.

'It's not that simple. A present has to be announced. Explaining something afterwards as a present is a deadly insult. Because you're insinuating that that the person who has received the object or service can't pay for it. I would be dishonouring her,' the priestess explained patiently.

Ahren still couldn't see the problem.

'So? She'll get over it.'

Jelninolan looked at him, her eyebrows raised.

'She was a slave for almost her whole life. Then a beggar, then a thief. The one thing that the girl possesses at the moment is her sense of honour, and her service to me. And I'm supposed to take both those things from her?'

Ahren's head was spinning and he decided to give up. The place where Khara came from seemed terribly complicated and unbelievably cruel. He really hoped he would never have to set foot inside the Eternal Empire.

'Do you still need me?' he asked finally. 'I should really carry on practising before Falk catches me dawdling.'

'No. Off you go,' said Jelninolan absently, and pulled the still-crying girl up to her feet. 'I'll calm Khara down and figure out how to proceed with her.'

Ahren left the two of them on their own and wondered how Uldini would react when he found out that the ex-slave was a now a fixed part of their group and bound to Jelninolan through an oath of service.

The sun cast the shooting range in a golden light, and Ahren looked with satisfaction over at the stuffed mannequins that he had peppered with arrows without missing once.

After the morning's sound thrashing, his pride had been in urgent need of some success, and so he had retired to the shooting range and engaged in some shooting practice. Culhen stayed with him and offered him companionship. The approving looks of the palace guards, who were training with their crossbows, had done him good. Ahren was calm and relaxed again at last, a condition that had been painfully missing over the previous few days. He had been tossed about like a ball by the many new experiences and turbulent events, but now all was well again.

Ahren had understood what he had done wrong in the alleyway, and the realisation was painful. Had he reached for his bow, he would have shot two of the scoundrels in the leg before they'd have even noticed. Instead of which, he had made the fatal decision to depend on Windblade because he had overestimated his ability as a swordsman.

At least everything had worked out well. Khara had been saved, and even her scars had been healed, and Ahren was closer to his master than ever before.

He silently thanked the THREE for his luck and noticed that this was the first time he had ever expressed his gratitude to the beings that had singled him out with their blessing. He glanced over at the cathedral and wondered if he should visit the house of the gods when he heard a sound behind him.

He turned around, and there was Khara, half a pace behind him.

He started and recoiled, and she frowned and pointed at him.

'Susekan hear bad,' she said haltingly. Then she smugly laid her hand on Windblade, which she had hung around her. 'Susekan fight very bad,' she goaded.

Ahren bit his tongue in an effort to avoid giving a foul-mouthed response. Then, as coolly as possible, he lifted his bow and shot without any effort an arrow into the head of the furthest mannequin.

'I'm more of an archer, really,' he said, a little too light-heartedly.

Khara ignored his tone and gave a slight bow.

'Susekan coward too. Hide behind bow,' she said.

Ahren was ready to explode and was on the point of uttering a string of expletives when he noticed a giveaway twitch of her exotic eye. The girl was making fun of him quite brilliantly and he had nearly fallen into her trap. He laughed in embarrassment and she laughed too, a sparkling laugh that Ahren found quite charming.

Then Jelninolan's self-proclaimed servant became serious again.

'Mistress said, give back to you,' she said. She took Windblade from her back and held it out to Ahren.

The young man quickly took it, happy to be its owner again. He wanted to thank her, but Khara was quicker.

'Bad sword. Head too heavy. Blade too wide. Bad weapon suit bad fighter.' Then she bowed slightly and went away, leaving a furious apprentice in her wake, who spent the rest of the day taking out his frustrations on innocent mannequins. And while he was peppering them with arrows, he kept imagining them in the form of a certain girl he knew.

Chapter 11

The following three days flew by in no time. Ahren trained diligently under Falk's eagle eyes and honed and refined his archery skills. Uldini and the king co-ordinated the suppression of the Illuminated Path and, despite some moaning and groaning, it wasn't long before the Arch Wizard had come to terms with the fact that Khara would accompany them for the foreseeable future. Ahren hardly ever saw her because the elf spent every waking minute drumming the basics of the Northern language into the girl.

The evening of the celebratory feast, in honour of Falk and Ahren, was now upon them. Preparations were in full swing and attendants were rushing hither and thither carrying out the many essential tasks such a feast required.

Ahren had just bathed himself thoroughly. Falk had insisted that his apprentice should appear in the best possible light that evening. He climbed out of the wooden tub, rubbed himself dry and walked towards his own little cell. There was a bundle on his bed with a folded-over piece of parchment with his name on it, written in his master's handwriting. Curious, he opened it up and read its contents.

Ahren,

Falk, Jelninolan and Selsena wish you a belated, happy Autumn Festival.

And don't dawdle! The guests of honour are expected at the second pealing of the clock.

184

Excited, Ahren opened up the bundle and saw an elaborately embroidered costume, decorated with the Falkenstein coat-of-arms on its chest. The material was of a much higher quality than the brown linen jerkin he had been given on their arrival. The evening was promising to be less uncomfortable and itchy than he had expected.

Delighted, he lifted up the clothing and gasped. He could now see two more things that had been hidden by the costume. A strange white cord which he couldn't figure out, and a material with a telling shimmer. Ahren put the feast day clothing aside and picked up the dark green material, shouted out in joy and hopped from one foot to the other in excitement. Jelninolan had made him a set of Elvin undergarments.

Humming happily, he slipped into the undergarments and asked himself why the bards never sang of the hard and uncomfortable life on the road when you had poor quality undergarments. He ran over the soft and smooth material with his hand and was convinced he had never been as happy as this in his life. No abrasive armour anymore! No more blisters or abrasions in the worst possible places after hours in the saddle! Ahren decided he would guard these clothes with his life, and quickly got dressed.

The garments fitted him to a tee. He moved his shoulders around contentedly and tested his freedom of movement. He took up the white cord with a frown of consternation and examined it critically. He really couldn't make head or tail of it and was about to put it down on his bed when he noticed two little loops, one at either end. Then it dawned on him.

It was a bowstring – but the material was unfamiliar to him. He held the string in front of his face, felt it with his fingers and saw a silver shimmer reflected by the light. He recognised the colour, and the fact that it was made from twisted hairs, and then the penny dropped. Selsena's mane shimmered in exactly the same way. Ahren was certain that the bowstring was made from the mane of the Titejunanwa.

He lay down on the bed and considered the present. He had never heard of this before and neither Falk's nor Jelninolan's bow had a similar string.

Full of curiosity, he took his bow from a corner of the room and fixed the new string. He checked the tension and to his surprise he groaned with effort. It was considerably stronger and Ahren was not sure if, or how often, he could draw the bow fully before his arm would grow tired. But there was no doubt it was a priceless gift, and he decided to thank Selsena as soon as possible.

Falk had been very specific in his instructions that morning, so Ahren buckled on Windblade, hung the bow over his shoulder and left the tiny room.

'The people want to see a hero,' he had said. 'So, enter with your weapons and deposit your bow at the entrance after everyone has seen you in full armour. And make sure you are vague when you're telling stories. Nobody wants to hear that the king's life was saved by a greenhorn.'

He left their quarters and immediately met Jelninolan outside. She was wearing the same clothes she had on the first evening of their stay in the capital. Ahren threw his arms around her.

'Thank you for the wonderful present, Jelninolan. I can't tell you how happy I am,' he said excitedly.

She smiled warmly in return.

'You're welcome, Ahren. These undergarments always attract the highest prices among human merchants, no matter how many we produce. The traders invariably take everything with them when they leave Evergreen and keep the first set for themselves.' They both laughed and the elf linked arms with him. 'Let's wander through the park while we wait for the bell,' she suggested. 'It would be very rude to appear too early. We don't want to spoil your big entrance.'

Ahren nodded and they stepped out and headed for the perfectly laid out green lawns, where Culhen loved to play, much to the gardeners' consternation.

The weather was getting gradually cooler and the first hint of winter was in the air. The sky was still clear, and the sun had some strength, but during the evenings now the temperature dropped noticeably. Ahren looked forward to the winter for some reason, and he hoped that after his first journey in the dark season he would still feel the same way.

'Where are the others?' he asked casually, more for something to say than out of genuine interest.

'Uldini is spinning a few court intrigues in order to reduce the damage Elgin's unwitting complicity caused, and Falk is probably hiding somewhere and sprucing himself up.'

Ahren almost stumbled with shock and gave Jelninolan a sceptical look.

'I'm sorry?' he blurted. 'Pardon?'

She smiled indulgently and tapped a finger on Ahren's nose.

'Your master has a dramatic streak, which tends to come to the fore when he's on King's Island. Also, this is his first official appearance in over seven hundred years. The old curmudgeon will pull out all the stops to remind people that the Paladins are still watching over them.' She frowned. 'At least, some of them.'

Ahren was now really looking forward to the feast, and wondered what Falk could possibly have planned. Jelninolan went on.

'Khara will stay in my rooms. She only has the rank of a servant and isn't allowed to come with us. Anyway, I want to keep her away from crowds until she has become more used to the Northern Kingdom. Otherwise it could quickly lead to misunderstandings.'

Ahren could imagine Khara giving a nobleman a bloody nose or hurling an aristocratic lady into the midst of the banquet because she'd misunderstood a remark. He knew exactly where the elf was coming from.

'But she seems very happy with the condition. When I left her, she was busying herself with her Autumn Day present.'

'You made her a present too?' asked Ahren a little sharply. He knew he shouldn't be jealous, but couldn't help feeling a little tinge of envy.

'We were at the weaponry market today and bought her a half-decent Windblade. Wherever we're going to be going there will be danger, and she needs to be able to defend herself. Anyway, it would be a crying shame if she weren't able to practise, with her talent,' she responded, smiling.

Now Ahren was truly jealous and remained silent while he tried to swallow his injured pride.

They wandered on through the park until they heard the first peal of the bell.

'Ah, the first bell. Can you accompany me to the entrance? All of the invited guests are supposed to go in now, so the herald has enough time to introduce everyone.'

Ahren began walking quickly and he couldn't stop grinning, Jelninolan put a hand on his shoulder.

'Steady on! We have time. The more important you are, the later you go in. That way most people get to hear the herald's presentation. There's a fixed order, you know,' she explained.

Ahren rolled his eyes.

'I'll be happy when we're gone from here. The rules of nature are a lot simpler and more sensible.'

Jelninolan laughed and kissed him lightly on the cheek.

'Dear Ahren. Hopefully, you'll never change,' she said affectionately, and for a brief moment the motherly Jelninolan he had got to know in Evergreen was back.

A large cluster of people had gathered at the palace entrance, where they were standing in little groups, laughing, talking, whispering, or arguing.

Uldini couldn't be missed – once again he was floating half a pace above the ground so that he could speak at eye level with the others. The Arch Wizard had decided on little green flashes, which darted down from his hanging feet and danced over the ground at irregular intervals.

Ahren noticed with amusement that the colourful discharges perfectly matched Jelninolan's dress and he saw once again how much of a routine they had developed in their long lives and how they were able to use it playfully and elegantly in moments like this.

Uldini floated over to them and embraced Jelninolan ostentatiously.

'Darling, you look wonderful this evening,' he said in an unusually soft voice. 'You wait here for your master until your grand entrance,' he whispered to Ahren and wiggled his eyebrows meaningfully.

The young man nodded, and the two Ancients disappeared into the crowd, where Uldini greeted a baroness in a gushing manner.

Directly in front of the palace Ahren could see a small line of people, for the most part in pairs, waiting patiently until they would be waved into the ballroom by the steward. Occasionally, Ahren could hear a loud voice speaking and calling out titles, and he assumed this had to be the herald, announcing the guests.

He looked around him, but there was no sign of Falk, and so he stood there, a little on his own, and studied the people around him.

The clothing and jewellery was even more extravagant than he had seen on first entering the court, and Ahren asked himself how some of the older ladies were able to stand upright at all, under the weight of all the gold and gemstones around their necks.

To the left of the guests and a little apart seemed to be their attendants. Ahren felt ill-at-ease among all the pomp and so he went near the liveried group and heard some of their conversation.

'Have you heard that there's supposed to be a Paladin here today. They say Dorian Falkenstein has returned to court', said a lady-in-waiting excitedly. 'Imagine all the things he must have done since he left.'

'I heard that he was fighting Dark Ones in the Borderlands. That's why there are so few,' said someone else, whom Ahren couldn't see.

'Nonsense. My lord says he was living the high life in the Southern lands. If you know what I mean...' said another attendant with a lewd grin.

Another one protested.

'Everyone knows that after fighting a dragon, he was locked up in its cave. He escaped during an earthquake a moon ago and that's why he's back.'

Ahren almost exploded with laughter but held himself together and continuing listening with amusement.

'I don't care where the old codger was hiding. I went to see the king's rescuer,' said a maidservant nervously. 'I hear he's very good-looking, muscular and as strong as an ox.'

'I heard he comes from Kelkor and only wears animal hides,' said another servant enviously.

'You're only jealous. I bet you he's carrying an enormous axe or a mighty two-handed sword, or something like that.'

Ahren couldn't suppress a giggle and then he felt a powerful hand on his shoulder.

'Do you find something particularly amusing or do you just enjoy listening in on honest people's conversations, boy?' grunted a large servant to Ahren as he swung him around.

Obviously, he took Ahren to be a fellow servant, and he was looking at the apprentice belligerently.

'Egbert, I really don't think he's a servant,' said the lady-in-waiting, and looked questioningly at Ahren.

Before Ahren had a chance to say anything, the large servant poked him hard in the chest, spurred on by the woman's doubts.

'Just look at him. He's not even sixteen winters old. Cleaned himself up a bit so no-one would notice him.' The man's breath reeked of cheap wine and Ahren took a step backwards. He wasn't in the mood for getting into an altercation with someone from the serving staff. Such a skirmish would really be childish after his previous injury in the alleyway in King's Island.

Most of the guests had gone in by now, leaving only the servants and a few of the nobility. Uldini and Jelninolan were standing in the queue before the ballroom. It was only the fact that the servants were more or less among themselves that gave the man the courage to continue harassing Ahren.

'Come on,' he commanded. 'Tell us who you belong to, or maybe you just weaselled your way in here,' he said in a mocking tone.

Then the second bell sounded and three heartbeats later Falk, in full armour, which gleamed in the golden evening light, rode along the main street and approached the palace. Selsena was in full armour too, only her head protection was absent so that everyone could see she was a genuine Titejunanwa.

In his closed fist Falk held an enormous lance, which glittered white and was supported by the right stirrup. A pennant bearing the insignia of the Falkenstein barony fluttered gaily in the wind.

Ahren ignored the uncouth servant. He just couldn't believe what he was seeing. The rider was wearing a helmet with a visor, and the pomp suggested that here was an imposter pretending to be Falk. Except for the fact that it was definitely Selsena – and she would never accept another rider.

Another couple of heartbeats and the Titejunanwa and rider stopped beside Ahren.

'What business do you have with my squire?' asked Falk in an imperious voice.

The eyes of all the servants widened in disbelief, and here and there Ahren could see shaking knees as it dawned on them who the young man was that the servant had been harassing. The man stammered a few incoherent phrases as an excuse but Selsena had already begun trotting again. Falk ignored the servant and nodded to Ahren, indicating that he should run beside them.

Ahren glanced back over his shoulder at the dumbstruck servants, shrugged his shoulders casually and smiled mischievously. Then he walked determinedly beside Selsena.

'What happened there?' asked Falk quietly.

'Well, I just think I'm not going to live up to some of their expectations. Their picture of how I should look doesn't really tally with reality.'

Falk laughed, a rumbling sound under his visor.

'Now you can imagine how Uldini's been feeling for hundreds of years. Everybody expects a wise old man with a big bushy beard and kindly eyes, and then they get…him.'

Ahren chuckled and then quickly tried to control his expressions again as they arrived at the entrance to the ballroom. Falk dismounted Selsena in a grand manner and Ahren used the opportunity to throw his arms around the Titejunanwa's neck.

'Thank you for the lovely Autumn Day present,' he said quickly.

Selsena sent waves of affection over him and Falk gave her an affectionate slap on her flank.

'The old girl insisted. Probably so that you won't try to let yourself be killed, sword in hand, again. Now you belong to the select few. Maybe thirty elves and humans possess a cord made from Titejunanwa hair. It will never become loose, works even when it's wet, and its traction is immense,' he explained.

They ascended the small step and were now standing in front of the steward. Falk took off his helmet and tucked it under his arm. Ahren noticed that his master's beard had been newly trimmed, and he even got the scent of eau de toilette. Who was this man standing beside him, and where was the stoic, simple Forest Guardian who had been training him for years?

Falk noticed the young man's look.

'It's only one evening, and it's not every day you come back from centuries of exile, so don't begrudge me the fun,' he said with a grin and a wink of his eye.

Ahren shook his head in dismay and walked beside his master. Jelninolan had hit the nail on the head in her prediction of what Falk had been up to. The apprentice really didn't know what to make of this

Dorian Falkenstein, who seemed to have dislodged his Master Falk so completely.

Then the steward spoke, and Ahren's train of thought was interrupted.

'Good evening esteemed and honoured guests. Are the gentlemen ready to be presented at court?' he asked in a formal voice.

Master and apprentice nodded. Satisfied, the master of protocol invited them to enter.

Ahren saw a wooden wall in front of them and was taken aback, but then he saw entrances left and right and realised that it served both as a protection from prying eyes and as a wind breaker. The steward guided them to the right and around the wooden wall where Ahren would have stood rooted to the spot were it not for Falk giving him a discrete push forward. The first things that struck Ahren were the many candles, torches and fireplaces that lit up the enormous room. A wide stairway in front of them led into the rectangular room with a large dance floor in its centre. At the edge of the stairway stood a man with an ornately decorated staff in one hand and a long parchment scroll in the other. He exchanged a glance with the steward and then gave a gracious bow.

Ahren and Falk were led up to the herald, and Ahren had a quick look at his surroundings. To the left and right of the dance floor there were tables and chairs at which the guests were eating and drinking, laughing and playing or simply chatting amongst themselves. The dancing had not yet started. At the other end of the room, which was a least two hundred paces in length, the young Forest Guardian could make out a throne behind a long table.

The herald banged the bottom of the staff three times into the floor, and the noise rolled in a wave throughout the hall causing the crowd to fall silent. Ahren had never experienced the silence of so many people and he found the situation eerie.

The herald cleared his throat loudly before banging on the smooth, polished wooden floor three more times with the base of his staff.

'Baron Dorian Falkenstein, Paladin of the Gods, Champion of the Dark Days, General of the Northeastern Allied Cavalry, Conqueror of Delsorus, Thousand Tooth and the Low Worm Jagged Scale.'

Falk stepped forward and walked slowly down the steps. There was a frenzy of jubilation and applause, and somewhere in the room a band struck up a military march. All of the guests were down on their knees and the apprentice was sure he could see that some were in tears. Some others had fainted, and Ahren found the celebration more and more unreal.

His master stepped across the dance floor and approached the throne. Once he had reached the last third of the room, the steward leaned over to Ahren.

'Just copy exactly what the baron is doing and nothing can go wrong.'

Ahren nodded uncertainly and once again the herald banged his staff on the wooden floor. All the heads turned in the room and Ahren had a queasy feeling at the thought that at this moment more than three hundred pairs of eyes were fixed on him. No, four hundred, he mentally corrected himself. Among the crowd were many servants in red livery, who were serving food and carrying jugs and bottles. And everyone was staring at him.

'Squire Ahren from the Barony Falkenstein, rescuer of our beloved King Senius Blueground.'

The introduction had been considerably shorter, and the applause was less enthusiastic than for Falk's progression, but that did not bother Ahren. He walked down the steps a little too quickly and waved a little awkwardly as he tried as much as possible to enjoy the applause.

Nobody had ever cheered him like this before, and Ahren thought he could well get used to it. Three or four beautiful admiring young ladies smiled at him invitingly and suddenly the apprentice thought this feast might be more enjoyable than he had expected.

He approached the other end of the hall, trying to imitate the graceful, measured steps of his master. When he reached the table before the throne, the music started playing again and the atmosphere in the hall returned to the previous jollity, with the conversations being struck up again once, Ahren was no longer the focus of attention.

The long table, situated in front of the richly decorated wooden throne, was overflowing with foodstuffs and drinks. Every one of the aristocratic guests sitting at the table was carrying enough valuables to buy Ahren's home village of Deepstone. In fact, Ahren reckoned that if all the people at the table pooled the jewellery they had on show, they would be able to acquire the city of Three Rivers. And the land around it, with a radius of one hundred and twenty-five miles. Many of the aristocrats had the confident look of people whose orders were carried out in double quick time. And all of these mighty and wealthy guests were staring at him.

Ahren broke out into a sweat and quickly positioned himself beside his master, suppressing the impulse to hide himself behind the broad, armoured back of the Paladin.

Falk it seemed had waited for him and now bowed before the king, who smiled at him benevolently. The friendly warmth he had exhibited towards Falk in the throne room had been replaced this evening by a statesmanlike smile, and Ahren asked himself again how the king managed to separate his kingly self from his true self.

The apprentice bowed too, and as he straightened up, there was a polite smattering of applause.

'We are thankful for the appearance of the Paladin Falkenstein at the royal court. We are similarly thankful to the Squire Ahren, who helped to save our life and to reveal the dastardly treachery of Brother Wultom,' intoned the king in a formal voice.

The applause grew a little louder and when it died down, the monarch gestured to the two guests that they should join the table.

Falk sat down after he had hung his broadsword over the back of the expansive chair. Ahren followed suit, although he took considerably longer because of his nerves and he also had to set aside his bow and arrows.

'Didn't I tell you to leave them at the entrance?', said Falk irritably and so quietly that nobody else could hear him.

'I forgot. This is all so overwhelming, master,' he mumbled apologetically.

Falk softened, nodded and took off his gauntlets.

'You'll get used to it in time. If you can disregard the pomp and ceremony, then you're left with a good supper and entertaining conversation,' he said, winking at his apprentice. 'Put them over there by the pillar, they won't be in the way.'

Ahren smiled back in gratitude, placed his bow and arrows by the pillar, took his seat and looked around the table.

The king was sitting opposite them, with Jelninolan to his left, and a plump, elderly man with thinning grey hair and wearing a flashy robe, to his right. He spotted Uldini at the head of the table on the left. The Arch Wizard was in lively conversation with half a dozen aristocrats, and every so often he would emphasise his words with some magic sleights of hand. All of his companions were following his performance with rapt attention. Falk leaned over and whispered into Ahren's ear, 'Uldini is in his element. Give him a royal court and he'll enjoy the next two years by

197

sweet-talking, intimidating and pressuring the courtiers until they are all dancing to his tune,' he said with an amused tone.

'He comes across as perfectly charming,' said Ahren in amazement.

'Oh, he can be very charming when he wants to be. The problem is that usually he doesn't.'

Then Falk turned away and began chatting to the nobles at the table.

Ahren tried to listen in but he was so overwhelmed by impressions he decided to concentrate on one thing at a time. And so he turned his attention to the guests closest to him.

Beside him was a young lady with eyes lowered to her plate, who looked as shy as Ahren felt. Like all the others, her clothes were richly adorned, and Ahren saw an enormous diamond which had been worked into her diadem. The gemstone sparkled with every movement, which drew his eyes automatically to her forehead. Because of this, her otherwise lacklustre appearance was not the focus of attention, which, Ahren thought, was probably the point of the diamond.

An older lady sat next to her. She too had a diamond, on her head. However, the cut and size of the latter stone was more subtle and drew attention to the lady's confident and dignified appearance. She caught Ahren's eye, nodded politely and pointed towards the younger lady.

'I couldn't help noticing you looking at my daughter, Squire Ahren. Allow me to introduce to you Ludmilla von Glarding, the sole heiress of the Glarding Barony.'

Her voice had a strangely furtive undertone, which Ahren couldn't make head or tail of. And so he decided that politeness was the best policy.

'It is my honour, Baroness Larding,' he said with a slight bow. Then he turned to her daughter, who gave him a shy look. Ludmilla was a few winters older than Ahren but her shy demeanour made her seem considerably younger, and when she greeted him with the same formality, he saw a hint of a smile, which gave colour to her otherwise blank expression. Perhaps the dinner would be quite enjoyable after all.

'Did you really save the king's life all on your own?' asked the baroness's daughter in a whisper.

When it came to showing off, Ahren had learned his lesson, and so he decided on a modest approach.

'I was the first to spot the High Fang's thorn, and so I could foil his attack on the king. It was the Ancient Uldini who incapacitated him,' he said, trying to look as humble as possible. He was sure that Falk was listening in and the last thing he wanted was for his master to give him a dressing down in front of the king and the assembled high nobility.

'Perhaps you'd like to tell my daughter of your heroic deed during the first dance of the evening,' suggested the baroness in a persistent, almost sly tone.

Ahren wasn't sure if he'd done something wrong, and was about to agree so as not to annoy the baroness when he suddenly felt a painful stabbing in his foot. Falk had stepped on his foot with his steel-clad boot, and when the apprentice looked up at his master with a pained and annoyed expression, his master shook his head unobtrusively, while continuing to feast on a piece of venison.

'I apologise, Baroness,' Ahren stuttered in a confused voice. 'But my master has issued clear instructions that I am not permitted to leave his side.' That sounded considerably less confident than he had intended, but it was the best he could do on the spur of the moment.

Falk winked at the confused apprentice and continued chewing contentedly. The baroness looked as if she had just been served some sour milk and acknowledged Ahren with a curt nod before turning away without saying a word. She then started a conversation with her neighbour at the table, an elderly gentleman with an array of medals on his formal uniform.

This was clearly a message to Ludmilla, who looked at him sadly and a little apologetically before staring down at her plate again in complete silence.

Everyone else around him was either deep in conversation or helping themselves to food, and so Ahren decided to still his hunger. There was game, pheasant, vegetables and bread, and Ahren also noticed a deep red wine in his goblet. He discretely smelled the drink, and his nose was filled with a strong, pervasive aroma. He tasted it carefully and there was an intense taste of fermented berries. Before he knew it, he had drunk a substantial mouthful. He quickly put back the wine and filled his plate. If he got drunk at his first evening in court, his master would have him running up and down trees until his hair turned grey, and he could really do without that.

And so he contented himself with the meat and listened in to any conversations he could catch. Most of them were too difficult to follow, and the rest seemed to be concerned with the events that had led up to Ahren's presence at the feast. Falk seemed to be talking about some old families in Knight Marshes and was trying to get up to date regarding the present state of the nobility in the royal court. His master's face was relaxed and contented, so Ahren concluded that the answers his master was getting were satisfactory.

Ahren slowly began to relax. Contrary to his expectations, he wasn't the centre of attention and apart from the odd friendly glance or polite nod, he was left in peace. Falk was just finishing a conversation, so the apprentice took his opportunity.

'Why exactly are they ignoring me now?' he whispered curiously.

Falk grinned and leaned into his ear.

'You are now a squire of my barony and as you are sitting directly beside me at the feast table, you are here as my adjutant. That means that you stay by my side and are ready to carry out my wishes during the festivities,' he whispered almost inaudibly. 'That means I can keep you away from trouble and protect you from the worst of the vultures, who would otherwise take advantage of your favour with the king,' he said, finishing his explanation.

Ahren gave a nod of understanding and looked in gratitude at his master.

'But why is the king ignoring me? I'm one of the guests of honour after all,' pressed the young man. Although he was trying his best, he sounded a little as if his nose was bent out of joint.

Falk's eyes narrowed and he became serious as he responded. 'A king cannot show any weakness, especially not when his kingdom has just been infiltrated under his very nose by an enemy cult. The fact that he was saved by a youth of tender age in his own throne room makes him appear weak. Which is why he's showing you the minimum of attention that good etiquette requires and he's hoping that the uproar over the cult and the manner of his rescue will die down as quickly as possible.'

He pointed secretly at Jelninolan.

'Why do you think he put our Elvin friend sitting directly beside him? Everyone has to see the strong alliance with the elves, and that the king has everything under control. You don't understand how important such symbolic gestures can be when it comes to keeping a kingdom together in times of crisis.'

Ahren looked over at the priestess. She was laughing merrily at a joke the monarch had just made, and had placed her hand on his forearm in a gesture of familiarity. The apprentice observed the long table, looking from left to right, and it was as if Falk's words had opened his eyes.

Everyone kept glancing over at the king and his guest, and every gesture and reaction of Jelninolan was examined and evaluated by critical eyes.

The realisation that court life was a series of complications, and that the power of the king depended so much on the acceptance and goodwill of the nobility, confused Ahren and shattered his view of the world. A king had always been for him some kind of force of nature, unbending and absolute in his authority. He had already got to know the fallible human being behind the title, and now he could see the limits of royal authority. He now had a better understanding of the monarchy, and Ahren was glad that they would be setting sail the following day. King's Island was certainly no place for him, and all the luxury seemed shallow on account of all the wheeling and dealing.

'Are all royal courts like this?' he asked, deflated.

'Absolutely not,' replied Falk.

Ahren breathed a sigh of relief.

'The Knight Marshes are relatively harmless. If you have the barons under control, then you can rule more-or-less unhindered. At the Sun Court or in the Eternal Empire, it's a different story altogether. No guest would turn up without a food taster for fear of being poisoned at the feast,' Falk added darkly.

Ahren gasped and swore to himself to keep well clear, if at all possible, of all the courts of the wealthy and mighty.

Ahren spent most of the evening eating out of boredom. After Falk's explanations, he was quite happy at being ignored, and because he had nothing else to do, he ate far too much of the good food and ended up slouched inelegantly in his seat, and was in constant danger of nodding off. Falk had warned him several times to sit up straight but had eventually given up.

202

Ahren considered whether he should nick a few bones from the table for Culhen, now that everyone was indulging in the wine, and the atmosphere was becoming louder and more boisterous. The dance floor was full, but the aristocratic dancing style seemed cold and formal to Ahren. The movements of the elaborately dressed guests were stilted and angular and bore no resemblance whatever to the joyful exuberance of the villagers of Deepstone when they had dances.

As Ahren sat at the half-empty table and had just hidden a deer-bone under the table, he heard a commotion behind him. A person in a brocade waistcoat embroidered with the insignia of the Falkenstein barony was storming through the dancers on the floor leaving a wave of indignation in his wake. The stocky man with a tiny goatee was heading straight for Falk. Ahren gave his master a shove and pointed at the incensed person who was no more than a few paces away.

Falk turned around, raised his eyebrows and rose to his feet in a leisurely manner. The newcomer was now in front of him and looked at the old Paladin in a disparaging way.

'So, you are the imposter who the king has granted a hearing to so naively. Everyone knows that Baron Falkenstein is lost without trace, dead in some godforsaken dragon's lair!' the angry man shouted scornfully.

Ahren was about to leap up but Falk stopped him with a sharp hand movement. The Forest Guardian stepped towards the guest, who was still shouting furiously. Falk, with his broad shoulders and tall figure and wearing his white armour, seemed to tower over his opposite number in every way. Remaining silent, the Paladin listened to the man's words.

'You may be certain that the Oblagon family does not recognise your claim and we shall do everything in our power to keep the lands safe from your fraudulent fingers. So long as an Oblagon is the custodian of the

Falkenstein barony, so long will you not set foot in its castle,' shouted the man, finishing his tirade.

Ahren had to give some credit to the man, for in spite of the aggressive manner of his entrance, there were not many among the cowed people present who could stand up to his master, who now had a ferocious look on his face. The man in blue fixed his eyes firmly on his master's narrowed eyes, and refused to flinch. The music had stopped playing, and you could hear a pin drop in the enormous hall. Only here and there was there was there an outraged whisper.

Falk reached behind him and without a word drew his mighty broadsword out of its scabbard, which had been hanging over the back of his seat the whole evening. There was a low gasp among the guests and for a brief moment Ahren feared that his master was going to cut down this disrespectful man in the same cold-blooded manner the king had done to Brother Wultom.

But Falk merely stared fixedly into the man's eyes, then grasped the hilt in both hands with the blade pointing downwards. Then he bellowed in a ritualistic tone: 'Paladinum theos duralas!' and thrust the blade into the floor, where it stuck deep in the stone, making a singing noise as it reverberated.

Then there was a deathly silence in the hall, and Ahren was sure that many of the people present had even forgotten to breathe. He too was shocked, but in his case, it was because he had heard that call before. Falk had uttered the same words during his fight with the Blood Wolf, but later he had laughed off the phrase when Ahren had asked about its meaning. The young man only knew that the words were something in Elfish, but judging by the reactions of those present, they were familiar with the phrase.

The effect on the troublemaker was dramatic at any rate. He trembled, dropped like a thunderbolt down on one knee, bowed his head and beat his breast with his fist.

'Forgive me, m'lord. It's just been too long a time, and I couldn't foresee that...' he began to stutter but Falk cut him off with a sharp voice.

'Of course you could tell who I was.'

His voice cut through the trembling man like an executioner's sword.

'Several portraits of my wife and me hung in my castle, by which you could have recognised me without any difficulty at all. But from what I hear, your great-grandfather banished these portraits into some musty store-room in the cellar, and from that day to this not one of your family, who live in my castle and manage my lands, had the common decency to right this injustice. Instead of which, last summer the king received a request from you personally to rename the Falkenstein Barony as the Oblagon Barony!'

The man had collapsed onto the floor as if he had been hit, and with his face on the ground, he repeatedly tried to stammer some kind of explanation. However, Falk was merciless in his fury and the cold rage of his words echoed through the hall as he continued speaking.

'You are right, Albrecht Oblagon. I refuse to set foot in my castle as long as your family are living there.'

He drew his sword, seemingly effortlessly, out of the ground.

'You recognise my sword of course, and know what deeds I have performed with it. The one reason that I will not use it to execute you here and now for your neglect of duty, is that I have no wish to sully this blade, which felled Dragons, Wyrms, Grave Frogs, Fog Cats, and Blood Wolves, when your forefathers were simple farmers on my land, with your worthless blood.' Falk looked around, and then pointed with the tip of his blade at the leader of the palace guard.

'You,' he roared. 'Come here!'

The addressee approached in double quick time and bowed before Falk. Ahren recognised him as the leader of the guards who had escorted them to the palace when they had arrived on King's Island.

'Your name, captain?!' Falk demanded to know.

'Erik Greycloth, your honour,' said the man, saluting nervously,

'Greycloth? Your family are manufacturers?' asked the Paladin.

The captain nodded and blushed. It seemed that such a background did not amount to much among the higher nobility present.

'My brother took over our father's weaving mill and I decided to try my luck in the army,' he explained, apologetically.

Falk nodded severely, then turned dramatically to all present.

'This courageous man welcomed the esteemed Jelninolan with open arms, and under his personal protection accompanied her to this palace in the full knowledge that his action made him a target of the cult. For this reason I declare him and his successors hereby custodians of the Falkenstein Barony for as long as I am absent from my lands.'

Albrecht groaned in shock and Falk added, almost casually: 'The Oblagon family are hereby banished from the Falkenstein barony. If any adult family member is found within the confines of my lands after six days, then they shall be put in the dungeons.'

Albrecht sprang to his feet and stared wide-eyed at Falk. The terrible fate that had befallen his family in such a short time could clearly be read on his face. He staggered, and Ahren realised that the man, now white as a sheet, thought for a moment of attacking Falk. But the Paladin looked at him calmly with his steel blue eyes, his sword still in his right hand.

The king rose from his seat and addressed the gathering in a similarly loud and authoritative voice.

'I recognise the pronouncement of Baron Falkenstein. My congratulations, Captain Greycloth. Let all present spread the word, how neglect towards the feudal lords will be punished and how friendship and willingness to help the weak, and our Elvin friends will be rewarded.'

Falk added in a lower tone, 'perhaps it would be wise to warn your family, Albrecht. The ride to Falkenstein takes at least two days when conditions are good, isn't that so?'

With an indistinct scream, the deposed steward spun around and fled, stumbling out of the hall in his rush to tell his family of their misfortune, which his impetuosity had caused to befall them.

The king raised his goblet.

'To Baron Falkenstein, risen again from the legends, who has reminded us this day, why so many tales of the Knight Marshes sing his praises!'

The hall exploded in thunderous applause and everyone with a goblet or tankard in front of them joined in their monarch's toast.

Ahren was dumbfounded and would have carried on sitting there in silence were it not for a stern look from Uldini, which brought him back to his senses before he hurriedly toasted his master. Falk continued to stand stock still however, his steely eyes fixed on the exit, with the completely befuddled newly selected steward of the Falkenstein barony standing beside him.

The apprentice took a small sip of the strong wine and looked at the old Paladin thoughtfully. It seemed to Ahren as if there were two people inhabiting this weather-beaten body. There was Falk on the one hand, his master, the strict but good-hearted Forest Guardian who had taken him on and trained him. The man he would happily have called father. Yet on the other hand there was Dorian Falkenstein, Baron of the Knight Marshes and Paladin of the Gods, who with the full force of his power and authority could change the life of a person in a heartbeat, just as others might throw a broken pitcher onto the scrapheap.

Ahren had been confronted by this aspect of his master for the first time when they had first entered the Knight Marshes, and it had taken him a while to find Falk again, hidden under his authoritative demeanour. Now the old man had taken on his task as Paladin again and Ahren worried about what would happen to the stoical, silent Forest Guardian he had become so fond of.

All these thoughts were racing through the young man's head when Falk tilted his head slightly and looked at him for a split second. During this heartbeat his master winked at him almost unnoticeably, before turning back and bowing before the king. Ahren gave a sigh of relief and looked over at Uldini and Jelninolan. The elf smiled at him good-naturedly and gave a slight nod and Uldini looked as contented as a Fog Cat in a darkened pigsty. Ahren looked at the king, more relaxed and at ease than he had ever seen him, and then the penny dropped.

When Falk had sat down Ahren could contain himself no longer and he had to struggle so speak in a whisper.

'The four of you planned all of this, didn't you?' he blurted out excitedly. 'That's the reason for the armour and everything. Was the feast just a smokescreen as well?'

Falk placed his hand on the apprentice's shoulder and pressed it so hard that it almost hurt.

'Quiet boy, or you'll ruin it all,' said Falk softly, and with an edge in his voice. 'Uldini overheard that Albrecht was coming and was going to challenge me, so we prepared for the opportunity. Tonight was all about making clear to everyone that the Paladins have returned, that the king demands absolute obedience, and that the dirty tricks against the elves will have to stop.'

He chuckled drily before continuing.

'I'd actually planned on dealing with the Oblagons later and have half of them thrown into the dungeons, because they've bled my barony dry in the past few decades, but the opportunity was too good to miss, and we were able to kill two birds with one stone. We've united the Knight Marshes with this little scene more quickly than half a dozen royal proclamations could have achieved in five years. The news of this evening's events will quickly do the rounds, and my idea of rewarding poor Greycloth for his good deeds will resonate with a lot of people. With a bit of luck, the people will start treating the elves in a friendlier manner in the hope of being rewarded themselves. Which will encourage more to do the same.' Almost with pity, Falk looked over at the captain, who was still rooted to the same spot and trying to come to terms with his change of fortune.

Ahren stood up.

'I'll go over to him for a moment. I know what it feels like to be in the middle of your machinations, master.'

Falk tried to look at him severely but could only grin approvingly at his apprentice.

The young man went over to Erik and put a hand on his shoulder.

'You should return to your duty, captain,' he said softly. 'I'm sure you're not expected to travel tonight, and I've learned that the normality of a familiar activity helps people to come to terms with important events.'

The new steward looked at Ahren in surprise and a little annoyance.

'I don't think you have any idea of how I'm feeling…,' he began but Ahren interjected brusquely.

'You'd be surprised. But perhaps you'd like to remember the fact that two days ago we met each other as simple citizens, yet now I am a squire and you are steward of a barony.'

Erik bit his upper lip and then his shoulders slumped.

'But I'm a soldier, not an administrator. What if I do everything wrong?' he asked helplessly.

Ahren recognised himself in the question he was being asked, and the feeling that he would be giving advice seemed almost unreal. He thought back to what Falk had taught him, shrugged his shoulders casually and then answered.

'If you don't know what to do, ask someone. The worst mistakes are always the result of false pride. I'm sure the Oblagons didn't do much themselves. Look for help from the attendants. Show them that you have the interest of the barony at heart, and they will teach you everything you need to know.'

All in all, he was quite happy with the answer he had given, and Erik was now looking at him with a lot more belief.

'And anyway, I think that a soldier is exactly what the barony is going to need over the next few years. Hard times are coming and Baron Falkenstein, a Paladin of the Gods, has selected you to assist him. That surely has to count for something, doesn't it?'

Ahren didn't wait for an answer, but turned and walked back to his place without a glance back.

'And, what's he doing?' he whispered curiously to his master.

'He's going back to his soldiers, and he doesn't look as if he's afraid of his own shadow anymore. Whatever you said to him worked. If I didn't know better, I'd say you were beginning to use your head,' said Falk mockingly.

Satisfied, Ahren took a drink of the strong wine and ignored the sarcastic tone.

Then all hell broke loose.

Everywhere in the hall attendants were whipping out daggers and short swords, and they were stabbing at the palace guards. Aristocrats were screaming and rushing to the exit, only to stop abruptly as figures garbed in the robes of the Illuminated Path emerged from behind the wooden windbreak, blocking the entrance. Each of them had either a bow or a sword in their hand and they began butchering the unarmed nobles with their weapons.

Ahren was on his feet before he even realised it. Instinctively, he reached behind his back, but his grasping fingers found nothing but air. Falk had simply thrown himself backward in the chair and rolled behind the back of it as it went crashing to the ground. His hand grasped the broadsword at the same time, and he pulled it out of its scabbard, using the swinging motion to land lightly on his feet again. Ahren was thinking he should really consult his master about this manoeuvre later, but his master was screaming at him.

'Don't just stand there! Grab your bow. Jelninolan, Uldini, we need shields here!' he screamed.

Ahren threw himself sideways to his bow, which he had placed earlier that evening against the nearby pillar. He slipped behind it for cover, pulled out an arrow and carefully looked around the cold stone, while pressing himself against it.

The cultists had already struck down more than ten guests and several of the palace guard were lying on the ground too. The archers were shooting at random into the crowd of nobles while the other cultist followers were shielding the archers and preventing the guests from escaping.

Ahren suppressed the rage that was overwhelming him. The lesson of his last battle was still fresh in his mind and so he sought out the Void, while at the same time setting his arrow and aiming at an archer.

A green shimmering shield was forming over the heads of the screaming guests as the two Ancients together created a protection against the cultists' arrows.

The apprentice saw the attackers' arrows bouncing harmlessly off the sparkling magic spell, and he quickly decided to alter his plan. As fast as he could, he volleyed his arrows into the dagger and sword-carriers who were threatening the nobles, all the time taking care that the flight path was low and flat so they would pass under the magic shield. The cultists didn't spot him at first, and his many hours of practice now came into full effect. Each of Ahren's arrows met their target, and as the attackers were wearing no armour whatsoever, the effect was devastating. Within only a few heartbeats the eight arrows shot had produced seven victims, at which point the line of attackers collapsed. The nobles stormed forward in wild panic, pushing their way past the cultist archers, who couldn't use their weapons anymore on account of the mass of people.

Ahren had two arrows left in his quiver, and he quickly glanced around the room to see how he could use them most effectively. The palace guards had withdrawn to the king's table, and had created a closed line at the foot of the shallow step that led to the podium where the members of the high nobility were cowering. The remaining cultists were trying to break through the line so they could get to the barons and the king. Falk was standing in the middle of the king's guard and his sword was crashing down on the attackers, who were disguised as attendants. The cultists were unable to counter the heavily armoured Paladin, and under Falk's command the battle was soon over.

From outside more palace guards were forcing their way into the ballroom and attacking the remaining archers from behind. The battle was over as quickly as it had started and was replaced by an unnatural silence, punctuated by cries for help and the groans of the wounded. Jelninolan had worked a second shield around herself and the king, which she now dissolved. She and Uldini ran into the middle of the room and called the palace guards to bring over all the wounded.

While the pair began to heal the nobles in order to save as many lives as possible, a stunned Ahren walked over to Falk. The suddenness and violence of the attack had been a bolt from the blue and now the realisation was beginning to dawn on him that he alone was responsible for more than half a dozen deaths. The fact that it took him less than twenty breaths to do it made things somehow worse. He stared at the bow in his hand. Then his fingers lost their strength, and the wood clattered to the floor.

Falk planted himself in front of the apprentice and pointed down at the weapon.

'Pick it up again,' he ordered quietly.

Ahren didn't budge and Falk repeated the command.

'Pick it up again, Ahren.'

His master's voice was more urgent, more commanding this time, and his eyes bored into Ahren, but the apprentice couldn't bring himself to take the bow in his hand. The bow was now a symbol of death and Ahren was shaken to the core by the carnage he had wreaked with this weapon.

'You have saved many lives this evening and because of this you have had to take a few. You have to come to terms with that fact, because it's going to happen again. If you surrender now, if you give up, then we are all lost,' said Falk insistently to the traumatised apprentice.

Then he stood up to his full height and looked at Ahren with a commanding look.

'Pick. The. Bow. Up!' There was steely determination in every word, and with every word Ahren flinched.

Ahren stood paralysed for several heartbeats, unable to move a muscle, then his resistance to his master's willpower broke and his fingers circled the wood of the bow. He had almost expected its polished surface to feel different somehow, but the bow was as familiar as ever to the touch, and with a sigh of regret, he slung the bow over his shoulder. There was no point in blaming the weapon. He himself would simply have to find a way of dealing with situations like this, for they would be a part of the monumental task that awaited him. He decided he would follow this tactic in future: if he acted cleverly, then nobody would need to die. But then, if he failed, it would result in battle, and lives would be snuffed out.

He stared over at the cultists, who lay on the floor motionless, the shafts of his arrows projecting out of chests, necks and heads of the dead. The new cord, made from Selsena's hair, had given the arrows far more power, and Ahren saw that none of his victims had stood a chance. The arrows had driven in twice as deeply as expected, and even fluffed shots had inflicted severe injuries.

'I should have aimed at their shoulders,' he mumbled sadly, 'then they would still be alive,'

Falk shook his head and looked mercilessly down at the bodies.

'That's wishful thinking, young man. These were murderers and traitors. If you had simply wounded them, they would have been executed later anyway, and probably more innocent lives would have been lost today.'

Falk laid his armoured hands on Ahren's shoulders and fixed his steel-blue eyes on the apprentice.

'You find it hard to come to terms with the fact that you have killed these people? Then just imagine how you would feel if an innocent person had died because you had hesitated before doing the necessary. That's the day when you will really hate yourself, and I really want to spare you that.'

Ahren was confused, and his opposing emotions were waging a private war within him. Falk's words were true. But Ahren was not sure if he was afraid of killing, or of the responsibility that went with it. He needed time to think things over, and all he wanted to do now was bury his head in Culhen's fur…

He spun around.

'Culhen! Selsena! The stables!' he shouted, and started running towards the exit. If there had been an attack here, then why not in other places?!

Falk followed him and tried placating him, tilting his head at the same time.

'Selsena says they're fine. Two attackers targeted them, but the wolf finished one of them off and the old girl dealt with the other one.'

Ahren slowed down but continued walking, nevertheless. He wanted to confirm with his own eyes that they were unhurt, and anyway, he also urgently needed to be with Culhen.

They passed by the healing magicians, and Uldini, his robe and arms bloodied, looked up.

'Go with Ahren. This here was the Illuminated Path's last desperate throw of the dice. There could still be the odd remaining assassin in the palace or in the gardens.'

'And bring Khara to us,' called Jelninolan after them. 'She still doesn't really understand our language and I don't want any nervous palace guard drawing the wrong conclusions.'

A wave of fear came over Ahren when he heard the girl's name. But surely, she was safe within the palace. Or was she?

He exchanged a concerned look with Falk, and they began to run.

The palace gardens lay dark and still in front of them. In the distance they could see many guards patrolling the expansive palace grounds, their torches casting streaks of light through the darkness of the night.

They could also hear sounds of fighting in all directions, and so they drew their weapons and ran on. It wasn't long before they reached the stables, and Ahren was relieved when he spotted Culhen, standing guard at Selsena's smashed-up stall. A bloodied cultist was stretched out on the floor. Bite marks provided eloquent testament that the wolf had overpowered him. Another attacker was draped across the dividing wall, looking like a rag doll. The indentations in his chest suggested that Selsena had kicked him full force with her hind legs and tossed him to his resting place.

Culhen looked a terrible sight, the embodiment of the blood-soaked wolf, but Ahren didn't care. He embraced the animal lovingly, and his friend reacted by whining cheerfully and wagging his tail.

Selsena was radiating scorn and indignation. Emotions that Ahren was feeling like prickly thorns.

'What's wrong? Is she injured?' he asked, concerned.

Falk snorted. 'Only her pride. If there's one thing Selsena hates, it's being attacked in her stall. She thinks it's very inelegant and quite unmannerly. I never really understood that.'

216

The Elvin warhorse gave an offended whinny and deliberately turned her head away.

'Let's go and check on Khara. Selsena's going to be sulking for a while yet. The mercy of the THREE on any attacker who comes near her when she's in this mood.'

He shoved the remains of the stall door to the side so Selsena could leave the stall whenever she felt like it, but the Titejunanwa still refused to look at him.

Falk sighed and murmured, 'women!', then he left the stable and trotted towards the palace.

Ahren smiled quickly at Selsena, who took no notice of him, then followed his master after giving Culhen the order to stay by his side. The wolf let out a joyful bark and the three of them hurried through the palace gardens.

As they were running through the trees of the park, Ahren imagined for a moment that they were back in the Eastern Forest of Deepstone in the middle of one of Falk's training sessions. He felt a stab of homesickness, but he pushed it aside when he heard a cry of pain the distance. There had to be still cultists on the grounds. Falk nodded in affirmation for he too had heard the noise, and so they hurried on.

The entrance to the palace was full of guards, but they quickly made room to pass when they saw the fully-armed Falk rushing in. The Paladin wasn't going to waste time on explanations and just stormed through them and headed straight for Jelninolan's rooms. Ahren and Culhen stayed close behind Falk and slipped through before any of the guards could stop them.

The way through the palace corridors seemed longer now to the young man, and the more he thought about Khara, the more concerned he became that something might have happened to her. His fears increased when they turned into the corridor containing the guest quarters and saw four palace guards and three attackers lifeless on the floor. The smell of blood hung heavily in the air and the stillness in the palace created an air of danger and threat.

Ahren placed an arrow on his bow and stormed forwards. The door to the elf's rooms was slightly ajar. Falk opened it and now they could hear the sounds of fighting. Ahren was overcome by blind rage when he heard Khara's scream of pain, and he rushed after his master through the doorway, his bow stretched as far as his new cord would allow.

The living quarters resembled a battlefield. Three figures, dressed as palace attendants were lying on the floor – two men with deep sword wounds and a woman with her head twisted in a terrifying way. Khara was fighting off two other attackers with Windblade in her left hand while her bloodied right arm hung uselessly by her side. The cultists had pushed her into a corner of the room and hemmed her in. A third, not in attendant's livery, but dressed in the white robe of the Illuminated Path, stood a little to the side and watched the scene, a horrible, contorted, bloody dagger in his hand.

The attackers reacted immediately to the new danger. The man with the dagger, obviously their leader, pointed at the new arrivals, and the two cultists stormed forward. Ahren instinctively let fly an arrow, which hit the dagger carrier in his left shoulder, spinning him around and throwing him against the wall. Falk let his blade do an elaborate dance, which fended the wild attacks of the other two fanatics. Khara leaped forward with a scream and plunged Windblade into the back of one of Falk's opponents, at which point the Paladin sent the other to the floor courtesy of three perfectly executed thrusts.

The cultist leader, however, took advantage of this opportunity and picked something up that had been lying behind Khara in the corner of

218

the room, before throwing himself out of the window. Ahren prepared his last arrow and as he crossed the room, Khara screamed in rage.

'Tanentan!'

As if electrified, Ahren drew back the arrow and stared out into the night. The cultists had been after the Elvin artefact, and if this man escaped in the darkness, then Ahren's Naming would be condemned to failure.

Two paces below him he could barely make out a movement. Luckily, the cultist was still wearing his white robe, but shooting from the brightly lit room of the palace into the darkness of the garden was hard enough as it was. Ahren could just make out the outlines of his target as it moved away while he set himself up at the open window. Any moment and the enemy would be swallowed up by the night.

Ahren breathed in deeply, sought out the Void and imagined where the man would be in following heartbeat. Then he let the arrow fly and was rewarded with a strangled cry.

As Ahren dropped his bow, Culhen was already leaping powerfully out through the window and then he ran growling to the place where Ahren imagined the fallen attacker to be lying. The apprentice called out a warning, but the wolf had already disappeared, and a few moments later all that could be heard were the sounds of a scuffle and a wet gurgling noise.

Ahren quickly clambered out while Falk supported the injured Khara. The apprentice wanted to rush to Culhen's aid, but the wolf was already trotting back, visible in the lights of the palace. His fur was covered in fresh blood, but he held Tanentan in his mouth, just as when he had secured the Artefact in the Weeping Valley.

'This is becoming a habit, my friend,' said Ahren. 'If it goes on like this, the bards will soon be singing your praises as the wolf with the lute.'

He carefully took the instrument from Culhen's mouth, and the wolf looked up at him proudly. Then he raised his head towards the night sky and gave a triumphant howl.

'I don't think your vain friend gives a hoot for the nickname. Just as long as the bards call out his name and praise his deeds.'

Ahren joined in as the old Paladin laughed in relief, and Culhen threw them a self-confident look with his proud wolf eyes, before walking in a stately manner away from them and in the direction of one of the palace ponds, where he had every intention of having a luxurious bath.

Chapter 12

54 days to the winter solstice

The seagulls circled the harbour above the hurly-burly of port activity. Wherever you looked, you saw wide-bellied cargo vessels being loaded or unloaded. Heavily laden carts hurtled over the cobble-stoned streets, sailors joked and cursed in half a dozen different languages, and traders haggled with them over shiploads of goods.

Ahren was completely exhausted, and all these sights and sounds overwhelmed him. It took all his concentration to examine the ship which would be their home for the following two weeks.

The Queen of the Waves was the flagship of the Knight Marshes' royal fleet and with her narrow hull and three tall masts she looked like a hunting animal among the heavy cargo ships, as she pulled impatiently at her ropes, eager to slide swiftly off on her adventures.

The sailors on board were similarly distinguishable from their fellow sailors in the harbour. They all wore impeccably clean and tailored uniforms. They too were laughing and joking, but nobody was dawdling or wasting time. Each member of the crew had an air of focussed discipline, and the apprentice, who was about to go to sea for the first time in his life, found their attitude very reassuring.

'If you've stared at everything enough, we wouldn't mind going on board,' mocked Uldini behind him, and Ahren hurried up the gang plank, which he had been blocking.

The wood moved under his feet to the rhythm of the waves, and for the first time Ahren was fully aware of the awe he felt for the vastness and power of the sea, a feeling that had been with him since he had first set eyes on it. He felt tiny when compared to this mass of water with all its inner strength. None of his training would be of any help if this collection of planks, nails and ropes succumbed to the power of the waves, and they were delivered helplessly to the ocean's dreadful deeps.

His face, as he looked around, spoke volumes, for behind him he heard Khara say something in her mother tongue, and then he heard Jelninolan laughing with her. By now, Ahren recognised the tone of voice that they used whenever they said something unflattering about the men in the group. The elf had really taken her new servant into her heart, and since Khara's fierce defence of Tanentan the previous night, their relationship seemed more like one of close friends, rather than mistress and servant.

Ahren stopped himself from asking for a translation of Khara's comments, as he suspected he wouldn't like to hear what it meant. He boarded the ship and stepped quickly to the left to hold onto the railing. The wood under his fingers was reassuring, and to distract himself he studied his travelling companions as they climbed on board.

They all looked as worn out as he felt. Uldini and Jelninolan had been healing the wounded until deep into the night, and the overdose of healing magic had made them listless and melancholy. Ahren had known that destructive magic could make its transmitters aggressive, even driving them into a frenzy, but he was surprised that healing magic could also affect them negatively.

Falk had only shrugged his shoulders and said, 'Healing magic joins what has been separated, takes the patient's pain away. It's alleviated by the healer, who absorbs the agony and then disperses it. Feeling the wounds of others for hours on end, and strengthening them in the process, has a powerful effect on the magician. When you get down to it, it's very

222

simple: there is hardly anything in this world that is healthy if you have too much of it. This is true for worldly things and also for magic.'

Khara stayed close to Jelninolan's side, holding Windblade, something she had been doing since the elf had healed her. She still didn't quite understand the events of the previous night, and since then she had looked daggers at every liveried attendant that they passed by. She had almost attacked a merchant on the way to the harbour because he had been wearing a white robe, but the elf managed to stop her in the nick of time.

Once everybody had finally been healed, they sat with the king until the early hours of the morning. They had talked about the events of the evening and considered the consequences of the attack. After the first shock, the king had been bizarrely overjoyed by the results of the attempted assassination.

'You were able to save the lives of all the nobles – bar two – and I hope that the Illuminated Path made the mistake of gathering its most fanatical supporters for this attack in the capital. We'll have to comb the countryside to track down the last few fanatics, but I am quite confident, because I can hardly imagine that there is anybody left who can really damage us or who even wants to. The cult has lost its support. Thanks to Jelninolan's healing arts, half of the nobility of Knights Marshes are still alive, and are bound to the elves in gratitude. It may sound cynical and cold-hearted, but yesterday was a wake-up call for the Knights Marshes and I will do everything in my power over the next two winters to unite all the barons, even the most stubborn, under my banner.'

Uldini agreed. He seemed to be just as happy as the king, if exhausted by the excess of magic.

'The followers of the Illuminated Path seemed to get their orders purely and simply from Brother Wultom. Once he was unmasked, they were leaderless and they made one last attempt to plunge the Knight Marshes into chaos,' said the wizard. 'Although I have to concede that the attempt to steal Tanentan was a stroke of genius. I have the uneasy feeling that there might be one mastermind who used the onslaught of the cultists as a distraction, so that Ahren's Naming could be prevented by the theft of the lute. It sounds suspiciously like a Doppelganger. As soon as Elgin has recovered, I'll have him look into it.'

King Blueground had been deeply grateful for all their help, but surprised that they still wanted to leave immediately in spite of the previous night's exertions.

'Our time is slowly running out,' Uldini had submitted, 'even if it was good that we were here and able to thwart the Adversary's plans. You know what's at stake if the Naming takes place too late. I think we've done well with our few days' work. An old fox like yourself should have no problem finishing off the job. Plus, you have Elgin at your side again, who can help you with his advice.'

So it was, they had said their goodbyes at the crack of dawn and headed for the harbour where The Queen of the Waves, seaworthy and laden with provisions, awaited her passengers.

Ahren held on tightly to the railing as the ship was unmoored and the crew set sail in the gentle harbour waves. The wind caught the sails, and the enormous rectangles veered and fluttered as the wind pushed the ship out of the harbour.

The wide ocean opened up before the awed apprentice as they left the horse-shoe shaped harbour, and the seemingly endless vast of water took the young man's breath away. As a Forest Guardian, he was accustomed to long distances. He had covered leagues and leagues of forest in the past with his master. But the sight of the broad expanse of sea made Ahren

224

realise how enormous the world really was, and how insignificant he was in comparison.

Uldini joined him and looked thoughtfully at the surface of the water.

'Beautiful, isn't it? I've gone to sea many a time, but the view always takes my breath away.'

There was a deep longing and warmth in the ancient wizard's voice and his words shook Ahren out of his paralysis. He loosened his grip on the railing and looked at the childish figure with interest. Uldini grinned wickedly.

'Surprised? I like to imagine that I would have become a sailor if magic hadn't flowed through my veins.' Uldini sighed. 'But that's only a romantic notion on my part. If I hadn't become a wizard, I would have led a short, hard life as a slave and would in all probability have suffered a painful death.' He sighed again and then smiled faintly. 'If you look it like that, I did alright, don't you think?'

Before Ahren could answer, the little figure floated away and disappeared into his cabin. The apprentice stared after him, dumbfounded, and jumped when he heard a voice behind him.

'Ignore that old curmudgeon,' said Falk in a reassuring voice. He had come up behind the apprentice unawares. 'He always gets a little maudlin when we're at sea, and the effects of all that healing make his feelings of melancholy even stronger. Give him a few days and he'll be back to his old, complaining, cynical self.'

Ahren turned around to the old man and noticed that at least three sailors were within hearing distance or were just hurrying past. Freedom of moment was significantly curtailed on a ship and this was something he wasn't used to. It would take him a while before he internalised the knowledge that behind every corner there would be two or three people working away, and therefore able to listen in on conversations.

He heard a strange noise above him, and when he looked up, he saw a sailor who was climbing up the ship's rigging with effortless ease. Ahren instinctively gasped and felt fascinated and imprisoned by the ship's boundaries.

His master had spotted his worried look and he gestured to Ahren to follow him.

'I too am no friend of these narrow confines. We are Forest Guardians but there are no trees to be seen far and wide, and we can't go running either.' Falk closed his eyes. 'And anyway, I miss Selsena,' he added quietly.

The Titejunanwa had not come on board but would be waiting for them in Kelkor. Ahren understood only too well that a ship was no place for Selsena, and she would be like a fish out of water in the caves of the Silver Cliff. And so Falk had said goodbye to her with a heavy heart and they had agreed on a meeting place inland from the Silver Cliff. The Elvin warhorse would doubtless make much quicker progress without their company and would probably be waiting for them once they had helped the dwarf on his Lonely Watch.

Now that King's Island was behind them, Ahren could concentrate fully on the next part of their journey.

'Master, you told us that time that you knew the dwarf we are going to help from before. How exactly did you get to know him?' he asked curiously.

Falk rubbed his beard and looked out onto the water as he led his apprentice onto the quarterdeck. It was quieter there and you could see what was around you more easily, which enabled the young man to relax a little.

'One of my favourite places on board ship,' explained Falk. Then he returned to Ahren's question. 'Telling the story of a dwarf is something very personal to the little folk, and without his permission I can only tell you this: in my wild days we were both in the same troop of mercenaries for a while, and we saved each other's lives a few times. In those days he was a young buck and still had his child name, and his beard didn't even reach his voice box.' Falk chuckled as he remembered.

'What's a child name?' asked Ahren bewildered.

'If you're a dwarf, you have to earn your name. With every Lonely Watch you gain a syllable for it, with more difficult Lonely Watches you can gain two or even three at once. The dwarf is called by his child name until he has his first Watch behind him. They're usually nicknames like "Little Pebble", "Rock Crumb" or "Sliver Stone." So, it's understandable that every young dwarf wants to get rid of it as quickly as possible. Many dwarves pick a Life Name as soon as possible. In other words, they plan what they are going to be called later and then work tirelessly towards their goal. It takes most dwarves over two hundred years to gather together their Life Name. And only then are they permitted to get married, and not even all of them. The length of their names determines the families they can marry into. They are an incredibly stubborn bunch, and that's reflected in all their traditions and customs,' he said approvingly.

'You seem to like them', said Ahren in surprise. What he'd heard up to this point sounded cold, severe and distant, and he was surprised that his master liked such a harsh culture. Even in his worst days, Falk's behaviour had never been as hard as the dwarves' way of life was, if he believed his master's description.

Falk simply shrugged his shoulders.

'They just aren't like us. Just as the elves aren't like us. You have to understand their strengths, weaknesses, and their peculiarities in order to value their culture. HE, WHO IS gave them an over-abundance of essence, so they're quite inflexible when it comes to form and feeling. There's an old proverb: "A human becomes what he is, an elf feels what he is, but a dwarf just is." The little folk have many qualities which makes dealing with them difficult. They're loud, blinkered, stubborn and often incapable of compromise. Even hard facts just bounce off their thick skulls, and they are very slow to pardon someone who offends them. I know of no case where a dwarf has ever changed sides or left his post. Treachery and falseness are alien to them, and their hospitality towards strangers is legendary. And while we are on the subject: if you have won over a dwarf as a friend, then this bond will last a lifetime. Their loyalty is limitless, as is their fury if you go behind their backs. If I weren't attached to Selsena, I probably would have sought my peace among the dwarves.'

Falk finished his monologue, and Ahren spent a little time digesting what he had just heard. He was now more curious about these 'complicated' folk, and he noticed that he was now really looking forward to their arrival at the Silver Cliff. The apprentice tried unsuccessfully to suppress a yawn, but his lack of sleep had caught up with him. Before retiring to his cabin though, he wanted to learn one more thing from his master.

'What kind of an exclamation did you utter in the hall yesterday? You know, the one you'd used against the Blood Wolf. 'His voice was shaking with curiosity, and he looked eagerly at the old man.

Falk was silent for a while, and Ahren feared that he would get no answer at all. Finally, after a long moment, the Forest Guardian spoke.

'That was the war cry of the Paladins. It means something like, 'Gods, see your Paladins!' We always shouted that before setting ourselves difficult tasks. Many of us had hoped that it would arouse the attention of the sleeping THREE, so their blessing would stir us on to victory.

228

Personally, I think the cry just gives us courage and reminds us of our task, and in the meantime, it has been uttered so often, in so many important battles that it has developed a life of its own. Dark Ones react aggressively to it, for they hear it is a challenge. And in the Knight Marshes and other kingdoms of the free peoples it has huge symbolic power, as you saw yesterday.'

Ahren nodded, grateful for the explanation, and suppressed another yawn.

'That's enough for now. Your head is tired, and if I try filling it with more things, you will forget it all again anyway. Go and have a rest, and this afternoon we'll see what happens,' ordered Falk good-naturedly.

Ahren couldn't and wouldn't contradict him. He went into one of the small, wooden cabins that had been pointed out to him by one of the sailors. Then he hung his bundle on a hook in the wall. A strong hammock dominated the small three-by-three paced room which was lit by a tiny light that swung squeakily from side to side in the middle of the ceiling. There was a small dresser with a metal washbowl, fixed to the wall with nails. The rest of the cabin was bare. Ahren took no notice of anything as he rolled himself together on the hammock and promptly fell asleep.

Had he known what would be awaiting him when he woke up, Ahren would have stayed sleeping for as long as possible. The tired apprentice stumbled his way on deck, having been driven out of his hammock by the call of nature. He had just relieved himself over the railings when he noticed Falk and Jelninolan on the quarterdeck, seemingly in conversation with Khara. Full of curiosity, he strolled over to them, rubbing the sleep out of his eyes.

'Oh, you're awake. Good. The three of us have just been discussing your further training,' said Falk merrily. There was a mischievous gleam in his eye and Ahren suddenly had a bad feeling in his stomach.

'You…three? What further training? There's no forest around here,' he said, confused, and realised immediately that Falk had been waiting for such a response.

The old Forest Guardian rubbed his hands together and looked firmly into Ahren's eyes.

'Good, we're agreed on that. Seeing as I can't teach you anything in the forest, and that running longer lengths is somewhat difficult on deck, we've been thinking about what other things we can work on. Khara is going to take over your training in sword fighting, and Jelninolan will teach both of you in the areas of balance, footwork and equilibrium. The ship is perfect for this. I'll take over the aspects of strength and endurance. I've a few ideas concerning the ropes and rigging on the ship.'

Ahren swallowed hard and considered raising an objection. But the wary look on Falk's face suggested that might not be the best idea. He gave an acquiescent nod, which sealed his fate for the next few days.

Ahren cursed silently to himself as he punched the railing repeatedly with both fists. He had expected that being trained by Khara in swordplay would be difficult, and the first few lessons had already ended in loud arguments. It wasn't just the fact that because of her limited command of the language she roared out all her commands in a staccato voice, but her face also betrayed her deep contempt for his abilities. It took Ahren all his self-control not to lose his temper.

But what really took the biscuit was her habit of giving him a slap on the face any time he made a mistake. His cheeks were burning in no time at all, and finally he had exploded. He had shouted at her long and loud and he certainly hadn't minced his words. When it came to insults, his vocabulary had blossomed thanks to Uldini's propensity to curse, and Ahren was certainly imaginative when it came to confronting Khara. Unfortunately, most of what he said was like water off a duck's back. Jelninolan, understandably enough, had not introduced bad language during her language lessons with Khara. The girl had just stood there, her face impassive and without showing any reaction to his tirade, until she recognised some unmistakable words that the furious apprentice was spitting out. At which point her face had hardened and she put her sword away.

'Lesson over,' was all she said. Then she disappeared into Jelninolan's cabin, leaving a speechless Ahren, full of rage that he could no longer give vent to.

Now he was punching away at the railing in hopeless anger, shouting himself hoarse and swearing that he would never again go rushing to the aid of a strange girl in a darkened alleyway.

'What an interesting choice of words,' he heard a voice say coolly behind him.

Ahren spun around and saw Jelninolan's face, which had disappointment written all over it.

'Is there any particular reason why the chosen aspirant for the title of Thirteenth Paladin has turned into a combination of a three-year-old and a drunken brawler?' she asked sarcastically.

Ahren's face went as red as a beetroot with embarrassment. The elf's aura was always very intense, but when the priestess scolded someone, you felt as if a thousand ants were crawling around under your skin.

'Khara doesn't explain anything and she hits me when I don't do what she expects,' blurted out the young man. 'How am I supposed to learn anything if she doesn't speak to me?'

He folded his arms and tried hard not to appear belligerent. After all, his arguments were pretty solid.

The elf priestess, however, seemed unimpressed. She looked at Ahren critically and tapped a finger on her thigh with exasperation.

'Khara has just come to me and said that she is turning you down as a student. And that, after not even one full morning. She says you're inattentive, answer back and have no discipline.'

Jelninolan threw her arms up in frustration and then continued.

'The girl has had years of training with Windblade, and that was from a real Master of Blades. Her training methods may well be unusual but remember where and how Khara grew up. What you would call a hit is for her a polite request to pay attention. You saw her scars. Her definition of punishment and pain is in a completely different dimension to yours.

Ahren tried hard to stay calm and to rationally think over what the priestess had said but as soon as he imagined the look of contempt on the girl's face, he became furious again. However, one look at Jelninolan's narrow eyes nipped any attempt at protest in the bud.

'I will have a word with her so that she continues training you and I will also suggest that she not hit you if possible, and you will behave towards her in an unbiased, polite and respectful way. If I come to the conclusion that you are being deliberately difficult because you don't want to be taught by a girl, then I will introduce some Elvin principles of apprentice discipline that not even Falk knows about.'

The elf's voice was now icy cold and Ahren concluded with a shiver that a few slaps on the face weren't the end of the world. He would just have to try harder and make as few mistakes as possible so Khara would have no reason to assault him.

The rest of the training ran remarkably painlessly. Ahren watched Khara's movements very carefully and realised that, unlike Falk, she instructed more by demonstrating than by words. By the time the midday sun was burning down on him, he was sweating alright, but had only received three slaps across the face, and they hadn't even been too hard.

Finally, she put Windblade away, and Ahren did the same. He went to the railing and felt the air blow through his hair for a moment before Jelninolan came onto the quarterdeck. She began practising the most varied movements with the two young people, cleverly incorporating the ship's pitching and rolling into the exercises, which really tested her students. By the afternoon Ahren had lost any feeling in large parts of his body, but then Falk came along whistling, and began shunting him around the ship and up and down the rigging in a most creative manner. And, although Khara hadn't been ordered to, she performed all the Forest Guardian's exercises too, in spite of the fact that she was surely as exhausted as Ahren. She watched every one of Ahren's movements carefully and imitated them quickly and confidently, and although she lacked experience in the precise implementation of climbing techniques, she learned remarkably quickly.

Ahren found himself unconsciously performing some of his movements just a little more slowly or with a little more exaggeration so that she had time to study them, and so, without even noticing it, he slipped into the role of a teacher. Falk allowed him to do this, and over the next few days an energy-sapping training regime was developed for Ahren and Khara. Having three trainers almost brought Ahren to his knees, and he was thankful that he had had the presence of mind to bring a full supply of healing herbs with him. Three days' training took their toll on Khara too, and Ahren overcame any reservations he might have had, and shared his energizing herbal soup with her.

He learned from her, and she learned from him, and even if they hardly spoke to each other, a kind of grudging respect for the other's abilities was developing between them.

Chapter 13

44 days to the winter solstice

Their voyage was slowly coming to an end. The weather had been good up to this point, the winds had been favourable, and although the lookout had twice spotted pirate ships, these had turned tail quickly. The Queen of the Waves was considerably bigger and clearly a warship, so that any pirate worth his salt would keep a wide berth from her.

One of the sailors had answered Ahren's questions regarding pirates by saying that there weren't many on the route to the Silver Cliff. They tended to stay further south, where, however, right old battles went on among them, over who should wreak havoc on which routes. Apparently, many merchants paid a considerable amount of money to the leaders of the big pirate fleets so that their ships would have safe passage. Ahren was amazed to learn that traders paid buccaneers, who in turn protected them from other marauding pirates by providing them with escort. And this courtesy cost a pretty penny.

Ahren's training was hard and demanding but it filled out his days, and all in all, Ahren was grateful for it. He was still amazed by the vastness of the ocean, and even though the captain travelled within sight of the coast, the apprentice was still glad he didn't have time to brood. He had come to the conclusion that it was better to help Khara learn the Northern language rather than wait for her to think of the suitable word in the middle of sword training, or for a slap in the face because he hadn't understood her staccato commands and then made mistakes. He was busy every waking moment now, learning Windblade techniques, climbing up and down the rigging, or teaching Khara phrases such as 'hold the blade higher' or 'please don't slap my face.'

They had been travelling off the coast of Kelkor for two days now, and the landscape was beginning to change markedly. Where before he could see the rolling hills and large fields of Knight Marshes, with little fishing villages and the silhouettes of castles barely visible in the distance, now he   was looking at coastal cliffs, craggy mountainsides and groups of fishermen's huts squeezed together. Sometimes Ahren could see the shadows of enormous shapes in the sky dancing among the clouds, and once he saw a giant, herding a flock of sheep. He was not surprised that Kelkor was called the untamed country, and he broke into a sweat every time he remembered that they would have to travel through it.

He was standing at the railing now looking out at the oncoming dusk. Large clouds were gathering on the horizon, and Ahren hoped that, despite the worried looks on the sailors, the bad weather would pass them by.

Suddenly the young man felt an urgent need to be alone. He climbed up the rigging, something he could now do in his sleep, and before he knew it, he had reached the crow's nest, which he happily climbed into. It was true that the pitching and rolling of the ship could be felt more dramatically up here but he was happy to have nobody around him for the moment. He looked again at the storm clouds and stared spellbound at them. The flashes of lightning and the swirling movements of the massive clouds were strangely hypnotic and soothing. Ahren thought about all the lives he had taken already, and all the effort he had endured, and he began to question the point of what he was trying to achieve. What if HE, WHO FORCES was just misunderstood? Perhaps he could talk to HIM and they could come to a peaceful solution? He stood up at the thought and leaned forward in the crow's nest while he stared at the storm. Images appeared in his head, and he saw himself smiling and walking towards the Pall Pillar, and inside himself he felt a warm, welcoming presence. He slowly walked towards it in his mind's eye. The thought of preventing all that bloodshed and looming conflict was truly seductive.

Without realising it, his feet had left the safety of the crow's nest and the young man was balancing and walking along the wooden beam of the mainsail, towards the Pall Pillar and away from the mainmast, further and further out over the foaming ocean waves.

His eyes were fixed on the seething mass of storm clouds in front of him, but inside he was only looking at the vision of himself approaching the Pall Pillar. Only a few more steps and peace would be at hand. A ceasefire, which would bring eternal peace to all of Jorath, freed from the threat of a devastating war…

Suddenly, his left foot was standing on air. He had reached the end of the beam and there was a piercing pain in his head as something attempted to seize hold of his thoughts and to turn them, so that they were only a poor imitation of his hopes and dreams. Ahren gasped in pain and fought with all his might against this mysterious force that was raging in his mind like an invisible clenched fist. Fully concentrating on the battle within himself, he lost his balance, and as the ship pitched to one side, he plunged silently into the dark water below.

The current caught him and tossed him about wildly, his clothes filled with water and he was pulled downward into the depths. Ahren knew he had to move, to force himself up to the surface, but pushing away the intruder who had entered his innermost being was costing him all his energy and he sank like a stone.

Then suddenly there was a hand in the surge, pulling him roughly by the hair, and slowly but surely raising him to the surface. The pain helped him shake off the trance he had been in, and the attack on his mind subsided. Instead he felt the ice-cold water and the pull of the current while his lungs screamed in vain for air. Disorientated, he instinctively breathed in and swallowed sea water. He began coughing, and more seawater entered his lungs while his field of vision grew smaller. He felt nothing but weakness as his head broke through the surface of the water and he heard Falk's voice in the distance.

'Good work, Khara. Wait, I'll help you.'

Strong hands wrapped around his chest, and the painful tugging of his hair was gone. The apprentice struggled to open his eyes, but he couldn't. His chest felt strangely numb, and he heard Falk calling anxiously, 'he's not breathing, Uldini, bring him on deck!'

'Bring him over the surface of the water. Water is too unstable and constantly moving. No magic can work precisely enough in those conditions,' shouted Uldini forcefully.

The last thing he heard was Falk complaining about useless magicians. He felt his body being exposed to the cold wind. Then everything went black and he lost consciousness.

The first thing Ahren was aware of when he woke up coughing was a sharp pain in his chest. He was lying under a blanket in the captain's cabin and Jelninolan was bending over him and placing both her hands on his chest. From wherever she touched him, a hot fire travelled through his body and burned the pain away. Within a few heartbeats Ahren had warmed up and was in a sweat, but otherwise he felt well.

His memories were strangely muddled, but something important must have happened. All his companions were around him, and Uldini had constructed a magic shield around them. It was burning a dangerous red, and cast the cabin in a strange light. Khara was sitting soaking wet on a stool, and she was shivering under a blanket. Falk too was wet, and was looking at him anxiously.

'He's waking up,' grunted his master in a dull voice, before giving a sigh of relief.

Uldini's shield flickered and went out, while his crystal ball hovered in the air before going over to Ahren and briefly grazing his forehead.

'What happened?' asked Ahren, confused. He tried to sit up but Jelninolan increased the pressure on him so that he lay rooted to the spot.

'If you stand up now, I'll have to start from the beginning again, so stay still,' she murmured, her face the picture of concentration.

Falk turned to Uldini. 'How does it look?'

The crystal ball released itself from Ahren's forehead and floated back to the Arch Wizard.

'Everything is in order. My charm has re-established itself and I've strengthened it in the process. HE won't break through again for the moment.'

Jelninolan took her hands away from Ahren's chest, leaving behind a comfortable warmth that radiated through his whole body.

'I'm finished with him,' said the elf curtly and went over to Khara to carry out the same process. Steam rose up from her attendant's blanket and clothing, and the girl thanked the priestess in a low whisper.

Ahren sat up and looked tensely around the room.

'What happened?' he asked again, frowning.

Falk wanted to answer but Uldini interjected.

'I'm an old fool, that's what happened. I told you before that I'd protected you from the influence of HIM, WHO FORCES until your Naming makes you immune to HIS Thought Manipulation, didn't I?'

The Arch Wizard paused briefly and Ahren nodded weakly.

'Now, I never realised that HE could not only absorb your blessing, but that through that, HE had a direct connection to your spirit, for so long as you have not been named. HE has used all the strength that HE had sucked out of you over the past few weeks to circumvent my protective magic. The storm that you saw outside was a manifestation of HIS will. HE almost succeeded in drowning you.'

The memories were returning in a blur. Snatches of images that awakened in him more of a feeling than a reliving of what had happened.

'HE wanted me to go to the Pall Pillar so that we could talk. HE had promised that there would be no war.'

Falk snorted. 'You can bet your life on that. HE is good at turning your own wishes against yourself. What happened then?'

'HE tried to control my thoughts and I defended myself, but because of the vision, I had walked too far out on the beam and I fell off,' said Ahren with horror in his voice. The memory of the alien will, that had wrapped itself so firmly around his own, was too hard to bear and made him feel sick.

Falk laid a comforting hand on his back.

'You're safe now. Uldini has strengthened the protection that lay on you. That should last for quite a time.'

His master looked over at Khara and continued.

'Luckily, she saw you falling in, shouted out a warning and dived straight in after you. One of the sailors alerted us and by the time I got to you in the water, she had already pulled you up to the surface. Uldini floated you on board and Jelninolan persuaded your lungs to get back to work.'

Ahren became dizzy again and looked in a daze at his companions.

'Thank you,' was all he could stutter. He had barely escaped death once again, and although it wasn't his fault this time, he wouldn't be here now if it weren't for the others. Culhen sensed how he was feeling and jumped without warning onto his bed and started licking the young man's face.

Khara looked at him impassively, and Jelninolan continued performing her magic. Finally, the girl said, 'Ahren bad student. Many lessons needed. He dead, waste my work.'

The others laughed and the apprentice bit his tongue to stop himself giving back a cheeky answer.

Uldini stood up and said in an exaggeratedly celebratory voice, 'If Khara is making jokes about Ahren too, she is officially one of us!'

The others laughed again and the young man hid his tired face in the wolf's fur. He knew they were only laughing out of relief that he had been saved, but he really wished they could find another way of expressing their feelings.

Happily, the night was uneventful. Ahren was woken up a few times as the sea was rough, and his companions changed watch from time, each one ensuring that he wouldn't be taking another enforced bath. But when the dawn broke, he felt as good as new.

He stepped on board and found the others huddled together at the starboard railing. The captain was there too, a thickset man with powerful forearms and short black hair streaked with grey. His navy-blue uniform always looked immaculate although Ahren had often seen him working alongside his men. As someone who managed to dirty his leather armour even when collecting water, the apprentice was curious as to how the captain managed this trick. However, when he saw the concerned looks on the group, he thought he might leave that question for another occasion.

The storm of the day before could still be seen on the horizon. It had gathered itself together into one large cloud, and in its middle was an inferno of lightning flashes which gave its whole appearance a dark purple aura.

'It's following us and slowly coming closer. We knew already that this was no ordinary storm, but it seems to have another function quite apart from yesterday's imparting of a thought-vortex,' said Uldini darkly.

'Can you not ward it off?' asked Ahren cautiously.

The ancient Arch Wizard shook his head.

'That there is highly concentrated magic, tied into a natural phenomenon. The storm arose naturally, it has just been hijacked. I wouldn't know where to begin. If I try to dissolve it and I fail, then my magic will only strengthen it.'

He turned to the captain.

'You may not like it, but we really have no other option. Jelninolan and I will protect the ship as much as we can, and we'll sit out the storm to the bitter end. If we have an opportunity to break out of it beforehand, I will let you know.'

The captain saluted without saying a word and went off to give his first mate orders, which the latter then bellowed out to the remainder of the crew.

'I'm not normally that keen on the military but I have to say one thing for them: they don't waste time on idle chatter when it comes to a crisis,' he said contentedly.

'I know you like it when we blindly accept your advice, but do we really not have any other options?' asked Falk caustically and with a nervous glance over at the seething mass of cloud.

Uldini shook his head morosely.

'I can't think of anything, and Jelninolan is at a loss. We could try to influence its course just a little, but the Adversary's magic is like a crossbow, and the storm is its missile. He gathers it together, aims it at us and shoots. At the moment it's some distance away but when it gets to us, then there will be no magic that we can charm it with. Our shields will hold off the worst of it. I hope so, anyway,' said the Arch Wizard morosely.

'You hope so?!' pressed Ahren in a shocked voice. 'What is that supposed to mean?'

'Let me just put it like this,' said the little figure. 'When it starts, there should be nobody below deck who can't breathe under water, and everybody on deck had better tie themselves tightly to something.'

Ahren stared at the conjurer, hoping to see a sign that Uldini had been pulling his leg. But his dark face remained impassive, and Ahren understood that his last words had been deadly serious.

'I need to make sure Culhen is safe somehow,' he blurted out fearfully, and called the wolf over to him. The animal approached with his tail wagging, and Ahren stroked him absentmindedly as he looked around. Culhen's head was up to the young man's hip now. The one-time blood wolf wouldn't know how to hold on to something for the duration of the storm. Fixing his weight somewhere on deck was practically impossible. Ahren spent some time searching the ship for a suitable place until the captain interrupted him.

'Stop running around the ship like a headless chicken and getting in the way of the crew. You can leave your animal in my cabin during the storm. It's on deck, and it'll be safe enough for him when the portholes open. It would be dangerous for a human in there, but your dog is large and strong and should be able to cope with a little water.'

Ahren agreed gratefully and gave Culhen a quick hug. The wolf was beginning to get nervous himself too as he sensed the impending storm.

Then there was the sound of thunder in the distance, which rolled over the water and broke over the ship like an explosion of the gods. Every head turned towards the horizon and the apprentice saw how the electrical storm front was suddenly racing towards them.

'The spell has spoken. Jelninolan, you go aft and I'll go 'fore. The mainmast will be our point of contact where we can smelt our protective shields together. That should cover the whole ship,' shouted Uldini over the sounds of the high winds.

The elf nodded and ran back to the quarterdeck where Khara was already waiting with a rope. She quickly bound the elf and herself to the railing. Ahren looked around and saw how Falk was doing the same for himself and Uldini. The crew performed their last few actions with the sails and ropes before following the others' examples. Ahren brought Culhen into the captain's cabin before finally tying himself to the mainmast in the middle of the ship, from where he would have a good view over what would happen. And if he were honest with himself, he wanted to position himself as far as possibly away from the railings. He tied two Elfish knots, just as his master had drummed into him, and he was now securely attached to the thick timber which held the mainsail.

The sun was swallowed up by the approaching seething wall of wind and rain, and the captain called out: 'Everyone, watch out for your neighbour! If you hear something crashing above you, get yourselves to safety! Put your faith in two wizards and in the gods! May we see each other again on the other side of the storm!'

The crew let out a roar and Jelninolan and Uldini saw this as a sign that their magic was working. A shimmering net of blazing lines was arcing in a low semi-circle over the ship, with bowsprit and rudder marking either end, and the crow's nest as its apex, so that the sails were almost touching the magic dome that enclosed them. Ahren could not feel any difference as the wind tore at his clothing with increasing force, but he had no other option other than to believe, along with the others, in the age-old wisdom of the two magicians.

And then the storm was on top of them. A wall of wind and water struck the ship with such force that it seemed as if the whole world had conspired against every living creature on board. Freezing rain stung Ahren's eyes and he hid his face in the crook of his arm while he frantically held on to the taut rope, which prevented him from being washed overboard. Hardly had Ahren recovered from the first shock, when the first enormous wave was on top of them, released by the seething mass of the ocean. The ship was tossed around like a cork, and danced up and down in a tempestuous chaos of surging water, as thunderbolts flashed down from the heavens.

Ahren screamed the fear out of his body and it bothered him not a whit if anyone could hear. Now the apprentice saw how the magic was working, that the ship was being protected, and this gave him courage. None of the lightning bolts that were flashing around them hit the ship directly, and although wave after wave crashed over them, the deck for the most part was spared the deluge, as if the water was being diverted at the last moment.

Ahren threw a worried look over his shoulder at the captain's cabin, but absurdly enough, Culhen seemed to be enjoying himself thoroughly. The wolf's tongue was hanging out of his mouth and he splashed around in the water that ran out through the portholes, then he sought refuge on the captain's hammock when the next flood of water surged in through the portholes, and finally he jumped back into the water when the levels dropped again. In spite of the dramatic situation Ahren had to smile. Then a gigantic wave made it past the protective magic.

It slammed him full force against the mast and he felt a crunching pain in his chest. Ahren took an agonising intake of breath and the dull pain indicated a painful bruising. He turned to face the next wall of water, better prepared this time, even if the next impact sent fiery darts through his damaged ribs.

He had just forced himself to control his breathing when he heard a terrified scream behind him. He turned his head and saw that Jelninolan, torn loose by the water, had been washed over the high body of the quarterdeck. Her rope must have loosened and now she was clawing at the railing, while Khara was furiously trying to tie another knot in the wet, slippery rope. Another wave was approaching and Ahren drew his knife out of his belt and got himself ready. He hoped that the elf would survive this wave, for as soon as the wave passed, he would cut himself loose. If he were quick, he would be with the two women before the next mountain of water rolled over the ship. With full concentration he watched the surge of black that seemed to want to swallow him up, and he steeled himself for the fearful heartbeats when the ocean would steal away his breath. As he waited in a state of tension, the wave seemed to get bigger and wider until his whole world seemed a seething mass of water. Behind him he heard frantic shouting, but he kept his eyes fixed on the wall of water. He wasn't going to miss the right moment.

The wave smashed into him like a sledgehammer and pressed the breath out of his lungs as it tried to break his connection to the mast. Ahren felt after a few heartbeats the tug of the wave slowly decreasing and so he cut the rope that had been preserving his life. The wave still managed to knock him off his feet and carried him a few paces towards the afterdeck before the apprentice managed to get up on his feet again.

246

He quickly pulled himself up onto the higher platform, ignoring the steps which would have cost him precious time. The wood was wet and slippery but Ahren had climbed in worse conditions, and so he pulled himself up with some agility. There were only ten paces to the back railing where Khara was trying in vain to pull Jelninolan back on board. The last mass of water had lifted the priestess over the railing, and it was only the girl's desperate grip that was stopping the priestess from being pulled into the black depths below.

Now the elf was hanging on the outside of the wet railing and her enraptured face told Ahren that on account of her magic she was in no position to help herself. He raced to the two women like a madman and grasped Jelninolan's wrists with force, while at the same time bracing his two feet against the wooden railing. Then he threw himself backwards and pulled with every muscle in his body. The body of the elf was thrown in a high arc and flung back onto the deck as Ahren's body weight and muscles worked in harmony to save the priestess from her certain death. Khara gave a cry of relief but Ahren leapt to his feet again as fast as he could and turned to look at the prow.

The Queen of the Waves was already diving into the next valley and another wall of seething water was racing towards them, which would sweep both Jelninolan and Ahren away if he didn't act quickly. He spun around. Khara had pulled the conjuring Jelninolan back up onto her knees. The priestess's rope was fluttering in the wind and he didn't have time to catch hold of it. With his knife, he quickly cut the rope around Khara's hips, ignoring her protests. He grabbed the new end of her rope and performed a scurrilous dance around the two of them and knotted his end of the rope into a complicated design that Falk had drummed into him again and again.

The wave was crashing over the front of the ship by the time he had finished his preparations. He embraced the two women in an almost ridiculous gesture and slung his prepared end of the rope around the strut of the rear railing. And just as the surge of the unfettered sea reached them, he pulled the Elfish knot tight and pressed himself and his companions against the wood of the railing. The complex coils of the rope intertwined with each other, and although on account of its tightness Ahren could hardly breathe, the wave was unable to shift them from their place. The pull of the water subsided, Ahren's breath came back into his lungs and when he opened his eyes, he was looking at Jelninolan's and Khara's thankful eyes, not a hand's breadth away from his face. Khara's almond-shaped eyes glistened and she shouted in all seriousness over the noise of the wind, 'you save my lady. Me thankful.'

Ahren tried to shrug his shoulders, which completely misfired on account of his self-created shackles, and he mumbled flatly, 'who's counting?'

Then the next wave crashed over them and they made themselves as small as possible in order to minimise the power of the storm.

Ahren wasn't sure how long the storm had them in its claws. He could have sworn that it had lasted the whole day, but when it finally died down, the midday sun broke through the clouds. Every breath had been torture, the wet rope had dug into his back, and his arms and legs were trembling from the effort of the enforced embrace he had maintained for the duration. Finally, a sailor came over and admired his handiwork.

'You tied yourself up well, squire. You do know there are easier ways of holding onto a woman,' he laughed, 'although I do admit holding onto two is trickier, especially when one of them is a magician.'

His good humour evaporated when he saw the two women's stony faces. He cut the rope quickly and disappeared as fast as he could to the other end of the ship, where he sought out some work that would keep him out of their sight for as long as possible.

The three newly released companions groaned and sighed as they rubbed their arms and legs, trying to reinvigorate their stiff limbs, and then they limped down to the main deck where Uldini, Falk and the captain were standing. Bits of torn rigging and sail were hanging loose everywhere and Ahren noticed with unease that there was a long crack in the mainmast, and one of the crossbeams of the mainsail had fallen off. His change of position had saved him from serious injury or worse, and he swallowed hard.

Culhen was scratching at the inside of the captain's cabin door, and Ahren released him as he approached the others. The wolf seemed to have survived the storm unscathed and was more relaxed than he'd ever been since they'd come on board. The animal had obviously enjoyed the pitching and heaving and Ahren came to the conclusion that his wolf was a real water rat. He wasn't sure if he'd ever share his friend's love for the water after the events of the morning, but he was glad that Culhen had enjoyed himself so much.

He came up to the others and saw concerned faces, staring at the horizon.

'Our plans are clearly making the Adversary nervous. First the attack on your spirit, then the attempt to destroy the ship, and to top it all off, this,' said Falk without looking at Ahren. Instead, he indicated to several shadows on the horizon, which Ahren took to be little islands making up an irregular chain.

'The Deserted Islands,' explained Uldini, unasked, into the stillness. 'Once the home of a peaceful and trusting tribe of fishermen and divers who had known no war. Until HE, WHO FORCES came to them at the beginning of the Dark Days with lies and promises. They believed his promises, for news of his terrible deeds had not yet reached them. The whole tribe gathered together, and each accepted a necklace that HE had brought to them as gifts. Once every man, woman and child had put on their necklace HE activated a treacherous trick. The pieces of jewellery contracted, and they couldn't breathe. Gills developed under the necklaces and the people ran into the sea so that they wouldn't suffocate. And so, HE enslaved a whole civilisation. The necklaces couldn't be removed, and anyone who tried, died. Anyone who disobeyed his orders died. And that was how the Lost Tribe came into being. They've been living for centuries in the waters around their erstwhile homes and no ship willingly sails into these waters, for very few make it back. The few who do, talk about nightly ambushes, of pale creatures that climb over the railings, pulling the crew into the water in ghostly silence.' Uldini's voice had become quieter and quieter, and when the captain gave him a meaningful look and indicated to the terrified crew, the Arch Wizard stopped speaking altogether.

'I've already plotted a course that will lead us away from the Deserted Islands. This time tomorrow we'll be in safe waters,' said the captain.

Uldini looked over at Jelninolan questioningly, but she just shook her head weakly. He sighed and addressed the mariner again.

'Unfortunately, we won't be able to support you in your fight with the Lost Tribe, should it come to pass. Protecting the ship from the storm has expended all our energy, and both of us are exhausted. We urgently need to relax, or we risk over-extending ourselves. If that happens to a wizard, then he loses control of his magic, And none of you want to experience Lady Jelninolan's power, or mine for that matter, unshackled on this ship.' An uneasy silence followed Uldini's words.

'The crew of this ship consists of seasoned soldiers,' said the captain loudly. 'We're no lily-livered merchants or cowardly pirates. We will protect The Queen of the Waves through the night and carry out our order of bringing you safe and sound to the Silver Cliff.'

Ahren was sure that the captain's little speech was primarily aimed at his own crew rather than the passengers. And so, with renewed courage and determination, the sailors were soon busying themselves by examining the storm damage and repairing everything that was salvageable.

Falk drew his apprentice aside and whispered, 'you'd better lie down. It's going to be a long night, and if we are attacked, then our bows and arrows will have a lot to do.'

Ahren gave a reluctant nod. In his mind's eye he could see again the moment in the ballroom when in the blink of an eye he had dispatched seven lives. The thought of perhaps having to kill again in the dark of the night filled him with dread.

Falk laid a sympathetic hand on his shoulder and pressed it gently but firmly.

'I know that you want to avoid bloodshed, but if you can think of no other way of keeping the Lost Tribe away from our ship, then we will have to fight as soon as they attack.'

His master's hand was on his neck now, and he pressed hard with his calloused fingers and fixed his steely eyes on Ahren.

'Whatever you do, remember that your actions have an effect on your companions too. I didn't want to mention it but I know that in Jelninolan's rooms you deliberately shot at the dagger-carrier's shoulder so as to spare him death. Imagine what might have happened if he had decided to stab Khara in the back rather than steal Tanentan. Or if his

251

theft had been ultimately successful. Would you have been able to live with the knowledge that your deeds had made this possible?'

Ahren went as white as a sheet and he held firmly onto the railing. His decision to shoot the man in the shoulder hadn't been a conscious one, and yet Falk's conclusions were correct. The young man had never considered all the things that could have gone wrong if things had worked out differently.

His master gave him a look that bore witness to the fact that he understood what was going on in Ahren's mind.

'This is one of the hardest lessons this world will present you with. The knowledge that you have taken a life is terrible. But the knowledge that you haven't saved a life because you haven't lived up to your responsibilities can destroy even the most battle-hardened warrior. So, decide wisely, which action you think is best to take when you are in a conflict situation.'

The stilted language the Forest Guardian was using didn't go unnoticed, and as he continued to speak Ahren understood the reason for it.

'These are the exact words my mother told me as she sent me on my way many hundreds of years ago, when it was my turn to do battle in the Dark Days against High Fangs and Low Fangs, Dark Ones and mercenaries, highwaymen and pirates. My mother's advice may be several hundred years old, but its value hasn't diminished with the passage of time.'

Ahren needed time to digest this information. He nodded as if in a daze and retired to his cabin, where he collapsed into his hammock. It was hard to imagine that Falk, when he started out as a Paladin, had been plagued by the same doubts as his apprentice. On the other hand, the old Paladin had had a considerable amount of time to come to terms with himself and his deeds. And even that hadn't been totally successful. He had only found his way to inner peace when he was with the elves and was made Forest Guardian. Even if it was hard for Ahren to accept, he alone had to figure out how to deal with his enemies and the obstacles that would lie in his path. And he would have to figure it out quickly. If anything were to happen to one of the others because he had hesitated or spared an enemy, he would never be able to forgive himself.

Falk's mother must have been an exceptional woman. His master didn't talk much about her, but she must have been one of the last Paladins able to pass down their service to their successor. She had been granted the right, after long service to the gods, to grow old in the circle of life and to finally die. Something denied to Falk and the other Paladins for centuries.

Ahren's thoughts went around in circles and the many questions and choices weighed him down so much that he couldn't solve a single problem satisfactorily. Exhausted, he finally dropped off to sleep and dreamed of the ocean waves crashing over him and in whose depths, he could see the faces of all those he would kill in order to save the others he had been destined to protect.

The night arrived more quickly than he'd hoped. A hand shook him roughly awake, and then the sailor was gone on deck again. Ahren could hear steps rushing to and fro and shouts of encouragement. There was the sound of hammering coming from different parts of the ship as the crew hastily continued their repairs.

Ahren took the bow out of the oil cloth, which protected it from the damp sea air, so that the wood wouldn't warp or become swollen. He felt the bow in his hands with a feeling of unease. He hadn't touched it since the night in the king's palace, either for practice or to maintain it. The wood glistened softly in the weak light that came in from outside, and the cord of Selsena's hair was in perfect condition.

He tested the weapon by extending it and realised that when it was stretched to the last third, he still didn't have enough strength to tauten it fully and keep it upright for an extended period. The thought that this bow still hadn't reached the limits of its capabilities frightened him, but he decided to push aside his concerns for the night. Unknown enemies might attack the occupants in this constricted space of hammered-together planks, whereas the whole ocean would be home territory for the attackers. This possibility made Ahren's desire to avoid bloodshed a little less attractive. But if, against all expectations, the opportunity arose to negotiate, he would grasp it with both hands. And if they were lucky, there might not be any attack at all. Having considered all the possibilities, he gave a sigh and stepped out on deck.

After three paces he stopped and looked around in amazement. The rigging had been completely repaired or bound together so that no rope hindered the sailors any more. There had to be replacement sails on board, for three of the four sails had clearly been changed. The mainsail had been reefed, no doubt to take the pressure off the mast, and the mast itself had been strengthened where it had cracked, with heavy planks which had been hammered on with enormous steel nails.

The true surprise however lay in the pointed spears that were affixed all along the railings, each a forearm apart from the next, and pointing outwards. As far as Ahren could see, the defence measures went all around the ship. The crew clearly didn't share his hopes for a quiet night and a peaceful solution.

The captain slapped him on the shoulder proudly.

'Surprised, squire? I told you, this isn't any old defenceless merchant ship. The spears are really designed against a normal boarding and the

254

angle is wrong because the tips are pointing upwards and we're expecting the attackers from below. Still, it should slow them down a little.'

Ahren nodded, dumbstruck, and the mariner continued.

'If you like, you can keep an eye out for danger from the crow's nest. Your bow would come in very handy, and you can store the arrows in the basket.'

The apprentice nodded again, blindsided by the speed of events. Obviously, the others had drawn up their battle plan already and his role had been decided on. The captain gave him another encouraging smile and then hurried away and proceeded to shout at a sailor who hadn't tied one of the defensive spears properly.

Ahren collected all his arrows from his cabin and brought them up to the crow's nest. The sun was a narrow streak on the horizon and shone golden on the water, now smooth as glass. There was a gentle wind and The Queen of the Waves was making good progress. The young man fixed his arrows firmly in the meshes of the basket, then climbed down to collect his bow and to consult again with his travelling companions.

Falk was standing with Khara on the afterdeck and seemed to be trying to instruct her, haltingly, in her own language. He saw Ahren and gestured at him to come over.

'Gods, this is hard. I urgently need to brush up on my knowledge of the empire's language,' he grumbled. 'Good that you're here. Has anyone told you what your role is?'

Ahren nodded and pointed up to the crow's nest.

'I'm supposed to use my bow from up there,' he said with as much self-confidence in his voice as he could muster.

If his master had heard the silent doubts he still had, he didn't acknowledge it.

'Khara is going to guard Uldini and Jelninolan. Both of them are lying in a sleep trance and are not to be woken up unless it's the end of the world. I'm going to put on my armour soon and help on deck, where I'll be needed. Ahren, keep your eyes peeled for any movement at all, no matter how small, outside the railings, alright? We have to be very careful with fire on a wooden ship so there will only be a few lanterns and visibility will be poor. The sailors have orders to call out your title three times if they run into difficulties. So, if you're aiming into a melee, only shoot at the figures that aren't shouting "squire"'

Falk was already walking to the steps and glanced back. 'Any questions?' he called over his shoulder and paused.

Ahren shook his head timidly.

'Courage, son. Imagine it as a trap we've set for Dark Ones. As if you were lying in wait on a hunt. Except that this is happening on the water. And we're being attacked by intelligent and co-ordinated enemies, and we've no escape route.'

He shrugged his shoulders, then descended the ladder and his last words were blown upward by the wind.

'You know what? Forget the comparison.'

'That was a great help,' mumbled Ahren. Khara looked at him questioningly but he gave her a dismissive wave. For a moment he wondered if he should put on his ribbon armour, then decided against it. If somebody managed to get past the sailors and climb all the way up the mast to his basket, then he would have more serious problems to be thinking about than not having armour on. And anyway, Jelninolan was sleeping and he didn't want to risk getting tangled up in his armour on the swaying ship, because he would be putting it on himself. He suddenly had an image of the helpless Jelninolan, as she had lain on the boarding-room floor that time, and in spite of the situation now, he couldn't suppress a smile. Then he climbed up into position and the smile disappeared, along with the last rays of sun, which were swallowed up by the sea.

Waiting for the battle to start was the worst part . Or so Ahren had heard old soldiers say, and he was inclined to agree with them. The tension that he had been feeling throughout his body since he'd positioned himself in the crow's nest, with his eyes constantly peering down into the darkness, had turned into pure torture within a short time. A third of the night had passed and Ahren now found himself beginning to get bored. It seemed he was only capable of remaining tensely nervous for a certain period before his reason began to accustom itself to the circumstances around him. The hope that there might be no battle at all slowly began to overcome his anxiety. To counteract his boredom, Ahren was counting the struts on the railings in the dim light of the lantern when he suddenly saw out of the corner of his eye faint movements in the darkness. His pulse started racing. White figures were slipping gracefully between the spears and jumping onto the deck in total silence.

He and two sailors simultaneously screamed out a warning and he let fly an arrow at the nearest attacker. The spectres seemed to be unarmed and Ahren hesitated for a moment with his second arrow. But it was then that Ahren understood with horror, the tactics of the Lost Tribe. They were carrying slim, narrow objects around their wrists, which they threw over the sailors' heads from behind while they were distracted by other attackers. The unfortunate sailors dropped their weapons and grasped their necks as they gasped for breath. Ahren understood what was happening below when he saw the first of the sailors who had been attacked in this way, jumping head over heels into the water.

The Lost Ones had necklaces with them, which they put around the crew members, so that they would join them in their cursed existence.

The horror he was witnessing was made even worse by the fact that there was complete silence as they performed their dastardly acts.

'Watch out for the necklaces! They're attacking you from behind!' he screamed at the top of his lungs, shooting off arrows at lightning speed at any attackers who still carried the necklaces in their right hands.

Ten heartbeats after the first of them had boarded the ship, the Lost Ones turned around at speed and dived elegantly back into the dark water where they disappeared without a trace. The next were already lifting their heads above the water and were preparing for the second attack. After missing two of the swimmers, Ahren gave up trying to hit them in the water. The lack of light, the movement of the ship, and the small size of his targets made a sure hit impossible and he would only be wasting his arrows.

Meanwhile, there were shouts on the deck as the mariners called out the names of their brothers- and sisters-in-arms, checking who was still on board and who had followed the Lost Ones down to their watery prison. They had already lost five of their thirty crew members and the attack was far from over.

Even from where he was, Ahren could make out the fear on their faces. An enemy that wanted to kill you was bad enough, but one that had the capability of changing you into a creature of the Lost Tribe, and to condemn your existence to a life on the dark ocean floor, was too much for even the most hardened veteran to bear.

The captain hurried through his ranks, giving courage or comfort where needed, and Falk re-organised their defence.

'Nobody is alone from now on!' he roared. 'From this point you're always in twos, back to back!'

The mariners nodded and gradually came to terms with the shock of the first attack, while at the same time dividing themselves into pairs so

258

that they could each cover the other's back. Ahren prepared his bow without tautening it, and anxiously counted the attackers as they bobbed up and down in the water, surrounding and circling the ship on her course through the night.

'They're gathering!' shouted Ahren down to the deck below. 'There are at least forty and they're circling the ship!'

Falk raised his hand briefly to show that he'd understood. None of the sailors dared to speak, and so the ship sailed silently through the night. Only the rhythmical slapping of the waves against the boat could be heard as everyone waited for the next inevitable attack.

It happened a hundred heartbeats later, but this time the crew were better prepared. Hardly had Ahren seen a movement on the side of the ship when he let fly an arrow and he screamed down a warning. Any reservations he had had about killing vanished when he contemplated the murderous tactics of the Lost Tribe. He let arrow after arrow fly from his bow, and the ship's crew carried out their actions with military precision as the Lost Ones swung themselves onto the deck.

If the sailors didn't succeed in mortally wounding the sea creatures, they swiped their short swords towards the right arms of the attackers, which held the insidious necklaces. At the same time, they provided cover for the person behind them. Ahren could only admire the interactions in each pair, and their co-ordinated defence seemed to have flummoxed their opponents. Their attack was fruitless and so the Lost Ones abandoned the sailors and jumped silently back into the sea.

This time nobody had lost their lives to the cursed necklaces, but instead, there were over twenty Lost Ones lying motionless on the deck. Shouts of jubilation filled the night sky as the sailors yelled in celebration of their victory. Ahren's heart beat faster with joy and he joined in the cheering while still keeping an eye on the attackers, who had gathered around the ship, but this time at a greater distance away. Even Falk seemed happy at the outcome of the skirmish, and Ahren gave him a broad grin from up high.

Falk looked up and saw Ahren's head leaning over the side of the crow's nest and peering down.

'Keep your eyes fixed on the water!' he ordered. 'We need you to warn us if they attack!'

Ahren nodded and stood up straight again. The clouds in the sky had broken up and now the moon was casting a dim light, not enough for Ahren to make out things in detail but allowing him to better identify movements in the water.

After some time Ahren noticed, much to his consternation, that more and more spectres were swimming along under the water and joining the waiting attackers, and he could also make out strange misshapen shadows that the sea creatures were pulling behind them.

'They're changing their tactics,' Ahren shouted down in a worried voice. He was unable to make out what the outlines were. 'They're bringing something with them, but I can't make out what!'

'They've probably realised that they need to try a different approach. They wanted new recruits earlier, but now they're probably thinking in terms of killing,' prophesied Falk darkly.

Ahren suddenly had an idea that he wanted to share immediately.

'If the unexpected puts them off their stride, then we should bring Culhen on deck. I bet you a wolf on the high seas will really irritate them!' he shouted down, keeping his eyes fixed on the water. The sea creatures seemed to be assembling in some sort of formation and Ahren was certain that they only had a few heartbeats before the next wave of attack would be upon them.

'Hang on a minute, so that's a wolf and not a wolfhound?' asked the captain with concern. Ahren flinched. Culhen was still in disguise – and it had completely slipped his mind.

'Long story,' said his master, sweeping aside the sailor's question. 'The animal is trained and can be of assistance to us. That's the only thing that matters. My apprentice has a good idea there, even if he is a little cheeky.' The last words were spoken with a little bite and Ahren was sure that the old Forest Guardian wouldn't forget Ahren's slip-up for some time.

Falk ran beneath deck as he spoke, and a couple of heartbeats later Culhen was scurrying around the main deck, sniffing curiously at the bodies. The wolf sneezed and then snarled quietly. Ahren chuckled until he saw the front line of attackers darting for the ship at top speed.

'They're back!' he screamed at the top of his lungs, and a wave of tension rolled through the assembled sailors, while Culhen crouched instinctively, preparing to spring forward. Ahren felt uneasy at the fact that he'd involved his friend in the conflict, but if Culhen could give them an advantage and thereby save lives, then it was a risk the young man had to take.

The sea creatures clambered on board and Ahren could make out at last, what they were holding in their hands: strange, wavy spears with lines of algae attached to their ends. He saw the harpoons boring through sailors, and the sea creatures jumping overboard and pulling at the algae-string, yanking the wounded over the railings and into the sea. Their victims were screaming and trying to cling onto the slippery deck, so Ahren concentrated his arrows on the Lost Ones who hadn't yet thrown their spears, while Culhen jumped up at the attackers as if possessed, biting in all directions.

Ahren's blood boiled when he saw a trio of Lost Ones slipping unnoticed through the melee and heading towards the lower deck. The thought of one of those cursed necklaces being put around Jelninolan's or Khara's neck filled him with rage, and with an inarticulate scream he riddled them with arrows before they could reach the hatch. From then on, he shot at any sea creature that came within ten paces of the opening while the fight raged on. Finally, Culhen, who had just wildly bitten and defeated yet another Lost One, let out a blood-curdling howl. Its companions covered their ears in shock before leaping overboard in fear. It seemed that the alien noise had been so painful for them that they had abandoned the fight immediately and run helter-skelter for the sides of the ship in an effort to escape. The sailors quickly cut the algae ropes of the harpoons and pulled their injured fellow crew members into the middle of the ship.

Ahren saw how all the shapes dived below the surface, and a few seconds later the ocean was calmly reflecting the moonlight, which was dancing over the wavelets.

'They're all gone!' shouted Ahren with relief.

The battle seemed to be finally over. Culhen was celebrated like a hero, and even from the crow's nest Ahren could see how the vain animal was lapping up all the demonstrations of affection.

The crew busied itself with treating wounds and started singing quietly. Their harmonies echoed through the sea and the sails, while Ahren remained at his post, watching the water around them.

The sailors were about to throw the bodies of their fallen companions overboard when Falk gave a shout of alarm.

'Take off their necklaces first, or they can be used again,' he ordered.

But for all their pulling and tugging they were unable to get the tightly bound shackles off them until one of the mariners took on the terrible task of cutting the necklaces from their victims' flesh. Once the necklaces had been separated from the bodies through brute force, they immediately decomposed into mouldy strings of algae. Falk didn't want to take any risks, and instead of throwing the remains of the necklaces overboard, the green matter was burned in one of the oil lanterns. Stinking fumes rose up from the charred algae and some of the crew were convinced that they heard distant cries of relief among the crackling of the flames.

The night passed by and everything was quiet. Every now and then Ahren would cast a curious eye on the corpse of one of the Lost Ones, which Falk was examining thoroughly by the light of one of the lanterns.

The corpse was male, his only clothing consisted of mouldy rags, tied loosely around his hips. Ahren could see, even from the crow's nest, that his eyes were unnaturally large , with enormous pupils and without any lids. He had a flat nose with strange slits at the side and a small mouth without lips. His arms and legs were muscular out of all proportion, and the same with his chest. The apprentice found it hard to imagine that this creature was once a human, before he had been condemned to live the rest of its days travelling in the depths of the ocean.

'It seems they only have gills,' he heard Falk say. 'Which is why their individual attacks were so short. They had to get back under the water to get more air.'

Ahren shivered and a feeling of pity overcame him, now that the immediate danger was over. These poor souls were condemned to a miserable existence in terrible slavery, and Ahren's determination to put an end, once and for all, to the dark god grew. He grimly continued his watch from up high, but no Lost One broke through the surface of the water.

When dawn finally broke on the exhausted defenders of the ship, there was another cry of celebration on deck. Ahren looked down and saw a throng of exuberant crew members surrounding Culhen and stroking and tickling him. The wolf was sitting on his hind legs with his tongue lolling, enjoying to the fullest, his new role as ship's mascot.

At noon the captain announced that they were approaching the safe coastline, and there was no fear of another night attack. Uldini and Jelninolan were still sleeping, and Ahren decided that at last he could do the same. His legs stiff, he clambered out of the crow's nest and was relieved by a sailor who greeted him with a broad smile. His unerring marksmanship, not to mention Culhen's surprising effect on the Lost Ones ensured that Ahren would be greeted with open, welcoming arms by everyone. It was only Falk who gave him a more critical look, but if he had greeted him in any other way, the young man would have been seriously worried.

While Ahren was doing some stretching exercises to get the stiffness out of his legs, the broad-shouldered Paladin, still in his white armour, came up beside him and looked out onto the waves, whose white crests were doing a wild dance in the fresh winds.

'That was good work you did last night. Have a rest now and I will keep watch for a while. Not that I don't trust our captain's judgement, but better safe than sorry.'

The grey-haired man looked over at Culhen, who was lying on his back and enjoying being tickled on his stomach by two sailors.

'Anyway, we also have our fearless hero who can save us all,' he added with a chuckle.

Ahren smiled too before rolling his eyes in mockery.

'Culhen will be unbearable for the next few weeks if they keep spoiling him like that.' Then he gave an exhausted wave to his master and disappeared into the cabin. He fell asleep immediately and slept calmly and without dreams, his right hand buried in the fur of the wolf, who had settled down beside his friend.

Chapter 14

37 days to the winter solstice

The rest of the voyage passed very agreeably.

Jelninolan and Uldini were still in a trance, and it dawned on Ahren how much effort it must have cost them to shield the ship from the mighty storm. He couldn't bear to imagine what might have happened without their help if the ship had encountered even a milder variation of the hurricane. Suddenly, he saw in his mind's eye an enormous wave smashing the ship to pieces and he had to force his mind to think of something else.

Such as, for example, the happenings of the morning. Ahren had woken up early and he h'd had an urgent need to do something active. The others were still asleep, so he went had gone on deck and decided to climb up the rigging without using his legs.

This exercise was always exhausting and would make him break into a sweat, but if Ahren didn't strengthen his arms and shoulders, then he would never be able to extend his bow to its optimum shooting position without wasting valuable time or tiring too quickly. The cultists and the Lost Ones had been unarmed, and the shooting distances short, so he had been able to manage without using the full power of his weapon. He surmised however that some day he wouldn't be so lucky, and he didn't want to be responsible if something happened to someone because he hadn't been able to use his improved bow to its best effect. Even if he could never have shot as well with his original bowstring, he felt that there was still a considerable untapped potential in his weapon.

And so he had tortuously made his way up and down the rigging again and again. Eventually, Falk had found him, soaked to the skin and worn out, with shivering limbs and panting breath, his teeth chattering in the biting wind, which carried with it the first signs of winter.

'I see you have decided to start the next stage of your training,' the old Forest Guardian had said, approvingly.

Ahren was too out of breath to respond.

'I'm proud of you. Today, for the first time, you've asked yourself what you can do to move your training along. You've spotted a weakness, and without being asked or ordered to, you have set about eradicating this weakness by using what you have already learned.'

Ahren could only stare at him speechlessly, as his master looked approvingly at his young charge.

'Some day I really will make a decent Forest Guardian out of you,' his master had said before turning and disappearing below deck without another word.

Ahren collapsed on the ground in exhaustion but couldn't stop a silly smile from spreading across his face. It was true that his master had prompted the apprentice to take this next step in his development by giving him the Autumn Festival present, but that didn't stop Ahren from basking in the praise he had just received.

Now Ahren was standing at the railing and squinting his eyes in the afternoon sun, hoping that he would at last see the silhouette of the Silver Cliff. He heard a loud yawn behind him and when he looked around, he saw Uldini floating beside him and closing his mouth. He blinked at the apprentice with sleepy eyes.

'I see we've won,' he mumbled indistinctly. The Arch Wizard was floating in a slightly tilted manner.

Ahren tried to keep a straight face and nodded silently. He knew from experience that it was never a good idea to pull the wizard's leg. At the very least, the ageless boy would attack him with his centuries' old knowledge of verbal sparring, and that was far from enjoyable.

'Don't just stand there, tell me what happened!' Uldini grumbled between two further loud yawns.

And so it was, that Ahren related the events of the previous night and of the attacks by the Lost Ones on the ship. Uldini listened with interest, and as the apprentice went on, his demeanour changed and he grew more awake and alert. By the time the young man had finished his report, Uldini was back to his old self.

The childlike figure opened his eyes wide one last time and smacked his lips contentedly.

'Thanks for the latest. If you sleep for five days, it takes a while to come back to normal again. At least I'm not a morning grouch like Jelninolan.' He rolled his eyes as he spoke.

Ahren was on the point of asking him what he had meant by that when Khara stormed on deck, her cheeks bright red, with a furious look in her eyes. She ran up onto the afterdeck and dug her nails into the railing.

Curious, and a little concerned, Ahren went over to her.

'Is everything alright?' he asked from a safe distance.

Khara had knocked him to the ground with an elegant throw on more than one occasion when he had taken her by surprise, and so he had learned not to approach her unannounced. He suspected that she was in control of her reflexes to a much better degree than she let on, but whenever he had confronted her about that, she had said, 'arena dangerous. Always careful.'

Her head spun around and her arms shot up into a defence position and Ahren doubted that on this occasion the moves had been deliberate. Something had really upset her.

'Mistress very angry,' she said. 'I not want talk.'

Then she turned back and stared out at the water, kneading the railing with her hands.

Ahren decided that retreat was the best policy, so he then approached Jelninolan's cabin carefully. When he was still a few paces away, he heard the elf uttering foul curses, and a wooden jug was hurled out the open door, where it smashed into the opposite wall.

'I said hot water,' the priestess snarled, and a distraught sailor came tumbling out of the cabin before picking up the jug. When he spotted Ahren, he gave him a pleading look and pointed at the cabin, and the apprentice was sensible enough to step back, shake his head vigorously and race back on deck.

Falk and Uldini were standing together and laughing over a joke. His master saw Ahren's distraught look and he laughed again.

'Did she catch you?' he asked wittily.

'No, but Khara and one of the sailors must have crossed paths with her,' said Ahren uncertainly. 'Is she always like that after a trance sleep?'

Falk and Uldini both gave an embarrassed nod.

'She suppresses many of the negative effects of her magic and then there's a reaction when she wakes up from her trance,' Uldini explained. 'The term 'unbearable' doesn't come near to describing it. The best thing to do is to leave her alone and after a few hours she'll have come back to herself.'

'If the ship is still in one piece,' added Falk drily.

He looked over at Khara, who was still brooding.

'I'd better explain to her what's going on. The poor thing idolises our elf, and I don't want her to blame herself.'

Ahren watched his master going to great lengths trying to explain the situation to Khara and calm her down. Suddenly, a wave of jealousy came over him.

Uldini chuckled mischievously.

'You should look at your face. Forget about Khara and look over there - that will lift your spirits.'

As he turned to look where Uldini had indicated, and was about to deny that he had been thinking about the girl, he gasped at the sight that presented itself.

The Queen of the Waves had sailed around a particularly jagged section of coastline which had jutted out to sea, and suddenly the Silver Cliff came into view. Ahren had always thought the name had some sort of symbolic meaning, referring to the riches of the dwarf enclave, but now the truth revealed itself before him. Hemmed in between two side cliffs was a narrow shingle beach in a little cove, behind which was a steep wall. This wall seemed to consist of pure gold, and it glittered brightly in the sunlight.

Ahren squinted and could make out huge openings in its surface, from which protruded enormous arrowheads as big as horses. He remembered seeing similar weapons on the palace in King's Island and then it struck him that they must have been gifts from the dwarves. He looked uneasily at the dragon longbows and he suddenly felt very vulnerable as the enormous arrows turned slowly in the direction of their ship.

Uldini noticed Ahren's anxiety and floated towards him.

'Calm down. The dwarves of the Silver Cliff like to show off their wealth, and they also like to impress upon their guests that they are well capable of defending it. They're actually a very pleasant lot, considering they're dwarves.'

Ahren looked again at the monstrous projectiles aimed at them and asked himself what a grumpier dwarf clan's welcome would look like.

Uldini turned around and caught sight of the captain.

'Sail slowly and steadily into the bay. The dwarves here are only used to heavily laden ships. The fact that we're sailing in a warship could lead them to draw the wrong conclusions.'

The captain looked nervously at the dragon longbows and then called out a series of commands. The ship slowed down considerably, and Uldini nodded approvingly before turning back to Ahren.

The apprentice had regained his composure and was filled with curiosity.

'Is the whole cliff really all made of silver?' he asked excitedly.

Uldini smirked and rubbed his bald head with his hand.

'No. This magnificent view is part of their intimidation tactics. They covered the surface with a thin layer of silver, and they then sealed it all with an alloy so that the wind and water would glance off it. Falk's armour has the same sealant on it, by the way.'

Ahren looked over at his master and a thought struck him as he put together bits of information he had learned over the previous few weeks.

'His armour is that of the Paladins, am I right? And his sword?' He knew the answer already, in fact, but he hoped Uldini would give him some additional information.

The Arch Wizard nodded. 'Every Paladin got their own armour and weapons that time, forged by the master blacksmiths in Thousand Halls. There is a chamber deep in the mountain where particular pressure ratios exist. There – and only there – can Deep Steel be forged. They say it consists of the pure essence of HIM, WHO IS, but I personally think that's just bragging. Dwarves have a tendency to exaggerate their stories if it can add value to the handwork they produce.'

Ahren looked thoughtfully at the silver-glistening material which made up Falk's armour, while Uldini carried on speaking.

'Don't get me wrong. I can understand the reasoning behind these myths. A Paladin's armour is very rarely breached, and then only through a violent effort. The bite of a giant dragon, a collapsing crag, things like that, and even then, the wearers have survived – if only just. There is an enormous strength in the material and even I, after all the centuries, still don't understand it.' The voice of the boyish figure died away as the Arch Wizard became lost in thought.

Ahren turned his eyes back to the dwarf enclave and tried to make out more details as they slowly sailed forward. The days had grown noticeably shorter and colder even though their southern course had counteracted it if only a little. The sun had just disappeared behind the cliff, and although the silver was no longer blinding, the long shadows cast across the bay made it difficult to see.

The apprentice squinted and thought he could make out extensive engravings on the surface of the cliff face, but then he was distracted by a tumult behind him.

Jelninolan had appeared on deck, her eyes flashing with anger, and miraculously all the sailors who had been nearby were now at the other end of the ship or were climbing the rigging to do some repairs. The elf stomped sullenly over to her companions and her angry eyes settled on Ahren as a whirlwind on four paws pushed between them and slid around on his stomach with a begging look in front of the priestess. Culhen's eyes begged piteously for mercy, and the wolf whimpered urgently.

The group had observed this ritual every morning since Jelninolan had transformed the conceited wolf's appearance into that of a wolfhound.

And every time the elf had sent him away with a smile and words of consolation, but now she looked down at Culhen irritably, made a gruff hand movement and spoke a few words in Elfish. Culhen's fur changed colour and returned to its normal white, at which point the delighted dog was unstoppable. Howling and barking, he jumped up at the startled elf, licked her furiously on the face while landing his front paws on her shoulders. The wolf had grown considerably larger and heavier and so he knocked her over and all Ahren could see was a ball of fur and green elf robes as Culhen continued to express his unbridled gratitude.

Uldini's face was the picture of horror and he whispered quickly, 'Considering her condition, I think you should get your wolf off her now before she does something that we'll all regret.'

Ahren quickly went over to Culhen and grabbed him by the neck just as he heard Jelninolan murmur something in Elfish. He tried to drag away his friend before the Wizard would turn him into a water rat, but then he suddenly heard the ancient priestess chuckle. He walked around the boisterous pair and saw that she was smiling at the wolf, using terms of endearment and ruffling his fur. She turned to Uldini and smiled at him, and he responded with a raise of his eyebrows.

'If I'd known that, I would have tamed her own personal wolf for her centuries ago. And even if I had to do it blindfold and with my hands behind my back. Do you have any idea how many mornings I've had to survive when she was coming out of a sleep trance.? I think I have to agree with the rest of the crew. Your wolf is a true hero. He has confronted a dragon and lived to tell the tale,' said the Arch Wizard in his typical, try tone.

Jelninolan pushed Culhen aside and stared at the childlike figure. Then she raised her hand and a little wave came over the railing, surprising Uldini by splashing him thoroughly with cold water. The Arch

Wizard stood there, dripping wet in his soaking black robe and gasping for air as the icy wind blew through the wet material. And without a word he floated below deck, leaving a few weak blue sparks dancing on the wooden planks, the only evidence of his suppressed anger.

Ahren tried to keep a straight face and went up quickly to Falk and Khara on the quarterdeck, leaving his noble wolf to cheer up the priestess.

Falk looked at him questioningly.

'What happened there?'

'Uldini and Culhen are cheering Jelninolan up a little,' said Ahren quickly.

If he went into detail, he would surely burst out laughing, and at the moment there were two irritated Ancients on board who might take it the wrong way.

When Falk realised that he wasn't going to get any more information out of the boy, he shrugged his shoulders.

'That's a good idea, the two of them have. Elves and dwarves don't get along with each other, anyway, their cultures are too different. It's hard enough without Jelninolan hitting the roof over every little thing.'

The old man looked over at the cliff.

'Also, she's always terribly ashamed of her outbursts afterwards. If the two are able to help her recover herself, then good for them.'

As if in response, a peal of laughter could be heard from the main deck and Culhen came running up, wagging his tail and rubbing up against Ahren's leg.

'I see you have your old fur again, greedy guts. No wonder you're so happy. I swear, I've never seen such a conceited animal,' laughed Falk.

Khara's reaction came out of the blue. She recoiled from Culhen and went into a low defensive posture, while she instinctively reached for her weapon. Her hand only grasped air as she had left Windblade in the cabin. A wild, almost panicked look was in her eyes.

Ahren went down on his haunches and embraced his friend so as to restrain him, when he suddenly understood what had shocked the girl. This was the first time she had seen Culhen as a wolf, and as an enormous and boisterous one. The apprentice stroked the broad head of the animal between the eyes, and his furry friend gave out a deep, contented growl.

'Culhen – this is Culhen,' he called out, trying to get through to the attack-ready girl.

After several heartbeats she understood and straightened herself as she tried to find the right words.

'In arena sometime wolf enemy. Dangerous fights. Many dead slaves.'

Ahren nodded, moved. He really couldn't even begin to understand how Khara had spent her childhood, but the more he discovered, the less he wanted to think about it.

Jelninolan came up to the afterdeck and joined them, speaking to Khara in the Empire language and bowing slightly. The girl returned the bow, but longer and deeper than the elf. Then she beamed at the priestess.

'You two were protected from my bad mood, so I don't need to apologise to either of you.'

She stroked Culhen's hackles gently with the tips of her fingers.

You've raised a real-life saver there, Ahren.' Then she looked the wolf in the eyes. 'Culhen, whenever you've had enough of this numbskull, you're always welcome in Eathinian.'

The wolf gave a cheerful bark and pushed himself up against the young man's legs.

Loud shouts could be heard from all over the ship as the crew prepared to anchor.

'We've arrived and we should head off as soon as possible,' said Falk. 'Winter is coming, and now that the sun is setting it's going to get markedly cold here along the coast. For my part, I've been freezing long enough and I urgently need to warm up.' He looked around. 'Where's Uldini?' he asked.

Jelninolan shrugged her shoulders guiltily.

'Oh dear. I'll go get him. Then we can get a rowing boat to bring us ashore.'

The elf disappeared below deck and Falk placed his hand on Ahren's shoulder.

'Now we're among dwarves. Anything you're going to learn about courage and stubbornness, you'll learn it here.'

The apprentice looked over at the Silver Cliff and asked himself what wonders were awaiting them.

Chapter 15

After a few friendly words of farewell from the captain, and an endless amount of cuddling for Culhen by every single one of the sailors, all of them wanting to bid farewell to the wolf, the companions clambered aboard the little boat.

Uldini did not go with them. He was still mortally insulted and had hovered over to the beach on his own, where he was now standing, arms folded, waiting for them. In his dark robe, barely visible in the twilight on the dark shingle beach, the little figure looked for all the world like the spirit of revenge ready to wreak vengeance on the nefarious people of the world.

Ahren looked longingly over at the Arch Wizard, as he held on for dear life to the edges of the boat while it tossed here and there. He tried to stay clear of the water, which had already risen a good foot on the inside of the wooden nutshell-like vessel. The others ignored the rising water and Ahren did his best to follow suit. He looked at Uldini again.

'Can he not just take us with him when he does that?' he grumbled quietly.

Jelninolan smiled at him indulgently.

'We're nearly on land. And no, he can't just do that. Uldini has perfected the magic of self-levitation almost to the point where de doesn't expend any energy. His whole body works in unison with each of his movements. If he uses this magic on someone else who doesn't have control over himself, then it's extremely tiring, because he has to balance out every counter action of the other person. I could float over there myself, but I haven't practised in a long time and it would really wear me out. On the other hand, I can invocate ten times as many healing charms as our bad-tempered friend there. "Practice makes perfect" is true for wizards too, you know.'

The keel of the boat crunched onto the pebbled beach, and the two sailors who had rowed the boat leaped out into the freezing water and pulled the vessel ashore.

Culhen immediately hopped out and jumped around in the surf, and the rest of the passengers disembarked.

Khara hopped elegantly ashore, and Jelninolan left the boat with practised moves, but Ahren was struggling. His attempt to leave without getting wet failed miserably and when he finally stood on shore with sopping boots and trousers, he tried to ignore the smirks on the women's faces. The two sailors heaved the two heavy trunks with all the group's possessions onto the beach, then nodded silently but thankfully, before climbing back into the little vessel and rowing back to their ship.

Ahren looked over at The Queen of the Waves and was surprised to realise how much he would miss the ship. Neither the constant fear of drowning, nor the storms, nor the murderous sea creatures, but the pitching and rolling of the hulk and the ever-present creaking of the timbers. These sounds and feelings had subconsciously become part of his being, and although there was a cold wind howling around the cliff and the waves were crashing against the shore, it seemed remarkably still here on land.

He turned towards the cliff face which had lent its name to the town, but the setting sun was behind the cliff and all its details were now hidden in darkness.

Disappointed, he joined the others, who were standing around the hovering Uldini. Culhen came from the water at Ahren's call and shook his fur heartily, causing the icy drops to fly in every direction. Ahren jumped quickly to the side so as not to get even wetter and so avoided the shower, but Uldini was the main recipient. Sparks flew between the wizard's fingers as he looked threateningly around the group.

'Great. Would anyone else like to wet me today?' he growled, with a strangely hollow bass sound in his voice, which echoed with an unnatural loudness back from the cliff. Culhen disappeared into the night with his tail between his legs, and not a soul said a word or moved a muscle as the Arch Wizard fixed his eyes on them. Ten heartbeats of absolute silence passed before Uldini nodded curtly and floated silently towards the cliff.

Falk cleared his throat.

'I'll go on ahead. His Dwarfish isn't the best, and we don't want the first impressions of us to be dependent on his diplomatic skills.'

The old Forest Guardian trotted after the Arch Wizard.

'Just leave the things on the beach,' he called out over his shoulder. 'The dwarves will bring everything in – as long as we're welcomed.'

Ahren nodded but Jelninolan quickly took Tanentan out of one of the trunks. She was not going to let her folks' artefact be minded by some unknown dwarf. She closed the trunk, then followed the others quietly up the shingle beach. Ahren looked around curiously, and out of the corner of his eye he noticed that Khara was straining her neck too, trying to make out more of their immediate surroundings. Ahren's heart was warmed by the thought that he was no longer the only one in the group for whom so many things in the world were new and strange. He threw Khara a conspiratorial look but she only looked back at him with a puzzled frown. Their moment of solidarity was gone, and with a sigh Ahren continued to look around.

The beach had looked very narrow from the ship, but now Ahren had to revise his impressions. He calculated that there were a good five furlongs between the two cliffs on either side and there were at least three hundred paces from where they had landed to the Silver Cliff. The shingle was slippery from the spray and stubborn algae, and as the sun of the autumn evening didn't reach them anymore, there was very little light. They walked forward slowly and carefully until suddenly, in the late evening gloom, a tongue of fire shot upwards in front of them.

Ahren crouched down instinctively, thinking they were under attack. But then his eyes became accustomed to the brightness and he was dumbstruck. What had started as a jet of flame had developed into a controlled fire that was shooting up the surface of the Silver Cliff. The way in which it spread out suggested some kind of gullies of oil, which the dwarves had lit, and which were brightening the entrance to the Cliff.

Two dozen heartbeats later and all the gullies were in flames and the result was unique and breathtakingly beautiful. Khara laughed with happiness and Ahren stopped for a moment to take in the view. The surface of the cliff was full of complex and strangely angled shapes that had been hewn into the silver. The lines of fiery oil were masterfully arranged so that they highlighted every detail, making them stand out against the darkness. The overall impression created by the complex silver-glittering mosaic of lines, light and shade was of power and majesty.

Ahren felt himself to be small and insignificant and he had the impression that this was exactly the effect that was intended for every onlooker, as if the dwarfish creators had calculated how best they could impress upon the visitor, no matter what time of day or night, the wealth and majesty of their dwarfish community. As it stood, the apprentice was not in the least surprised when he heard Jelninolan's disapproving voice.

'Garish. Far too garish!' He also heard a slight undertone of marvel in her voice, but in the interest of self-preservation, he thought better than to mention it. He had neither the loyal eyes nor fluffy fur of a young wolf with which he could charm an irritated elf-priestess.

They walked towards the brightly lit rectangle in which Falk and Uldini were standing, together with four small, squat figures. Ahren couldn't see an actual door, just an entrance, five paces wide and two paces high, around which he could see simple but finely worked symbols with motifs that suggested hammers, shields, hilltops and pickaxes

They heard Falk saying something in the rumbling and hollow-sounding Dwarfish language. In the backlight of the cliff interior only the outlines of the dwarves could be made out but Ahren recognised the jangling of chainmail as they moved, and the silhouettes of their axes and spades were threatening enough. Luckily, the body language of the four small mountain dwellers didn't suggest any hostility.

When Falk had finished, one of the dwarves responded. He spoke twice as quickly as the Forest Guardian and with strangely flat cadences in his voice, but also twice as loudly. His voice was thrown back by the walls, and the echo of his words combined with the sound of what he was currently saying into a harmonious whole. Ahren was amazed when he realised that the dwarf chose his words carefully, so that their tone and rhythm would echo in perfect harmony with the words yet to be spoken.

The conversation ended and Falk grasped the dwarf's forearm with his hand, and his opposite number did the same. Ahren could see that the mountain dweller's arms and hands were disproportionately large and that his master's powerful hand looked almost like that of a child.

Once they'd released their grasps, the guards stood aside and Falk waved at his companions to follow him inside. They entered the Silver

Cliff and Ahren caught a glimpse of the four sentries standing on either side of the entrance, who let them pass with a smile.

Ahren had already seen a dwarf in the trading town of Three Rivers and so he wasn't surprised by their appearance. Bushy eyebrows, long plaited beards which covered most of their faces, heavy chainmail protecting their torsos and extremities – all of which reminded him of the jewellery merchant he had encountered that time. Although there were also differences. Their armouring was considerably thicker and was further strengthened in vital places by steel plates. He observed also that, while the merchant had two small hatchets on him, these guards were carrying massive two-handed axes and thick spades, which looked three times as heavy as those humans would carry. They also had a much stronger physique. But despite their ferocious appearance, their faces expressed a straightforward friendliness, which he had never seen on a human guard when confronted by strangers.

Culhen sniffed curiously at the chainmail and the calloused hands, and the dwarves reacted with rumbling laughter and heavy slaps on the wolf's flanks.

Falk noticed the wonder in Ahren's face and grinned.

'I told you already that Culhen would be welcome here. Dwarves love seeing wolves because the skin of the little folk is too thick and their bodies too strong for any normal wolf to present a danger. So they're looked on more as domesticated animals who live in the wild. The dwarf scouts who keep an eye out for enemies outside the mines sometimes train them as sniffer dogs.'

He looked at the wolf affectionately.

'Dwarves also value size and strength. Culhen has both, and the fact that he obeys you will counteract your own weaknesses in their eyes.'

Ahren sighed. His master had succeeded once again, and quite casually, in bringing him down to size. Then he noticed that the guards, on seeing the two women, had bowed respectfully and even blushed a little.

'Why do they behave so strangely?' he whispered to Falk, but he walked on and only replied gruffly, 'I'll explain it to you later.'

And so, without further comment, the apprentice followed his master along the short corridor. The surfaces of the walls were smooth and plain, and Ahren was a little disappointed at the absence of splendour, until eight paces later the corridor opened into a large dome-shaped hall.

Here the magnificence that Ahren had expected following the impressive exterior of the cliff revealed itself in all its glory. The apprentice saw walls and ceilings decorated with gold and silver and depicting marvellous mosaics, all of which were somehow connected with trade. There were coins and gemstones and stylised pictures of merchant dwarves, humans and even elves. They were haggling, evaluating, paying for or exchanging a multitude of goods whose outlines, depending on their worth, consisted of semi-precious or precious stones.

As he looked around, Ahren even saw measuring tapes made of pure gold set in the wall, in one section of the dome at about hip height. And to top it all, he saw a cord of thick silver which ran along the ground through the middle of the hall, neatly dividing the entrance through which they had come and the exit directly opposite.

The dome itself was empty, except for two elongated plain stone blocks on either side of the cord and a stone throne which, situated on the left of the room, stood precisely on the line, and from where both halves of the hall were clearly visible. Ahren could see a lonely figure sitting on the throne in perfect stillness. The whole scene was lit by a strange red flame that burned quietly in a basin hanging from the ceiling in the middle of the room.

'What sort of a place is this?' asked Ahren quietly and gave a surprised start as his voice echoed back loudly off the walls.

Falk stood still and spread out his arms.

'This is the Trading Hall. Nine out of ten merchants never get past this point and don't make it deeper into the mountain. The goods that you want to sell are placed on the block on this side, and the things that the dwarves want to exchange for your goods are placed on the block over there. Once you have agreed terms, the goods are moved along the silver cord on the floor simultaneously to the other side, and the deal is done. The rules of trading are depicted in the mosaics on the walls. The dwarves have calculated exactly the relative values of the gemstones, coins and all other valid currencies, and they have even developed a system of measurement that all visiting traders have to adhere to.'

Ahren looked around again and now he could see the deeper meanings behind many of the pictures. Here was an elf handing over two sapphires and receiving a gold ingot in return. Over there were two dwarves, exchanging various combinations of semi-precious stones. Ahren was impressed by the directness and the thoroughness of this system. But he had seen enough traders haggling in his time to know that they would find such fixed regulations far from attractive.

While Khara seemed to be just as impressed as the apprentice, Uldini hardly gave the chamber a second glance and Jelninolan looked positively nauseated by the exhibition of wealth. Ahren knew that the elves only traded when they needed products that they thought would be useful, or sometimes to satisfy the greed of human traders when it meant keeping on good terms with them. It suddenly struck Ahren that were it not for the brisk trade between the elves and Knight Marshes and the consequent abundance of wealthy merchants, the defamatory messages of the Illuminated Path would have had a much more fruitful reception. Nevertheless, the elf priestess's demeanour betrayed disgust at this place of ritualised trade with its greed etched into its walls. Culhen, on the other hand, trotted around the hall sniffing hopefully before finally giving up, as the hall didn't provide any morsels to eat.

Falk indicated to them to follow, where they arrived at the exchange line and finally reached the stone throne on which the motionless dwarf was sitting, his eyes staring seemingly at nothing in the distance.

'Is he dead?' asked Ahren as quietly as possible and this time it was Uldini who answered him, while Falk planted himself in front of the sitting figure and performed a peculiar, angular, ritual bow.

'No. Dwarves sleep differently to humans or elves. They can bring their bodies into a sleep-like condition, in which they can still see and hear. Their bodies do not age during this time and many dwarves take advantage of this ability during their long watches. This is why the life spans of dwarves can vary so much, and their ages can range from three hundred to two thousand years.' Uldini thought for a moment. 'Although the later dwarves must have been living very boring lives,' he added with a wink.

The figure on the chair moved and sat up straight once he saw the visitors. The light now fell directly on the dwarf and Ahren could see a long grey beard falling over an enormous stomach. Intelligent, steel-blue eyes set in a deeply wrinkled face examined them carefully and widened considerably when they fell on Jelninolan and Khara. His chainmail was covered by a red material which gave the figure a strangely threatening demeanour, although he appeared to be unarmed. He spoke in an incredibly deep, rasping voice and Falk answered tersely and with a shake of his head. The dwarf looked reproachfully at the Forest Guardian and he began to speak again, but this time in the Northern tongue.

'If your companions don't possess the basic manners of speaking the language of those from whom they seek aid, then I will just have to speak in your tongue.'

The biting undertone in the old dwarf's voice immediately reminded Ahren of dressing-downs he had received from his master and he wondered if Falk had learned a few tricks from the dwarves.

'I know you, Dorian Falkenstein, Baron of Falkenstein. You are a Paladin of the gods; you have fought in fifty-three battles alongside the dwarves and have in the process saved one hundred and thirteen from certain death. You have insulted our dwarves eighteen times and you have atoned for them eighteen times. You have killed eight Cleft Skulkers and two Pit Mantises. You are a known friend of seven dwarves who live in these halls, and therefore you may pass.'

He then turned towards Uldini, who rolled his eyes and cut off the old dwarf before he had a chance to speak.

'For the love of the THREE, this is going to take all night. Just give him your guarantee so that we can be on our way, because I swear, if he starts adding up my story, there will be two hundred and thirty-seven insults against the dwarf folk'.

Falk raised his eyebrows in surprise, and Jelninolan put her hand in front of her mouth and giggled quietly. Then an oppressive silence descended on the hall.

The old dwarf drew in his breath deeply, his face was the picture of fury, and Falk quickly jumped in.

'Most noble Garmatulonok, you honour me with your remembrance of my deeds. I hereby place my companions under my guarantee. What they do, I will have done. What they say, I will have said.' He shot Uldini

286

a warning look, who responded with a grin and an innocent raising of his hands.

The dwarf nodded grumpily and said grudgingly: 'so be it. You may pass. Your deeds will be reflected in your history.'

At these words a dwarf guard appeared out of the shadows of the passageway which led into the mountain and began, without moving a facial muscle or saying a word, to light a lantern which he held stretched out in front of him. Garmatulonok slumped back into his chair and stared blankly into the distance again, while the dwarf turned around and marched into the mountain without saying a word.

Falk bowed quickly and then hurried after the dwarf guard.

'We'd better stick closely to him. Personally, I don't want to get stuck on the wrong track,' he said hastily.

'Wrong track?' interjected Ahren anxiously and looked nervously around.

Uldini floated up beside him, giving him a shove forward at the same time.

'A precautionary measure of the dwarves,' he said. 'If anyone has the brainwave of attacking the mountain, first their ships are sunk by the dragon arrows, then they're peppered with crossbow bolts, after that they're slaughtered in the narrow passageway we've just come through, and finally they're surrounded in the Trading Hall and butchered. If a few lucky sods manage to get past all that, then there's the maze waiting for them made up of corridors and passageways consisting of trapdoors, tumbling rocks, not to mention the slides, which bring them down into ice cold potholes filled with water and with no way out.' The little figure pointed at their guide. 'Hence the guard. He knows his way. If you take a wrong turn here, you're finished.'

Ahren felt distinctly uncomfortable. All of a sudden, he was very conscious of the massive rock that surrounded them, and he felt buried alive and imprisoned at the same time. The steady glow of light from the Trading Hall disappeared once they rounded a corner and now it was only the flickering light of the lantern before them that kept them from darkness. They passed by empty corridors which prompted Ahren to imagine unknown dangers lurking in the shadows, and he felt that if he took one false step, he would feel the grip of icy hands coming from the darkness. He brought Culhen firmly to heel and the wolf stuck close to his master, who looked down at him in amusement.

Uldini continued speaking with scorn in his voice.

'No doubt Falk has told you about the dwarves' legendary hospitality. That can be explained very easily. Once they've led you through here, you'll feel as if you've been locked up and a dragon has swallowed the key. At which point, of course, they can be generous hosts, because if the guest doesn't behave, well…' the Arch Wizard didn't finish his sentence, just smiled maliciously as Falk threw him a furious look.

'No wonder you've collected two hundred and thirty-six insults, if you keep stirring things up. You know well how seriously they take such things. How many have you atoned for?' he asked grumpily.

'Not a single one.' The pride in Uldini's voice was unmistakable, and Ahren was sure that the dwarf leading them had paused for a moment, having heard the enormous affront levelled against his folk.

Falk turned and looked at the Arch Wizard in disbelief, but Uldini merely shrugged his shoulders nonchalantly. 'Dwarves love size and strength, that's what you said yourself. I possess neither one nor the other. My abilities as one of the Ancients means nothing to them, and diplomatic niceties just bounce off their thick heads. So how far do you think I can get with the dwarves before I get on the wrong side of one of

288

them? And if I then defend myself, it's not according to their rules, and so the next notch is scored in my list of insults against Dwarfdom.'

The Arch Wizard's voice had grown louder and louder as he spoke.

'Do you know that they wanted to force the Emperor of the Sun Courts to sack me as his adviser once? Their ambassador made an ultimatum and it was only a very large, very heavy casket of gold that got them to change their minds. Of course, not one of my so-called insults was cancelled.' Uldini finished his little tirade with an angry snort before settling into a brooding silence.

Ahren made a decision to take special care of every word he said and of every action he took down here. He couldn't imagine what might happen to him if he called his master's reputation into question among this uncompromising folk after Falk had acted as guarantor for them all, and so he asked a question which he hoped would be harmless enough.

'Who was the old dwarf who let us in earlier?' Ahren couldn't remember his complicated name anymore.

Falk answered without turning around.

'You mean Garmatulonok? He is the Clans Guard of the Silver Halls. His memory is perfect, that's the prerequisite for this position. He knows the history of every dwarf who lives here, and the histories of all the friends of the Silver Cliff dwarves in his head. He decides who may pass through the Trading Hall and into the Clans Halls, and who may not.'

'With a long name like that he must already have...' Ahren paused and counted the syllables in his head, '...five Lonely Watches behind him if I'm not mistaken.' Ahren found the ritual whereby the dwarves could prove their worth endearing.

Falk hesitated and then nodded.

'In principle, yes, but there are exceptions. His last three syllables were honorary awards, one for every century he remained sitting in that chair back there.'

Ahren thought that his master was pulling his leg, but the expected laughter never came.

'Are you telling me that he's been sitting on that chair receiving visitors for over three hundred years?' he asked in disbelief.

The length of time itself was unimaginable, but the thought of performing this single, monotonous activity for so long seemed quite incredible to the apprentice.

Jelninolan muttered something about barbaric rituals and Falk continued hastily and loudly as he tried to drown out the elf's comment. The dwarf guard's lantern threw flickering shadows on the walls of the seemingly endless passageway, whose twists and turns were leading them ever deeper into the cliff.

'You mustn't forget that his perceptions are different. He spends his time in a state of torpidity, and he has been fully awake for perhaps ten of the last three hundred years. For many dwarves, long watches at remote entrances or honour watches in the Clan Hall are a tried and tested means of doing their bit in gaining a name-syllable, and at the same time, only sacrifice a small period of their lives,' explained the Forest Guardian in a conciliatory tone.

In the beginning the air had been cold and damp, but the further they penetrated the cliff, the drier and more stifling it became. The salty sea air was replaced by a strangely dusty smell, and Ahren had the feeling as if a sack of flour was slowly being pressed onto his chest. He began to breathe more quickly, and he noticed that Jelninolan and Khara were doing the same. Eventually, the feeling became unbearable and the apprentice, thinking he was going to suffocate, hit his master's armoured back, breathlessly. In his panic he hit the forest Guardian with much more force than intended and a loud clash echoed down the dark corridors and passageways.

Falk spun around with a curse, but when he realised what was happening, he stopped and indicated to their guide to do the same. Then he spoke quietly to his three breathless companions, all of whom had sunk down onto their knees.

'What you are experiencing at the moment is what is called Mountain Lung, or Depth Breath. Uldini and I know how to deal with it, but you still have to become accustomed to the different air and also to your thoughts regarding the rock surrounding you. Close your eyes and hold your breath for a short time, even if you find it uncomfortable.'

Ahren did as he was told and broke into a sweat. It took all his willpower not to gasp for breath, so he fled into the Void. Immediately, the cool benevolent peace of the emotionless condition came over him, and even if his lungs were still pleading for oxygen, at least he was no longer in a panic.

Culhen sensed the discomfort of his friends and ran around between them, planting encouraging, if quite useless, slobbery licks of his tongue on them.

Ahren heard Falk's voice giving them further instructions.

'Very good. Now, breathe in, hold your breath, count to five and breathe out. If you feel a pressure on your lungs, try to breathe slowly and in a controlled way through the pain.'

At the start, it was almost impossible to follow the old man's instructions, but it gradually became easier and finally the pain on Ahren's chest was gone and it was as if he had never experienced it. The apprentice opened his eyes and his master gave him an approving nod. Khara was the next to be ready and finally Jelninolan opened her eyes.

Soon Culhen too had calmed down and Ahren wasn't the only one wiping away panicky beads of sweat from his face, not to mention dog saliva.

'I hate mountains,' whispered Jelninolan, who was drenched in sweat. She grabbed onto Culhen's fur and pulled herself up.

Falk grunted. 'I thought you were down in the mines a few times during the Dark Days,' he said with a questioning undertone.

'Only in Wyrm Caves or Packtooth nests. Never deep in the rock,' she said shortly.

Ahren pricked up his ears and decided to ask his master later. He really needed to broaden his horizons regarding the various Dark Ones.

They went on in silence, and after what seemed like an endlessly long and boring time, the tunnel suddenly ended with a rectangular shaped hall, whose roof was held up by mighty pillars hewn into the stone. Attached to each of them was a deep bowl in which burned the same strange red fire. There were almost two dozen rectangular walls because of the many corners of the room, each with an entrance as wide as it was high, and each protected by several guards. To the left and right of each entrance were angular symbols, each door having its own special pattern. The dwarves wore the symbols of their respective doors on mighty broad shields, which stood before them. Ahren recognised some of the symbols from the entrance door to the cliff and he studied them curiously.

'The Grand Junction. Here you find the entrances to every clan in the Silver Cliff, each recognisable by its unique symbol,' whispered Uldini to Ahren.

While Falk was speaking to their guide in Dwarfish, Ahren took the opportunity of leaning over to the Arch Wizard.

'Who are all the dwarves here? Are they all guards?'

Uldini nodded. 'These are honour guards of the individual clans. If you look at them carefully, you will see that they're all standing in torpidity. Most of them are greenhorns who want to earn their first syllables in a safe environment.'

Ahren carefully studied the vacuous countenance of the dwarf guards. He wanted to remember the qualities of their strangely unfocussed looks so that he could recognise more quickly if a dwarf was in a state of torpidity. Then he quickly called Culhen back, who was sniffing at one of the young guards curiously. The apprentice wasn't sure how a guard would react if it was yanked out of its torpidity by a wet tongue, and he didn't want to risk finding out.

Falk, meanwhile, had said goodbye to the dwarf who had safely led them through the labyrinth, and now turned to the others.

'That way leads to the guest caves. We're allowed to move freely there. We can also request to have conversations with members of individual clans if we wish.'

Falk looked around and scratched his beard thoughtfully.

'It's quite late already. Why don't we take up quarters and have something to eat? Then we can discuss our next steps,' said the old Forest Guardian.

'Why can't I shake off the notion that you're hiding something important from us again?' grumbled Uldini.

'Come with me first', said Falk firmly.

Ahren was hungry and tired, and the idea of eating and sleeping was very attractive. Anyway, he was glad to have a little time to digest his experiences of the past few hours. And so he followed his master, and the two women did the same. After some hesitation and a few softly spoken curses about stubborn Forest Guardians, Uldini followed his companions through the only unguarded entrance.

This entrance was no different to the others. Ahren calculated its dimensions to be four paces high and wide. Behind it was a short tunnel with heavy doors placed at regular intervals along it.

Falk stood at the main entrance and looked at the doors. He was unsure of which one to open.

'I was only here once before, and that time I was the guest of the clan of silver workers. I was never actually in this spot.' Then he picked out a door at random and opened it.

Ahren was standing directly behind him and gave a low gasp of surprise when he saw the spacious chamber which the heavy wooden door had revealed. Even Falk seemed impressed and stepped inside. Ahren almost pushed past Falk in his excitement.

'Come in,' he shouted excitedly, 'You have to see this!'

The chamber was at least fifteen paces long and fifteen paces wide and the ceiling was over five paces above them. The walls were made of hewn rock, but that was as far as the simplicity of their accommodation went. The cross section of a square shaped quartz vein in the ceiling spread an orange-red uniform light which fell on pillars decorated in gold, silver-plated trunks and enormous wardrobes. The solid tables and chairs were made from the same robust wood as the heavy door.

The travellers looked around in curiosity. Several entrances led from the main room to individual guest rooms, which were smaller but decorated just as opulently as the common room. Each contained a comfortable looking bed which extended the length of the wall.

There were tankards placed everywhere containing a dark brew which Ahren identified as some kind of strong beer, and on each table there was a dish containing smoked fish and dried mushrooms, each the size of a saucer. A separate plate contained a strongly smelling gold and yellow cheese. The intensive smells caused Ahren's mouth to water.

294

The aromas had the same effect on Falk and Uldini and before twenty heartbeats had passed the men were sitting together and helping themselves to the food. Khara sat with them, although she ate with a little more scepticism and avoided the cheese altogether.

Only Jelninolan couldn't be won over by the choice of food, but a short while later they were surprised to hear a little cry of delight, and when Ahren went over to have a look, he saw the reason for her exuberance.

One of the entrances to the main room led over a long, gently-bending hallway to a small, hewn cavern with gently steaming flowing water. Somehow, the little folk had managed to tap into a hot spring and direct it to this cavern.

Jelninolan was clearly so keen on taking a bath after two weeks on board ship that she had already begun undressing herself when Ahren came around the corner. Her appearance was far from indecorous at this point but nonetheless, Ahren spun around and made his retreat before the elf noticed him. Ahren kept catching himself being embarrassed by the priestess's new, athletic body, and the young man found it hard to reconcile her new appearance with the motherly feelings Jelninolan's earlier self had radiated.

He told the others about the hot spring, and Khara jumped up without saying a word and ran towards it, not forgetting to take a drumstick for provisions.

Ahren sat with Falk and Uldini, with the sound of splashing water occasionally echoing from the cavern nearby. Now the apprentice asked the questions that had been at the back of his mind.

'Master, you say there is a purpose to the openly displayed wealth of the dwarves. But what is it? Do they not just attract outlaws?'

He chewed on the surprisingly aromatic cheese while he waited for an answer. Ahren had discovered that it tasted remarkably good as long as you avoided smelling it beforehand.

Falk was just in the process of chewing on a hock, and he spoke while he ate.

'Ye Gods, how I love Dwarfish food. My heart belongs to the elves, but my stomach is definitely Dwarfish in origin.'

He took another serious bite before addressing his apprentice's question.

'The maxim of the small folk is very simple: present what you can do, and what you can protect. Everything you see here, the dwarves consider to be justifiable grandiosity and absolutely safe from theft. Their business tactic is very simple but effective: a merchant who sees their riches will automatically offer more for Dwarfish goods because they assume that a lower offer will arouse no interest. As for the fortifications and the dragon bows, it makes it clear to the merchant that he will only obtain the Dwarfish goods by engaging in trade.'

Falk chewed his meat for a moment.

'It seems to have worked very well for the past couple of centuries.'

Ahren nodded and took some more cheese and mushrooms, washing them down with some of the beer, which made him light-headed without clouding his senses.

'And what kind of a light is that?' he asked, pointing up at the quartz rectangle.

Falk paused and looked up for a moment, then put his knuckle of meat aside.

'That is a really good sleight of hand, if a damned expensive one. You saw the red flames when we came in? In the Trading Hall and the Grand Junction?'

Uldini and Ahren nodded. Ahren was astonished, for it seemed that the Arch Wizard couldn't answer Ahren's question either. This was the first time the ageless magus was ignorant of anything that was based on facts.

'It's Deep Fire,' said Falk, interrupting Ahren's train of thought. 'It's made from Deep Steel which has been saturated in various oils before being set alight. Only Deep Fire can set other Deep Fire alight. But it doesn't consume itself and its flame is practically eternal. It's difficult to prepare and as such, extremely costly. They have a lot of it here, which suggests that the Silver Cliff is doing extremely well financially.'

Falk's calloused hand pointed upwards.

'Up there behind the quartz there must be Deep Fire burning, which makes for continuous light. As I said, a trick, but a very good one, and very impressive.'

Then Falk took up his hock of meat again and continued eating.

Uldini looked thoughtfully up at the ceiling.

'Eternal fire? Why don't I know anything about it? You could do a lot with that.'

Falk put down his food again and gave Uldini a firm look.

'That's exactly why. If you really want to burn something, throw a fire charm. Deep Fire is extremely expensive and its temperature is so high that the bowls in which it burns have to be manufactured using a special alloy.'

He pointed at the cave walls that surrounded them.

'One big Deep Fire can keep all of the rooms in the Silver Cliff warm and dry with the help of narrow shafts set into the walls. The Grand Junction is kept at a stable temperature by a few torches even though there are over twenty passages through which the heat can escape. The bowl in the Trading Hall serves as a bulwark against the sea air. They

297

may come across as stubborn and inflexible, but they're not stupid. By the time you've thought of two ways of solving a problem, they will have come up with three, and will already have implemented them.'

Uldini rolled his eyes. 'If you love the little folk so much, why did you end up with the elves then?' he asked bitingly.

Ahren looked down and held his breath. He'd been asking himself the same question ever since they'd arrived, and he was eager to hear the answer.

To his surprise Falk was not enraged by the question but instead he gave a slight smile.

'It's deep respect rather than love. I was a broken man and that didn't bother them as long I stuck to the rules. They gave me a few years of stability when I needed it urgently. But I was never welcomed in Thousand Halls, and the dwarves here are purely merchants and crafts people. Neither of which gave me happiness or peace. So, I headed off again and a few decades later I landed with the elves. They saw my pain and weren't indifferent to it. My conviction in Eathinian, where the punishment was to work off my guilt, saved me. Ultimately that was of more value than culinary preferences.'

Then he continued eating and they sat for a while in silence.

Ahren already knew about the terrible events surrounding the death of Falk's daughter. It was only thanks to the patience and sensitivity of the elves that the old man had found inner peace again, and he felt a deep affinity with the forest folk. Had they not saved Falk from himself, then the cantankerous man would not have been able to save Ahren.

Chapter 16

37 days to the winter solstice

When Jelninolan and Khara finally came out of the bath, they found their three companions in contemplation, each one pursuing their own thoughts. Culhen's barking was the only sound that broke through the silence, a tell-tale sign that the wolf had gulped down the enormous portion of food that Ahren had handed out to him, following his constant begging.

'See, I told you, too much meat causes depression and inertia,' said Jelninolan to Khara resolutely, who nodded eagerly, but still glanced longingly at the meat on the table.

The elf looked up at the ceiling and screwed up her face.

'Oh, dear goddess, how I miss the sun and the wind already! How can anyone live in a place so far apart from everything living?' she sighed.

Falk roused himself out of his thoughts and looked sternly at the priestess.

'You have a tendency to only accept points of view that are similar to yours. Humans, dwarves and elves have all been created differently and so they each have rules that only apply to them. A dwarf sees the forest as fickle, volatile and threatening, and a human settlement as primitively built, unplanned and chaotic. So, make judgements about their values, not their way of living. They are hard but fair, ostentatious and at the same time frugal, direct but consistently honest. I would like to have someone like that on my side; don't you feel the same way?'

Uldini intervened before a serious argument could flare up.

'I take it that your friend, whom we are supposed to help, possesses all these qualities you're raving about?'

Falk nodded.

'In those days he was called Tor. He had just earned the first syllable of his name and he had been hired out for several years to the Mountainshield Clan as a sapper to a company of mercenaries. I was new to the company as well and we got on well together. We laughed, drank and ate a lot and now and again we would save one another's life. I was pretty reckless in those days and he got me out of more than a few scrapes with his strength.'

Uldini frowned.

'Hang on a minute. The Mountainshields don't actually hire out young dwarves. What are you not telling us, old friend?'

All eyes were on Falk, who looked uncomfortable for a moment.

'He's one of the Pure Ones,' he said finally.

Uldini gave a whistle and Jelninolan was stunned.

'No wonder you're thinking of him as Ahren's Einhan,' said the Arch Wizard and gave a concerned look. ' Pure Ones always mean big trouble though. Have you thought about it properly?'

Falk slammed his fist down on the table. The sound echoed loudly from the surrounding walls, and everyone looked at him in shock.

'He's my friend and he's asked me for help. We help him, he helps us. I'm not going to turn my back on him just because it's easier.'

None of the others were willing to express their doubts, so Ahren cleared his throat and spoke.

'I'd like to know what a Pure One is, and why that could be good or bad for us,' he ventured, trying to speak as calmly as possible.

It was now well into the night and the beer was making him fretful. He just wanted an explanation, then a quick dip in the hot spring, and then bed.

'The term is a little misleading. The Dwarfish word is Kulkumharan'thur. And if you translate that directly, it means 'he, in whom the pure essence lives.' They have an excess of strength from HIM, WHO IS. This makes them stronger, more resistant and longer-living than normal dwarves,' said Falk reassuringly.

'And more stubborn, opinionated and surlier than your normal dwarf. Which is probably why he was hired out to the mercenaries that time,' added Uldini with fury in his voice.

He turned to Ahren but said to Falk instead: 'the Pure Ones are deviations from the norm, and that goes completely against the Dwarfish culture. They automatically become members of the Mountainshield Clan, who are responsible for the defence of the little folk, and they are usually to be found at the most difficult posts that exist. No Pure One has ever died in their dotage. Their own folk have a love-hate attitude towards them. They're of great value to their community on account of their fighting strength, but because of their peculiarities they are never considered fully-fledged members of their community.'

The little Arch Wizard gave a deep sigh.

'Which means of course that with their not-so-sunny disposition, they become even more uncommunicative with the passage of time.'

'We have some experience of difficult travelling companions,' murmured Ahren.

The beer and the cave walls ensured that the comment resonated more strongly than intended, and both Uldini and Falk gave him an offended look. Jelninolan had to hide a smile and Khara used the distraction to quickly shove a piece of meat into her mouth.

'But then he'll surely want to come with us, won't he? If he doesn't properly belong here anyway and Falk is his friend?' said the apprentice quickly and with as innocent a face as he could muster.

'Pure Ones are always given the most difficult tasks when they are sent on a Lonely Watch. If it were a normal dwarf, our help would probably be much easier. But however monumental the task my friend has to perform is, it will be a hard and time-consuming job to help him finish it.'

Ahren's master turned to Uldini.

'I've kept in contact with him over all this time, and in his last letter he said that he would be busy for the foreseeable future. That was five summers ago, and as he didn't meet us at the Grand Junction, he still has to be at his Lonely Watch. I think helping him is the right thing to do, in more than one respect.'

Uldini was about to protest, but he was cut off by Jelninolan.

'If I have to travel with a dwarf anyway,' said the priestess, 'then rather it be with one who has our cantankerous Forest Guardian as his friend and who, as a Pure One, will provide considerably more protection to our travelling party. I'm in favour.'

The Arch Wizard folded his arms but said nothing.

'Then it's decided. Tomorrow morning we'll go in search of the Mountainshield Clan and ask them where the dwarf, once called Tor, can be found,' announced Falk ceremoniously.

Ahren gave a tired nod and stood up. He was tempted for a moment to slip into the water, but the lure of his bed was too strong. He wished his companions good night and went in search of his chamber, where he could lie down. Hardly had his head hit the pillow on the large bed, when he was out like a light.

When Ahren woke up, he was completely disorientated. The room looked exactly the same as it had when he had fallen asleep, and there was nothing around him that could indicate how long he had been slumbering. The reddish light was still the same and the timeless stillness that hung over the chamber weighed heavily on the young man.

His companions' voices could be heard coming from the common room, and he leaped out of bed gratefully and went towards the sounds. The feelings of loneliness and timelessness that had possessed him disappeared with every step, and Ahren was relieved when he yanked open the door and found everyone sitting around the breakfast table. However, when he saw the choice of foods available, he grew irritated. Meat, cheese and mushrooms. Somebody had obviously been in the room during the night and had replenished the provisions, but the menu hadn't changed.

Falk was just biting into a large piece of cheese and glanced in Ahren's direction.

'There aren't any mornings or evenings down here. And as a consequence, they don't differentiate between the meals. If you're hungry you just help yourself.' Then he took another big bite.

The rest of the party weren't quite so enthusiastic, and nibbled at a few bits of mushroom.

Such a breakfast being an acquired taste, Ahren decided to abandon it in favour of a bath, and trotted on to the bath cavern, where the hot spring bubbled a merry welcome. And not just the spring. Ahren laughed when he saw the soaking wet wolf, who was splashing about happily in the large basin.

'Don't let the ladies catch you,' he whispered conspiratorially as he undressed quickly and slid in beside his friend into the delightfully warm water.

'They'll be far from happy if it stinks of wet wolf in here.' Culhen threw him an offended look and gave a snort, but then licked his master right across his face.

After a while Ahren had finished giving himself a thorough wash and playing energetically with the wolf. Now he was floating in the warm current and was just holding onto the edge of the basin. Heavy iron bars on both ends slowed down the current of the subterranean river as it passed through, and here, at the edge, he could resist the pull of the current effortlessly and allow himself and his thoughts to float freely. He tickled the wolf's fur absently. Culhen was lying outside the basin beside his master and was growling contentedly under the apprentice's fingers. The smell from the wolf's mouth suggested to Ahren that Falk had fed him a substantial portion of smoked meat, and the animal's half-closed eyes reflected his relaxed, satiated contentment.

Ahren tried to remember the last time he had played around with Culhen. It was when they had departed from the elves before their journey to King's Island. So much had happened over the intervening two months that he felt quite dizzy thinking about it. And now at last, they had reached the dwarves. If everything went well, they would have all of the Einhans together and they would make their way to the secret Place of Ritual. Not even Uldini knew where it was. How the Wild Folk of Kelkor were to help them still wasn't clear to Ahren, but at this stage of the journey he was happy to have learned to accept that it was better to take one step at a time. Everything was so new and so strange that he had his hands full trying to understand what was going on in front of his nose.

His training too, had stalled through the circumstances of the last few weeks. Instead of running around the forest, there was now sword training with Khara and Jelninolan, and the latter kept them both on their toes, instilling the ground rules of Elfish lightness of foot, and all of that was rounded off by Falk's gruelling strength exercises.

Ahren heard steps behind him and he quickly sank up to his neck in the water, but it was only Falk, who looked down at him critically.

'Other people want to get in there today too, you know, so get a move on!'

Ahren quickly got out of the water and used his old shirt to rub himself down.

'The dwarves brought our things over earlier. Your rucksack is on your bed,' his master added.

Ahren gave a nod in gratitude and went past his master, who hummed quietly to himself and began to get undressed. Culhen followed the apprentice, and the young man hurried quickly through the common room so that he could dress properly. Khara was sitting at the table and she gave the half-naked apprentice a critical look.

'Chest like chicken,' she giggled and threw Culhen a piece of meat while her eyes sparkled mischievously at Ahren.

The apprentice was sensible enough not to get involved in a verbal duel, dressed as he was, and so he went on to his sleeping cavern without saying a word. He stepped into his new clothing and realised it had been cleaned before being deposited. This meant that somebody had been going through his things, but at this point he happily accepted cleanliness over privacy.

He hurried back into the main room and found Culhen contentedly chewing at Jelninolan's feet.

'Stop! Nobody feeds this wolf!' he called out in a firm voice.

The others looked at him in amazement, and Ahren began questioning them about how much Culhen had already managed to beg off them. To everyone's surprise, the greedy animal had already scrounged enough for three days.

Ahren raised his finger and looked sternly into Culhen's eyes.

'Bold wolf!' he scolded, but Culhen merely licked his mouth contentedly as he swallowed down the last of his ill-gotten gains. Realising his final source had finally dried up, the wolf curled up into a large ball of white fur and fell asleep, completely unperturbed by his master's scolding.

'I think you may need to polish up on your authoritativeness,' said Uldini drily.

The apprentice looked at him furiously and the Arch Wizard raised his hands in defence.

'Merely a suggestion,' he added innocently. 'I'll shoo Falk out of the water. At this rate our dwarf friend will have finished his Lonely Watch before we've even left these lodgings.'

Much later than originally planned, as Uldini had pointed out no less than six times, everyone was ready to depart. They had all wanted to free themselves of the patina of dirt and salt that a long sea voyage had laid on every inch of their bodies and had also made their clothing stiff and scratchy.

By now they were all fully fed, rested, freshly dressed and beginning to feel restless, the young man included. The monotony and constant timelessness of their accommodation was beginning to wear him out and he was longing to see other things. Even a short sword-training session with Khara couldn't distract him from this feeling, and she'd given up in annoyance after she'd slapped him across the face for the tenth time and declared the lesson over.

Now they were standing again at the Grand Junction and Falk was explaining the layout of the Dwarf kingdom to them.

306

'You're already familiar with the Trading Hall. That's something like the outskirts of a human city. The Grand Junction leads to all the individual Clan Halls, which can only be entered by invitation. These halls make up the residential areas of the dwarf settlements. Being a member of a particular clan depends on birth and occupation. If you are born a steel worker, you remain one all your life, unless you develop an exceptional talent in another area. It's quite rare but it does happen. Then it's possible to change clan through marriage. Which is how they make sure that the greatest talents aren't simply wasted, and fresh blood is introduced into the clans' cloistered existence.'

Ahren realised that this was the first hint that there were also female dwarves. He wanted to find out more about this, but Falk had already continued to speak.

'That entrance over there, with the eight sentries in front of it, leads to the mines, the smelting, the smithies and the workshops of the Silver Cliff. Everything in there is the property of the enclave, and visitors are only allowed in with the permission of one of the clan elders.'

Falk moved on and the others followed, as he headed towards one of the clan entrances.

'We're going to try and talk to the clan elder of the Mountainshields. He can answer all our questions about my friend and also give us the permission we need to go to him. So, let me do the talking and don't touch anything,' he instructed them.

They reached an archway, beside which was a resplendent square with a stylized mountain top. The drawing itself was simple but the carving in the wall was diamond-studded and it sparkled in the shimmering reddish Deep Fire light.

The two young dwarves guarding the entrance were dressed in heavy plate armour, which was so weighty no human could possibly wear it, let alone fight in it. They held long axes in their armoured gloves, and their ferocious faces with their still-short beards stared stubbornly forwards. Ahren recognised their characteristically torpid look and asked himself yet again; how the dwarves could keep watch that way.

Then Falk stepped forward and suddenly, as if he had stepped across an invisible border, life came back into the guards' features, and they looked at him seriously and officiously, the left dwarf asking him a question in his rumbling sounding language. This little being too used the echo of the hall to make his voice sound harmonious. Falk stood to his full height and intoned an answer, which sounded very formal, yet crude when compared with the sounds of the dwarf, the Paladin not being able to manage the basics of the echo technique. Nevertheless, following a short consultation they were permitted to pass, and Falk nodded respectfully. Ahren had wondered earlier why his master had put on full armour and had strapped on his broadsword, but now he realised that without the old man's impressive appearance they would never have been granted permission to enter.

'Hero of the Three Gorges? Really? Are you not laying it on a bit too thickly?' whispered Uldini to his companion.

Falk threw an almost apologetic look over his shoulder.

'I wanted to play it safe so that they'd let us through. I've fought in so many battles, I'm not going to be locked out by a pimply dwarf youth just by being modest.'

Uldini gave an ironic bow and murmured, 'but of course, Your Mightiness.' Falk snorted and walked on as Uldini floated behind him laughing sarcastically. Soon they'd reached the end of the short corridor and were entering the Hall of the Mountainshield Clan.

The first thing Ahren saw was the enormous fire in the middle of the large vault. The room was at least one hundred paces in length and

308

breadth and its roof stretched up roughly twenty paces. There were dozens of doorways along the four walls, and short wide steps led up to impressive galleries that ran all around and offered entrance through yet more doorways. Four stories towered one above the other in this manner, and the apprentice made out well over two hundred doors leading into this room.

The hall was a hubbub of activity. The room was filled with long tables, along which dwarves were drinking, eating, laughing, throwing dice, messing about, and polishing their axes and shields. It was just like in the old sagas with dwarves around the campfire, and yet it was also quite different to how Ahren had imagined it. Their tone of address was polite, almost friendly, everything was neat and tidy, and the general impression of civilisation put many a human tavern into the shade. In the human ballads about dwarves, the little folk were seen as pugnacious drinkers with dubious morals, but there was no sign of that here. If it reminded him of anything, then it was of the hall in the barracks on King's Island, which he had caught a glimpse of once.

Falk noticed Ahren's expression and he gave him a wink, and then they approached the fire in the centre of the enormous room.

Gradually the noise died down as the conversations subsided, the dice cups were placed on the tables, and the tankards were set down. Many of the dwarves stared openly at them, and the apprentice saw some of the little folk bowing respectfully towards Jelninolan and Khara, in the same way that the guards at the Cliff entrance had done. Culhen sniffed along the rows of benches and received many strokes along the way and, of course, more to eat once he had given his best impression of a starving wolf. Ahren remembered what Falk had said the previous day concerning the respect dwarves had towards domesticated wolves. He decided not to scold Culhen but instead he gave a clear, shrill whistle, and when the wolf's head flew around to see his master, the young man gave him a steely look and gestured towards his heel. Culhen obediently trotted over to him and Ahren noticed, to his satisfaction, how some of the dwarves gave him an approving nod.

'You're good for something, anyway,' he whispered to the white animal and ruffled his fur lovingly. Culhen gave an annoyed snort but stayed by his side nevertheless.

The two women were still being bowed to respectfully as the group neared the fire, and Ahren's curiosity got the better of him. 'Why are they being so unbelievably respectful to Khara and Jelninolan? I thought dwarves weren't particularly close to elves and humans,' he asked.

'It's nothing to do with their origin, but with their sex. Women are very special phenomena to dwarves. Only one in every twenty dwarf children is female. The only reason they haven't all died out is that dwarf women usually give birth to quadruplets or even quintuplets. Hence, their respectful behaviour. Many of them have never seen a female in their lives, with the exception of their mother.'

'Which is why the female dwarves decided thousands of years ago to hide themselves from the world.' Falk's voice sounded sad as he continued. 'If too many of them die within one generation, whether through war or disease, then the whole race of little people will die out.'

Ahren looked at the polite, almost longing looks of the bowing dwarves and a feeling of melancholy came over him. Almost everyone of these dwarves would spend their life without a partner. Friendship and camaraderie, they would certainly have, but never togetherness. And the realisation that their own race always had the threat of extinction hanging over them had to be difficult to live with.

310

Ahren now understood some of the dwarfish qualities better. Everyone of them wanted to prove something to the others, put their value on show and perhaps become one of the lucky ones to win the favour of a she-dwarf. Even the grim willingness-to-fight that every dwarf radiated made more sense now. A dwarf would undoubtedly give everything to protect their homeland and the precious female custodians of the future dwarf generations, who were hidden away in the depths of the enclave.

They arrived at the crackling fire, over which were hanging enormous pots at different heights, attached to cables that were operated by hoists. Ahren could smell a multitude of earthy aromas as he watched a dwarf, with a singed beard and a red face, turning several cranks, which lifted and lowered some of the metal containers. The dwarf reached to the side and turned over a large hourglass before drawing strange angular shapes on a slate that was standing beside him.

While Ahren was still pondering if it wouldn't make more sense to have several smaller fires for stewing the food instead of one big one, he noticed a dwarf who was bent over, with a blanket over his back, standing directly in front of the fire and stretching his hands forward as if to warm them. The apprentice's eyes fell on the dwarf's hands, with their knotty, bony fingers and pale age-spotted skin stretched tight over his knuckles.

Falk cleared his throat respectfully and the figure slowly turned around. Ahren looked in shock at the old dwarf's face and tried hard to hide his feelings. His bald head looked more like a death mask than a living face, and his incredibly long beard, which resembled a snow-white waterfall, reached all the way down to his ankles. His translucent skin revealed deep bluc veins and it was only his intelligent, lively eyes that betrayed that there was life in the body standing before them. Ahren was flabbergasted to see that he was wearing chainmail, albeit one that was thinner than normal. It was made of pure gold and instilled respect towards the dwarf in spite of his decrepit appearance.

Falk bowed deeply and spoke formally and at length, remaining all the time in his stooped position. The dwarf listened impassively, the time passed by, and Falk continued his monologue. Ahren looked around without attracting attention and noticed that almost all the dwarves had returned to what they were doing, with just the occasional secret glance, filled with respect and longing, at the two women.

Uldini glanced at Ahren in annoyance.

'The dwarves' introductory ceremonies are pure torture. First Falk has to relate to the venerable Fulretedurkolok the story of his life, which the dwarves know about already. Then he has to relate the life story of the dwarf we're looking for, to prove that they're friends. It's very important for the dwarves to hear the details of a dwarf's life because it's very hard to tell them apart until they have their own names. Falk's description is as detailed as possible, not only because it's a reminder of all his services to the dwarf folk, but also to show the Elder of the care he is taking in respectfully, upholding their traditions. It's not forbidden for outsiders to help a dwarf on his Lonely Watch, but if the Elder tells us the way to Falk's friend, it could be presented, according to the dwarf traditions, as interference in a dwarf's Lonely Watch. If the Elder decides against us, then we will neither gain access to the mines, nor find out what the Lonely Watch's task is, nor where our dwarf is.'

Jelninolan prodded the Arch Wizard's foot once Falk had finished with his torrent of words. Uldini stopped speaking abruptly and looked down to the ground with as neutral a face as possible.

It was only then that Ahren noticed that the dwarves were taking practically no notice of the Arch Wizard. It had to be a surreal experience for the ageless wizard not to be the centre of attention – he, who dined

312

with kings and queens and had the upper nobility wrapped around his little finger. Culhen, on the other hand, who had slipped away, was being stroked and given portions of meat by the dwarf warriors. They had obviously fallen for his impression of the starving wolf.

The Clan Elder began to speak, and in spite of his age, his voice rang clear and precise.

'You come to us with great deeds and a little request, Dorian Falkenstein, friend of the dwarves and of all free folk. And, though you need to polish up your pronunciation of the Cliff language, I very much enjoyed your story of your life. He, whom you know, and was once called Tor before he left, has concerned himself with the Ancestry Name.'

There had been total silence in the room since the old dwarf had begun talking. Uldini gasped when he heard those words, and Falk stiffened, as if he had suddenly been plunged into an icy bath.

'The task was selected as appropriate to the honour he sought, and as he is a Kulkumharan'thur, we expect greatness from him. He has taken on, as befits a Mountainshield, the greatest danger that the Silver Cliff is currently facing. He has been keeping watch for five summers and must do so for another ninety-five, unless he succeeds in overpowering our enemy once and for all.'

The Elder stopped speaking, and Ahren feared the worst. He looked with concern at Uldini's and Falk's stony faces. Then he looked appealingly at Jelninolan, who laid a hand on his shoulder to support herself and pressed the surprised Khara into her chest. Ahren swallowed hard and concentrated on the Elder who spoke again.

'You'll find him on the deepest level of the northern shaft, far beyond the Warning Runes. Help him, and he has the blessing of the Clans to accompany you'

The Elder gave a dignified nod and then turned back to the fire.

Ahren saw that the aged dwarf's hands were shaking as if from the cold as the stooped figure stretched his fingers out towards the blazing flames again.

Falk gave a deep bow behind the Chief of the Mountainshield Clan and stiffly signalled to the others to follow him out of the hall. Everyone in the group, with the exception of Khara and Ahren, seemed to be in a state of complete shock, and the girl threw the apprentice a quizzical look, but he only responded with a puzzled shrug of his shoulders. The silence that followed the Elder's words continued as they walked back towards the entrance. The lines of dwarves bowed respectfully as Falk passed by, and Ahren's master tried to reciprocate as many bows as possible without slowing down his pace. The others followed him like a royal household rushing after their hurrying king.

They were hardly back at the Grand Junction when Uldini shook off his state of shock and exploded with rage. He floated directly in front of Falk's nose and sparks flew in all directions as the Wizard tried to regain his self-control.

'An Ancestry Name!? What by all the gods was your dunderhead friend thinking of? As if it wasn't difficult enough being one of the pure dwarves, he wants to lay claim to the most important name in Dwarfdom? Dwarf generals and master blacksmiths need aeons to have an Ancestry Name bestowed on them by the Clan Board, and your dwarf friend, who isn't even two hundred years old, expects to be granted one at the drop of a hat?' the Arch Wizard shouted in frustration. 'Oh, Falk, what have you ridden us into? Are we going to have to hollow out a mountain? Or take over Southern Kelkor? Or exterminate every Gorge Spider from here to Thousand Halls?'

Uldini was discharging little sparks, which were exploding on the ground and ceiling.

314

Jelninolan laid a calming hand on the raging Ancient's forearm.

'You really need to control yourself. Half of the Honour Guards have awoken from their torpor and are giving you fearsome looks. You know what dwarves think of magic, and at the moment there are over forty hostile eyes looking at you and at this very heartbeat they're wondering if you might be a threat to their Clans,' she implored.

The priestess's urgent words finally brought Uldini to his senses. The discharges suddenly stopped, and the Wizard floated away from the old Paladin, who was standing there grinding his teeth. Ahren could see that his master was in a state of shock, and so he did what he always did, to defuse a fraught situation. He asked a question.

'What exactly is an Ancestry Name?', he interjected.

Uldini's response was to curse quietly, but Falk pulled himself out of his lethargy.

'There are names that are so important in the history of dwarves that it is forbidden to form them from the individual syllable that a dwarf gathers in the course of his life. The names of heroes from a bygone era, of the original Clan founders, or of legendary blacksmiths are all to be found in the Ancestry Names. The king of Thousand Halls, Holwortunur, for example, bears such a name. At this time there are two dozen Ancestry Names, and each can only be borne by a single dwarf. As far as I know, there only three in use at the moment along with the king,' explained Falk in a monotone. 'Achieving an Ancestry Name is the almost unattainable pinnacle of a hard but successful dwarf life. Only exceptionally honourable, not to mention talented dwarves have ever achieved them. They're only bestowed by the Clan Board, the ruling council of the dwarf kingdom. Theoretically you can claim one for a Lonely Watch but that's…unusual, because performing a task worthy of an Ancestry Name usually results in death,' said the Paladin as he concluded his explanation.

Uldini raised a sarcastic eyebrow but remained silent.

Falk shrugged his shoulders helplessly.

'It makes no difference. We've permission to enter the northern mine and to help him. We also have a licence to bring him with us afterwards. I only hope the task is not one of the ones Uldini fears. That could take longer than planned. We should at least listen to what he has to say. If worse comes to worse, we'll just have to leave him here and hope that another dwarf will help us,' he said with a worried voice.

Ahren stopped in shock and stared at his master's back. The apprentice had assumed that Uldini, in his rage, had exaggerated wildly, but it was obvious that Falk shared the wizard's worries concerning the enormity of the task that the nameless dwarf was currently faced with. The old man's doubts were so strong that he was even toying openly with the idea of abandoning his friend.

Ahren stomped after the others with mixed feelings and earnestly prayed that they hadn't bitten off more than they could chew this time.

Chapter 17

The blackness in the tunnels under the Silver Cliff was endless. There were too many passages, corridors, quarries, smelting areas and tunnels for them all to be lit. And so the dwarves only took their lanterns and oil hoses to where they were currently working, and everywhere else was left to silence and darkness.

Uldini provided them with light through his crystal ball, which emitted a faint brightness and which floated along over their heads and just under the ceilings. Ahren had noticed early on that the dwarves' love of imposing structures played second fiddle to their pragmatism, and so the tunnels, while wide, were not particularly high. Ahren had to duck his head repeatedly, and Falk was almost constantly walking in a stooped position. Having banged his head several times, his master had resorted to putting on his helmet. From time to time they would hear a scraping, metallic sound when Falk was too near the ceiling, but at least there was no danger of him doing any serious damage to his head.

They had taken all their armour with them and put it on as they had no idea what task awaited them. Khara had been a little disgruntled and looked at the others with envy, because she was the only one who hadn't taken body armour with her when they left their quarters. With the only option left to her, she had grasped Windblade firmly, and Ahren was certain that her hand had been on the hilt ever since.

During the first few hours of their journey, Ahren and his companions had seen the hustle and bustle of work everywhere. Carts filled with ore, or rocks streaked with precious stone, were pulled up from the depths of the tunnels on their way to large smithies and workshops where the majority of the dwarves were working away within comfortable distance of the Clan Halls. The bustling activity gradually diminished however, during the course of their first day travelling in the mines. Ahren huffed and puffed more and more loudly under the weight of the enormous rucksack full of provisions. Falk had tied it onto his back before they had set off, but Ahren couldn't complain because his master was carrying a similar load of foodstuffs on his broad shoulders, and even Jelninolan and Khara were heavily laden. Ahren realised with a sense of unease that Falk and Uldini had calculated on their journey taking several days, and the thought of their little group stumbling through the dark bowels of the mountain, far from any help, filled him with gloom.

The first night Ahren lay under his blanket surrounded by darkness, and the oppressive feel of the rock all around him almost caused him to scream in panic. It was only Culhen's soothing presence that prevented him from losing it. The quiet calmness of the wolf helped him to drop off to sleep as he snuggled close to his furry friend.

The group pushed further and further into the northern tunnel, following the angular line drawings that marked each turn off and passageway. Every one of these tunnels, hewn out of the rock, looked the same to Ahren, and with every hour that they progressed, Ahren would imagine that they were walking around in a circle. No Deep Fire kept the cold of the rock at bay here in the mines, and he felt a clammy dampness in his bones. This part of the tunnel seemed abandoned, and only occasionally would they come across a dwarf scurrying along, clasping a pickaxe and looking at them suspiciously.

Then they started their descent into the depths. The corridors and tunnels looked as if they were on the level as the descent was very gradual, but thanks to Ahren's balance training with Jelninolan, he sensed the downward direction. The air and the pressure which he felt on his chest changed subtly with every hour they walked, like a constant whispering that you grow used to, but which changes its volume or tone ever so slightly.

They had rested for four nights by this point. In the morning, the square-shaped hewn tunnels had disappeared, and yet, in spite of the many angled warnings etched into the walls for a stretch of over sixty paces, they had carried on walking. Once they had passed the warning signs, the tunnels changed dramatically. They were now circular, three paces in diameter, and the surface of the rock was smooth. Ahren had seen no signs of pickaxes and the rock looked as if it had been worked on by some incredibly fine machinery before being polished. Ahren asked himself why somebody would go to so much trouble to smooth a tunnel in the depths of the earth.

In order to fight the monotony and danger of their slow, gruelling progress, Ahren had again begun to practise the Northern Language with Khara. Jelninolan helped out when he ran into difficulties but she seemed happy that Ahren had taken on the task of helping the girl.

'These mines have been abandoned for some time, and the warning runes make it clear to any traveller that it's dangerous here. If you practise with Khara, then I can concentrate on establishing if there are other beings present. Other creatures live in the mountain and they spread out unhindered in areas where the dwarves have withdrawn their guards. We don't want to walk into an ambush down here, do we?' she had said.

These words had made Ahren uneasy, but Uldini and Falk seemed to have blind faith in the elf's abilities and so they proceeded, more bored than frightened, down the endless passageways.

They were now resting for the fifth time, at least that was what Ahren guessed, for he had lost all feeling for time. Falk had insisted that they bring along as many provisions as possible, but this didn't stop him from rationing their supplies. Drinking water would have been a problem under other circumstances, but Uldini possessed a magic charm that sucked all the moisture up to the surface of the rock. The water was extremely cold and had a strangely metallic taste, but the Arch Wizard had promised them that it was palatable.

Ahren ignored Culhen. The wolf saw the rationing of their food as a personal affront and so he approached everyone in the group, whining and yelping piteously until Jelninolan finally gave in and fed him a little portion of her meat.

Falk gave her a reproachful look, but she stopped him with a wave of her hand.

'The dwarf cuisine does nothing for me anyway. The mushrooms and cheese are more than enough to keep me going, and if I have to starve down here for another two weeks, I might be able to fit into my old armour again.' The priestess said this with a twinkle in her eye but everyone else in the group had the good sense not to make a comment in response.

Communication had generally abated during the days of their descent. They only spoke when necessary and often the only sounds to be heard echoing through the darkness were their steps and the voices of Ahren and Khara as they carried on with her language classes.

Every now and again they would come to a crossing, and it was at one such crossing that Falk suddenly stopped with a feeling of unease.

'We really should be finding our dwarf by now. These tunnels are certainly not natural, but neither do they look to me like dwarf work. We've been out of the Silver Cliff mines for over a day now,' said Falk.

Then he turned to Jelninolan.

'Are you sure we haven't missed him somehow?'

The elf thought for a long time before answering - too long for Ahren's taste. When she finally spoke, however, her voice was full of confidence.

'Hardly anything lives down here, which makes it easier to sense anything nearby. So far, we've passed by two Gorge Spiders, but they didn't notice us, so I just ignored them,' she said calmly.

Falk nodded, satisfied, but wasn't finished yet.

'Could you cast a Charm Net to find my dwarf friend, Uldini?'

The little figure swayed his head left and right and then looked at the elf.

'I've most practice in sensing out magic or Dark Ones. Maybe I could improvise something with Jelninolan's help that specifically searches for dwarves.'

The priestess looked very doubtful, but then she went down on her haunches and the two began to draw complicated drawings on the ground which glimmered dimly in the faint greenish-blue light.

Khara became uneasy.

'It makes me nervous when they do things like that,' she confessed quietly. Ahren had picked up a few words of the Empire language and he and Khara were using a colourful combination of the two languages at the moment.

'You mean the magic?' responded Ahren uncertainly. The word for magic in her language was similar to that for 'prohibition' and he wasn't sure if he had pronounced it correctly.

Khara had understood him and nodded. Ahren then distracted her by saying 'magic' in the Northern language and made her repeat it until she had internalised the word.

'I was very nervous about it at the start too,' he explained in a confidential tone. 'But up until now, it's only helped us. Remember how Jelninolan healed your wounds?' 'Have a little faith.'

It took a few heartbeats for Khara to understand his words, and she instinctively hugged herself with her arms. She stood in that position for a while and was the picture of fragility.

'Thank you from stopping me from running away that time. Without you, the magic would have misfired. I only understood that later when Mistress Jelninolan explained it to me,' she said, almost inaudibly.

Ahren didn't know what to say. He was embarrassed, and it still irritated him that Khara only described Jelninolan as her mistress. Of course, he had a master, but somehow this was different. A master trained you, a mistress gave your orders. The priestess had explained her attitude by saying that the ex-slave needed some sort of structure so that she could gradually get used to having a free life. But the young man found it hard to see the justification in the adjustment phase the girl was going through.

Before they could continue their conversation there was a sudden flash and a bluish-green streak of light ran along the walls. Blinded, Ahren and Khara were jolted by the shock. Then they heard Uldini's voice behind them.

'Careful. It could get bright,' he said, a little embarrassed.

Flecks of light danced before Ahren's eyes and he heard Culhen's distraught whining, and his master cursing indignantly.

'You could have warned us, you little upstart,' he grumbled irritably.

Ahren knew that his master's description of Uldini always infuriated the Arch Wizard, and while his eyes returned to normal, a foulmouthed argument echoed down the tunnel walls as the two ageless friends went for each other, hell for leather. Ahren used the time to calm down his panicked wolf, who had been totally thrown by the sudden flash of light.

Finally, Jelninolan intervened.

'It's nice to see that some things haven't changed after eight hundred years. Have the gentlemen finished, and would they like to hear what has transpired out of the magic, or do you want to keep bleating like two old billy goats and, by the way, attract the Gorge Spiders to us.'

The two brawlers were silenced by the reprimand and looked over anxiously at the priestess. She waited a moment to make sure she had the undivided attention of the group, then pointed to the right.

'A good hundred paces in this direction there is a little nest of Gorge Spiders. Seven or eight fully-grown animals, all of them in satiated sleep. If we don't wake them, they won't present us with any problems, but we should definitely warn the dwarves about them on our return.'

Ahren felt shivers run down his body. At the beginning of their journey through the tunnel, Falk, at Ahren's request, had told him what could be lying in wait down here, and the spiders, two paces in length and capable of folding in their bodies, had given him nightmares. The creatures would wait for their prey, sleeping in tiny fissures in the rock, and when the unsuspecting victims walked past, the spiders would pounce on them from behind, which made them even more malevolent. Falk had explained that the Gorge Spiders were nature animals and not creatures touched by the Adversary. They were hunters of the highest order and not to be underestimated in these confines.

Just as Ahren was trying to shake off the image of his body suddenly being embraced from behind by a multitude of long, hairy legs, the next words of the elf, who was now pointing to the left, brought welcome relief.

'I can sense in this direction, about five furlongs away, a single dwarf. It must be Falk's friend, because his vital strength is the equivalent to that of ten oxen.'

There was a tone of grudging respect in the elf's voice, and she finished her charm by wiping away the symbols on the ground.

The prospect of meeting the ominous dwarf and of hearing about his task, which would now be theirs too, caused them to pick up speed as they walked.

After a while, Jelninolan announced that she could sense his vital strength even without the Charm Net, and she positioned herself at the head of the group and led them forward, using the increasing number of crossings that they met to bring them closer to their goal.

Finally, through the darkness, they saw a faint red light in the distance, and they walked towards it. They quickly approached it. It was then that Uldini's crystal ball revealed a motionless figure, standing with its back to them in the middle of the tunnel. A little beyond and on the ground was a tiny bowl of Deep Fire.

As they got closer, the solitary silhouette spun around and raised a massive hammer in a threatening manner.

Ahren could see in the magical light, a dwarf with stone-coloured hair, and the typical plaited beard of the little folk. Similarly coloured grey eyes peered out from under bushy eyebrows and examined them with a piercing and searching look. A barrel-shaped chest with massive arms and legs gave the body an even stockier and broader build than the other dwarves that Ahren had seen, so the impression was one of looking at an almost square shape.

The figure lowered its weapon and stepped forward, a look of curiosity on its face. The apprentice now saw that the dwarf's grey beard was forked and ran over both shoulders towards the back. The dwarf dropped his hammer, and laughter lines were now visible around his eyes as he walked surprisingly nimbly towards Falk. At which point Ahren could see that the two lengths of beard were plaited into a complicated thick knot, which then fell thickly down his muscular back.

'Dorian, you old waster,' he called out merrily as he lifted up the heavily armoured Paladin and spun around with him, as if he were spinning a child.

'What brings you to this godforsaken place? Did you miss me that much, or have the fumes from the fire gone to my head and I'm just imagining your withered self?' The dwarf's voice was so full of life and joy that Ahren couldn't help smiling.

Falk's reaction was the same. He grinned broadly and slapped his hands on his friend's shoulders.

'Gods, it's great to see you again, old friend. We were just in the area and we thought we might as well help a useless excuse for a dwarf get his Ancestry Name,' called out the old man exuberantly.

The dwarf spun around on his own axis again and then placed Falk back on the ground.

'Have you heard of it? Stupid question, of course you have, or you wouldn't be here. Did old Fulretedurkolok really give you directions?'

'I told him your story, also the bit about the twin sisters in Stubbornnag. He'd no choice but to accept I was your friend,' said the Forest Guardian with a twinkle in his eyes.

The squat figure released him and placed his hands on his heart in mock sorrow.

'Dammit, old man, you shouldn't have done that. Now I can never look the good dwarf in the eye again.'

Then he laughed again, coarse, rough and full-throated.

'I've been standing here for five summers, and the first bit of company that's offered to me is your ugly face? The gods really do have a strange sense of humour.'

He examined Falk in all his armour and looked at the rest of the group.

'You all look like the beginning of a rude joke. A young man, an elf, a girl and a weakling go into a tavern…' He stopped himself and laughed coarsely again.

Ahren couldn't help but like the dwarf. He was like an avalanche that you could try resisting but that would pull you along anyway. The choice was simple: you could fight against the force of nature or enjoy the ride down into the valley.

Khara seemed to react the same way, as Jelninolan smiled politely. Only Uldini looked distinctly miffed. The fact that the dwarf had referred to him as a weakling made a disagreeable first impression on him.

Falk turned around and pointed to the group.

'I'll introduce the others to you first. The elf is Jelninolan, priestess of HER, WHO FEELS, and one of the Ancients. This is Khara a one-time slave who freed herself of her own accord. The young man with the silly smile is Ahren, who I had the misfortune of taking on as my apprentice, and at the back is Uldini Getobo, another one of the Ancients, even though he looks very young.'

Falk lowered his voice conspiratorially, but everyone could still hear him as he said, 'he's three times as old as you are, and age is making him crankier all the time, so behave yourself.'

The dwarf stomped over to the ladies and embraced them both simultaneously in a bear hug, sighing exaggeratedly. Khara couldn't suppress a giggle and Jelninolan looked irritated. Then he planted himself before Uldini and for a few heartbeats they eyed each other critically.

'You're the magic trickster who rescued the third company under the command of General Vankulorunar from the Blikton Gorge? The one who blew up the mountain?' asked the dwarf briskly.

Uldini gave him a hostile look but nodded.

'I only lit the gasses that were contained within it, nature took care of the rest. But yes, that was me.'

Ahren was astounded. He had ridden by the shattered mountain when they had travelled along by the Red Posts, but the Arch Wizard hadn't said a word about having been responsible for its destruction.

'Then let me say, better friend than foe.'

He held out a knotty paw to the wizard, who grasped it after a moment's hesitation. The dwarf looked down at the Arch Wizard, who was a head smaller and not even half as broad, and they shook hands. Ahren was certain that he heard a slight crunching sound in the process. Finally, the dwarf turned towards the apprentice while Uldini hid his right hand in his left and grimaced with pain.

The squat figure looked him up and down, and Ahren did the same. The dwarf was wearing chainmail that had plenty of holes and patches. Shabby leather boots, also with holes, peeped out under ragged linen trousers. The dwarf's clothing emitted a strange, biting smell. Before he knew what was happening, Ahren was lifted up by the shoulders and shaken vigorously. The dwarf easily held him a pace up in the air and studied him from both sides like a farmer would his breeding pig. Then he looked over at Falk, without putting Ahren down.

'There's really not much to him. How long has he been your apprentice?' he asked humorously.

'Too long,' responded Falk in the same tone. 'But you should have seen him beforehand. He's developed well, all things considered, and besides, I'm not a magician.'

The two friends laughed again, and the dwarf unexpectedly let Ahren go, causing him to flop unceremoniously onto the ground. The nameless dwarf good-naturedly handed him his paw-like hand and pulled him with a swing into a standing position.

'You're lucky, son. As an apprentice, you are under Dorian's protection, and therefore also under mine. You can hide behind my back whenever you want.' And he twinkled good-naturedly at Ahren, who smiled uneasily, determined to bear the mocking tone with stoicism.

'And who are you, my big friend?' asked the squat figure with a lot of warmth in his mouth, as Culhen sniffed the warrior's chunky leg and sneezed on account of its sharp smell.

'This is Culhen, and he's saved our skins on more than one occasion,' said Ahren proudly.

The nameless dwarf grasped Culhen's fur with both hands, left and right, directly under his ears and rubbed his head against the wolf's. Animal and dwarf purred contentedly and after a few heartbeats, the warrior let him go again. He then pulled his hammer up into the air and called out in a rousing voice, 'now that we all know each other, who fancies killing an Ore Worm?'

Chapter 18

'You're joking! An Ore Worm? Those creatures were eradicated during the Dark Days. The early wizards helped the dwarves in that regard if I remember my history lessons correctly,' said Uldini emphatically. He looked over to Jelninolan for support.

The elf gave a dismissive wave of her hand.

'I was a child then. And in those days, we elves had even less truck with the dwarves than now. I heard the creature's name mentioned once, but that's all.'

'The fact is that one of them lives down here. And he's a pretty tough nut to crack.'

The dwarf shrugged his shoulders stoically.

'He should be here again shortly if my sense of time isn't mistaken. Then you can see for yourselves.'

Everyone, with the exception of the miniature warrior, looked around nervously, and then the dwarf gave a hearty laugh and pointed in the direction he had been staring at previously.

'Why do you think I've been standing around in the middle of this tunnel? The worm comes here every day and we do a little dance and then he disappears again to feed on a vein of copper. He doesn't grow any bigger with it, but it keeps him alive. We've been playing this little game for the last five years.'

He looked at himself with a look of disgust.

'Had I known that from the start, I wouldn't have worn my best chainmail.'

Suddenly a dull vibration filled the tunnel, and immediately Ahren thought it was an earthquake. Panic came over him. Uldini and Jelninolan instinctively created a defensive dome of glimmering energy which surrounded the group, but the dwarf simply shouldered his weapon and grinned good-naturedly.

'Nothing to worry about, it's just our daily visitor. Stand there and I'll deal with him. Then you can decide for yourselves if it's an Ore Worm or not. If you know a magic spell that will kill him, then feel free to use it.'

He walked contentedly a few steps into the tunnel and then glanced over his shoulder at Uldini.

'But I'd be grateful for a little light. The skinflints only gave me this bit over here, and it would be nice not to fight in semi-darkness for a change.'

The dwarf's jovial manner was grotesque in view of the vibrations which were shaking the tunnel and growing more powerful by the heartbeat, signalling the approaching danger. Suddenly a shimmering metallic mass without any recognisable face heaved itself into view and Ahren screamed at the top of his voice. It seemed as though the very mountain had come to life and was about to swallow them all. The creature propelled itself forward with jerky movements and the apprentice could see a surface, gleaming dimly and seemingly made up of tiny scales, coming inexorably closer. The creature's movements were strangely fitful – two paces forward and one back – and Ahren could see under the worm's metallic skin, massive rings of muscle that would contract, only then to expand a moment later, pushing the creature forwards.

The nameless dwarf took a run-up of four paces and smashed his weapon against the very tip of this domed creature. To his horror, Ahren saw how its tip divided itself into four equally sized quarters, and a shimmering ring of ever turning, jagged teeth was revealed, each tooth as big as Ahren's foot. The inside of the creature seemed to be made of the same material as the outer armour. Ahren saw a pulsating throb race through its body as it contracted and then expanded, moving forward another two paces.

'We are lively today, aren't we?' roared the dwarf, smashing his hammer against its teeth. The impact resulted in a metallic sounding echo, but that was the extent of the blow's effect.

Ahren looked over pleadingly at Falk but his master only shook his head. Then the apprentice glanced at Uldini, but he looked equally nonplussed.

'The thing is made from massive iron or some other similar ore. I wouldn't know where to start,' he shouted over the sound of the fighting.

Jelninolan too looked dumbfounded.

'It has practically no reason, and all it can think of is eating. My magic is useless here, as is that of Tanentan,' she called out over the rhythmical hammering of the dwarf.

He was humming quietly to himself and hammering away at the enormous worm. His blows didn't seem to be having much effect other than keeping the enemy at bay. Anytime the worm would contract, the warrior would hammer with all his might and direct the thing a little way back down the tunnel. When the worm expanded again, it would be back up at its original location.

Ahren found it hard to imagine that the dwarf stood there every day in the semi-light and on his own, waiting for the appearance of this creature, and that he'd been doing it for five summers already! Even if the dwarf didn't follow them later, Ahren just couldn't, in good conscience, imagine leaving him here to battle it out for another ninety-five years in this ever-repeating combat.

Even as he was thinking this, the worm pushed itself dramatically forward, its mouth circled itself around the figure with the hammer and then closed around the dwarf!

Ahren was dumb-struck, and Falk stormed forward with his broadsword to come to his friend's assistance. His strikes left minimal dents on the worm's surface, and apart from that, didn't seem to have any effect on the monster. Horrific sounds could be heard coming from the creature's innards and Ahren's mind was filled with terrifying images as he imagined the dwarf being choked before being corroded away by the monster's gastric acids. Feeling nauseous, he tried desperately to cast out the images.

Jelninolan looked the picture of misery, and Falk roared in rage as he laid into the beast, which was now pushing back at the Paladin.

Uldini had never had such a helpless look on his face, Khara was hiding her face behind her hands and Ahren stood there in shock, digging his fingers into Culhen's fur to stop the wolf from doing anything reckless.

Then they heard an almighty, hollow smash coming from the inside of the worm. Its mouth shot open and the dwarf was spat out. The sharp smell that Ahren had got from the warrior's clothes earlier was now filling the air in its intensity and steam was rising up from the squat figure, who, soaked through, picked himself up and began smashing his hammer again against the worm's head. The monster withstood three more blows before pulling its massive body backwards without warning and disappearing into the darkness.

'You seem to have excited him, he was particularly grumpy today,' said the dwarf lightly and wiped the acids from his face.

The others stared at him in disbelief. His skin was slightly redder than before and his clothing looked even more dishevelled, but he was uninjured.

'How did you manage that?' asked Falk in disbelief.

The nameless dwarf shrugged his shoulders.

'The first time was pretty frightening. I'll give you that. That time I hit and kicked all around me until I was out of breath, but just before I lost consciousness, I found a slightly softer spot at the top of the gums. I hit that spot and the creature spat me out. Seems to be some sort of reflex. Plus, my tough skin helps of course, and with every spittle bath, it gets tougher. Luckily, the thing isn't capable of chewing. That would be too much of a good thing.'

As he spoke, he wiped his hands clean before finally running them along the walls of the tunnel. Ahren heard a low hissing sound and saw how the surface of the rock became smoother with the effect of the saliva.

So, these round tunnels must have been dug out by the worm. Now some of the occurrences were beginning to make more sense to Ahren, but he still had so many questions. 'Why do you confront him every day at this spot? Why does he come back? What dangers does he present to the dwarves? Why can we not just drive him away without killing him?' The questions tumbled out of him. What he had just seen had put the young man into a frenzy of excitement, and the result was this torrent of questions.

'My goodness, you certainly can't be accused of not being curious,' laughed the dwarf before looking over at Falk. 'Does he always ask so many questions?'

'Welcome to my world,' said Falk drily. 'You gave me a real fright there,' he added seriously.

'Not my intention. He was a lot more stubborn today than usual. Maybe, because I have reinforcements now,' suggested the dwarf.

This was the first time Ahren had seen the warrior not in his normally exuberant mood. The serious thoughtfulness that he was now displaying showed the young man that there was more to the dwarf than a wicked tongue and an unbridled toughness.

'First, come with me. We won't see him again until tomorrow,' said the nameless dwarf thoughtfully. 'I'll tell you everything I know when we have something to eat. Maybe you can think of a way of breaking the deadlock.'

He led them a few paces into the tunnel, where an opening appeared to the left, hewn roughly into the rock and so small that the dwarf could barely fit through. On account of his substantial body build, the opening was wide enough for the others too. On the other side was a craggy cave with a woollen blanket and an enormous bundle.

'Someone brings me provisions once a month. I'm so far off the beaten track that even the most stubborn dwarf has to acknowledge that I'd starve if it weren't for the deliveries. But they never look at me when they come, and they don't talk to me. At the end of the day, the old traditions have to be respected.' His voice was dripping with irony.

'You really haven't changed a bit. Even in those days you had no time for orders or rules,' scolded Falk but in a soft tone.

The nameless one laughed aloud.

'There's just too much vitality in me. Do you know why I want the Ancestry Name? So that nobody can tell me what to do anymore. My name will be Trogadon and finally the orders will stop.'

Ahren had heard that name somewhere before. Then the penny dropped.

'Didn't we want to collect this Trogadon's shield to use it for my Naming Ritual?', he asked eagerly.

The dwarf pricked up his ears and looked impishly over at Falk.

'What do you want with that old piece of metal? And what kind of a ritual is your apprentice talking about? I'm slowly beginning to think that you didn't just come here to say hello and to help me eliminate an Ore Worm.' His eyes twinkled humorously, but his tone of voice had become serious.

Falk's look became sober. 'We need your help, my friend. Much as I value being with you, if you couldn't help us, we wouldn't have come here.'

Ahren gasped, but the dwarf seemed untroubled by the unvarnished truth. On the contrary, his mischievous demeanour returned, and he spread out his arms demonstratively.

'Then make yourselves at home. My shabby cave is your shabby cave. There's fresh water back there that runs down from the roof, and in the ground is a fissure where it runs off. You can follow the call of nature there too, so that the smell doesn't last too long for those with a sensitive nose.' He bowed before Jelninolan, who struggled to keep a straight face and to maintain her dignity as she looked down at him with a superior look.

'I think before we discuss our request, we should deal with this worm, which shouldn't in fact, exist at all anymore,' said Uldini aloofly.

The travellers laid down their belongings and found a spot for themselves and their sleeping mats, while the nameless dwarf walked up and down at the cave opening and began telling his story.

'It was the Elder Fulretedurkolok who gave me the task of slaying this Ore Worm that time. It had turned up just ten years ago at the outer reaches of the mines and had started eating up the deposits we had just been mining. Hammers, axes, pickaxes, Deep Fire, and even a damned Dragon Bow – nothing would stop it. Finally, we had to seal up the lower levels of the northern mine even though there's still plenty to be mined there. The Clan Board in Thousand Halls was called on for advice, but nobody could think of a way of dealing with the thing. The old texts only say to use the essence of nature against it, but they don't say how. It was just too long ago. Some of the archives were submerged during an earthquake and nobody has yet gone to the trouble of digging them up again. I was presenting my head on a silver tablet when I requested an Ancestry Name. It didn't take them fifty heartbeats and I found myself on my way here with the order to kill the worm, or to hold him back until the old library has been exposed again, which they reckoned would take a hundred summers.'

He drew breath and then continued while the others lay down and listened eagerly.

'I followed the worm into his tunnel and watched him for a while. He digs the quickest route to the deposits and he weighs up the amount of deposits against its quality. Low quality ore just keeps him alive, but ore of a higher quality helps him to grow and makes his armour stronger. There's a profitable copper vein nearby and when he made his way there, I was waiting for him. A few dozen hammer-blows later and he retreated to strengthen himself on some copper, and then he came back the next day. It took me a while to find the perfect point, so that the beast wouldn't try to dodge into another tunnel. There were two or three close shaves and he almost escaped. So long as I stop him here, his instinct is to come back this way again, day after day. He isn't intelligent enough to

336

dig his way around me. And so we fight every day, and then he retires to his copper in order to replenish himself. I can't move forwards because it would influence his route, and he can't get past me. It seems he only eats enough to attack me again, so our stand-off could last quite some time yet. All in all, I think I'm doing quite well.'

The dwarf looked with self-satisfaction at the travellers, then raised his eyebrows.

'Now tell me your story,' he commanded.

Falk drew breath to prepare himself to speak, but Uldini was quicker.

'The young lad there is the future Thirteenth Paladin. HE, WHO FORCES is gradually waking up day by day and we have to carry out Ahren's Naming before the Adversary gets the chance to suck the blessing of the gods out of our apprentice's body. And for this we need an artefact and a representative of each of the god's three folks. Human and elf are present here, we're just missing a dwarf. Falk had recommended you and so here we are,' he explained quickly, and in a droning, almost bored tone of voice. Then he folded his arms.

'We have little more than a moon to carry out the ritual and so we don't have much wriggle room to be scrapping every day with an Ore Worm.' His last words were not only aimed at the dwarf, but also at Falk, but the Forest Guardian looked away and remained silent.

'So, the Thirteenth Paladin? And isn't it about bloody well time. I know over a hundred dwarves who, ever since the end of the Dark Days, have been standing in torpidity, waiting for the return of the Adversary. But they're all in Thousand Halls and the way there is far too long, or you could have asked one of them instead. Tough luck for you, but good luck for me,' he exclaimed.

Falk cleared his throat and the nameless one grew serious.

'Of course, I'll help you, you can be sure of that. But without my name, there is no way I can ever get to an artefact of the dwarves. And anyway, this Ore Worm is a real danger. When they get to a certain size, they divide. Then we're dealing with a pair of them, and in a few years, there will be no ore anymore. No ore, no weapons, no weapons, no half-way decent war against Dark Ones.'

It seemed to Ahren as if the dwarf found it impossible to suppress his exuberant style for any length of time and, although the apprentice liked him, he wondered if the squat figure he was looking at really was the right choice for this post of responsibility. On the other hand, Uldini hadn't exactly been over the moon at the thought of Ahren being a Paladin aspirant, and so the young man decided to reserve judgement for the time being.

Uldini seemed focused for the first time since they had seen the worm. He wasn't going to abandon his hostility towards the dwarf in the immediate future it seemed, but nonetheless he understood the importance of stopping the creature.

'Right then,' he mumbled, 'we have an enormous worm that likes eating ore and that we have to prevent from reaching platinum, or our problems will multiply. The only thing that drives him is his hunger, and so we can only manipulate him in a very restricted way.'

'What about magic?' asked Falk. Can you not melt him down, or something?'

Uldini shook his head. 'Much too big and solid. Anything powerful enough to damage the worm would collapse the walls around us. His body is metallic and generally magic doesn't work very well against him. The denser the material, the less penetrable it is. That applies to magic too.'

A brooding silence descended on the group and the rest of the day was spent exchanging ideas and then dismissing them. Finally, they all retired, irritated, to bed.

The next morning, they all sat together again and finally hammered out a plan. Uldini would use his magic to create lances out of the rocks, which would impale the worm as soon as he came along the tunnel. The two magicians would strengthen the tips of the lances using magic, and that would hopefully prove sufficient to bore through the worm's body. Bows, wolf's teeth and swords would be of no help whatsoever and so Ahren, Khara, Falk and Culhen were condemned to doing nothing. A nervousness descended on the whole group as the vibrating walls announced the impending arrival of the worm.

All were at the ready as Ahren peered through the gap in the rock which separated their den from the passageway where the dwarf and the Ore Worm slugged it out every day. Jelninolan and Uldini were both kneeling on the ground and had spent hours carving signs into the rock, which would shoot up a mighty rock spear as soon as the worm broke into the carved magical circle. With a little luck the magically enhanced stone arrow tips would have enough strength to bore into the huge creature.

Khara pushed in beside him and tried to shove him out of the way so she would have a better idea of what was going on outside. Ahren gave her an angry look but reluctantly made room for her, while at the same time ordering Culhen for the twentieth time to lie down and not make a sound. The apprentice had to admit that the role of onlooker no longer suited him very well. He was itching to help and when he glanced at Khara he could see that she too was desperate to get involved. At last the tunnel began to vibrate violently and the whole group was gripped by a wave of anxiety. The worm had arrived and soon they would know if they could leave the tunnel, or if they would fail in their task.

Chapter 19

The following days were full of frustrating setbacks.

The worm had effortlessly destroyed the magic rock-lances and had become considerably more aggressive in his efforts to get past the dwarf and his companions. This had been their best plan, and their following efforts only became more desperate.

The Ancients concocted walls of ice, filled a section of tunnel with poisonous gas, threw a potpourri of magic into the gaping mouth of the worm and tried to play with his inferior mind, but all to no avail.

The worm seemed to be a force of nature and nothing or nobody was going to stop him. Nobody apart from the nameless dwarf, who after every failed attempt would lay into the monster, humming to himself and seemingly without a care in the world, until the monster would retreat, leaving his opponents to ponder the next day's encounter.

Uldini and Jelninolan ventured into more obscure magic, and Falk did his best to help drive the snake away. While all this was going on Ahren and Khara decided to explore the tunnels nearby in the vague hope of finding something that could be useful in the fight against the creature. Culhen played his part as a sniffer dog, who could alert them to any other creatures around.

The dwarf had given them the little Deep Fire to use and so they stalked quietly and carefully through the underground domains, and with the help of the faint red light, they could make out unimagined wonders. It seemed that the worm had the ability to detect not only veins of ore but also cavities in the rock, for his tunnels often led through natural caves. Ahren presumed that the creature was able to preserve his energy that way by not boring through more rock than was necessary. That would also explain the stubborn repetition of his movement patterns.

On their reconnaissance trips they came across subterranean rivers full of blind fish, crystal formations in the most marvellous colours and even a current of molten rock, winding its way sluggishly to a fissure into the depths.

After a while, they had explored everywhere that was in the vicinity without having ventured too far from the safety of their companions. Every evening Ahren would sketch with a piece of coal, a crude drawing of where they had explored on the back wall of their cavern and explain to the others about their discoveries. The magicians would listen half-heartedly, but were too caught up in their own dilemma to respond to the apprentice's enthusiastic reports with anything more than a faint smile. Ahren brought pieces of the crystal with him and even caught one of the blind fish in the hope that one of them might be of use in poisoning the monster, but no matter what was thrown into the worm's mouth, it had no effect whatsoever.

In the end Khara and Ahren just stayed, downhearted, in the cavern and practised each other's language, or went through various Windblade manoeuvres. After half a dozen failed attempts, the two magicians admitted defeat and they all sat down together to discuss the situation.

'We can't think of anything else, and time is against us. We have to get back to the Clan Halls, then go to Kelkor and find one of the Wild Folk, and then on to the Place of Ritual,' complained Uldini.

Nobody said anything in response. Even the dwarf had a serious look on him, his cheerful nature defeated. It seemed to Ahren that their new companion would see it as a personal disgrace that his task was holding them up for so long, and yet he was performing extraordinary feats on a daily basis, pushing back the worm.

'Maybe we should alter the direction of our attacks,' suggested Falk in a resigned voice.

'His head is in some ways his hardest part. If we attack him from the side or the back, maybe that will change things.'

The others didn't seem particularly convinced. After all, they had already tried an attack from the bottom with their magic, but nobody had a better idea and so they decided to try it.

The familiar tremors which announced the impending arrival of the worm grew more powerful, and everyone, with the exception of the dwarf, was crouched in the little cavern which had been their home for days and waited for the enormous body of the monster to push past them. The Nameless dwarf stood a few paces upwards, ready to drive the worm back, should their experiment fail. Jelninolan and Uldini had cast a mighty spell on the Paladin's weapon and they hoped that the blade they had strengthened by magic would somehow pierce the worm's armour when Falk attacked the creature's flank through the cavern opening as he passed by.

The rumbling intensified and Uldini whispered, 'now's the time, get ready, everybody!'

Then they saw him – the head of the worm had reached the crevice – and Falk prepared to strike. His sword-arm was shaking as he drew it back to strike, and the worm contracted. For a moment the view through the gap was clear again. A heartbeat later and they would see the creature's flank as he pushed himself forward.

Ahren held his breath and concentrated completely on the hole in the wall. It was now or never.

Suddenly, their cavern trembled violently, and rocks tumbled from its roof. Everyone threw themselves to the ground and covered their heads with their hands as the worm began to smash his head against the cavern wall.

Falk lunged his blade forward frantically, but the magic discharged itself uselessly in a scornful violet on the beast's head as the animal opened its mouth and began grinding the outside of the cavern wall with his teeth and digging into it.

There was a bone-shaking crash and the thin wall of stone disappeared into the worm's mouth, which was now directly in front of them. They were now totally unprotected and at the mercy of the beast that for some reason had turned his attention to them.

The dwarf stormed into action and hammered against the side of the skull but the worm seemed completely oblivious to him.

Khara was hit by a falling piece of rock and tumbled dangerously towards the worm's mouth but Jelninolan leaped forward and pulled the girl to safety behind her. Ferocious flashes of magic darted along her staff as the elf fired dart after dart of charm power, which came down in a magical shower on the shuddering body of the worm.

Ahren's limbs were paralysed by fear but his brain was wide awake and he forced himself to bring the animal part of his nature to heel, which was urging him to curl up into a screaming, helpless ball. With effort he slid into the Void and then he had a brainwave.

'Master, jump out to the dwarf!' he roared.

The worm contracted. The next moment he would be in the middle of the cavern and no blow of a hammer, no matter how strong, nor no magic charm would be able to force back the incoming monster. They were caught in a trap and the animal would swallow them as easily as flame extinguishes a snowflake. Jelninolan dropped her staff and bent down protectively over Khara, as a mother would protect her child, and frantically tried weaving a protective spell.

Time seemed to pause as Falk and Ahren exchanged looks, the one questioning, the other urging. Within the blink of an eye his master made his decision and threw himself out into the tunnel and beside the dwarf.

The beast's head spun around, looking back once more into the familiar tunnel, and the Nameless One hammered away at his head, full of energy and at twice the speed of his normal rhythm. The worm pulsated forward, and forward again. The beast seemed to be driven this day by a frenzied voraciousness and the dwarf's chest rose and fell in a forceful tempo, his breathing like that of a blacksmith's enormous bellows.

At last the massive body retreated down the system of tunnels and disappeared into the blackness. The rumbling died down until all that could be heard was the panting of the companions. The panting and another sound. Everyone turned and looked at Ahren in disbelief.

The apprentice was chuckling, and a broad smile had spread across his face. He looked at them all, his eyes bright, and he said in a low voice, 'I know how we can beat this cursed creature.'

He had spent the rest of the afternoon and most of the evening persuading the others of the value of his idea. And the rest of the time they spent sleeping, planning, and packing their belongings.

One way or another, they would be leaving the area the same day, because they only had one chance. Which was why it had been so difficult for Ahren to win everybody over. Should they fail, the predictable deadlock that the dwarf had achieved all this time, and which had prevented the worm from making progress, would be gone. On the other hand, there was the alluring prospect of victory, and in the end, it was that which had decided things.

'I'm in favour of giving it a go,' said the nameless dwarf in support of Ahren. Falk too had expressed his belief in the plan, and much to Ahren's surprise, Khara had said shortly, 'good idea. Might work.' In the end, Jelninolan and Uldini gave in, not least because they could put forward no other proposals.

Now they were all standing at the ready and awaiting the first sign of the approaching Ore Worm. The soles of Ahren's feet tingled and he turned to the others.

'It's happening. Everybody knows what they have to do?' he asked nervously.

Uldini folded his arms, his head tilted.

'It was your idea but don't milk it, young man. Jelninolan and I did things like that hundreds of years ago,' he grumbled complainingly.

'Give him his moment,' said Falk reassuringly. 'It's an idea, and if it goes wrong, then he'll have to explain to the Elders why their ore veins are lost.'

Ahren looked forlornly at his master, who winked back at him before putting on his helmet. He looked quite silly there, dressed in his linen clothing with the clunky headgear on him.

Ahren straightened the unfamiliar chest guard, which didn't fit him properly and had a tendency to flap. Somehow it looked lighter on his master, he thought nervously, as the worm came ever nearer. Then the silver, shimmering head of the beast appeared and Ahren ran ahead of it.

The others followed his example and at the first crossing, Khara, with Culhen at her side, an improvised torch and Falk's forearm guards in her hands, veered off into the left tunnel. The others ran straight ahead and Ahren risked a glance over his shoulder to see what the Ore Worm was up to. The head of the beast swayed to the left and it pushed itself into the tunnel that Khara had taken.

'It's working,' he called out, and increased his pace. They had impressed upon themselves the pattern of tunnels and had practised the routes in the run-up several times and now everybody had to take up position at the right place and at the right time. Khara was the only one who could run the wide arc in the short time available to them, according to the plan. Ahren was probably the faster runner over longer distances but the girl was a born sprinter. The apprentice ran another twenty paces exactly, then stood still and counted slowly up to thirty-nine.

Nothing happened.

The apprentice broke into a sweat and his head was full of doubts. Had something gone wrong? Had he miscalculated? He saw a picture in his head of Khara, alone in the darkness being grasped by the worm, and he was on the point of abandoning his post.

Then the glimmering body of the monster appeared behind Ahren and he breathed a sigh of relief as the creature moved towards him.

With his opponent on his heels, Ahren ran on with fresh courage. He came up to the crossing where Uldini was waiting for him, who beckoned to him with Falk's sword.

The apprentice gave him a grin and ran on, while the little figure remained floating where he was and waited for Ahren's pursuer.

Now every heartbeat counted. Ahren had run the furthest. Up to now they had used up a lot of time, although they had done everything as planned, but the simple truth was this: there was no other way. Each member of the group was wearing one part of Falk's armour and they had positioned themselves so that the worm would instinctively follow whoever had the biggest and nearest piece of armour. The animal smelled pure ore, and Falk's armour was made from hardened Deep Steel, the purest and noblest metal that existed. And so the creature followed the path laid out by the armour carriers. Through clever interplays and pre-timed positioning, they had created a route which would lead the worm to a point in Ahren's plan in which they would have a real chance of defeating the beast. The young man wore the largest and heaviest piece of armour and if everything ran smoothly, the creature would be facing him at the end.

Ahren raced over jutting rocks, ducked under stalactites, pressed his way through fissures in the rock as he neared his final position. The others would hopefully distract the worm until Ahren was in position.

Finally, he reached the last cave and breathed deeply. Now it depended on the others and particularly on Uldini and the dwarf.

It was sticky in the cave and Ahren was becoming warm in the armour, when the ground began to move. In the natural reddish smouldering light of the cave, Ahren spotted the silver shimmering colossus, as it rolled inexorably towards him. His breathing quickened and he watched every movement of the rhythmically contractive mass of muscle and steel-hard armour. When the Ore Worm was two paces in front of him, Ahren took two paces to the side. The head swayed around and the creature followed him slowly but with determination. Ahren was soaking in sweat by now and the moisture was running into his eyes, but he kept his eyes fixed firmly on his opponent. The ground near the abyss was uneven, and slowly the apprentice felt his way backwards, step by step, on the edge of the vertical drop.

The surface of the worm playfully reflected the light, and for a heartbeat Ahren had to admire the simple beauty of the creation whose existence they were being forced to extinguish. The young man took a few steps backwards and the Ore Worm followed him. The creature, ten

348

paces in length, had followed him a good twenty paces along the ridge of rock and the enormous body was now parallel to the chasm.

It was time for the last part of his plan.

A glance behind and he knew he had a bare six paces until the end of the cave and he would be caught in a trap.

'Now!' he roared at the top of his lungs. The dwarf and Uldini stepped out of the darkness of the uneven rock walls and ran along the side of the shimmering mass.

The Arch Wizard raised his arms in conjuration and the rocks, the length of the ledge along which Ahren had stepped, began to glow. Then the Ancient called out a command and the glowing cliff edge broke away, pulling the worm with it, down into the stream of lava, which was rolling inexorably and smoothly through the cave, and which Ahren had dismissed only a few days earlier as beautiful, yet useless.

Ahren was on the point of cheering, but the Ore Worm rotated on his own axis and held on to the last section of rock, stopping himself from falling. The rock having fallen away, the heat of the boiling lava rose directly up to them and Ahren could hardly breathe in the searing heat. Ignoring the danger, the worm moved towards him again and the young man realised to his horror that there was now no way he could skip around the beast. He had missed his chance. Either the Ore Worm would fall, or he would be swallowed.

'Help!' he screamed as loudly as he could, but the dwarf was already in position. Then he smashed his hammer with such force into the worm's flank that a piece of rock came crashing down from the roof of the cave and Ahren had to cover his ears against the deafening clangs of the hammer.

Slowly, like a gradually unfolding avalanche, the enormous creature began to tip over to the right. The worm stretched once more in Ahren's direction and opened its greedy mouth. The biting smell of the corrosive saliva hit the apprentice forcefully and he pressed himself against the wall, making himself as thin as possible. The dwarf carried on hammering at the side of the Ore Worm until finally the imbalance became too great. In surreal silence, the massive figure of the worm tipped over the edge of the ridge. His mouth snapped one more time, directly in front of Ahren's nose, and then the enormous worm was gone and splashed into the lava, where he curled together before he finally sank like a stone. The fiery mass closed over the creature and a heartbeat later the cave was quiet and still. As if the monster had never existed.

The journey back to the Grand Junction seemed strangely unreal to Ahren. The others had congratulated him euphorically, and the dwarf had embraced him with a bear hug, but everything seemed blurry to him, as if he were under water. Jelninolan had finally looked into his eyes and, turning to her companions had said, 'that was a close shave. He's in shock and he also breathed in some of the moisture from the poisonous saliva. He'll need time and then he'll be back to himself.'

And so they had headed off, someone always at Ahren's side, leading the apathetic young man while Culhen pressed in beside the other leg of his friend. They followed the round tunnels, then the dwarf passageways. The further they ascended, the clearer Ahren's mind became. When they finally came across the light of an active smelting works and saw dwarves for the first time, the apprentice was almost back to his old self.

Many questions were asked and answered, but everything was spoken in the rumbling language of the dwarves, so that Ahren could only guess what they were talking about. But the tumult that ensued suggested to Ahren that the news of their deed had certainly created a stir. Their dwarf friend's back was repeatedly slapped in recognition and the miners bowed before the travellers, even before Uldini.

A little retinue of dwarves accompanied them, and there were always some running ahead to announce the good news. When they finally arrived at the Grand Junction, over two hundred dwarves were already waiting for them, squeezed into every corner of the large hall. Ahren saw that the entrances to all the Clan Halls were bursting with dwarves, all eager to catch a sight of what was about to happen.

'Now that's what I call an impressive entrance,' whispered Uldini.

'This is a full meeting of the Silver Cliff Elders. There's nothing more official outside of Thousand Halls. Only the Clan Board and the King of the Halls are of more importance than such a gathering,' whispered Falk.

Their Nameless Dwarf appeared so self-satisfied, that Ahren feared he might say or do something silly through cockiness, but he simply walked through the cheering dwarves and then planted himself in front of the Elders.

A circle of twenty dwarves, all of them very old and dressed in golden chainmail, stood in the centre of the Grand Junction, and each of them was holding a decorated object.

The Mountainshield Clan Elder held a golden shield, other ones had a bejewelled tankard, a priceless blacksmith's hammer, silver ingots, copper staffs and so on. Each object seemed to represent the respective crafts of the clans, and each of the Elders looked at their dwarf friend with a mixture of veneration and distrust.

'They don't seem to be as overjoyed as the other dwarves,' mumbled Ahren, confused.

Falk snorted. 'He's going to outstrip them in rank any moment now, and Pure Ones have a reputation for not taking their precious rules particularly seriously. Imagine you opened the door to a provisions room for Culhen, and it was filled with delicacies of all description, then you can imagine how they are feeling at the moment.'

Culhen licked his chops and looked at Ahren expectantly. The young man tousled the wolf's head and asked himself if the wolf deliberately misunderstood them when it suited him.

The Elders began to speak to the Nameless Dwarf, and all of the other dwarves present radiated patience. Ahren noticed Falk's relaxed stance and figured that the ceremony would take some time.

Half a day later and his legs were aching, his bladder was bursting, and a certain starving wolf was constantly standing on his master's right foot and begging for food. Ahren couldn't help looking over at Falk for assistance, but his master's eyes were fixed firmly on the ceremony's guest of honour. At last the final one of the twenty-four dwarves stopped talking, and the Nameless Dwarf opened his mouth.

'Trogadon,' he said, and a murmur went through the hall, awestruck and disbelieving.

While the dwarves quietened down, Ahren took the opportunity to shake out his legs a little and he quickly asked Uldini who Trogadon really was. 'They all seem to be really impressed,' he added.

'He was their best blacksmith. Lived for over two thousand years and discovered the secret of Deep Steel. He forged weapons and armour for half of the dwarves in the old days. One of his last deeds was the creation of his own clan, that of the Hall Smiths. Many of the greatest dwarf architects came from their ranks, I'm talking about dragon arches, new enclaves and the famed fortifications of Thousand Halls. The founding of the Silver Cliff was his dream and his direct descendants founded this enclave for that very reason,' said Uldini casually.

Ahren looked at him in surprise and the childlike figure raised his finger like a schoolmaster.

352

'I'm no great fan of the dwarves, but of course I know about those who have achieved something.'

Before Ahren could respond, an expectant silence fell over the hall. All of the Elders stepped forward, and each laid their hand on the head of the lonely dwarf in their midst.

'Reg vulan Trogadon,' they intoned, and a thunderous sound filled the hall as the dwarves started stomping on the ground with their boots, growling throatily, hitting their armoured hands off their shields or clanking their metal tankards together.

The noise made Ahren see double, and he placed his hands protectively over poor Culhen who was whimpering wildly, but then looked gratefully back up at his master.

After a while the celebratory noises died down and the Elders drew back wordlessly from the newly named dwarf. He beamed with such self-satisfaction that Uldini at his best looked like a shy Godsday pupil in comparison.

Trogadon turned to Falk and gave a broad grin.

'It's a wrap. Let's get our things and clear off'.

Chapter 20

23 days to the winter solstice

As the tumult died down, Trogadon turned to the group with a conspiratorial look.

'Wait a moment,' he whispered and before one of his companions had the chance to congratulate him, he disappeared into one of the Clan Halls, which had a symbol of an anvil and a stylised mountain beside it. As he left, he was surrounded by jubilant dwarves who slapped him on the shoulders and back, bowed before him or simply stared at him reverentially.

'What's he up to?' whispered Uldini mistrustfully, but Falk simply shrugged his shoulders helplessly.

'At least they're not wasting any time,' said Jelninolan snippily and pointed out a troop of over fifty dwarf workers, decked out in brand new outfits and marching through the entrance to the mines, doubtless with the intention of restarting work in the northern mines.

The elf had been in a foul mood ever since the worm had plunged into the lava. She had hoped to the very end that they would find a non-fatal solution even though she had gone along with the suggestions of the group. But now the deed had been done, and Ore Worms were gone from the face of Jorath. The elf knew that their battle with the worm had been necessary, but that didn't alleviate her feelings. Ahren felt the same way, even if he saw things in a more pragmatic manner. The fact that the worm had almost eaten him up twice, helped him to keep his guilty feelings in check.

While they were waiting, Ahren remembered that this was the perfect opportunity to repay an old debt. He craned his neck so he could examine the Clan Elders above the throng of dwarves and he asked Falk quietly, 'which of them is responsible for trade with Three Rivers?'

'Hmm, good question.' Falk scratched his beard thoughtfully. 'Why are you asking?'

'The weapon mistress Falagarda, who gave me Windblade, asked in return that I should present her wish to the dwarves that she might purchase more wares from them, and not just jewels,' said the apprentice, and he remembered the enormous, friendly woman whose gift and brief lessons had saved his life several times already. He wanted to return the favour, and now that the dwarves were well-disposed to them, it seemed to him to be the perfect time.

'She can only have meant Dwarf Steel,' said Falk in admiration. 'If she manages to strike a deal with the dwarves, she'll be the only blacksmith north of Thousand Halls making weapons from that material. They'll be breaking down the doors to buy things off her.'

He pointed over to a dwarf with particularly bulky plate armour.

'That's Balanukurotom, chief of the Smeltore Clan. Give your request to him, then Falagarda will have the best chance with her proposition.'

Ahren nodded nervously and pushed his way through the boisterous crowd towards the dwarf, then hesitated and looked back. His master had stayed put and was giving him an amused grin while his eyes remained deeply serious.

'Just go. You're in Falagarda's debt, and so you should pay it.'

Ahren nodded and continued on his way, all the while formulating what he had to say in his head. When he arrived before the Elder, whose reddish-grey hair billowed out from under his steel helmet, he stopped, bowed deeply and then looked fixedly into the steel-grey eyes of the dwarf. Then Ahren spoke.

'I am Ahren, Aspirant to the title of Paladin, Chosen One of the THREE, Squire to the Paladin Dorian Falkenstein and Fellow to Trogadon. I drew up the plan to bring about the Ore Worm's downfall and put my life at stake in this venture.'

The figure of the old dwarf in his thick plate armour was impressive, he was at least twice as broad as Ahren, yet the young man made every effort not to be cowed, at least outwardly, by the dwarf opposite him.

Balanukurotom looked him up and down for a moment, then planted his heavy paw-like hand, weighed down by a massive armoured glove, heavily on Ahren's shoulder, and his bushy beard opened up in a smile. Ahren was sure that he heard something crack in his maltreated shoulder, but he kept a straight face and listened to every word the dwarf spoke.

'It's true that you only have measly fluff on your chin, but you have proven yourself more than many a young beard. I recognise you as a friend of the dwarves.'

There was a roar of approval from the surrounding dwarves and Ahren almost burst with pride. Full of confidence he addressed the Elder again.

'The blacksmith and Mistress of Weapons Falagarda Regelsten from Three Rivers wishes to enter a trading relationship with you in order to purchase your steel. She is already known to your jewellery traders and in my estimation, she is a person of the highest honour.' Ahren was really pushing the boat out at this point, but she had been so generous and sensitive towards him that time that he believed that she would behave in a similar way to her future business partner.

Balanukurotom gave a friendly nod and straightened his beard.

'I shall make enquiries of the Silver Cliff traders. If I hear she is a person of loyal character as described, then one of our Clan shall approach her.'

Then he folded his arms and the conversation was over. It had gone better than he had hoped and so he bowed again, gave his thanks, and withdrew quickly. The Elder gave another friendly nod before turning to his fellow Clan Elders, who were having a lively discussion.

Falk was waiting for him with a quizzical look and Ahren smiled triumphantly. Falk slapped him on the shoulder and Ahren flinched. There was no doubt that he would have an enormous bruise on his shoulder-blade the following day.

'I'm very proud of you, boy. This is the second time you have done a favour for another without thinking of yourself. First with the elves, when it came to the question of my banishment, and now this. That was worthy of a true Paladin,' said Falk quietly.

Ahren swallowed hard and felt a lump in his throat. For a moment he thought of embracing his master, but Trogadon was already returning to the Grand Junction. He was wearing bluish chainmail, carried a strange looking hammer on his shoulder, and in his other hand he had a shield that was far too big for him. A wave of indignation and outrage spread before him.

Falk turned away from Ahren, looked at what was happening and gave a big sigh.

'I knew he was too tame during the ceremony,' he said in a tired voice. 'Get ready. We'll have to make ourselves scarce in double quick time.'

The Elders looked at Trogadon with disbelief. Some of them looked as if their eyes were going to pop out of their heads, while others gasped in astonishment. Half of them looked threateningly red-faced and the other half deadly pale.

Trogadon marched past the Elders, grinning with self-satisfaction and he didn't even bother to look at them, which in turn led to a threatening silence in the hall.

'Are we ready?' he asked, all innocence, and walked contentedly on.

Falk was about to say something, thought better of it, and joined him.

'I don't know what you think, but in my opinion the sooner we're in Kelkor having it out with giants and hydras, the sooner we'll be in safety,' prophesied Uldini.

The Arch Wizard's dry toned voice carried clearly through the silence of the hall in the Grand Junction, and when Ahren looked into the stony faces of the dwarves, he couldn't but agree.

They stepped out through the entrance and left the Grand Junction behind them. Ahren felt as if he had a hundred daggers in his back as the hostile eyes of the Silver Cliff watched them leaving.

'But they only just welcomed us like heroes,' he stammered. The sudden change in mood had been too much for the young man and he felt hurt and deceived. Over the previous few days, his imaginings of their triumphant entrance into the Hall of the Dwarves had helped him work through his encounter with the Ore Worm. He had just been proclaimed a friend of the dwarves, but the bearded figures he had just looked at seemed anything but friendly.

'Have we been banished now? What happened?' Ahren tried to make his voice not sound too accusatory but he failed dismally. The thought that his request on Falagarda's behalf would fail on account of the dwarves' attitude was too much to bear.

358

'Our glorious hero was over the top, and not for the first time,' grumbled Falk. 'That will have no effect on us because we're not under his command, but with the mood the way it was in there, it's good that we're going.'

Ahren breathed a sigh of relief, happy that he hadn't done the blacksmith a disservice, while the eyes of his master were fixed on the heavily armoured dwarf. Falk's scowl, however, seemed to have absolutely no effect on the dwarf, who was humming away contentedly, oblivious to the Forest Guardian's anger, just as he had been to that of the two hundred dwarves he had walked blithely past.

Once it became clear that Trogadon was not going to react to Falk's criticism, the old man clenched his fists and gritted his teeth. Then he spoke.

'My old friend has taken not only Trogadon's shield, as was agreed. But he's also taken his armour and his forging hammer,' he said, gnashing his teeth. 'Did you really clear out the whole of the Silver Cliff artefact chamber?' he asked, facing Trogadon. The old Forest Guardian's voice suddenly sounded terribly weary.

Trogadon laughed loudly and looked back over his shoulder.

'Of course not. They still have the anvil. Much too heavy and impractical. And at least they can use that whenever they want. Nobody has used these things in hundreds of years. What a waste.'

'You could at least have left the shield there!' shouted Falk, exploding in anger. A vein in his face was pulsating angrily. 'You said yourself it was far too impractical, and as far as I know, the hammer is more than enough for Ahren's Naming.'

The group stopped as Trogadon turned around. The dwarf was still smiling but there was determination in his eyes.

'The shield isn't for me,' he simply said.

Then he stuck the handle of his hammer into the metal handles of the shield and pulled forcefully a few times at the smith's tool while he worked on the shield. The handles creaked and crunched loudly as the dwarf flexed his muscles and mauled the millennia old artefact.

The group looked on in horror and Ahren was only too glad that they were standing in a deserted tunnel with no members of the little folk in the vicinity to avenge this atrocity. Even Ahren, with his limited knowledge of their culture was certain that there would have been trouble in an instant.

Trogadon lifted the shield up and looked at the considerably warped handles with satisfaction, then stretched it out to Falk.

'For your aid I give you this shield as an Ancestral gift. May it protect you until the next Trogadon demands it be returned to him.'

Falk stared at the dwarf in disbelief before putting his hands behind his back in a gesture of refusal.

'Have you completely lost the plot?' he hissed. 'The Elders would never allow it.'

Trogadon opened out his fingers and the shield clattered to the ground.

'I have hereby given it into your custody. Leave it there if you will. It's far too big for a dwarf, besides, I've been staring at it for the last few decades and have always thought that it would suit a human very well. If you ask me, the first Trogadon wanted it to be used for settling a debt,' and he waggled his bushy eyebrows meaningfully.

Ahren and Jelninolan snorted with laughter and Khara and Uldini grinned broadly, while Falk looked at the shield as if it were a poisonous Dark One. Trogadon smiled good-naturedly and then walked on cheerfully, leaving the Paladin standing there.

'Courage, old man!', chortled Uldini. 'It's unmannerly to turn down a present, and you've been complaining about not having a shield ever since you lost it to the Great Wyrm of the Threespiked Mountains.'

Falk continued to look down uncertainly at the large rectangular object lying at his feet.

'At least try it,' said Uldini, urging him on in a surprisingly gentle voice.

Gingerly, as if it were a precious jewel, Ahren's master raised the shield and ran his hand along its surface.

'It's so light,' he whispered in surprise and he looked at it in wonder.

Trogadon turned around again and clapped his hands once in satisfaction.

'It looks good on you, old friend. According to legend, the first Trogadon worked gases into the shield that are lighter than air. I think that's a load of codswallop but there's no doubt he was a damn good blacksmith, and the thing is lighter than it should be.'

The dwarf looked wistful for a moment.

'Someday I'll outstrip him.'

Then he spun around and strode onwards.

The others followed him with Ahren walking beside his master. 'Are you going to get into trouble with the dwarves now?' he asked in a concerned voice.

Falk slowly shook his head. 'Not as long as Trogadon is with us and can attest that it's an Ancestry gift. Which means it belongs to me until his successor in name claims it back. When the last Trogadon was dying, he left it to the Mountain-Smith Clan. And they brought it here together with the other artefacts. Now our Trogadon has claimed it for himself.'

The old man was probably unaware of it, but his right hand was continuously stroking the surface of the shield.

Now that Ahren was able to examine it up close, he noted the details of the masterpiece. The shield was rectangular in shape and looked big and cumbersome, but Falk seemed well able to handle it. It was polished smooth, without decorations or a crest, only four lines which indicated a smaller and a larger mountain peak. The surface glimmered in the same blue tone of Trogadon's chainmail. Or the chainmail of the old Trogadon. The dwarves' rules for names made things unnecessarily complicated, thought Ahren in irritation.

'Where does this blue colour come from?' he asked curiously.

His master was lost in old memories and it was always at moments like these when he would freely share his knowledge.

'The first Trogadon discovered Deep Steel that time. These are his first works. It was later on that he perfected the anti-dirt alloy which is where the whiter colour came from,' he answered absently.

Falk was now deep in thought and Ahren didn't want to push it, so he strode forward and joined his new travelling companion.

Trogadon gave him a good-natured smile and glanced mischievously over his shoulder at Falk.

'It was obvious he was going to put up a fight, but you can see clearly how much he was missing a shield.'

Ahren could hear a real fondness for his master in the dwarf's voice and his liking for the little man increased.

'You really are a good friend, Trogadon,' said Ahren sincerely, 'and congratulations on your Ancestry Name.'

The broad-shouldered dwarf grinned.

'It sounds good, hearing this name, and to know that it's me you mean. And thanks for the compliment, but I can't claim that for myself. We dwarves just are like that, loyal friends and ferocious enemies.' There was something wistful in the sound of the warrior's voice, and Ahren couldn't stop himself from commenting on it.

'You seem different to the other dwarves somehow. Less...rigid.'

'I'm a Kulkumharan'thur. Do you know what that means?' The wistfulness in his voice was even more prominent now.

Ahren shook his head. 'Not really. You're more resistant and stronger than the other dwarves and you live longer. That much I understand.' He didn't want to say too much in case he offended the dwarf.

'It's more than that. What you're describing is what you see on the outside. HE, WHO IS gave me an overdose of life. It's as if every moment I experience is new and full of wonder. My joy at living bubbles over with every breath and a belief that it could be such a fantastic life.'

He stopped himself and took a deep breath.

'But we dwarves lead a very ordered life. Everything has its place and there is a place for everything. Since birth I have been a member of the Hammer Clan, the smiths of our folk. When it became clear what I was, the rules were unambiguous. I went to the Mountainshields, although I had a burning enthusiasm for the art of the blacksmith. Other dwarves find me uncontrollable and volatile. It's impossible for me to stand in torpidity for more than two days at a time without waking up. And then I find myself in a clan whose job is to do nothing more than guard tunnels, corridors and passageways for years at a time. Trouble was inevitable.'

Trogadon glanced over at Falk again.

'And so I was hired out to a troop of human mercenaries for an obscene amount of money – and I was delighted. I could see and experience other things, even if they were dangerous. Your master and I quickly became friends. We were both running away from lives we didn't want to lead, and I'm quite willing to admit we saved each other's skin on more than one occasion. He destroyed many a shield in those days, because he simply couldn't get used to them, as they broke far more quickly than this Deep Steel shield. He was always complaining that their cost was being taken out of his wages. His nickname was 'Paladin,' but the others thought it was just a joke. It even took me years before I realised that he really was one.'

His voice lowered to a whisper.

'He was in a very poor spiritual state in those days. You need to know that.'

Ahren thought back to the withdrawn, grumpy Forest Guardian of Deepstone that he had got to know then. That was how his master was after he had found peace with the elves. He shuddered to think how the ageless Paladin had been in earlier times.

'Our ways parted eventually, and we swore that we would meet again sometime. We stayed in contact through a few letters every summer, but by the gods, it's great to see the old warhorse again with my own eyes. Even if he's drinking considerably less than he did, it seems.'

The dwarf chuckled.

'Did you see the look on his face when I presented him with the shield? I thought the eyes were going to pop out of his head.'

Ahren agreed and the dwarf laughed heartily. Falk looked at the pair suspiciously, and Ahren quickly stifled his merriment.

'Don't be afraid of the old curmudgeon, he won't bite you,' chuckled Trogadon.

'It's easy for you to say. He doesn't make you climb up and down trees until you're ready to collapse, just because you've annoyed him,' said Ahren quietly.

The dwarf gave him a friendly slap on the back and Ahren stumbled forward, gasping for breath.

364

'And now you know my story, there's no need for you to stalk me as if I were a wounded Dark One,' he said frankly.

'You're so different to what I imagined. Pure dwarves are supposed to be grumpier than normal ones,' Ahren blurted out before he could stop himself. Trogadon's disarming honesty was infectious and enormously liberating, so that the words came out as soon as they were thought of.

The dwarf chuckled.

'That's true you know. Most of the Pure Ones are sour pusses, but they've all experienced what I have. However, unlike me, they haven't found a useful way out. Centuries of unhappiness can put you into a very bad mood. I, on the other hand, swore that I would carry my joie de vivre around with me like a shield and free myself from the yoke of tradition. The fact that I was able to do that with our oldest tradition was an unexpected bonus.'

He looked at Ahren mischievously.

'But if you like, I can be grumpy from time to time, if that's what you're missing.'

The young man blushed and stammered an apology, but Trogadon stopped him with a casual wave of his hand, and grinned when Khara suddenly came up to him and gave him a warm hug.

'You free you with own strength,' she said haltingly. 'Me very happy you.'

Surprised, Trogadon smiled at the girl and gently returned the hug. Ahren stood there and was annoyed, both at Khara's poor choice of words and at the warm embrace she had given him.

The two separated and there was a moment of understanding which even Ahren clearly recognised. Here were two individuals expressing their admiration for each other, both of whom had escaped from slavery, which had pressed them into terrible bondage for so long. Khara bowed, before running back to Jelninolan, and the scene was over.

Finally, they arrived at the entrance that would take them out of the kingdom of the dwarves and lead them into the wild mountains of Kelkor.

Trogadon led them through a veritable labyrinth, and he seemed to enjoy explaining to them all the traps they passed by. It took them two days to make their way through the tangle of passages with its dead-ends, pitfalls, hidden spears and gullies. When they finally arrived at a smaller, and considerably less decorated version of the Trade Hall, Ahren decided to dig deeper.

'Why is everything so different on this side of the mountain?' He was looking anxiously at the eight fearsome-looking dwarf guards who were guarding the entrance and in a state of torpidity.

'No outsider can enter the Silver Cliff through the land route,' Trogadon replied quietly. 'Non-dwarves can't get past the Little Trade Hall. Anyone who wants to reach the clans must go by sea. It's a precautionary measure to stop anyone from getting the idea of exploring the route before returning later with an army.'

He looked thoughtfully at the guards.

'It's better if we go. The guards that are situated here are generally of a ferocious disposition.'

And so they quickly stepped out into the light and Ahren immediately became dizzy. For a start, the light was particularly glaring following their extended stay in the caves of the dwarves, and apart from that, they now found themselves on a mountain path which wound its way at a great height along the side of a mountain range. As far as the eye could see, Ahren looked at jagged mountains, low-lying valleys, smooth plateaus and raging waterfalls. The whole landscape presented a primal

366

wilderness, one which he had already sensed when he had seen it as they had sailed along the coastline. This impression was further strengthened by the heavy snow that covered everything.

He looked over at Uldini with concern.

'I thought we had more time, but it's already winter. Are we too late?' he asked ruefully.

Uldini tried to play down the situation.

'In Kelkor it snows for half the year. But you're right, we're running out of time. It's less than a moon to the winter solstice. We need to hurry, not least because we have no pack horses or riding animals and the terrain is difficult.'

Falk rubbed his beard and looked thoughtfully at the Arch Wizard, who was still talking.

'The first thing we need to do is find someone from the Wild Folk. A fay would be best, they're the most cheerful. A satyr would suffice too but I'm not sure if his magic would suffice to answer our question. As a last resort, a goblin could help us.'

Although Ahren was shivering in the cold mountain air, Uldini didn't seem to be cold in his thin robe. He looked over at the ageless figure enviously, who was just pointing down at a nearby valley.

'We should climb down. It's reasonably sheltered from the wind and I sense powerful magic. If all goes well, we'll strike it lucky, before we have to deal with a griffin, a rock partridge or a belligerent giant.'

Falk nodded and his eyes glazed over.

'Selsena is very near, I can sense her already. Not near enough for a message, but she should be able to sense where we're heading for.'

He turned to face the others.

'Before we head downwards, everybody should dress as warmly as possible. It's better if you wear your clothes rather than carry them on your back.'

Everyone heeded Falk's advice and to Ahren's surprise, the old man changed too. Finally, they were all ready, and the old Forest Guardian was standing before him in his leather armour, and wearing the fur cape he had made from the skin of the Fog Cat he had killed many years before in the Eastern Forest.

Falk noticed Ahren looking at him and approached the young man.

'I'm a Guardian of the Forest and that's what I'll always be. Being a Paladin is my destiny, but Forest Guardian is my vocation. And how am I supposed to climb properly and go on reconnaissance missions if I'm wearing my Paladin gear? You and I have a few tiring days ahead of us. We're going to have to run ahead all the time and explore the area, keeping an eye out for any dangers. Half of the creatures in Kelkor have highly magical natures, they would sense Jelninolan or Uldini if they tried using their clairvoyance. And anyway, we don't want to have any Dark Ones on our tracks, now that we're outside of the mountains again, so we're going to have to protect ourselves the old-fashioned way.'

Even if Ahren was cold and a little anxious, he still gave an inner leap for joy at Falk's words. The thought of traversing the wilderness with the old man again evoked a feeling of homeland and familiarity, which he had so painfully missed over the previous few weeks.

He nodded eagerly, while still trying not to appear too enthusiastic. He wanted Falk to know that his apprentice was taking his imminent responsibilities seriously. The old Forest Guardian seemed content, and the two marched wordlessly ahead of their companions and into the wilderness where they were soon to be swallowed by blankets of snow.

The following two days were cold but clear. A blue sky accompanied the two Forest Guardians and Ahren enjoyed every second of their strenuous excursions. Whenever it was possible, Falk would quiz him on animals, plants, the weather and the wilderness in general. He was generally happy with his apprentice's answers and in return the young man learned much about the peculiarities of the mountains.

'Be under no illusion. Learning about an area can take your whole life. I am only a semi-informed guest here. But for the moment, you'll have to make do with the most important facts and figures,' said the old man on one occasion, before they set off again.

They encountered the six-footed track of a Storm Mammoth, and Falk showed Ahren an abandoned Griffin nest. The apprentice looked at the nest, four paces in diameter, in disbelief. It had been built from a combination of twigs and mighty branches and the speckled shells of the recently hatched chicks looked so iridescently beautiful in the noon-day sun that Ahren reached out to touch them. But his master held him back.

'The smell of the eggs sticks to you easily and lasts for weeks. You wouldn't like a scornful Griffin mother coming after you because you smell of her chicks now, would you?'

Ahren pulled his hand back at lightning speed and they continued their march. The majestic beauty of the landscape was breath-taking, and Ahren felt better than he had done in a long time.

'According to the priests, Kelkor is the first land the gods created and peopled. That's why it feels so primordial. Nowhere else has so many creatures. Grief Winds, Golems, Fays, Goblins, whatever. Kelkor is dangerous and unpredictable, but that's why there are so few Dark Ones in this country. They'd become prey before they knew it,' said Falk one evening, as they were sitting around the camp-fire.

Ahren absorbed every last piece of information that came from the old Forest Guardian and asked many questions about the creatures that lived here. It seemed to Ahren that with every question Falk answered of his eager student, the old man was becoming more and more like the contented man who two years ago had taken on a shy village youngster as his apprentice.

'I know what you're up to,' whispered Jelninolan to Ahren on the third evening as she was setting up camp. The young man was about to protest his innocence but then thought the better of it. The elf was very experienced when it came to feelings and knew him too well at this point for lying to be of any benefit at all. And so he decided on an impassive look and remained silent. If she had anything else to say, then no doubt she would.

Jelninolan started lighting the campfire and smiled good-naturedly.

'You're improving slowly. When we met first you were always instinctively apologising.'

She spent a few moments giving the little fire some fuel until the fire was burning steadily.

'I welcome what you're doing for Falk. It's important for him to remember what he has achieved in his life as Falk the Forest Guardian. Your master has almost found the balance between what he has to be and what he wants to be. You, Trogadon, Uldini and I are all part of his centuries of development. He has to learn, just as I do, that the way to his goal is to combine both parts of his life, and not to ignore one of them.'

Ahren had watched her carefully during her little lecture and noticed the subtle changes hinted at in Jelninolan's own person. Her facial features had become softer and rounder and her eyes were not quite as hard as they had been over the previous weeks. The young man could see that the priestess had managed to amalgamate her two identities, the carer and the warrior. Ahren believed that Khara had provided the impetus for this amalgamation. The warrior in Jelninolan admired and fostered the girl's expertise, and yet there was also no doubt that the one-time slave was in urgent need of a mother-figure. Without her knowing it, Khara had somehow managed to bring both aspects of Jelninolan closer together and they were now one harmonious whole. He was amazed at the emotional depth and the strangeness of the elf's being and he looked doubtfully over at Falk. There was no doubt it would take longer for his master to achieve his balance.

She laughed when she saw the expression on his face.

'Give him time and just be his apprentice. He doesn't need any more from you, and by the THREE, you certainly need a master.'

Then she ruffled his hair and turned to Khara again, leaving Ahren looking more than a little miffed.

Chapter 21

20 days to the winter solstice

That night Selsena found her way to their camp. Falk had announced that she would be there the following morning, but the Titejunanwa had travelled on after dusk so that she could be at the old man's side again. As she galloped joyfully, whinnying and with her hooves flashing, up to the weak embers of the dying campfire, there was almost a disaster.

Trogadon reacted with lightning speed to what he thought was a sudden attack of an unknown creature. The dwarf had been in a state of torpor and therefore wasn't lying on the ground like the others and so he raised his hammer and raced towards the Elfish warhorse.

'Trogadon, no!' roared Falk and quickly climbed out from under his blanket.

The dwarf paused as he was about to strike and Selsena pranced lithely to the side, lowering her head in a threatening posture. Then the two eyed each other suspiciously. Trogadon still had his hammer ready, raised over his right shoulder and ready to strike, and Selsena was ready to charge forward, her horn and the two wooden blades aimed directly at the dwarf's chest.

'Selsena, may I introduce you to Trogadon? I've often told you about each other,' gasped Falk breathlessly, his arms raised in a placatory gesture as he ran between the two opponents.

The rest of the group gasped, still half-asleep, at the confusing picture before them. Selsena was the first to raise her head, and she sent out a wave of happiness at her reunion with the others, so that all the others had to smile. Except for the dwarf, who remained unmoved and ready for action.

Falk cleared his throat. 'He can't hear you, old girl. Dwarves are more or less immune to empathetic or thought magic. They're much too stubborn and set in their ways.' And he gave Trogadon a severe look until the dwarf at last lowered his weapon.

The miniature warrior had a truculent look on his face.

'You say that as if it's something bad.'

He looked at Selsena and then said airily, 'I apologise, Selsena. He always only used to talk about you when he was drunk and that's why I thought, if truth be told, you were just a figment of his imagination. There were plenty of braggers among the mercenaries.'

The Titejunanwa whinnied cheerfully and the others laughed in relief when they sensed Selsena's happiness.

Falk scratched his beard indignantly.

'We should all go back to sleep now. Tomorrow is going to be a very testing day. We've arrived at the bottom of the valley and we have to keep our eyes peeled for signs of life that might lead us to the Wild Folk.' With that, the old Forest Guardian lay down again and the others followed suit.

Ahren looked at Falk for a while and could see that his master was having a silent conversation with Selsena and was smiling. Satisfied, the apprentice curled up under his blanket and fell asleep.

The following morning the snow came down heavily, reducing their visibility to less than ten paces. It was true that Uldini could strengthen the fire with his magic but it wasn't much protection against the wind and the snow, as their resting place was relatively exposed. There was nothing for it but to travel onwards.

Now Falk and Ahren had two tasks they had to complete. Either they had to find the Wild Folk or a secure encampment which could offer the travelling party better protection. It was a pretty critical situation and so with a heavy heart Falk decided to let Ahren go on by himself, with the strict proviso that the apprentice turn back should there be any sign of danger.

Ahren was delighted at the faith the old man had put in him, however reluctantly. And so the apprentice and Culhen stalked on through the snow-covered wilderness, eyes concentrated on every bush and every crevice in the rocks. The wolf had his nose in the air and he sniffed curiously whenever Ahren stood under the shelter of a tree.

Time passed, and only when the late afternoon sun was struggling to break through a thick cover of cloud did Ahren find success. At the bottom of the face of the mountain, which they had been descending for the last few days along a narrow path, was a cave which seemed large enough to provide a refuge for all in the travelling party. It was true that there was a musky scent within, but it seemed that its occupants had moved on, or fallen victim to some of the hostile wildlife in the area, for it was empty and the scent was old.

Ahren excitedly took note of the spot and they made their way back, taking care to remember points along the way so that he could find the place quickly again.

It had been agreed upon that the others would go in a south-westerly direction until the Forest Guardians had returned, and just as it was getting dark Ahren reached his companions, who were warming themselves around a small fire they had lit behind a jagged rock.

They greeted him with questioning and hopeful looks as he squeezed in between them and warmed his numb hands at the fire. Their relief when he silently nodded was tangible, and Ahren was filled with pride.

'There's a really cosy cave about seven furlongs from here. Uldini will have to light us, but it's worth taking the risk. As soon as Falk is back, we can go.'

'I am back,' a voice said above him, and Ahren instinctively looked up. His master was sitting in one of the nearby trees and had been keeping watch. He had hidden himself up the trunk, squeezed in among the branches. Now he slowly lowered himself and stood among the others.

'Good work, boy. I had no luck looking for a place for us to rest and I wasn't really happy about us lighting a fire in so open a place. But if you hadn't been successful then this spot would have had to do,' he said in a low voice. 'Uldini, create only as much light as enables us to barely see, and keep it low to the ground. Ahren, quench the fire and with as little smoke as possible. Jelninolan, Selsena, sense for living beings in the surroundings, but do it as gently as possible. We need to know if anything is approaching us, even if it does increase our risk of being discovered. Khara and Trogadon, you secure the flanks. Ahren leads, I'll stay at the rear and keep our backs free, and the wolf keeps his nose to the wind,' commanded the Forest Guardian in hushed tones.

In no time at all they were on their way, and Ahren had his hands full, trying to make out the route to their place of refuge in the dim light. Uldini kept the light extremely small, and on more than one occasion Ahren had to ask him to float it over to a particular rock or tree so he could make out if they were still going in the right direction.

The air had become even colder, and the icy wind was blasting through every gap in their clothing. Ahren was used to the winters in the Eastern Forest and quite proud of how he would stoically handle the hostile weather, but the icy surrounds of Kelkor in winter were significantly more unpleasant. The knowledge that they were traversing a wilderness populated by dangerous creatures added to his nervousness. Suddenly, nothing could have prepared him for what was to happen next.

They were half-way to the cave when the young man heard a quiet crying sound which seemed to be coming from the air directly above him. Irritated, he looked upwards but could make nothing out. The surreal sound became clearer as it approached, and now the apprentice could hear that it was actually several voices, all of whom were crying, wailing, whimpering, and sobbing. The mournful sounds went right through Ahren and spoke directly to his heart. He breathed deeply and looked around to the others to warn them. They too seemed to have heard the sounds, and Jelninolan had a look of horror on her face. The elf tried to say something but then her face became the picture of sorrow and she began to sob uncontrollably.

Shocked, Ahren tried to go to her, but the sounds of the keening sucked all the will-power out of his body, and he closed his eyes in an effort to fight it.

The sky was a perfect blue and the sun burned mercilessly down. It was the kind of weather Ahren had loved above all other in his childhood days. He and Likis, his mischievous friend, would spend their days fishing and swimming, or eating goodies, which his wily friend had pilfered or scrounged, in their tree-house.

Now, unfortunately, things were rather different, and the intensive heat meant only more effort as he carried out his tedious work. Ahren looked down at his hands, which were holding a rusty plough, as he tried to break up the hard ground under his scratched and tattered feet. Using all the strength of his arms and back, he pushed the plough forward.

The Southern Fields were notorious for their unmanageable topsoil, and anyone working here had it twice as hard as the others, and as Trell, the mightiest landowner of Deepstone paid per ploughed furrow, Ahren's pay was more barren than the field that lay before him.

With a sigh he pushed the crooked steel a further step forward. He breathed heavily and tried to ignore the pulsating pain in his left hand. Every push of the stubborn farming implement sent a wave of agony through his crippled wrist, which had been broken ever since his father had fractured it the night before the Apprenticeship Tests.

In the many hours since then, that he had spent labouring on the farm, he had asked himself if it wouldn't have been better had he participated in the test. But who would want a cripple anyway, and his father had been clear at the time – turn up on the farm at dawn.

So, he had acquiesced, and taken on every task he was designated without complaint, while his hand shrivelled through the hard work into a useless appendage. Edrik, Ahren's father, knew how to reap the rewards of his son's labours for himself and at the same time ensure that any failures were laid firmly at Ahren's feet. The confirmed drunkard managed to be promoted to foreman and was leading a very comfortable existence while the other workers laboured hard.

The target of his chicanery was, for some secret reason known only in Edrik's black heart, his son. For several summers now he had been given the driest fields, the rustiest equipment and the paltriest food, and all the while Edrik made his life hell, during the day and even at night when they had left the farm and returned to the dark hut they shared. Over time, rage, grief and hate had become Ahren's truest friends, and even Likis had turned away from him the previous summer, once he had become mayor of Deepstone.

Ahren had been spending his time alone, but for an ever-present nagging brooding.

Until now, that is. For the last while an idea, both breathtakingly simple and frighteningly urgent, had been forming in his head. He had begun, almost mechanically, to whet one of the simple kitchen knives they possessed in their sparsely furnished home, on a stone in the forest. He would sit there for hours swaying backwards and forwards, backwards and forwards, while his crippled hand held the knife and the scraping sound of the sharpening blade took over his mind. The pictures in his head became clearer with every passing day. A soft shove between the ribs or a loving stroke across the throat was all that was needed to be free. Free from his father.

So far though, he had not found the courage to do it. His hand had never carried out the necessary action, no matter how many times he had tip-toed over to the sleeping man's bed. He would stand there for hours, dreaming of doing it, yet never quite managing it.

Here and now, in the scorching midday sun on the Southern Field of Trell's farm, it hit him like a thunder stroke.

He would never be free. Unless it were his own throat, his own heart that his knife would lovingly caress.

He pulled the blade out from the folds of his clothing and raised it in the blazing light of the sun. The reflection on the finely-sharpened blade promised salvation and peace. He placed the tip of the knife on his chest and almost with pleasure he increased the inward pressure and imagined the disappointed face on his father when he realised that his son had at last escaped him.

Ahren awoke, gasping with the cold. Frozen tears were burning his face and his hunting knife fell with a clatter from his hands, numbed with the

378

icy temperature. There was a coolness pressing in on his skin, where the tip of the blade had cut through the thick clothing. Ahren stood up and pulled the leather tiles of his ribbon armour back over the hole so he would be protected from the biting wind.

He looked around, confused. He was kneeling up to his thighs in snow, and most of the others were in the same position. Only Uldini was standing, eyes ablaze, in a little crater free from snow, and there was a lost look on his face with fresh scratches on his cheeks, which had been caused by his own fingernails. Falk was staring blankly while Jelninolan was curled over in the snow, her face hidden in the powdery substance. Khara was sitting back on her heels in what seemed to be some kind of ritual posture. She had opened her clothing at her stomach and the tip of Windblade was placed on her skin. She was blinking owlishly as if she had just woken up from a deep dream. Selsena and Culhen were nowhere to be seen.

Trogadon, however, presented the strangest picture. The dwarf was standing, his massive frame in a crouched position, and his arms and legs seemed to be jerking uncontrollably. He suddenly leaped against a rock and in seeming disgust he began hammering his head against the stone surface.

Totally confused, Ahren leaped to his feet, leaving the accusatory knife on the snow beneath him. He could hardly fathom what he had almost done, and the thought was too much for him to bear.

Thankful for the distraction, he rushed over to the others to help them. He turned Jelninolan on her back, who immediately began gasping for the freezing air. He carefully took Windblade out of Khara's hand and pulled her up onto her feet. Then he went over to Falk, who was now speaking reassuringly to Uldini.

'Breathe in deeply, good man. You're among friends and there's no need to pronounce magic spells. A Grief Wind caught us by surprise and you're just coming back to yourself now,' he whispered imploringly to the childlike figure with the burning eyes.

Ahren gasped. A Grief Wind! Falk had told him about this being. The first attempt of the gods to create life without the others' help, and it had failed spectacularly. These first beings were full of blemishes or horrendously ugly and very often dangerous.

The Grief Wind was an ethereal creation, formed by HER, WHO FEELS. It had no physical body and was therefore nothing more than a collection of concentrated emotions, imprisoned in something which, when seen clearly, was similar to a shimmering vortex of air. It was almost impossible to fight against it, and even Falk's advice had been quite sobering to hear.

'If you see one, run. Warn everyone in the vicinity and sit things out until it has moved on. A Grief Wind moves like a cloud, and if it gets no nourishment, it floats on,' the old man had said.

And that was exactly why the thing was so dangerous. A Grief Wind found its nourishment in hopelessness and despair. It filled up the spirit of a person and sprinkled it with the deepest fears and most terrifying images that could be drawn up from the memories and imagination of the victim. Either the afflicted person would die through a broken heart or take their own life.

This one here had caught them completely unaware and they had had no time to protect themselves. There were stories of very strong-willed people managing to survive a Grief Wind by locking themselves into empty rooms where they could not be harmed. But here, in the darkness of the wilderness, they should all by rights have died.

Falk seemed just as dumbfounded as Ahren, and so the apprentice left his master to deal with Uldini while he went over to Trogadon, who was still jerking wildly, although the movements were not quite as powerful as earlier. The dwarf's eyes were rolling in his head, and he was smashing it again and again against the rock. His forehead was decorated with large bruises, and it was only thanks to his thick skin that his face wasn't lacerated.

'What should I do?' shouted Ahren helplessly and looked over his shoulder at Falk and the others.

Much to his surprise it was Uldini who answered, whose words, hoarse through anger, came out through gritted teeth.

'He must not open his mouth. The lunatic has breathed in the Grief Wind and has imprisoned it. I have to banish it as soon as I've regained control over myself, but he must on no account exhale until I'm ready.'

Ahren stared at the compact figure of the warrior dwarf in disbelief. It was true that his chest wasn't rising and falling and slowly it dawned on the apprentice what was happening. The Grief Wind was controlling part of his squat body and was trying to force the dwarf to breathe out. The grimace on Trogadon's face showed Ahren that his strength was fading fast.

Ahren spoke encouragingly to the dwarf even if he doubted that his opposite number was taking anything in. Ahren stood there helplessly and could do nothing more than trust in the strength of will of their new travelling companion. He shoved his arm between the head of the dwarf and the rock, trying to cushion the blows that Trogadon was hammering under the increasing control of the Grief Wind.

After what seemed like an eternity, he heard a hoarse growling voice.

'Out of the way,' ordered Uldini urgently and Ahren spun to the side.

'Khuldat throl sundalar,' intoned the Magus with a voice so powerful that the snow tumbled off the surrounding trees. Then a bluish-violet flash of light came in a ghostly silence from the skies and hit the dwarf directly between the eyes.

Trogadon stopped jerking, blinked once and collapsed like a house of cards.

Falk cursed and ran over to him, and the others joined him with worried looks on their faces.

'Was there no other option? What if you've killed him...' began the old Forest Guardian as he scolded Uldini.

'No time for remonstrating, we have to act now. Jelninolan, your healing hands, please' said Uldini briskly.

The two Ancients laid their hands on the dwarf's chest and began uttering a charm.

Before they had even spoken three syllables, a dull, droning rumbling sound began to develop, growing steadily louder and stronger. Ahren glanced around in panic until he finally understood. The dwarf let out an almighty belch which left everyone around him in petrified silence.

Then Trogadon sat up and looked around in satisfaction.

'Everyone still here? Excellent! It would have been terrible if my headache had been a waste of time.'

Then his eyes rolled again and he collapsed on the ground.

'I think he'll survive,' said Uldini drily.

He and Jelninolan completed their charm, but Ahren could see from their expressions and the weak glowing of their hands that they were now preserving their magic strength, now that the dwarf had so impressively put his constitution to the test.

Uldini began giving orders even before he stood up.

'He needs to be carried and we have to get out of here immediately. The banning of the Grief Wind was no walk in the park and it certainly hasn't gone unnoticed. A cosy cave for hiding in is exactly what we need now.' He looked at Ahren expectantly and the young man picked up his knife and started walking again and so they moved on. Falk, Khara, and Jelninolan carried the snoring dwarf and after a slow and exhausting march they finally arrived at their new refuge.

The night seemed to last forever. They all crouched, shivering from the cold in total silence, and nobody dared to light a fire or to sleep. Twice they heard enormous creatures tramping by the cave and once Ahren was convinced he saw enormous wings beating heavily directly above the cave.

He spent the whole night worrying about Culhen and Selsena, both of whom had fled during the attack of the Grief Wind. Falk had explained to him that animals fled instinctively from the creature, but the longer the night wore on, the more concerned the apprentice grew. During this time, Uldini and Jelninolan had interlocked the fingers of their hands with the others,' which created a magical barrier deflecting others away from their place of refuge.

When dawn broke, they let go of each other and closed their eyes in exhaustion.

'We're not going anywhere today,' mumbled Uldini irritably, at which point the two Ancients fell asleep.

Falk took over temporary command.

'Trogadon, Khara, you guard the cave and our two sleepy-heads. Ahren and I will try to find someone from the Wild Folk and also see if we can catch sight of Selsena and Culhen. Yesterday I thought I'd seen signs of goblins. Maybe not Uldini's first choice but after the Grief

Wind's attack I think we're all agreed that we need to disappear from here as quickly as possible.'

The apprentice nodded and gathered his bundle as he prepared to trot off. He was glad to have something to do, after having spent the whole night with nothing but his thoughts. He had been deeply affected by the fact that he had nearly ended his own life, and by the terrible visions the Grief Wind had presented to him, and he was almost going mad with worry concerning Culhen's whereabouts.

He was halfway out the cave when Falk stopped him.

'Ahren, you're staying by my side today, I don't want to push our luck any further than necessary.'

The young man gave a respectful nod and all in all, he was happy with that. He wasn't in the best frame of mind, and he wasn't sure how reliable he would be carrying out his responsibilities after his sleepless night. On the other hand, he really wanted to look for Culhen as soon as possible. Falk saw his concern and placed a hand on his shoulder.

'There's no need to worry. He will probably have stayed with Selsena and the old girl really knows how to look after herself.'

He gave a look of encouragement, but Ahren couldn't shake off the impression that his master's words were primarily aimed at giving his master himself courage.

Ahren decided that he would first keep his eyes peeled for wolf or hoof traces and then look for the goblin later. But they'd hardly left the cave and trotted out into the snowy landscape when their animal companions came galloping out of the undergrowth and up to them. Ahren embraced Culhen with a firm hug, and Falk welcomed Selsena with a gentle stroke on her nostrils.

After a short exchange of thoughts with the Titejunanwa, the old Forest Guardian gave a groan.

'But of course! The magic charm of our wizards duped Selsena and Culhen just as much as the other nightly visitors. They knew we were in the vicinity but couldn't find out exactly where.'

He shook his head energetically.

'Uldini and Jelninolan must have been really worried if they didn't even leave a tiny hole in the protective shield for Selsena.'

Content that everyone was more or less safe and sound, the two Forest Guardians continued on their way, with wolf and warhorse by their sides. They spent the whole morning exploring the area that Falk had seen the day before, and shortly before noon they made a find.

'Over there,' whispered Falk and nodded his head in a westerly direction. Ahren concentrated on the snow-covered ground but couldn't make out any tracks. He frowned and looked more carefully, but there was nothing of interest apart from a couple of rabbit tracks.

Tut-tutting in annoyance, Falk grasped his apprentice firmly by the back of the neck and then turned his head, first to the left and then upwards. The young man immediately saw three boulders, stacked on top of each other in an impossible act of precision and balance, considering they were totally different to each other in size and form, and none of them appeared to have been sculpted. The second and third boulder hardly seemed to be touching each other at all and it almost seemed as though the top one was floating in the air.

'Goblins don't leave behind footprints if it doesn't suit them. If you want to find them, then you have to keep your eyes peeled for practical jokes like the one you're looking at,' he whispered.

'That was a goblin's doing?' Ahren was completely taken aback, not to mention impressed. 'Are they really that strong?' He began to feel somewhat queasy.

'You mean physically?' Falk shook his head. 'No. Definitely not. A goblin did that with a click of his fingers. They are highly magical creatures with a direct connection to the source of all Jorath's magic. Some scholars say that the goblins are magic.'

He rubbed his beard with his hand and then frowned in annoyance.

'Unfortunately, they not only have extraordinary powers, but they're also highly impulsive and their ability to take responsible decisions would be equivalent to that of a spoiled child.'

He pointed over at the rocks.

'It's quite possible that the boulders there will hop up and down if we pass by them, or that they will beat us to death. Goblins are unpredictable.'

He slapped Ahren on the shoulder and turned him gently around.

'We should go back to the others. Two Forest Guardians on their own will certainly not be sufficient to persuade them to help you, and it's questionable if my authority as Paladin will carry any weight. The Wild Folk hardly got involved in the battles of the Dark days. Anytime that HE, WHO FORCES tried to put down roots here, they would chase him and his creatures out, but nothing more than that. HE tried to conquer and destroy Kelkor out of revenge on three occasions, and every time HE got nothing more than a bloody nose.'

Falk frowned as he continued speaking.

'Unfortunately, every delegation from the Free Folk was also rebuffed. We sent people, elves, and dwarves here on more than one occasion, but they could never negotiate anything more than a ceasefire. At least the dwarves are friendly with the giants, but even that hasn't helped us. Personally, I think the Wild Folk shy away from forming alliances because they're afraid that the individual races on Kelkor will start arguing and fighting with each other.'

'Giants and dwarves like each other?' asked Ahren in surprise.

Falk shrugged his shoulders. 'Dwarves like everything that's big and strong. Giants love glittering objects. From time to time they send the giants a chest filled with semi-precious gemstones, and in return the giants protect the few trading caravans that take the land route to the Silver Cliff. You've seen how dangerous it is in Kelkor. A fully laden trader wouldn't get very far here without help, no matter how many mercenaries he might have hired from outside.'

Ahren considered how important relationships between different tribes were, even in this untamed part of the world, and his respect for Senius Blueground, the king of Knight Marshes grew even further. The monarch had to keep the interests of so many barons, guilds and neighbouring countries in harmony and at the same time look after the simple people and their welfare. All of a sudden, the young man was happy that he was only going to become a Paladin and all he had to do was hunt down the Adversary. That seemed a lot simpler when compared to a king's responsibilities.

They returned to the others and to his relief Trogadon was already awake. His head had a bluish-violet colouring on account of all his bruises, but the dwarf seemed in a cheerful mood and as unfazed as ever.

Falk greeted the squat warrior by striking his chest lightly with his fist.

'You gave us a big fright, you old warhorse. How did you come up with the crazy idea of swallowing a Grief Wind,' he exclaimed!

'Actually, I breathed it in,' said the dwarf jokingly. 'It's an old dwarf solution to a Grief Wind attack. Normally we spit it out again and it flees, but our example from yesterday was quite old and stubborn. The mind games of those things can't do us much harm, in fact we think of them of nothing more than an annoyance. Some of our more secluded clans even find them useful because they can keep unwanted visitors at bay.'

He nodded his head airily.

'I see things differently. Anyone who doesn't survive isn't a potential customer.'

Then he smiled mischievously and Ahren had to laugh at the dwarf's black humour.

'Still, you've saved our bacon, and thank you for that,' said Falk.

'So now it's nineteen to twenty-six, isn't it?' joked the dwarf.

Falk puffed himself up before responding. 'Twenty-six? How did you arrive at that number?'

'Don't tell me you've forgotten the siege of Shallow Ford? If I hadn't rescued you from that, you'd have ended up being burned at the stake!' bellowed the dwarf.

Ahren listened to the pair of friends as they continued to exchange stories of their derring-do in mock argument, and hoped that at least half of them were invented or at the very least exaggerated. The feeling of camaraderie connecting the two was real and tangible, and clearly seemed to do Falk a lot of good. Uldini and the Paladin didn't seem to have ever achieved that level of closeness, or if they had then it had been buried by the Night of Blood and Falk's flight from his own past.

The apprentice hoped that sometime in the future he too could exchange stories of shared exploits with them, but for the moment he was content to listen to the pair and absorb some of the air of invincibility which their anecdotes conveyed.

Chapter 22

Uldini and Jelninolan only awoke from their sleep trance the following day, but even then, they were still exhausted.

'If we're really going to be dealing with a goblin, then it makes no difference if we're not back to full strength, so we might as well get going,' said Uldini stoically, after Falk had brought him up to date regarding their search.

The Arch Wizard was still suffering the emotional after-effects of the magic he'd used to hold the Grief Wind at bay. Attack magic made you aggressive, healing magic made you lethargic, but when you exorcised a being, it seemed to bring forth a stoical indifference.

'What does that mean exactly, exorcising a being?' asked Ahren quietly as they were gathering their things together.

Falk scratched his beard for a moment and then spoke.

'You can only exorcise things that are without material existence. That's how Uldini described it once. So, other magic, curses, spirits, and heat and cold in small quantities, things like that. To put it in a nutshell, the conjurers wish the intended target away, and if they do it powerfully enough, it dissolves. Uldini explained to me that performing an exorcism is extremely difficult and always dangerous, because you are interfering with nature. That's why as a rule only non-substantial things are exorcised, and even that is hard enough.'

That explained Uldini's current apathy. He had wished something away, and now his emotions were gone too, or at least not in the immediate vicinity. In time, Uldini would be back to his old self, but for now he wasn't up to much.

Jelninolan, on the other hand, while weak and a little irritable, was still willing to share her knowledge with them.

'Goblins are also fay-creatures. To be precise, they're male fays, even if they don't look fay-like. The female fays keep the goblins in check, making sure that they don't put a hole in creation with their pranks by mistake. Eathinians have good relations with the fays, so I will try to speak to him. I have one or two ideas which might persuade him. Thankfully, Uldini isn't such a mystery-monger as a certain odd Forest Guardian, which meant I was able to prepare myself a little before our journey,' as she looked over accusingly at Falk, who looked back at her guiltily.

She rummaged around in her rucksack and put something small in her jerkin. Ahren craned his neck and could make out a small flower.

Jelninolan looked at him furiously and stamped her foot.

'Is there something under my jerkin that you find particularly interesting?' she fumed.

Ahren gasped and went a deep red.

Eh...no...I didn't mean to...' he stammered.

Then he gave a quick bow and fled out of the cave, the elf's icy stare following him.

Soon the whole group set off on their way. Ahren and Falk were a hundred paces ahead of the others and kept an eye out for potential dangers while Trogadon and Khara kept close to the two conjurers.

'The nearer we approach our target, the less we need to fear other creatures. Nothing and nobody hangs around in an area inhabited by a goblin.'

390

Ahren was nervous enough as it was, and Falk's statement only made him more anxious. The trick with the rocks may have been impressive, but the fact that the monstrous creatures of Kelkor fled from a goblin was, to put it simply, terrifying.

They found the strange boulder tower quickly again and steered a wide berth around it. Then they came upon an increasing number of signs suggesting they were nearing the goblin. A tree that was rammed into the ground with its roots in the air on which were growing small flowers, a little river with a powerful current that circled around a rock, but which had neither a source nor an outlet.

They were proceeding with more caution now because the pranks against nature were testing their nerves, when suddenly they heard a loud, complaining laugh behind them. Ahren spun around, as did all his companions.

Right on top of a throne of snow, exactly where they had passed by a few short heartbeats previously, sat a blue-skinned, tiny figure, who from a distance looked like a mixture of human and frog. He had long limbs and a bulbous body with shiny, oily skin with big pores and filled with wart-like growths. His bald head with enormous lidless eyes which were almost laterally positioned, and the lack of ears or a nose, strengthened the frog-like impression, as did the broad mouth with its few stumps of teeth which could be seen, now that the creature was beginning to speak to them.

'So many visitors in the one day. What could you possibly want here? Too meagrely laden to do trade with the short ones. Too poorly armed to go dragon-slaying. You really are a puzzle.'

The goblin's voice produced a curious echo, as if another person were whispering what he had said half a heartbeat later and in a shrill tone. A primeval fear came over Ahren when he heard this sound and he felt paralysed.

The enormous eyes of the fay-creature stared at them and a curious look came over the goblin's face.

'I love puzzles. So you may speak.' He wagged his hand about, and Ahren felt an unbearable urge to speak. He began chattering wildly and began telling his whole life story in random sentences while staring fixedly at the frog creature. The others were doing exactly the same - even Trogadon seemed unable to escape the charm.

The goblin listened to the chaotic sounds for a while, then wagged his hand about again and immediately everyone closed their mouths.

'My goodness, but some of you are old. You wouldn't guess it by looking at most of you.' He looked over at Falk derisively. 'We'll be here for years if we carry on with this method and I'm getting bored already.'

He pointed at Khara.

'You. Explain why you're here.'

The girl stood for a moment frozen and then began to speak in the Empire language, so quickly that it seemed to Ahren to be one continuous sentence. After something like thirty heartbeats the goblin made an abrupt hand movement and she stopped speaking abruptly.

His unyielding eyes were now fixed on Falk.

'I knew I recognised your ugly mug from somewhere. You hung around here for a while after the Dark Days and you slaughtered a few of the large creatures that lived here. For trophies, if I remember rightly.'

Falk turned and said, 'they were a danger to the farmers who lived on the borders…' but the goblin interrupted harshly.

'Lies don't pay, Paladin. Let's be nice and truthful here,' he cackled.

'After a hundred years of resting on my laurels as a Paladin, the memory of our deeds began to lose their significance. I began to fall into debt and a few of the exotic animals here brought in good money if you sold them as trophies, so I came here, until I grew tired of fighting again,' said the old man through gritted teeth.

Ahren was shocked by the brutally honest words of his master. He knew that Falk had lost hope and his moral compass after the Dark Days, but he had had no idea of how low his master had sunk during his crisis.

The goblin sat motionless in his throne for a while. Rather than look at his guests, he stared up at the skies and hummed. Nobody could move and when Ahren tried to whisper something, he noticed that his tongue was paralysed.

The pale eyes of the goblin now fixed themselves on the apprentice, and Ahren could do nothing but stare back at the creature's strange pupils. Ahren forgot to blink, his whole world was held spell-bound by the two yellow-white pools.

'You really think you can defeat HIM, WHO FORCES? At any price? Even if you have to pay for it with your life or the lives of your friends?' The voice, which sounded like two, bored in through his head and into his very being.

Ahren saw flashes of his life appear and disappear, as the creature sought out the answer in the young man's reason, an answer that the apprentice himself didn't know.

The goblin clicked his fingers and released everyone from the spell by which he had held them captive. Ahren collapsed into himself and fell down on one knee. The threatening feeling that the goblin had radiated was slowly diminishing. Falk leaped two paces forward and was pulling his sword out of its scabbard when Uldini intervened and a sudden gust of wind threw Falk backwards to the ground.

'Use your head, old man,' whispered the Arch Wizard and gestured to the snow in front of the goblin's ice throne. Translucent snakes were wriggling around and they had already bared their fangs in Falk's direction.

The fay-creature cackled with amusement and the snakes disappeared.

'Spoilsport,' he said to Uldini and hopped off his throne. With an odd waddling gait, he walked in among the travellers and turned to face Falk.

'I have done no harm to your precious apprentice. He is remarkably honest for a human, if more than a little naïve. I even like him in some odd way. So, ask what you wish to ask and we'll take it from there.'

Ahren picked himself up. It was hard to fathom the goblin's strange facial gestures, but still, Ahren didn't believe him for a heartbeat. His furtive tone suggested that he was only toying with them.

The young man went over to his master and pulled him to his feet. They exchanged looks, and Ahren gave a reassuring nod to indicate that he was fine. Falk placed his heavy hand on his apprentice's shoulder for a moment, then they turned to face the goblin, who was now looking up in surprise at Jelninolan, who was now standing upright before him and looking down at him with a stern look.

'With the first flower of the springtime, a gift from your mistress Tillimandra Jul-Jilran, I command you to tell me your name, goblin!'

Jelninolan had intoned with the full authority of a life-time's experience as a priestess and Ahren trembled at the power of her words even though he wasn't the target of her command.

'Tlik, my name is Tlik,' called the goblet out hastily and then clapped his hands over his mouth, his face a picture of rage and respect.

Jelninolan spoke on before the fay-creature had a chance to react.

'Tlik, by your name I bind you to our task. Help us achieve the Naming of the Paladin Ahren, and you shall be free.'

The wind that had been blowing all day suddenly died down, the sun darkened for a heartbeat and it seemed as though the whole countryside was holding its breath. Then everything returned back to normal, only the goblin continued to stare at the elf, his hands still in front of his mouth.

Jelninolan looked down sadly at her own hands. Withered petals slipped between her fingers and onto the ground - dried out and without any life, they settled in the snow.

Uldini whistled out as the penny dropped.

'A powerful trump you had there, auntie. And you played it excellently if you don't mind me saying so.'

A triumphant smile flashed across her face, chasing away her sorrow, and she curtsied playfully.

Ahren was completely baffled but his master took mercy on him and explained what had just happened.

'Every summer Eathinian gets a blossom from the mistress of the fays. Supposedly it's the first flower of the spring and its power is simple yet powerful. With it you can compel a member of the fay court to be of assistance. Usually, selected elves seek out a friendly fay and their wishes revolve around things like eternal love, peace or the healing of a serious illness.'

Uldini pushed his way into the conversation, an admiring spark in his eyes.

'Our scheming priestess actually used the blossom on a goblin. That's certainly never happened before. Why ask a goblin, when you can ask a fay? But Jelninolan unlocked his name with her wish. And unlike fays, goblins are bound to their task through their name.'

He looked with an air of superiority down at the goblin.

'And she's just done that. Our recalcitrant friend here has to help us until your Naming has been achieved.'

Ahren looked down at the goblin, who had dropped his arms and now looked the very picture of blue misery. The fay-creature looked piteously up at Jelninolan and asked with his croaking voice: 'would you not like to reconsider it, your highness? I'm sure I can fulfil many wishes for you, if you only let me free…'

Jelninolan shook her head firmly.

'No thank you.'

The figure of the goblin seemed to shrink even further, and he nodded respectfully.

'As you wish, your most high and mighty.'

Trogadon let out a rumbling laugh.

'He's very cute now, isn't he?' he asked his companions.

Ahren was about to agree but Uldini interrupted. 'Please don't antagonise him. Once he's carried out his tasks, he won't be so friendly, and we don't want to give him any more reasons for wanting to wreak his revenge after he's been set free.'

The dwarf's laughter died down and he eyed the goblin thoughtfully, while he nodded in agreement.

'So, Tlik. Where exactly is the place that Ahren's Naming must be carried out,' asked Jelninolan firmly.

The blue figure examined Ahren thoroughly by looking him up and down, and wagged his hand once. In an instant the apprentice was surrounded by a pattern of incredible colours and shapes. He flinched in surprise but was frozen to the spot when the goblin snapped his fingers.

'No fidgeting, please. Your aura is complicated enough to read without everything becoming blurry.'

The goblin floated up to him, his ugly face coming nearer and nearer until finally it was only two hands away from his own. The apprentice wanted to flinch backwards, but the goblin's magic was ruthlessly effective, and he couldn't move. He began to sweat.

Tlik looked over his shoulder at Uldini.

'What sort of bungling chaos of strength lines did you cobble together that time? This is your amazing ritual that sent HIM to sleep? It's nothing short of a miracle that HE hasn't already sucked the young lad dry and that he isn't dancing around on your graves.'

A knotty finger rose before Ahren's right eye and a black line shot from it and off to the west from where Ahren was standing where it faded away into the distance.

'This strength line could have led you there with the help of those two. Then he would have strangled himself with every draught he had taken of the young man. Instead of which he has free reign and the connection between the two is getting stronger by the heartbeat.'

Ahren found the goblin's presentation hard enough to take, but the embarrassed looks on Jelninolan's and Uldini's faces made matters worse, as did the gleeful undertone in the fay-creature's voice.

'Is there any way you can lock HIM out, somehow?' asked the elf urgently but the goblin shook his head. 'The connection remains. If I separate them now, the young lad will explode and you'll have a shower of Paladin ragout.'

Ahren went pale and he really wished the goblin would stop talking.

Uldini cleared his throat and folded his arms impatiently.

'All well and good, but this isn't helping us. If you fays had helped us that time, then the Great Spell would have been more successful, but that didn't happen. We have to live with what we've got. Am I right in assuming that the lines will dissolve as soon as we've named Ahren?'

Ahren held his breath and fixed his eyes on the dwarf, who cast a fleeting glance at the apprentice's aura. Then the goblin nodded and Ahren felt a wave of relief.

'Certainly, but you need to name him urgently before the winter solstice or the cord will become too thick. After that day he would have to share the Blessings of the gods with HIM, WHO FORCES and that would really spoil the fays' days. And the rest of Jorath's too.'

For the first time Ahren could hear real fear in the voice of the magical creature as he spoke on.

'Not only would HE awaken more quickly, but he would achieve direct access to the power of the gods, and nobody wants that to happen.'

A horrified silence descended on the group. Jelninolan was the first to recover from the shock.

'Then we're agreed. I'll repeat my question: where can we carry out the Naming?' she asked in a voice that brooked no dissent.

The goblin turned around to her in surprise.

'I thought you knew that already. You have to go back to where the magic started which connects your precious aspirant to HIM. You have to go to the Borderlands.'

Ahren sat on the ground and tried to control his breathing by inhaling and exhaling slowly. The goblin had released him from his state of rigidity at last, having finished reading his aura. Now the goblin was reluctantly discussing things with Uldini and Jelninolan. Falk, Trogadon and Culhen were kneeling down beside the young man, and each in their own way was trying to console him, while Khara observed him with an enigmatic look on her face.

The apprentice wasn't really taking in what the others were doing. He was trapped in his own little world, and the name of the place they would have to search out was echoing endlessly in his head.

The Borderlands could be reached by marching for two months if conditions were good. But if they didn't get there within three weeks, then he would become a danger for the whole of Jorath because the

Adversary would be able to use the blessings of the gods, which Ahren now possessed, against creation.

Before he had the chance to sink into total despair, Uldini came floating over to them.

'We've found a solution. It's not without its dangers, but we've no other choice,' he began.

Ahren was hanging on to his every word in desperation.

'Tlik will open the Wild Paths. They follow the Strength Lines of this world, and other laws apply on this journey. If we go quickly, we'll get to the Borderlands in barely two weeks.'

Ahren threw himself forward and embraced the childlike figure of the Ancient with a cry of joy.

Uldini was totally taken aback and awkwardly patted the apprentice on the back.

'Don't worry about it, son. We Ancients made a right dog's dinner of it, so we'll help you get out of it.'

He gently released himself from the young man's embrace.

'It's best if we head off straight away. Jelninolan and I will figure out what safety measures we need to put in place. The Wild Paths are not designed for mortal ones, but I've one or two ideas.' He winked encouragingly at Ahren.

The apprentice got back up to his feet and decided to put all his faith into the two Ancients' ability to find a solution. But in his heart, he also reached another decision. If they didn't manage to get there in time, he would prevent his blessing being used against the free peoples. His hand reached down to the hunting knife which only two days before had been on the point of boring into his heart. If they didn't manage it, Ahren would point it at his chest again, but his time it would be of his own free will.

While he was thinking this, he noticed the goblin looking strangely into his eyes for a heartbeat and Ahren was sure he saw the fay-creature give a barely perceptible nod before returning to his conversation with the two conjurers.

Chapter 23

Ahren looked anxiously at the mysteriously shimmering pool of powerful energy that lay before them.

Tlik had measured out an area three paces in diameter and was circling it again and again. The icy surface had lain there unchanging at first, but every time he circled it the surface of snow became glassier and somehow more translucent. Eventually a bluish-white smooth fog began to arise from the pool.

The morning sun was just rising and when the goblin had finally stopped walking, Uldini and Jelninolan returned, after having left the cave in the early hours.

'We can't do anything before dawn,' Uldini had said the previous evening. 'First Jelninolan and I will have to rest. And even Tlik will need time to create a sturdy opening without drawing attention to us. Other creatures travel the Wild Paths too, and we certainly don't want to meet them.'

Ahren had intended remaining awake, but the events and revelations of the day had caught up with him. His decision to offer himself up if necessary had given him a feeling of melancholy peace, and his sleep had been deep and unusually calm.

He had woken up under the weight of Culhen, who had rolled in on top of him during the night, and as he carefully sat up the next morning, he saw Trogadon's cheerful face.

'You have a true friend there who has locked you in his heart,' the dwarf had said, pointing at the sleeping wolf. 'Be careful that you don't hurt him,'

Then the squat figure had stood up and marched out into the snow. The apprentice sat there stunned, until it dawned on him that the dwarf had sensed the apprentice's dark intention of the previous day.

Now they were all standing around the entrance to the Wild Paths, ready to depart. Everybody had their belongings securely fixed to their backs, and under Uldini's instructions, they had all dressed warmly.

'The Wild Paths are different to all others that you know of,' explained Uldini in his schoolteacher's voice. 'We want to proceed quickly and silently, and so Jelninolan and I have decided to lay magic upon you, which will help us. It will be a little uncomfortable for you but it's the best solution.'

He gave them all a blindfold as he floated past.

'Please tie them over your eyes and nose. They contain smells, sounds and pictures which will help conserve you. We've created earplugs out of candle wax for you as well.'

Falk was about to protest but Jelninolan cut in.

'It's for your own protection. Uldini and I have to hide you, and the less you move the better. You'll understand as soon as we're over there. Also, we'll be coming out into the middle of the Borderlands, and Uldini and I are going to be exhausted. You, on the other hand, will have to be as rested as possible when we arrive, so you can handle everything that will be awaiting us over there.'

Tlik nodded enthusiastically in support of the elf's words. Since the decision had been reached to travel along the Wild Paths, the goblin had become unusually amenable. Ahren smelled a rat, but Uldini and especially Jelninolan trusted him, so Ahren decided he had to do the same. He saw the others looking doubtfully too, but they too remained silent and resigned to their fates.

Jelninolan pulled a rope out of her bag and tied it around Trogadon, who looked at her in astonishment. She knotted it securely and then took a pace back to Falk and tied the next section of rope to the old Forest Guardian. Then she repeated the pattern along all the travelling party so that in the end they were all bound together, one behind the next at a distance of one pace each time.

Uldini pressed the wax earplugs into their hands and issued his final instructions.

'First the ears and then the blindfold. Hold on to the rope leading to the person in front, then you will know if you need to stop or walk on. Under no circumstances are you to loosen the rope. If you get lost in the Wild Paths, nobody will know whether or how you will ever escape.'

Jelninolan gave everyone an encouraging smile.

'Trust Uldini and me, then everything will be fine. We'll bring you safely to the other side.'

Ahren looked doubtfully over at Selsena and Culhen, who were both standing there, quite free and untied. The wolf was sitting in his usual pose, on his back legs, his tongue hanging out of his mouth as though he were laughing at Ahren.

'What about those two?' he asked uneasily. The more he heard about the Wild Paths, the more nervous he felt.

'Don't worry about them,' answered Jelninolan. 'Animals read the place in a different way. They'll follow us quite safely.' She said this with such certainty that Ahren didn't pursue the matter.

Then it became serious, and the travellers who had been strapped in began covering their senses. Ahren put the wax in his ears and tied the blindfold firmly over his nose and eyes. The material was thick and heavy and Ahren could recognise and smell nothing more than the slightly musty aroma of the blindfold.

He breathed deeply through his mouth and he hoped he would soon get used to the feeling of being blind and half-deaf as he snatched for breath.

Now that he was devoid of the two senses, he gripped firmly to the rough rope that connected him to Falk. He became ever more concerned about Culhen and was on the point of pulling off the blindfold when suddenly Tanentan's song took hold of his reason.

Jelninolan was playing her murmuring and calming melody on the artefact, and the music was flattering his understanding and leading him into a dusky half-sleep. His thoughts were becoming heavy and indolent. And nothing could reach him anymore except for the song from the soundless lute.

He trotted forward as if sleepwalking once he felt the rope tightening around his stomach and along with the others, he walked carefree and docile into the shimmering light that was pushing through the material on his blindfold. The feeling of cold and heat that overcame him simultaneously, pushed for a heartbeat through his befogged spirit but then it was over, and they were standing on the Wild Paths.

It was day and it was night. He felt snow and he felt sun on his skin. He heard colours and tasted every step he took. All of his senses were in a tangle, and of course that should have disturbed him, but he didn't even know where he was, and anyway there was this song in his head that held him safe and warm, like a loving mother. It murmured and it tugged at his heartstrings: 'come, oh come, step after step – come to your destiny,' it seemed to cry, and he would obey.

He was vaguely aware of standing still from time to time when the rope became loose in front of him.

Sometimes he felt a woman's hands pressing him to the ground, where he would curl into a ball as his senses were in their tangle, and he tasted enormous creatures moving past him with smells that made his skin tingle. Forwards and forwards he went, carried by Tanentan's song, an endless succession of steps, carrying him through this strangest of countries, to a place whose name he had forgotten, as indeed he had forgotten his own name.

When their journey along the Wild Paths finally came to an end, the crossover was uncomfortable and abrupt. He had just felt heat and cold on his skin again, when the magical song stopped playing in his head and he came around.

He sank to the ground whimpering. His legs were so weak that he could hardly move. He quickly pulled the blindfold off and the earplugs out of his ears. The noonday sun blinded him, and Ahren quickly closed his eyes again and massaged his aching knees. In front and behind he could hear quiet groans of pain, so he thought the others had to be feeling the same way.

'I told you, we were travelling too quickly,' he heard Jelninolan scolding quietly.

'We arrived on time and that's the only thing that counts,' snarled Uldini's complaining voice in reply. 'When it gets dark, I'll be able to tell by the stars how much time we still have. Even I find it hard to keep track of the days in there.'

Then he heard Tlik's voice butting in, with its tone of self-satisfaction.

'I can tell you if you like. There are still three days until the winter solstice.'

Uldini breathed a sigh of relief while Ahren gasped in shock. They had been in this trance for almost two weeks? No wonder he felt so exhausted.

'Then it was worth taking the risk,' blurted Uldini excitedly. 'How far is it still to the Place of Ritual?' he added more quietly.

The croaking voice of the goblin sounded again.

'Maybe another nineteen miles northward and then we're there. There was a Dream Snatcher on the Wild Paths. I thought you'd better avoid that and so I led you out a little earlier than I'd planned. You'll be able to manage the rest of the way yourselves, surely.'

Ahren still couldn't open his eyes without being blinded by the sun and so he couldn't see the face of the fay-creature, but his sarcastic tone was more than evident. Tlik, it seemed, was enjoying the prospect of making their final part of the journey more difficult.

Ahren forced himself to open his lids, even if only a little bit, so that he could recognise something, but the pain was too great. With a sigh he put his hand over his face and lay down on his back.

'You should all keep your eyes closed until evening time' Jelninolan called out in a firm voice. 'They were out of action for too long in the darkness and you'll only damage yourselves if you try too hard.'

'Where are we? Is it safe here?' Falk asked in a husky voice.

'We're in the middle of the Borderlands, so no. I wouldn't say any place within a one hundred- and twenty-five-mile radius is safe,' answered Uldini irritably. 'But Jelninolan and I have taken precautions. You lie there and stay quiet and nothing should be able to discover us.'

'All the laws of nature are turned on their head in the Wild Paths. Your bodies need to readjust quickly to normality and then the pains in your legs will disappear,' said Jelninolan comfortingly to the group. 'You should be fully recovered by early tomorrow if you use the right herbs from Ahren's bag.'

'Well, I'm fine anyway.' That was Trogadon's voice, and there was no trace of pain or hoarseness in it.

The apprentice heard the dwarf getting up and cheerfully speaking.

'I want to thank you for the delightful song. Without that melody it would have been deadly boring.''Then he began humming snatches of the melody Ahren had heard in his head the previous days.

'I should have known that Tanentan wasn't going to keep you quiet, Trogadon,' said Jelninolan contritely. I hope your experiences on the Wild Paths weren't too traumatic.'

'Don't worry about that for a second. I did stick my eyes out from under the cloth the first day but the sight of all those…things that looked so different to how they should have, well that was enough for me. I prefer to stand upright on the ground, and hands that grow out of plants do nothing for me, so I covered my eyes again and marched on dutifully.'

Ahren shivered at the creatures the dwarf had so casually described. Suddenly, he was grateful that he had been in that enforced twilight state and he made a mental note that he had to thank the elf as soon as he could see again.

'If you've recovered so well, then you might as well keep watch,' Uldini urged. 'These are the Borderlands after all, and I really don't want to be only dependent on our magic. And it's high time you were all quiet,' he hissed in an irritated voice.

The dwarf gave a satisfied grunt of agreement, and following the Arch Wizard's warning concerning the dangers that surrounded them, an uneasy silence fell over the party. Nobody wanted to risk alerting anything or anybody to their presence as long as half of them were lying on the floor, quite vulnerable to attack.

The afternoon crawled by. Ahren flinched at every sound and soon he was dripping in sweat. His legs were still aching but he knew he couldn't talk to the others about it for fear of endangering them all, and this only increased his anxiety.

At one point, Jelninolan came over to him and placed a calming hand on his chest. Ahren had to stop himself from holding on to her for dear life. Instead, he gave a thankful nod and presented a brave front.

'It's not much longer until dusk. If it's alright by you, I can take some of your herbs and prepare you three an invigorating brew. Then you can drink something as soon as the sun has gone down and you can take off your blindfolds,' she whispered in his ear.

Ahren nodded again, and again he broke out in a sweat. The elf being so close to him, not a finger's width from his face, made him incredibly nervous. When she began tugging at the bag of herbs which was hanging on his belt, his pulse began to race.

'I'll do that,' Ahren said quickly, and hurriedly untied the bag of herbs and handed it to her. She took the bag before leaving, and the apprentice gave a sigh of relief.

The priestess hadn't been lying. A short time later and Ahren was sitting upright with a cup of herbal brew in his hands and he blinked with some effort at the oncoming night. Twilight had already progressed considerably, but he couldn't see anything clearly, as even a small amount of light stung his eyes.

They were cowering in a sort of depression, in the middle of which was a pond, from which which they had come when they had risen up from the Wild Paths. Steam was still rising from its surface on account of their entrance into the normal world. A thin covering of snow was on the outer edge of the depression and Ahren realised that the warmth of the pond ensured that they wouldn't be miserably cold.

Tlik came over to them in his strange gait, sometimes waddling and sometimes hopping.

'I had a little look inside your head while you were eavesdropping on the elf melody. It was very revealing, I must say,' he said in a provocative voice as he pointed over at the pond.

The thought that the goblin had been rummaging around in his reason while Ahren was powerless, enraged the young man, and he hit the creature without even thinking. Ahren's fist smashed right into the middle of the fay-creature's face, and there was such power in the blow that the little body flew several paces through the air before landing with a splash in the pool and sinking out of sight.

Ahren looked in amazement at his hand, which was still balled into a fist and shaking with anger, when Falk towered over him and stared down at him in a furious rage.

'Have you gone totally mad?' he growled, with a look of incomprehension on his weathered face. 'We never hit our allies, no matter how infuriating they may sometimes be. That applies especially to fay-creatures who can make mincemeat out of us in a fit of raving madness.'

While Falk continued to scold, trying hard to keep his voice down, Tlik clambered out of the pool, now soaking wet, and staring directly at Ahren. The goblin looked more than ever like an odd kind of frog now, and Ahren couldn't stop himself from smiling.

The rest of the group had sprung to their feet, and Uldini and Jelninolan were about to position themselves between Ahren and the goblin, but the fay-creature made a quick hand movement and they were all thrown to the ground where they were held fast, even Falk, who had been taken completely by surprise in the middle of his tirade. Tlik took a surprisingly long leap and landed right in front of the flabbergasted, not to mention terrified young man. The strange looking eyes bored directly into his own, and the young man could see that the skin, where his fist had met the creatures face, was beginning to turn an even deeper blue.

The apprentice was frantically considering what he could do to appease the unpredictable creature, when the goblin broke into a bleating laugh.

'And here I thought you couldn't fight your way out of a paper bag,' the little figure called out. 'Everywhere in your head it's all about protecting and evading and avoiding violence and all that. Oh yes, and also about a certain elf, but that was amusing at least.'

Ahren's face went a deep red and he avoided looking in Jelninolan's direction, but Uldini's sarcastic laugh was impossible to miss, and Trogadon giving him a wink of recognition didn't help the matter.

'If you want to succeed against HIM, WHO FORCES, then you urgently need to become harder, boy. You won't be able to save everyone, and you're going to have to fight, and those fights will be long and hard. That sometimes includes boxing someone who appears to be weaker than you,' added the dwarf.

Then he snapped his fingers and Ahren began to sink down into the ground. The earth just didn't seem to want to carry him anymore and the more the apprentice tried to escape, the more quickly he went down. Three heartbeats later and he was already having to stretch his chin upwards to get air while the earth was beginning to cover his ears.

Just as the first crumbs of earth were forcing their way into his mouth, the goblin snapped his fingers again and the sinking stopped.

Ahren was panicking as he tried to breathe, feeling the ground around him pressing into his body and preventing his lungs from expanding

410

sufficiently for him to inhale properly. Over his own panting he could hear the voice of the goblin speaking quietly and slowly to him.

'If you touch me again, I will, once I've honoured my vow, leave you just like this in the wilderness for the ants and the birds to take care of you.'

The goblin wanted to continue talking but suddenly there was a threatening, deep snarling sound behind him.

Culhen had crept up towards the fay-creature and was standing now with fangs bared and hackles raised, ready to pounce.

The frog-like creature pursed his thin lips, which made him look even stranger, and clapped his hands.

Ahren was spat upwards and out of the earth in a high arc and came down in the pond. He came up to the surface of the unnaturally hot water coughing and spluttering and looked into the eyes of the goblin, who pushed himself passed the still snarling Culhen.

'I think we're quits now,' said Tlik and with another snap of his fingers, he was gone, and the group were left to consider what had just happened.

While Ahren was drying himself off, he was glad that the others couldn't be too loud as they scolded him. His companions showered him with accusations and warnings. Even Khara admonished him by repeatedly saying, 'stupid boy.' Selsena did her bit too, submerging him in a wave of disappointment. Trogadon was the only one who occasionally threw him a sympathetic look from where he was standing guard.

Ahren quietly let his companion's criticisms wash over him, all the while stroking Culhen's fur, while the wolf stood, a bastion of calm, his head leaning in against the apprentice's leg. Ahren knew he had deserved his dressing-down, and couldn't work out why he had overreacted so impetuously.

They had finally expended all their negative criticism and were now looking at him with expectant or demanding faces, but all he could do was shrug his shoulders.

'He spent the time that we were on the Wild Paths prowling around in my head, and I was completely unable to defend myself. The thought of it threw me into a blind rage. First the Adversary, trying to control my mind on the ship, then the Grief Wind playing with my emotions, and then only a short time later a frog-faced creep rummaging around in my innermost thoughts.'

'It was just too much!' he blurted out.

His eyes caught sight of Jelninolan, who gave him an understanding smile.

'Sometimes I forget how young you are,' she said in a friendly voice.

'Tanentan's song put you into a twilight state, but if Tlik was really browsing around in your reason, then he would have pulled some powerful feelings out of your memories up to the surface, which are now wreaking havoc.'

She turned to Falk.

'He should really spend the night in the Void, and at the same time you can run through his past with him. The last thing we need is another eruption in the wrong place and at the wrong time.'

Falk nodded thoughtfully, and Uldini laid a hand on Ahren's shoulder.

'Once you have been named, the blessing of HIM, WHO FORMS should protect you from most tricks of the mind. All going well, you'll be safe in three days' time.'

Ahren knew the little wizard well enough by now to recognise the statement as his version of an apology, and so he thanked him with a nod of acknowledgement.

Falk waved him a few paces away from the rest of the group and indicated to him that he should sit. He too sat down in a cross-legged position and looked soberly into Ahren's eyes.

'We call this phenomenon Shadow Anguish, and it doesn't happen often. But there's been a lot of tinkering around going on in your skull the last while, and you're still too young to have got over the traumas of your childhood, so there's no doubt that it's hit you hard.'

A wave of anger came over Ahren as he heard himself being described as weak and inexperienced, and he was just about to protest vociferously when it suddenly occurred to him that he was over-reacting again. He bit his tongue until it hurt and was thus able to keep his emotions in check.

Falk recognised his inner conflict and nodded approvingly.

'Have no fear, you'll be fine. We might need more than one night, but by the time of your Naming, we'll have put your old self back together again.'

They began their work, with Ahren forcing himself towards the Void. It took half an evening for him to battle his way past all the disturbing pictures from his past, which were preventing him from achieving the trance-like state. Things he thought he had overcome a long time previously were now painfully present. His father, his days as an outsider in Deepstone, even Holken, who had become his friend by the time he had left his home village, surfaced as a threatening figure before his inner eye.

When it was finally time, Falk began asking him questions about his past, going back so far into Ahren's childhood that the apprentice was

413

sure he wouldn't be able to answer them. But to his own surprise, he was able to give long and detailed answers to each of his master's questions. The goblin had brought many things to light that Ahren had gone to great lengths to forget, and only the Void enabled him to speak on, confidently and in a firm voice.

He spoke until deep in the night of the lonely days with his father, who was regularly violent to him, and of how he was bullied by other children in the village. Finally, Falk said he had spoken enough.

When Ahren emerged from the Void, he felt strangely exhausted and jaded, as if a storm of emotions had swept over him, while he had sat tight, under the surface, and so had escaped its devastating force.

Falk seemed contented and even smiled for a moment.

'That wasn't bad. But you still need your sleep, so we'll carry on tomorrow evening. I've taken the opportunity of killing two birds with one stone. Every aspirant is supposed to think back over their lives before their Naming in order to purify their spirit, and in preparation for their future tasks. My mother prepared me that time, and now I'm doing the same with you. I'm just being a little more thorough, because I also want to rectify the damage that Tlik has done.'

His master stood up and Ahren followed suit. His head was heavy and light at the same time and he could only give a dazed nod. Falk grasped him by the arm and led him to his blankets, which the others had already prepared for the young man. The apprentice quickly finished off his herbal brew, and then fell into a deep, dreamless sleep brought on by emotional exhaustion.

Chapter 24

2 days to the winter solstice

Ahren woke up to the smell of roast meat and fresh bread.

At first, he thought he was in a dream, but when he opened his eyes there was a wooden bowl with venison and millet cake in front of his face. He sat up quickly and the painful stabbing in his stomach made him realise how hungry he was as he set greedily to his food.

He looked around as he gobbled up large chunks of meat and bread. The others were eating just as heartily, except for Jelninolan and Falk who were observing their companions with a look of satisfaction.

'Eat as much as you can. Once we set off, we won't be able to enjoy a proper meal until the Naming has been carried out,' said Falk quietly. 'Uldini weaved a small charm net this morning and the route between us and the Place of Ritual is teeming with Dark Ones. Around here is safe enough, but from now on, proceeding quietly and carefully is the name of the game. A fight is always dangerous anyway, but any kind of a skirmish is likely to attract more creatures, and then we'll have to fight them, and on it goes.'

'According to Tlik, it's nineteen miles to our destination,' explained Uldini. As far as Falk, Jelninolan and I can make out, we're on the foothills of Geraton, a town that was destroyed during the Dark Days.'

Concern could clearly be seen on the faces of the three ageless companions when the town's name was mentioned, and Ahren asked himself if they had experienced its fall.

'The most direct route is through the town and so we have to be doubly prepared. There are so many hiding places and many opportunities for ambushes.'

A silence followed Uldini's words of warning until finally Trogadon spoke.

'On the other hand, that can also be an advantage, isn't that right? If we use the ruins as cover, then they won't spot us so quickly.'

Falk nodded reluctantly. 'It could turn into quite a dangerous game of cat and mouse. We have to make sure we avoid turning into the mouse'.

There was nothing more to be said. In total silence, and with full concentration, the travelling party broke camp and began their journey to the ruins of Geraton.

No sooner had they set off when Ahren was badly shaken by the sight of the ruined city. He had felt relaxed and calm after waking up, the pain in his legs had gone and the bright sun had had no effect on his eyes. But as soon as he raised his head over the top of the depression in which they had spent the night, his good humour was gone.

Together with his companions, he walked through the ruined streets in disbelief. The cobbled paths were covered in moss and their stones were hidden or pushed up by little plants. To the left and right were ruined buildings, some small and others towering above them, all of which seemed to have been destroyed by fire in the dim and distant past. The architecture seemed strangely contoured in a style that he had never encountered before. Sometimes the stumps of delicate pillars were visible, at other times mighty pedestals, which once had statues standing proudly on them. A porous covering of snow bedecked everything, strengthening the impression of decay and loneliness. Ahren had so many questions on the tip of his tongue, but as the group made its way slowly

416

from ruin to ruin, constantly seeking out cover, he knew that this was neither the time nor place to ask questions.

Falk, ever alert, led them through the ghostly city, which was a timeless reminder of the destruction wreaked during the Dark Days, which seemed to be telling them that the tragic events of the past were soon to be repeated.

In the distance they could hear the cries of strange creatures, and sometimes they heard the scraping of claws on stone or the beating of mighty wings. Each time Falk would indicate to them to make themselves as small as possible and not move a muscle, while he would wait with steely expression until the sounds had died away, and the group could move onwards again. If he thought a street looked too dangerous, they would take a wide detour and so their progress was painfully slow. Culhen and Selsena were invaluable helpers when Falk needed to decide on a direction and more than once the powerful senses of the two animals saved them from certain discovery.

The constant danger the Dark Ones posed, and the mournful backdrop of the city began to upset the emotional equilibrium which Ahren had felt since he'd woken up. He became irritable and impatient and at one point he was about to jump up and scream madly and wave his arms in the air, just so the terrible tension would come to an end.

It was Khara of all people who stopped him. He had tensed his muscles and was about to leap, when out of the blue he felt a slap on his face from his left, which left him flabbergasted. It was Khara looking at him pleadingly, and unusually, there was neither scorn nor accusation in her eyes.

'Fear makes Reason dead. Fight against it,' she whispered quietly.

The sight of the one-time slave, down on her haunches with Dark Ones all around, doing not her own bidding but her mistress's, brought

Ahren back to his senses. Khara had had to wait for so many battles in the arena in those days, that this game of hide and seek they were playing now could be little more than a walk in the park for her. At least that was how she was behaving.

And so Ahren bit his lips and made his way into the Void so that he would do no harm to himself or to others.

The longer the afternoon went on, the more times Falk made the group stop. He looked sourly over at a large ruin which had to have been the impressive dwelling of a nobleman once. The travellers hid behind a plinth on top of which was a little stump, which might once have been a memorial to a knight, and Falk gestured to Ahren to approach him.

The young man crawled up to him as quietly and carefully as he could. Falk nodded approvingly once his apprentice had reached him, then pointed silently at two points on the walls of the ruined house.

Ahren squinted and was able to make out two Swarm Claws that had settled down on the dilapidated stone walls and were watching their surroundings. The blood-red beaks of the large black birds glistened in the sun. Bad memories resurfaced in Ahren's head. The monstrous birds had tracked them down once before, when they had been on their way to Eathinian. A whole swarm of Dark Ones had almost hunted them down that time. And later, in the Elfish forest, Ahren himself had been involved in a daring duel with one of the creatures as he fought to save the life of the Voice of the Forest.

He looked around nervously but could see no other Swarm Claw. Falk pulled the apprentice up to him.

'Scouts', he whispered in the young man's ear. 'No doubt the swarm is perched all over the city, and if there's any worthwhile prey, they call to each other.'

Falk pointed to his bow and to the animal on the right, then he pointed to Ahren's bow and to the bird on the left.

'Simultaneously,' he whispered in a warning voice.

Ahren's hands were suddenly sweating. His master expected him to hit first time and at exactly the same time as the arrow of the old Forest Guardian. There would be no second chance. There was no possibility of hiding from the razor-like beaks and claws of the swarm here, and if Uldini had to protect them with some powerful magic, then that would attract all the other Dark Ones, which they had so far successfully avoided.

The Void collapsed under the feeling of increasing tension and he was left with his trembling hands. Uncertain, he drew his best arrow from his quiver. His fletching had been excellent, and the shaft was perfectly smooth and straight. The tip was sharp and glinted in the sun as he positioned the arrow on the bowstring. He remembered to hold the tip pointing downwards so as not to reveal himself, just as Falk had taught him.

Falk nodded his appreciation and encouragement, then he raised four fingers of his bow-holding hand.

Ahren wanted to protest that he wasn't ready yet, but his master raised his bow and aimed at the target, bending his finger around the wood of his weapon.

Three.

Ahren quickly copied him and searched out the Swarm Claw on the left. He aimed directly at the animal with the tip of his arrow and saw his master curl a second finger around the bow.

Two.

Ahren breathed deeply and went down a little on his knee to find a secure stance, watching his master at the same time and correcting his own bow position as he did so. Another finger moved.

One.

One of the Swarm Claws looked curiously in their direction and suddenly became aware of the glittering metal on their arrow tips. Like an old friend who returns at just the right moment, the Void was back just for a heartbeat in Ahren's reason. He took a deep breath, drew the arrow back until the bow was fully tensed.

Out of the corner of his eye he saw a tiny movement as Falk lowered the last finger.

The apprentice ignored every doubt, suppressed any indecision and let his arrow fly in deadly unison with that of his master. The Void vanished. Doubt and fear came over Ahren, but it had already happened.

With an almost synchronous crunch, the arrows hit their targets and both Swarm Claws tumbled from the walls, making no sounds but the leathery rustle of wings.

Falk slapped his apprentice hard on the shoulder and grinned broadly, then indicated to him to crawl back to the rear of the group again. Ahren grinned at him then made his way almost too exuberantly to his place at the back. Trogadon gave him a congratulatory box on his upper arm, and even Khara gave a respectful curtsy. For a short time the young man was at one with himself and the world.

Hardly had they reached the outskirts of the city, when the evening encroached early and fast. Falk increased his pace, and Ahren was surprised at how different the Borderlands were to how he had imagined them. In the fading light he could make out woods, grassy hills and rocky highlands on the horizon. When he thought back to the tales that had done the rounds back in Deepstone, he'd imagined sulphur mines, muddy barrens and volcanoes. What he saw in front of him was so…well, normal.

Only the monumental pillar of smoke, five furlongs in width and stretching upwards into the heavens, shattered the illusion of normality.

Up until that point there had always been ruins in the way, but now he had an unhindered view of the prison in which his arch-enemy had led his existence for centuries, chained through a powerful magic to a sleep made of smoke and darkness, a sleep from which he was gradually awakening. A shiver ran down Ahren's spine and when it became clear to him that Falk was walking directly towards the Pall Pillar, he heaved a sigh of resignation.

Somehow it was fitting that his Place of Naming lay in the shadow of the Pall Pillar, just as everything else had that he had experienced over the previous months.

They marched on for a while after the onset of night until Falk found a deserted farmhouse which hadn't completely collapsed or been burned down.

'Must have belonged to a frontiersman who realised a few years ago that there are better places to live,' said the old Forest Guardian quietly.

'Or somebody caught by the Pall Pillar,' said Uldini in a prophetic voice.

Falk gave him an angry look, but the Arch Wizard, as always, wasn't going to be silenced. 'What's wrong? You know just as well as I do, that we're far too close to the Pillar for anyone to spend their life here without eventually being called by HIM.'

Ahren began to shiver. The experiences on the ship seemed like only a moment ago, and the feeling of helplessness, when his spirit seemed no longer to be under his control, overwhelmed him again.

Jelninolan placed a comforting hand on his arm, and Falk stepped up to him.

'I think it might be best if we continue from where we stopped yesterday, before our sensitive conjurer starts relating ghosts-stories as only he knows how.'

That night proved one of the most difficult in his short life. Falk asked him questions relentlessly and confronted him with his worst moments. The evening his father broke his hand. The moment Edrik refused to recognise Ahren's right to an apprenticeship. The attack of the Swarm Claws, his duel in the forest with the Warden of the Weeping Valley, and the moment he first had to kill a man. Falk grilled him relentlessly and the Void collapsed on more than one occasion under the emotional pressure, leaving Ahren in tears until he managed to slip into the trance again. In the darkest hours of the night he had to remember being under the control of HIM, WHO FORCES and of the Grief Wind, and the men he had killed so quickly and ruthlessly in the ballroom of King's Island.

At that point it almost became too much for the apprentice. In the weeks following that attack he had dreamed of them again and again, and of their surprised faces under their hoods. Ahren knew that he was only imagining things - he had never seen the faces of the attackers hidden under the dark material of their capes and from that distance. But their spirits had tormented him mercilessly.

Falk leaned back exhausted when Ahren began sobbing for the umpteenth time. The young man was incapable of continuing or of answering any more questions. The Void seemed a million paces away, and were his master to question him about any more memories, they would crash in on top of him unfiltered. He just wanted to crawl away into a corner. But Falk continued mercilessly.

But now the questions had changed, and also the memories which they evoked. Falk invited him to remember his first night as an apprentice, the first time he had succeeded in getting to the top of the ribbon tree. The day he was presented with his bow, at the Autumn Festival in the company of his best friend Likis. He reminded Ahren of his first day in Eathinian and of the elf ceremony held in his honour after he had saved the Voice of the Forest. Falk spoke to him about Uldini's jokes, Jelninolan's goodness and Trogadon's laughter. And to cap it all, just as the first rays of light transformed the snow into a glittering landscape, he talked about Culhen.

How Ahren had found him and fed him.

How he had defied his master in order to save the young wolf.

How, with Selsena's help, he had broken the Adversary's spell.

Finally, Falk was silent and he released Ahren from the interrogation. But something had changed. The heavy clouds that had hung over the young Forest Guardian had lifted, and it seemed as if Ahren was able to breathe easily for the first time in a long time.

Falk leaned down towards him and fixed his eyes with a steely look.

'For moons now you've been concentrating on the bad things that have happened to you in your life, and that you may well have to face. But that is no way to go through life, and especially not when you have such a colossal task awaiting you. Believe in what you're doing. If you want to save everybody, then try to do just that. We are going to be with you on your journey every step of the way. And maybe we won't be able to save everybody in the end, but I'll be damned if we're not going to at least try.'

Falk stood up and presented Ahren his forearm. Ahren seized it in the warrior's greeting and pulled himself up to his feet. An overwhelming gratitude towards his master, and a feeling of triumphant exhilaration had come over him and he smiled as he followed the old Forest Guardian.

They went over to the others and Falk said loudly, 'right, let's get going and name the Thirteenth Paladin. '

For Ahren the rest of the day was like a dream. His enforced confrontation with the events of his past life had been exhausting but also liberating. Falk, with his experience of centuries of self-criticism, brought him to the understanding that Ahren had been seeing things over the previous few months with too much darkness. He had been close to losing that part of his person that made up his innermost being: Ahren did not want to cause suffering and did not want to kill beings that could still perhaps be saved.

As they slowly travelled through the Borderlands, he promised to himself that he would keep to this goal, even if it meant weighing up every battle and every skirmish scrupulously.

Once he had clarified this position for himself, he looked thoughtfully up at the Pall Pillar, which soared ubiquitously into the leaden skies suggesting the onset of rain.

Now that Ahren had found himself again, he felt the same serenity that he had experienced at the very beginning of their journey. Uldini had once said that it was the blessing of the gods that gave him the courage to take up the task so willingly. But Ahren knew there was a second reason as well, which no blessing could help him with: you had to know yourself, the manner in which you were going to perform your task.

Unknown to Ahren, Uldini and Jelninolan were watching him with a critical look.

'I keep thinking Falk expects too much of him,' said the elf disapprovingly.

Uldini shrugged his shoulders serenely. 'He's the master, he'll know what he's doing.'

The Arch Wizard looked over at the old Forest Guardian, who was leading them through the wilderness of the Borderlands and was currently inspecting a ford they needed to cross.

'Besides, I think it's helped him. Ahren had to figure out how he was going to fight this battle. You're too soft, I'm too hard, and Falk is too grumpy. My hope is that the young lad will absorb all of our best qualities and ignore the parts that keep us all bound to ourselves.'

Jelninolan looked over at the Arch Wizard in surprise.

'I haven't heard you being so philosophical and so self-critical in many centuries,' she teased.

The childlike figure pointed at the Pall Pillar, which looked from where they were standing like a massive black wall of cloud, and which blocked most of the heavens.

'I'm standing here in the shadow of my greatest failure. There isn't a day that passes when I don't ask myself if I could have woven the spell ban more skilfully, so allow me my bit of humility and regret. It won't last long anyway,' he said quietly.

Jelninolan gave him a hug.

'You don't have to carry all the responsibility yourself. I was there, and so were the other Ancients, and none of us came up with a better idea.'

She looked over at Ahren.

'Once he's been named, then the years of waiting and doubting will be over. Then we'll be finished with treading water and we'll be able to look forward instead to finally bring this war to an end.'

Uldini looked over at Ahren again.

'I was eaves-dropping and I think I know what decision the boy will reach.'

Jelninolan smiled. 'I've always known. He'll choose the most difficult path of all. Either, while trying to do his best for everyone, he'll fail disastrously in the attempt,' she took a deep breath and suppressed a shudder, 'or he'll become the greatest Paladin of all.'

They had spent the whole day marching onwards in a serpentine line.

Selsena had sensed Dark Ones at regular intervals and communicated the news to Falk so that he could lead the travellers past them unnoticed. Luckily, the land they were traversing was hilly and woody, which made it easier for the Forest Guardian to sneak the group past every danger.

Now they were crouched in a little copse waiting.

'With the best will in the world, I really couldn't tell you where we should go next. We've almost travelled nineteen miles from the pond we came out of,' said Falk for the fifth time.

Uldini shook his head angrily.

'I thought the goblin was supposed to be helping us? Where is the wretch anyway? I can't imagine that Ahren's little boxing demonstration has freed him from his oath.'

He looked questioningly over at Jelninolan, but she shook her head.

'No, he's still bound. The fact that he's not making an appearance is all part of his little game. It also means, though, that we've been on the right track up until now.'

She thought for a moment and continued speaking.

'I think we should rest here for a while. Our young aspirant here could certainly do with forty winks after last night, and we could all do with a little recovery time. I'll dish out the last of our cold venison and then we'll wait for the goblin to appear. Once time becomes tight, he'll turn up and lead us.'

Uldini's eyes nearly popped out of his head.

'The time is tight already. It's not long until the eve of the winter solstice. And you seriously want us to sit around here?'

'Have you got a better idea?' said Falk, intervening. 'Wandering aimlessly around the place, only to have Tlik appearing and croaking to us that we should have gone the opposite direction is not going to help things. I agree. We should stay here.'

'To wait and preserve your strength whenever you have the chance, is something you learn quickly as a mercenary. The elf is right,' rumbled Trogadon cheerfully.

Then he leaned firmly against the trunk of a tree and went into torpidity.

Uldini was boiling with rage, but knew he had been outvoted.

'Of course, we have no time left, so let's all take a little nap,' he said sarcastically but took the piece of meat the priestess offered him anyway.

Ahren quickly downed his dinner and snuggled up under his blanket. The nervousness that had kept him awake all day disappeared, and now he wanted to enjoy every precious heartbeat. He closed his eyes and was asleep in an instant.

It was the smell of old fish that woke Ahren abruptly from his sleep, and when he opened his eyes, he found himself staring into the lifeless eyes of a rotting trout. He threw off his blanket with a scream and had his hand on Windblade before he realised who it was that had awoken him.

427

The others spun around to face him and from behind he heard a bleating laugh.

'Ha! You should have seen your face. It was wonderful! Now I think we're really quits.' Tlik was now doubled over with laughter. His strange two-part voice sounded like fingernails scratching on slate.

Ahren's heart was in his mouth, and the goblin's laughter was giving him an earache, but he still managed a pained smile and said as quietly as possible, 'hello Tlik, we all missed you.'

The laughter stopped suddenly, and the goblin eyed him suspiciously.

'What have they done to you? Where's the fire, the scorn, the single-minded darkness that you need to perform your task?'

He looked at the others and pouted.

'I'd built him up so beautifully, and you destroy him.'

The creature theatrically covered his forehead with the back of his hand.

'As if Jorath needs yet another do-gooder who fails at the end. What will happen the next time HE, WHO FORCES catches one of you Paladins. A Pall House? A Pall Fence?'

Disgusted, the goblin turned around and pointed reluctantly eastwards.

'The place where the Naming must take place is five furlongs in this direction. You'll recognise it when you see it. Have fun.'

Then he disappeared in a stinking cloud of smoke, which spread the smell of rotting fish and caused everyone present to start coughing and spluttering. Culhen yelped and placed one paw over his nose before sneezing loudly, and waves of displeasure from Selsena were felt by all.

'What could the gods have been possibly thinking of when they let goblins loose on the world?' cursed Uldini as he wheezed.

428

'We elves believe that they were drunk that time. Or they had colds. Or both,' added Jelninolan and she covered her nose with a cloth.

The others quickly followed her example, and then they gathered together their things and left the stinking copse.

Ahren only now noticed that the night had crept up on them and now, outside their leafy shelter, he could see a light snow falling steadily. There was no wind, and the smell of new snow filled his nostrils and replaced the stench that Tlik had given them as his farewell present. The moon shone weakly through the cloud-cover and they wouldn't have been able to see more than ten paces ahead, were it not for the thin blanket of snow reflecting the moonlight.

Falk looked over at a nearby mound which blocked their view in the easterly direction.

'We should climb up there, and maybe we can recognise something,' he said hopefully.

They crept up the rise as quietly as they could and then looked down on the surrounding countryside. The black of the night swallowed almost everything but Ahren believed he could make out a few faint outlines which were possibly rising up from the surrounding snow.

'Could they be ruins in front?' he whispered into Falk's ear.

His master strained to see.

'Their position and distance tally with what Tlik said. That could be it.'

He gestured to the others to follow, and they set off on their way. Once they had descended the mound again, Selsena gave a timid whinny and Falk stopped suddenly. His shoulders slumped and he looked miserable.

'What's the matter?' asked Jelninolan with a worried expression.

'Selsena recognised the place,' said Falk and walked onwards.

The others followed with gloomy faces. Ahren had already been nervous enough, and Falk's ominous overtone increased the uneasy feeling in his stomach. He stroked Culhen's hair as he tried to calm himself and the wolf pressed his head against Ahren's leg, as he always did when he sensed that his human friend needed comforting.

Slowly they approached their destination, and gradually the outlines of a ruined country house began to emerge. It had been almost completely destroyed, so that only the foundation walls remained, except for one wall, which was completely undamaged. As they crept along it, Ahren could make out weather-beaten mosaics and ornamentations in the wall which presented leaves, vines and the sign of the THREE.

'Was this a temple once?' he asked quietly.

'No, they were only strong believers,' said Falk sadly. The way he said it, suggested he was referring to some people in particular.

'Did you know the people of the house, master?' asked Ahren, digging deeper. The house looked old enough to have been destroyed in the Dark Days and he was curious to find out who had lived here.

Falk nodded, rounded the corner of the wall and led them into what had once been the inside of the house. Shards of broken earthenware were scattered around the floor. Here and there, Ahren could make out bent door hinges and nails lying around. Everything else that had been in the house must have been destroyed by Time's decay.

Uldini and Jelninolan gasped for air, and the Arch Wizard slapped his forehead forcefully with his hand.

'Of course. This is where the Naming must take place. It begins where it ended.'

The elf turned to the bewildered apprentice, placed her hands on his shoulders and looked at him with her eyes filled with tears.

'Ahren. This is the home of the Thirteenth Paladin. This is where he was murdered.'

Chapter 25

Winter Solstice

While Ahren was still getting over the shock of discovering that his predecessor hat met his violent end centuries previously at the very spot where they were standing, Falk, Uldini, and Jelninolan quickly began clearing out the floor space of the ruin. They then started drawing elaborate symbols on the floor with charcoal, in which they placed the artefacts of the three gods that they had collected on their travels.

Jelninolan gently placed Tanentan in the western part of the pattern and placed herself behind the object. Trogadon did the same on the eastern part with his hammer. Uldini positioned himself and his crystal ball on the northern part, and Falk, having put on his armour, stood on the southern section. Ahren didn't need to be commanded. As soon as he saw the circle in the centre of the pattern, he knew what he had to do. The others nodded and he stepped in.

'We can now begin with the ceremony. Selsena, Culhen and Khara will watch out for any sign of danger. The Naming can easily be sensed by any creatures receptive to magic. As soon as we're finished, we should disappear with no delay,' warned Uldini.

Ahren wiped the sweat from his hands and carefully stepped over the lines of the drawing, being careful not to smear them. This was the moment he had been longing for, for many months now, and also the moment he had been most dreading. Nothing would be the same after this, and he really wasn't sure if he was ready for it.

432

Uldini spread out his hands and raised them shoulder high, at which point the lines of charcoal began to burn, casting the whole area in a shimmering golden light.

'The wording of the Naming won't be exactly right, but we'll do our best to stick to the original in order not to risk complications, so don't be surprised,' whispered Falk to him.

Ahren nodded weakly and then Uldini began to speak in a singsong voice.

'We have gathered here today to see how the burden of the Paladin passes from father or mother to daughter or son. We ask the gods to bless this transference and to grant their true servant a long and happy life, he having served THE THREE so truly.' The Arch Wizard paused, and everyone looked in a corner of the room.

Ahren suspected that that was where his predecessor's bed had stood, the bed in which he had been stabbed to death. He gulped heavily and forced himself to concentrate on the here and now.

'We further ask for the blessing of THE THREE on their new champion, who is now taking on the heavy burden to fight for creation, to halt the progress of HIM, WHO FORCES, and to wipe HIM off the face of Jorath.'

Now everyone looked at Ahren, and he shifted uncertainly from one foot to the other. Should he bow or say a few words?

Not knowing what to do, he looked at Uldini, but the wizard was speaking again.

'To show that he is worthy, the Einhans have gathered to intercede on his behalf, and also a Paladin, who will welcome him into the circle of his kind.'

He was stopped from continuing by Selsena's shrill whinnying.

'Dark Ones! They're approaching from all sides!' Falk called out in horror.

'It's an ambush. HE knew that we would come here,' groaned Uldini. 'You're going to have to defeat them without me. I'll keep the Naming in position. If I break off now, the magic will crumble and Ahren can never be named. Then it will be a piece of cake for HIM.'

Trogadon grasped his hammer with a questioning look at Falk, who nodded hesitantly. The dwarf picked up his weapon and went over to Falk, who changed places with Selsena.

'Ahren, come out of the circle,' said Jelninolan quickly. 'Uldini will keep the Ritual in limbo until everyone is back in their place. We've no other choice. But be careful! Don't step on the lines.'

The apprentice left the Ritual Circle and tiptoed out, avoiding the lines. Then he snatched his quiver and bow, strapped on Windblade, and joined the others. Khara came down from the wall, where she had been standing guard, and pointed to the sky.

'A swarm is flying in from Geraton,' she said carefully. Although it was absurd to be thinking of such things in their chaotic situation, Ahren couldn't help but be proud of her new-found grasp of the Northern language.

Jelninolan looked grimly up at the heavens. Nothing could be seen from where they were standing in the light of the Ritual Circle, but if you listened closely, you could already make out the whoosh of leathery wings, which were approaching swiftly like an oncoming storm.

'I can keep them at bay for a while but I'm going to need cover.'

Khara nodded immediately and drew her weapon, making it clear with a look that she was going to stand by her mistress through thick and thin. Jelninolan closed her eyes and began singing quietly in Elfish.

Suddenly the wind freshened up and a single gust turned into a terrific storm which whipped up over their heads, turning the sky above them into a bubbling chaos of spinning air masses. Even on the ground, the gusts of wind were powerful and bitterly cold. It was true that the Swarm Claws were enormous birds, but Ahren was certain that they would not be able to fly through the storm at them. He breathed a sigh of relief and turned to Falk, who smiled grimly.

'It's a start, but neither Jelninolan nor Uldini will be able to maintain their magic for long. We're going to have to deal with all sorts of enemies who will be on top of us in no time at all. Selsena is sensing two dozen Low Fangs and something large, perhaps a fully-grown Blood Wolf. They're coming from all sides so be at the ready.'

Ahren and Trogadon nodded, and the three separated into a semi-circle in order to protect Uldini and Jelninolan in so far as it was possible. Khara too, walked two paces away from her mistress and joined the semi-circle in preparation for the battle.

The storm was raging unabated over their heads, and a quick glance at Uldini reassured Ahren that the Arch Wizard was quietly concentrating on stabilising the magic circle and awaiting their return.

Ahren place an arrow on the bowstring and waited, all the while trying to find the Void, but without success. The turbulent emotions of the last few days were still too fresh, and he simply couldn't slip into the trance. However, much to his surprise, he realised that he was remarkably calm, even without the Void.

Suddenly the first pairs of red eyes became visible in the darkness beyond their light, and Ahren and Falk didn't waste a heartbeat. Arrow after arrow flew into the night and bored into the Low Fangs, who went screeching to the ground. But for everyone they felled, another came into sight, and soon the two Forest Guardians were no longer able to keep them from encroaching on the ruins.

Those who got through were received by Trogadon and Khara. The pair were like fire and water as they stormed into battle. The dwarf simply ignored his enemies' claws, which slid off his chainmail, and he hit them with mighty hammer blows, either into their chest, sending them crashing back into the night, or on their skulls, silencing them forever.

His direct brutality was in marked contrast to Khara's graceful fighting technique. She evaded their dangerous extremities with graceful dancing steps or else simply cut them off when their claws reached out to grasp her. She leaped and she stabbed. She swayed, first left, then right, and Windblade drew elaborate patterns as it weaved and bobbed in the air. In no time at all she had sent three Low Fangs crashing to the ground.

Now there were fewer attackers coming up from behind and Ahren breathed a sigh of relief. He was running out of arrows, and once they had both shot their last ones, they drew their close combat weapons. Culhen and Selsena were nothing more than flitting shadows beyond the light, dealing with the Low Fangs who approached them in their own way. Ahren braced himself and stood back to back with his master as they prepared to cut down their enemies when suddenly his sight became blurry and his legs gave way.

I've found you at last, little Paladin, a voice droned in his head.

The ruined house, his companions, even the attackers seemed suddenly to have slipped into the background. Ahren knew they were present but he could concentrate on nothing. On nothing but the tall, emaciated figure, clothed in black ribbons, that was rising up out of the ground before him, in the middle of the ruin. The ends of the material were fluttering in the storm and made it difficult to make out the creature's contours. The figure was a good two and a half paces tall but only half the breadth of a human and it seemed skinny and fragile, as if there were not enough substance to fill out its frame. This impression was in sharp contrast to its razor-sharp will, which was boring into Ahren's reason and almost causing him to break down on the spot.

Ahren found himself being forced to look into the depths of the hooded being, but was unable to make out a face. Out of the corner of his eye he could see that Falk had thrown himself in front of his apprentice and was desperately fending off the three Low Fangs that were attacking them, but without taking any notice of the figure in front of them. None of the others seemed to be aware of the stranger in their midst either.

Ahren made every effort to get back up on his feet but to no avail. The stranger's will was too powerful, and it slowly dawned on the apprentice who he was looking at.

You've recognised me at last, little Paladin? I am your deadliest enemy, said the presence in an amused voice. The self-confidence and certainty in the Adversary's voice were so striking that Ahren doubled up instinctively.

Images of ravaged landscapes flashed past before Ahren's eyes. He saw King's Island with all its inhabitants churning down into the depths of the sea, dragging down the Lost People; men, women, and children being dragged mercilessly down into the depths. He saw Eathinian ablaze, the colourful ribbons of the Elfish villages looked like burial shrouds, laid over the charred bodies of the elves and the animals.

And finally, he saw Deepstone, attacked by a multitude of Swarm Claws and torn to shreds until nothing was left but abandoned houses with their roofs ripped apart and their doors hacked to bits from which pools of blood were slowly flowing out onto the streets...

The apprentice gave a sudden sob. And behind all these pictures he could hazily make out how Falk was fighting hard against the Low Fangs and being assisted by Culhen, and calling out Ahren's name again and again.

If we fight, all this will happen. All this and much, much more. Tens of thousands will die because you will have made the wrong decision today, the voice of HIM, WHO FORCES continued. But it doesn't need to be like this. My offer still stands. Follow me of your own free will and together we shall save many, many lives.

That thought ran like a sword through the weak point in his armour and through the young man's resistance. This was everything that Ahren wanted – to save lives. Perhaps he could persuade the god to protect creation if they worked together. HE was once the guardian of the world. Surely it was possible to bring HIM to the point where HE would recognise the beauty of creation and HE would take HIS rightful place as its guardian once again.

Torn, Ahren looked into the hooded darkness, searching for a sign of goodness or mercy, but could see literally nothing.

In the meantime, Falk and Culhen had defeated the Low Fangs. The last one crashed to the floor a hand's breadth away from the apprentice and blood splattered his face. He turned his head away instinctively and caught sight of the corner that the others had been gazing at earlier. The corner where the bed must have stood. Where his predecessor had died, because his wife, out of her love for her child, had acquiesced to the offer of the dark god for one terrible heartbeat. Ahren was heartbroken as he thought pitifully of the poor woman who had been faced with an impossible choice, and in the end had lost everything. And suddenly, defiance exploded within them.

HE had deceived her that time, had used her love against herself and had broken her will, HE had perverted her desire to save lives and stamped his will upon her.

438

Just as HE was trying to do now to him.

Ahren turned his head back again and stared into the hooded blackness. He wanted to shout out to the figure all of his resistance and all of his ideals and his love for life and his gratitude to the multifaceted, living and breathing world that he was a part of. But all that came out of his mouth was one word. 'NO!'

The Adversary's reaction was instant and powerful. HE, WHO FORCES let out a loud screech, and his ribbons of material whipped through the air. For a brief moment Ahren caught a glimpse of the god's grey skin. He saw eyes where no eyes should be, he saw mouths and teeth, all of them in flux in a constantly changing nightmare of meat and bones.

Then the head swooped out from under the hood and stopped a finger away from Ahren's face. Then you are of no use to me and I will satisfy myself with your blessing without using your shell as the puppet to my will, he hissed.

Ahren felt his heart beginning to be pulled, as if a metal barbed hook had placed itself in his soul and was now trying to wrench it out of his body.

'He's stealing my body,' the thought shot through Ahren's mind. The apprentice became weaker with every heartbeat, and the figure before him filled itself out and became more material.

At the same time, he saw behind the god an enormous figure of smoke and corporeality pushing itself into the ruins while Falk and the others flinched back some paces. Whatever that thing was, even his master seemed afraid, and Ahren's understanding became filled with despair.

HE, WHO FORCES laughed and instantaneously Ahren knew what he had to do.

439

If he was to be responsible for making the god mightier, then he must prevent HIM from stealing more of his blessing from the gods.

With all the willpower he could summon, he slowly slipped the hunting knife from his belt while the Will of the Adversary was completely concentrated on the blessing of the gods within the young man.

The apprentice was possessed by fear. He didn't want to die, he wanted to live, to enjoy the world to the fullest and to save all the beings of creation from this evil thing that was currently feasting on him. But the only thing he could do now was to buy the others' more time in the hope that something would occur to them to prevent the oncoming Darkness. The best he could do now was to die.

He raised the hunting knife with excruciating slowness up to his heart and placed the blade on his chest in a gap in his armour. Falk and the others were focused only on their opponent in its covering of smoke and nobody saw what the young man was about to do.

Trembling, Ahren inhaled and then drove the dagger with all his might into his heart.

At least that's what he'd planned.

His muscles failed their duty at the last instant and beside his ear he heard a croaking voice.

'You really wanted to do that, didn't you? Offer yourself up and give Jorath another two or three summers before everything went down the river?'

Ahren couldn't believe his eyes when he saw Tlik floating in his field of vision and blocking his view of the dark god. The pressure on Ahren's chest vanished as the goblin made some peculiar hand motions and his edges began to fray, as though his own soul and not Ahren's was being sucked up by the black figure.

440

'Woe betide you if you don't save them all,' whispered Tlik.

And then his figure was sucked under the god's hood and an almighty explosion threw the apprentice backwards while the silhouette of the Adversary burst into a thousand pieces.

Ahren heard an echo of derisive cackling as the goblin's final practical joke dissolved, leaving Ahren as lord and master of himself again.

The ruin descended into chaos and darkness. Aghast and confused, Ahren looked up at the enormous, smoking shape that was coming closer to them step by step.

'What sort of a thing is that?' he called out as he pulled himself up and picked up his weapon.

Falk glance around quickly. 'The gods be thanked you're back,' he said with relief.

Then he nodded towards the figure that was furtively approaching.

'That's a Glower Bear. Ten tons of pure muscle and fury. Its skin is incredibly hot, which explains the smoke rising up from him. Be careful, he's faster than he looks.'

Ahren swallowed hard. Glower Bears were one of the most dangerous Dark Ones he'd ever heard of. According to what Falk had told him, they were particularly intelligent.

Which was why the bear had been holding himself back, thought Ahren. He'd waited until we'd run out of arrows.

The figure with its height of four paces and its width of two looked so massive that it resembled a smoke-covered wall, rather than a creature of flesh and blood. The Glower Bear stood on his hind-legs and produced such a bone-shaking roar that the walls of the ruin started crumbling.

'Ideas, old friend?' asked Trogadon nervously. Even the dwarf had changed his approach to fighting in view of the sheer size of their opponent and was standing with the others.

Falk frowned. 'He's behaving strangely. Normally they attack in a fit of frenzy once they've trapped their prey.'

Ahren had an idea, even if it was nothing more than a wild hope.

'Maybe he's not under the control of the Adversary at the moment,' he suggested gingerly.

Falk spun his head around while the Glower Bear, still standing on his hind legs, stretched up his nose in an attempt to catch their scents.

'Tlik stopped him from ripping the blessing of the gods out of my body. He sacrificed himself and there's been a kind of recoil…HE, WHO FORCES has simply disappeared.'

The old Forest Guardian's eyes suggested he believed what the apprentice was saying. He looked critically at the Glower Bear, then gave a cautious nod.

'You could be right. He's behaving like a normal bear at the moment.'

'And what are we supposed to do with a giant bear standing right in front of us?' asked Trogadon urgently. 'The beast is still dangerous, damn it.'

Falk scratched his beard.

'We'd better think of something quickly, he won't hold on to his free will for much longer.'

'Is there any way that Selsena can calm him down?' Ahren asked quickly. After all, the Titejunanwa had helped him free Culhen that time. The circumstances might have been different then, but the principle was still the same.

Falk looked as if he'd just bitten into a lemon.

'She can try, but she's not going to like it.'

442

'I couldn't care less if she likes it or not', snapped Trogadon. 'If it works, then I personally will comb her down every day for the whole of the next moon until her coat is shining all over.'

Falk nodded and tilted his head while he made his request to Selsena.

A short time later, and they were all feeling calming waves of gentleness and contentment rolling over them.

Everyone dropped their weapons with the exception of Trogadon, who looked around irritated.

'Has she started?' he whispered.

Ahren nodded and tried to disregard the Elvin warhorse. He watched the Glower Bear, who had gone down on all fours, intently. The bear grumbled contentedly, and Falk hurried up to the smoke-covered beast.

'Shoo, shoo,' he called and waved his arms in front of the bear's enormous face, which was the same size as the broad-shouldered man's upper body.

The Dark One turned with a grumble and trotted away into the night.

'He was almost going to curl up into a ball and settle down,' said Falk, while he was reading Selsena's thoughts. 'The last thing I need during the Naming is a sleeping Glower Bear that could attack us at any moment. Selsena is going to escort him for a while. She says the other Dark Ones are also behaving like normal animals and are not under HIS control.'

They turned towards Jelninolan, and Falk gently shook her by the arm. She opened her eyes and looked at him with tired eyes.

'You can stop now. The connection between HIM, WHO FORCES and his servants seem to be impaired. They're behaving like normal animals at the moment and you've probably blown the swarm all the way to over the Eastern Sea,' he said with a wink.

The elf looked at him in wonder and finished the spell.

'What happened?' she asked, confused.

'Later', said Falk tersely. 'We don't know how long of a breather we have, and Uldini doesn't seem as fresh as a daisy. Let's complete the Naming and get out of here.'

Everyone was back in position and Uldini continued with the ritual.

The Arch Wizard was bathed in sweat by now and his voice was hoarse with exhaustion.

'May the Einhan of the dwarves impart to us if he supports the selection of the aspirant here present, and if he considers said aspirant to be worthy of bearing the burden of a Paladin conscientiously and diligently,' he intoned.

Trogadon stood there with arms folded and winked at Ahren.

'Sure, why not,' he responded.

Uldini cleared his throat impatiently and the dwarf quickly added: 'the Einhan of the dwarves considers the aspirant to be worthy.'

'May the blessing of HIM, WHO IS be upon the aspirant and may the sacred armour and weapons serve the Paladin well,' continued Uldini.

Trogadon made an apologetic gesture with his hands.

'Sorry son, at this point you'd be getting my armour, but as was already said, we're improvising here. When we get as far as Thousand Halls, I'll forge you something decent, and that's a promise.'

Uldini looked daggers at the dwarf, who promptly stopped talking.

'May the Einhan of the elves impart to us if she supports the selection of the aspirant here present, and if she considers said aspirant to be worthy of bearing the burden of a Paladin conscientiously and diligently,' said Uldini.

'The Einhan of the elves considers the aspirant to be worthy,' said Jelninolan simply and with a warm if tired smile, which Ahren responded to by nodding gratefully.

So far, the apprentice felt no difference at all, which seemed somehow strange to him.

'May the blessing of HER, WHO FEELS be upon the aspirant, and may her servant protect him from all dangers in his travels, be they physical or spiritual,' Uldini's voice intoned.

Ahren waited with bated breath. They had explained the ritual to him beforehand, and now the time had come when his companion animal should appear. Ahren was secretly hoping for a Titejunanwa so that he could ride off with his master and Selsena, but perhaps it would be a Griffin. Only one Paladin had managed to earn a Griffin until now and the thoughts of flying was very exciting. Several heartbeats passed by. Everyone kept their eyes peeled on where their light met the darkness, but nothing stirred.

'There is no normal animal in the surrounding area,' said Jelninolan in a comforting but almost apologising voice. 'I'm sure it will come to you in the next few days.'

'I, as human Einhan, consider the aspirant to be worthy of bearing the burden of a Paladin conscientiously and diligently. May the blessing of HIM, WHO FORMS be upon the aspirant, and his form prove itself against coercion from within or without.'

Ahren felt a small but subtle change for the first time, once he had heard these words. Like a door closing quietly because it was caught by a breeze, it seemed as if a diffuse connection to the Adversary had been cut, a connection that had been ever present, if barely tangible, his whole life long. Suddenly he was breathing more freely and the air around him smelled more intense. The colours were brighter, and a surge of joy overwhelmed him. His eyes welled up with tears as Uldini finally said: 'Dorian Falkenstein, do you accept this aspirant as Paladin, and are you willing to teach him everything he needs to know?'

Ahren turned to face Falk, who looked at him with a dignified look and scratched his beard for a moment as if considering his answer.

'I accept the aspirant as one of our own,' he finally said, and Ahren could do nothing but give a laugh of relief.

'Then I hereby seal the Naming,' intoned Uldini in a loud voice.

'Welcome, Ahren, the Thirteenth of the Paladins.' Everyone shouted with joy, and merry laughter echoed through the ruins in the shadow of the Pall Pillar for the first time in nearly eight hundred years.

Chapter 26

Day 1 after the winter solstice

They were all snuggled under their blankets and were enjoying the warmth of the campfire and its comforting crackling sounds. Once Ahren had been named, they had taken to their heels and Falk had found an abandoned cave, which Uldini and Jelninolan had camouflaged with the strongest magic they could manage.

Now they were all sitting together and gazing contentedly into the fire. Selsena was scouring the area outside and reporting back that Dark Ones were gradually coming under the control of the Adversary again, beginning with the weakest and smallest.

'We have about three weeks of a cat and mouse game ahead of us before we've left the Borderlands behind us. The quickest route is from here to Hjalgar,' said Falk.

Ahren's head shot up. 'Can we drop in on Deepstone then?' he asked hopefully.

Falk nodded. 'I think so. Uldini and Jelninolan really exhausted themselves yesterday and need a couple of weeks to rest. A sleepy little village would be just ideal'. And he winked at Ahren while Uldini gave a pained sigh.

'I was counting on the Sun Court. Decent food, attentive servants and cultured conversations on intrigues and politics,' he grumbled half-heartedly.

Falk dismissed him with a wave of his hand and changed the subject.

'Now that we're safe, tell us what happened in the middle of the battle, and don't leave anything out.'

All eyes were on Ahren as he explained in detail how HE, WHO FORCES had tried to sway him and had used the young man's own convictions against himself. When he got to the point where he had been convinced that the only way of achieving anything worthwhile was by his own death, Falk went grey in the face, and Ahren hurried on. When he had finished his report, there was a silence in the cave as everyone took in what they had just heard.

Uldini was the first to speak.

'Was the vow strong enough to make Tlik sacrifice himself? Was the oath that powerful?'

Jelninolan shrugged her shoulders before shaking her head.

'I don't think so. It might have released the impulse in him to want to help – but allowing himself to be killed? Definitely not. It's more probable that he really wanted to help, and his deed was the only way of saving Ahren.'

'But what exactly did he do?' asked Ahren insistently. He still couldn't understand what had happened.

Uldini spoke again.

'He, to put it metaphorically, threw himself in the path of the arrow that was intended for you. The dark god wanted to suck up your blessing of the gods, and instead he absorbed a whole lot of goblin magic. If I understand your description correctly, he set free all his power at the very moment the Adversary was sucking it up. Like an enormous juicy roast that suddenly transforms into a fireball in your mouth.'

In spite of the troubling theme, Uldini couldn't help a little whoop of joy.

'That will set him back considerably. We successfully had Ahren named at the winter solstice and the little goblin's prank will have done HIM, WHO FORCES considerable harm. We surely have at least five or perhaps ten years before HE wakes up. That gives us a great chance of finding the others and uniting ourselves before it becomes an all-out war.'

Ahren was confused. 'Finding the others? What do you mean? I thought that now I'm a Paladin we can tackle the Adversary.'

Jelninolan interjected before Uldini could speak.

'Let me explain,' she said, looking into the apprentice's eyes.

'Ahren, we've discussed this already, that first all the Paladins have to be gathered together before we can be victorious against HIM, WHO FORCES. Isn't that right?'

The young man nodded. He was waiting for the catch and expecting it to be big.

'The rest of the Paladins have to be found first, and then persuaded. Many of them have been missing for hundreds of years, they've withdrawn from the world, or are leading completely different ways of life now. One of them is the Eternal Empress, two others have become pirates, one is a pretty successful mercenary, to give you a few examples. It's going to be difficult to find them, and to persuade them to join us. Each and every one of them lost their families in the Night of Blood and had to watch how the world continued to turn, and how the peoples of the world gradually banished them to the kingdom of legends,' she explained with sympathy in her voice.

'Five years may sound like a long time, but we have to find eleven immortal warriors who do not want to be found or have settled down somewhere in their own place where they can live comfortably. All in all, a difficult task', added Falk quietly.

'But they're Paladins. Now that I'm the thirteenth, they'll want to meet us, won't they?' asked Ahren, who was beginning to feel frustration creeping in.

The others just gave him a knowing look.

'The Ancients already sent forth a magic call several moons ago. All Paladins were to gather together after we had found you that time. But nobody came,' said Uldini in the stillness.

Ahren shook his head in disbelief, and Falk continued trying to explain the situation to the fledgling Paladin.

'I had only been living in Deepstone for a few decades, but you remember how set in my ways I was. I didn't want to leave, and I even slammed the door in Uldini's face when he came to warn us. Now imagine what it must be like for those who experienced the Dark Days, and centuries later, having built up their own lives, then having to go into war again, having already lost everyone who was dear to them.'

The thought of it made Ahren dizzy. Over the last few moons, he had seen enough violence and death to last him a lifetime. How could he sit in judgement on the men and women who had suffered far more than he had? He nodded respectfully and looked at the others.

'Good,' he said, 'Where do we begin?'

There was an immediate avalanche of names and places, and Ahren couldn't sort them out. There were too many, and the others were speaking too quickly for him to take in all the suggestions. Even Trogadon threw in a few ideas and soon there was a lively discussion in the cave as everyone put forward their ideas for the travel route.

Ahren was simply too exhausted following the events of the previous few days, and all he wanted to do was sleep. He still couldn't comprehend how the cantankerous goblin had helped him to the point of offering up his own life. Had the fay-creature seen the destruction that the

450

dark god was doing to his reason? Or was it the goblin's last act of defiance. 'You can't save them all,' he had said to Ahren. And by offering himself up, he had shown the apprentice this to be true.

Ahren shook his head, confused. Maybe it was that, maybe it was a combination of all those reasons. All he wanted to do was lie down and leave the planning to the others, but a buzzing sound on the edge of his reason was troubling him. He shook his head, but the buzzing remained, like a mosquito that had made itself at home inside his head. It became stronger, and Ahren massaged his temples and closed his eyes. But nothing helped. For a moment he considered telling the others, but then Culhen came over to comfort him. Ahren ruffled the wolf's neck hairs and looked down thankfully into his yellow eyes.

That was the moment the buzzing stopped and was replaced by something else. As he looked into the depths of the wolf's eyes, and as the wolf looked loyally and lovingly up at him, the apprentice heard a voice in his head.

Ahren? asked Culhen timidly.

__Epilogue__

Khara had withdrawn to the entrance of the cave and was standing guard.

The others were discussing which Paladin they should seek out first, and they were speaking so quickly that it was difficult to follow the conversation. She was still a little mistrustful of the Ancients' magic and so she had slipped out to the cave entrance to keep guard in spite of the protective magic that surrounded them.

Every now and then she would hear a snuffling sound or the scraping of claws when a Dark One would pass by their refuge, but none of the creatures came up to the entrance, and the girl began to relax.

She looked back thoughtfully at the dreamy looking young man who was cuddling his wolf and who had his head tilted as if he were listening to something. Tears were running down his face, and he was smiling.

Was Ahren blubbering again? Khara rolled her eyes and looked back out into the night. She swore to the gods that she had never seen such a cry-baby as this young Paladin! Well, at least he could shoot arrows well, and his tea wasn't bad.

Her thoughts were interrupted by a figure appearing out of the darkness.

Khara was wide-awake in an instant and had already half drawn Windblade when she realised that it was an old woman approaching the cave, whose features were hidden by a black veil. She was dressed in mourning clothes and walked in a stoop. She didn't step into the cave, however, but remained at the entrance and lifted a finger to her lips.

Khara had actually wanted to call for help, but there was no sense of danger coming from the woman, mostly a sensation of deep sorrow, which seemed to permeate her every movement.

'There's no need to disturb the others, my child,' she said in the Emperor language. 'I shall not stay long and merely wished to deliver a message. Out here, there are too many creatures on the hunt and an old woman needs to take care of herself.' She laughed like a billy goat, as if she had just told a very good joke, but there was also a terrible bitterness in her voice.

Khara was alarmed and fascinated at the same time. How had this little old lady survived in the Borderlands? And what was she doing here? Was she one of the frontiers women who had been driven mad by the presence of the Pall Pillar?

'Madness is only another way of understanding the secrets of the world,' said the old woman, as though she had just been reading Khara's mind.

The girl recoiled and the old woman raised a placatory hand.

'I am sorry, my dear. I did not mean to frighten you.'

She lifted her skinny hand to her chin as though she were contemplating something deeply.

'Now I remember what I was going to say. If you all want to be successful in your plans, then first you must go to the Brazen City. If the Sun Emperor is successful with his siege of the city, and if the captain of the Blue Cohorts is executed before you have arrived, then once again there will only be twelve Paladins walking the earth. The Emperor is very angry and is looking for blood. So much so, that he is willing to starve a whole city.'

Then she looked past Khara and clapped her hands together in delight.

'Look, he has learned to answer Culhen. How quickly they grow.'

Khara looked over her shoulder back into the cave and saw Ahren, sitting in the same position as earlier, drooling over his wolf and blubbering. Khara shrugged her shoulders and turned back to the old woman. But she was gone.

The girl stayed sitting there for a time and tried to understand what she had just seen. Then she went back to the others to pass on the message from the mysterious woman.

At least she knew now where they had to go next.

And that was something.

The journey continues in:
The Brazen City (The 13th Paladin Book III)
Available Summer 2020

Dear Reader:

If you enjoyed this book, please leave a short rating in the shop, where you bought it. As I am an independent author with no backing of a publisher, every positive comment helps to convince others to read my novel.

Acknowledgements

Thanks to my reader Janina Klinck for her considerate companionship on my first steps as an author, and to my illustrator Petra Rudolf for her enchanting work in transforming my crude guidelines into a breath-taking cover. Without them, the Paladin volumes would not be what they are.

And of course to Tim Casey and Neil Mc Court, who laboured hard to bring the English version of this story to life.

Printed by Amazon Italia Logistica S.r.l.
Torrazza Piemonte (TO), Italy

60927316R00258